She broke into a run but before she got to the front door, Jenny opened it. 'I saw you coming from the kitchen, Eva love. Don't worry. Miss Blake's all right.' She lowered her voice, casting a quick glance over her shoulder. 'I wanted to warn you. There's a fellow turned up two days ago, said he was Miss Blake's nephew – well, he may be, I don't deny that – but from the way he was eyeing the house before he rang the bell, you'd think he'd come to sell it. And she asked him to stay. If he had any thought for other folk, he'd not put an extra burden on us at a time like this. I've given him the big room in the attic.' She winked. That room had the most uncomfortable bed and was next to the plumbing pipes, which gurgled and moaned at times.

Eva stared at her in surprise. It wasn't like Jenny to take a dislike to someone. She'd been with them for several years now and was only a few years older than Eva herself, more a friend to her than a maid.

A door opened at the rear of the hall and a man came out, smiling. 'Ah, you must be Eva. I'm Gus Blake, Alice's nephew.'

She could not help staring at him. He was tall, about six foot, and quite good-looking though rather lanky, with dark eyes and brown hair parted near the middle and kept in place with hair cream. He had a couple of bad scars on his forehead, but a fresh complexion otherwise. She had never liked moustaches, though, especially thin ones like his. Was he really the son of Alice's step-brother? And if so, why was he visiting? Her friend had always said that all the relatives she liked were dead and she didn't care if she never saw the others again.

He moved forward with one hand extended and when Eva shook it, he held hers for longer than she liked, clasping it with his other hand and staring down at her.

ANNA JACOBS

Our Eva

CORONET BOOKS
Hodder & Stoughton

copyright © 2002 by Anna Jacobs

First published in Great Britain in 2002 by Hodder and Stoughton
First published in paperback in 2003 by Hodder and Stoughton
A division of Hodder Headline

The right of Anna Jacobs to be identified as the Author
of the Work has been asserted by her in accordance with the
Copyright, Designs and Patents Act 1988.

A Coronet paperback

11

A CIP catalogue record for this title
is available from the British Library

ISBN 978 0 340 82132 9

Typeset in Plantin by Hewer Text Ltd, Edinburgh
Printed and bound in Great Britain by
CPI Group (UK) Ltd, Croydon, CR0 4YY

Hodder and Stoughton
A division of Hodder Headline
338 Euston Road
London NW1 3BH

To Helen and Al Frewin,
Relatives, friends and fellow curry addicts

I

August 1921

Eva stared out at the Pennine foothills as the new motor bus chugged slowly towards Heyshaw. It had been wonderful to see all the family at her sister Polly's wedding, but she had come away envious of her two sisters' happiness. She was angry with herself for that, not wanting to be mean-spirited, but could not help wishing she too had a husband to love, children tugging at her skirts and calling, 'Mam, Mam!' in that insistent way you could not ignore.

She smiled at the thought of children, then sighed. Why would any man fall in love with shy, prim Eva Kershaw, former schoolmistress, who was neither beautiful nor remarkable in any way? She was twenty-four now, had never attracted a suitor and wasn't likely to, either, now that so many young men of her generation had been killed in the war.

Oh, heavens, she was getting maudlin! Pull yourself together, my girl, she scolded, and sat very upright, relieved to be nearly home – and yet fearing what she would find there.

She got off the bus in the centre of Heyshaw, a place

not large enough to be called a town or to have its own railway but still larger than most villages. She enjoyed living here, loved the rolling sweep of the moors just above the village and even loved the magnificent lowering skies that brought rain sweeping in.

She was anxious now to get back to Alice, who had been more of a mother to her over the past ten years than her own ever had and who was slowly dying. Eva blinked away the tears that would well in her eyes every time she thought of that, hoping none of the other passengers had noticed. She had given up teaching the previous year to care for her friend – willingly – and although Alice had lived for longer than the doctors had predicted, they both knew it could only be a matter of weeks now.

What Eva didn't know was how she would cope afterwards without Alice's wise guidance and motherly affection.

Picking up her suitcase, she set off to walk up the rise to the outlying district known as North Hey, glad of a chance to stretch her legs after the morning's journey from the Fylde Coast.

But as she passed an alley something caught her eye and, hearing children's cries, she stopped automatically to peer along the narrow space between two rows of houses. At the far end three girls had a smaller one trapped. She was cowering against the wall, tears pouring down her face, and they were clearly threatening her.

As Eva watched, the tallest girl darted forward to punch the victim in the arm, taunting, 'Dummy! Dummy!'

If there was one thing Eva hated it was bullying! She had been bullied as a child herself for being cleverer than the others and could never pass by when someone was suffering the same treatment. Without thinking she began to run down the alley, shouting, 'Hoy! Stop that at once!' as if she were still a teacher.

The trio turned towards her, glanced at one another, then started to run. The largest girl pushed past, nearly knocking Eva over, and while she was struggling to regain her balance, the others followed. By the time she'd turned round, all three were clattering out of the street end of the alley.

She didn't try to chase them, though she'd recognised two of them from her days as a teacher. The large one was called Christine and was the leader of a rough group of girls who were always in trouble about something or other.

Their victim slid to the ground and buried her face in her hands. The whole of the child's body was shaking with her weeping and yet she was making no noise. Automatically Eva knelt to put an arm round the child's shoulders, whispering, 'It's all right. They've gone now.'

Gradually the flow of tears stopped and the girl wiped her face on her sleeve, hiccuping as she did so.

'Here.' Eva took out her own handkerchief and offered it. 'What's your name?'

The reply was only a whisper. 'Molly.'

The child must be new at school since Eva had taught there, because she didn't recognise her. She was poorly dressed, with a hole in one sock and a tear in her skirt, and she was staring at the neatly pressed and folded handkerchief as if she had never seen such a thing. Taking it gingerly, she looked at Eva for permission to use it.

'I don't mind if you dirty it, dear. That's what handkerchiefs are for.' She watched the little girl mop her face and blow her nose vigorously, then offer the handkerchief back. 'No, you keep it. I have plenty of others at home.'

The child said nothing, but clutched it tightly and began to chew one corner of it.

'Where do you live?'

There was a shout from the end of the alley and a bigger girl came pounding down it. 'I've been looking for you all over, our Molly. Why didn't you wait for me outside the shop?' Then she recognised Eva and gasped. 'Miss Kershaw!'

'Hello, Gracie. Is this your little sister? I found her being bullied.' She named two of the girls responsible and asked, 'Why would they do that? They were so much bigger than Molly they can't even be in the same class.'

Gracie shrugged and grabbed her sister's hand. 'I don't know, but thanks for helping her, miss.'

Knowing Gracie's brusqueness of old, Eva didn't try to question her further, though she could tell the girl did know something. She picked up her suitcase and handbag. 'Come on. I'll walk with you to the end of your lane. They may be waiting for you down the street.'

Gracie scowled at her. 'There's no need. They won't

dare attack her when I'm here, because I can beat them lot any day.'

'It's on my way, so we may as well stay together.'

Gracie grunted something and Molly gave Eva a shy smile.

Ten minutes' brisk walking brought them to North Hey, which was mostly inhabited by the better class of people, who lived in large detached houses set back from the road. It always made Eva smile when she thought of that, because although she lived here now, she had grown up in the mill terraces of Overdale and her family had been desperately short of money after her father was killed. The smile faded as she tried to remember his face and failed. She had been only eleven when he died, about the same age as Gracie now. It all seemed so long ago.

Just before they got to Eva's house she stopped to say goodbye and watch the girls turn down the lane leading to Linney's Farm, where their father was a labourer. A little way along Molly stopped and gave Eva another tentative smile, but her sister jerked the hand she was holding so that Molly had to do a little half-run to catch up with her.

Eva watched them go with a sigh of regret. She really missed teaching, loved being with children. She walked slowly back towards Rose Villa, which had once belonged to Alice's uncle and would, her friend said, belong to Eva one day. As if she cared about that! She wished Alice could live for ever. But she did love Rose Villa, which stood in two acres of well-tended gardens, surrounded by high stone walls. The house was square, built of creamy millstone grit, with a grey slate roof. Alice always joked that it was a back-to-front sort of place, with the main gardens at the rear looking out towards the moors and sheltered by a wall, just as the main rooms were on that side as well.

When she went through the gates Eva stopped for a moment in shock at the sight of a car parked in front of the house, a gleaming black Riley tourer with its hood down. Surely Jenny hadn't had to call in the doctor again? No, this wasn't the doctor's. Whose was it, then? You didn't see many cars in Heyshaw, or visiting strangers, either. Had something happened to Alice? If her friend had died with only their maid to keep her company, Eva would never be able to forgive herself.

She broke into a run but before she got to the front door, Jenny opened it. 'I saw you coming from the kitchen, Eva love. Don't worry. Miss Blake's all right.' She lowered her voice, casting a quick glance over her shoulder. 'I wanted to warn you. There's a fellow turned up two days ago, said he was Miss Blake's nephew – well, he may be, I don't deny that – but from the way he was eyeing the house before he rang the bell, you'd think he'd come to sell it. And she asked him to stay. If he had any thought for other folk, he'd not put an extra burden on us at a time like this. I've given him the big room in the attic.' She winked. That room had the most uncomfortable bed and was next to the plumbing pipes, which gurgled and moaned at times.

Eva stared at her in surprise. It wasn't like Jenny to take a dislike to someone. She'd been with them for several years now and was only a few years older than Eva herself, more a friend to her than a maid.

A door opened at the rear of the hall and a man came out, smiling. 'Ah, you must be Eva. I'm Gus Blake, Alice's nephew.'

She could not help staring at him. He was tall, about six foot, and quite good-looking though rather lanky, with dark eyes and brown hair parted near the middle and kept in place with hair cream. He had a couple of bad scars on his forehead, but a fresh complexion otherwise. She had never liked moustaches, though, especially thin ones like his. Was he really the son of Alice's step-brother? And if so, why was he visiting? Her friend had always said that all the relatives she liked were dead and she didn't care if she never saw the others again.

He moved forward with one hand extended and when Eva shook it, he held hers for longer than she liked, clasping it with his other hand and staring down at her. This made her feel a little uncomfortable and she tugged her hand away, taking a hasty step backwards. She was not used to holding hands with strangers. Well, she didn't meet many new people because they led a very quiet life here. Mr Blake was still blocking her way, however, and she didn't like to push past him.

Behind her Jenny cleared her throat. 'I'll take your suitcase upstairs for you, miss, shall I? Excuse me, sir, but Miss Kershaw needs to get past.'

Only then did he move. The glance he threw towards the maid was not at all friendly but when he turned back to Eva his smile reappeared. 'Cousin Alice is waiting for you.'

He waved her along the hallway as if she were the visitor and he the one who lived there. He seemed too big and masculine in their feminine household. Even the dainty sprigged wallpaper looked wishy-washy beside him and his tread made the polished floorboards creak in protest.

As he opened the door for her, Eva paused in the doorway of Alice's cosy sitting room with its sweeping views over the moors. It looked different, somehow. The chair she always thought of as hers was pulled over beside Alice's daybed and two of the small tables had been shoved back so carelessly that the china figurines and enamelled boxes were askew, one of them danger-ously near the edge.

Alice, who was lying on the sofa, turned a glowing face towards her. 'Eva, darling, look who's come to see us – my half-brother Simon's son all the way from London. I thought Gus had been lost in France, but it seems he was just missing for a while.'

Eva hurried across to hug her friend and study her anxiously, worried at how tired Alice looked – or had she been this bad before? It was hard to tell when you lived with someone day in, day out, but after three days away Eva felt as if she were seeing everything with fresh eyes. 'Are you all right? You mustn't overtire yourself, dear.'

'Oh, I shan't. It was so mild Gus carried me out into the garden yesterday, right down to the far end so that I could see the stream on the other side of the wall. I can't tell you how much I enjoyed it. There were a couple of trout, only as big as my hand, lying behind a rock, just moving slightly, the way they do. We're going to go outside again tomorrow after I've had my rest.'

'That's lovely for you.' Eva smiled at Gus, grateful for anything that made Alice's life more enjoyable.

'Now, sit down and tell us all about the wedding. Did the sun shine? What did your sister wear? How is her poor little son?'

So Eva launched into a description of her sister Polly's wedding to Captain Richard Mercer, late of the North Fylde Rifles. Her eyes grew misty as she spoke of the love that was so visible between them and the beauty of the summer's day in the little village church, with her two brothers and other sister all gathered for the occasion.

'I wish I could have gone.' Alice sighed. 'It's lovely to think that Lizzie and Polly are both happily married now.' Her eyes rested on Eva thoughtfully. 'It'll be your turn next, dear.'

She didn't like Alice saying such things in front of a stranger, so said brusquely, 'You know I've no intention of marrying. I'm quite content as I am.' Her friend was looking so exhausted she added gently, 'And I think you need a nap now.'

Alice sighed again, but nodded.

Gus Blake left the room at once, but was waiting in the hall, blocking Eva's way again.

'If you'll excuse me, Mr Blake, I'd like to go up and unpack.'

'Oh, do call me Gus. We're almost related, after all. And I'd like to ask you about my aunt. Let's go into the small sitting room.' He pointed to the right near the front door.

'We'll use the garden room, if you don't mind, Mr B—Gus, I mean. That sitting room is my own private domain.'

He stood back with a flourish of one arm to let her lead the way. 'Certainly. Sorry to have intruded. I didn't realise it was yours.'

Alice's uncle had built the garden room at the side of the house. It had windows along two sides and there were several ferns in pots, not flourishing now that Alice was no longer able to care for them. Eva did her best, but knew she didn't have green fingers.

'What is it we need to discuss?' she asked, impatient to get on with her unpacking.

'What does the doctor say about my aunt? She won't talk about it, but she looks – well, as if she hasn't got long to live.'

Eva could not prevent tears from welling in her eyes, too many to blink away so she fumbled for her hand-kerchief, only to remember that she'd given it to the child.

'Here, take mine.' He thrust a crumpled piece of white cotton into her hand.

Eva wiped her eyes and handed it back to him. 'Thank you. Alice has a growth in the stomach, I'm afraid, and she's already lived for much longer than the doctor expected, so we just – take each day as it comes.'

He stared down at the handkerchief, which he was still holding. 'I wish I'd known earlier. Aunt Alice is the only close relative I have left now. I lost my parents a while ago so I can sympathise with what you're going through.'

'I'm sorry. That must have been very sad for you.'

He nodded, taking a deep, shaky breath before continuing, 'It was. Which is why I thought I'd get in touch with my aunt. Only I'm just in time to say goodbye, it seems.'

Eva gave him a moment to pull himself together, bending to nip some dead leaves off the plant next to her.

'Sorry. Didn't mean to unload my troubles on you. You must have a sympathetic face.' He looked at her with a wry half-smile.

She knew she didn't have that gift. It was one of her personal regrets that she could not overcome her innate shyness, except with children – but she didn't challenge his remark. She realised he was waiting for her to say something and searched desperately for words. 'It was a long war and a lot of people suffered, not just the soldiers. Alice and I were quite lucky, really. We had larger classes to teach and there were food shortages, but we were glad to do our bit. She's not one to complain, so it wasn't until after the war that I realised that it wasn't just indigestion that ailed her.' She paused for a moment, then decided to ask him bluntly, 'Might I ask how long you're intending to stay?'

'Oh, I'm not in a hurry to rush off. I've been helping

a couple of chaps out with this and that since the war, but that's finished now. I'll probably start up some sort of business of my own eventually.'

Eva tried to hide her dismay. That sounded as though he were planning a long stay in Heyshaw and she didn't want to share Alice's last days with anyone except Jenny. This man might be a relative but he wasn't really close to Alice, who hadn't seen him since he was a child. 'Well, that's very kind of you, Mr Blake, but I think a couple of days' visit will be more than enough for your aunt at the moment. She gets very tired, as you've no doubt noticed.'

'I keep asking you to call me Gus. And yes, of course. I'll leave whenever you say. I don't want to outstay my welcome.' He stood up. 'I think I'll take a stroll down into the village and get a breath of fresh air, leave you to unpack.'

She nodded and went into her own sitting room to watch him stride off down the drive, trilby perched jauntily on his head. What was a man like him doing in Heyshaw? He was so different from the locals he made her nervous. And she hadn't expected Alice's nephew to have such a pronounced London accent because he'd only gone to live there when he was nine.

With a sigh she sat down at her desk, still feeling unsettled. The mail lay to the right, as always, a letter from an old teaching friend who had married and moved to Bristol. She reached automatically for the paper knife then frowned as she realised it wasn't there. It took her a moment or two to find it under a pile of papers. The papers were in their usual place, so how

had the knife got under them? She was certain she
hadn't left it there. Alice often teased her about being
incurably neat, but when you were a teacher you had to
set standards and keep track of many bits and pieces.

She slit open her letter and skimmed through it. Not
bad news, thank goodness. She'd read it properly later
after she'd unpacked, but first she'd better confer with
Jenny about meals.

'He eats like a horse, that one does,' Jenny said
gloomily, leaning back against the kitchen dresser
and folding her arms. 'I've done a potato pie for
tonight. Nice and filling, and the butcher had a piece
of lovely suet to make the crust with. Miss Blake sat up
for dinner with him yesterday, but perhaps you can
persuade her not to do that tonight. She's worn out by
teatime these days.'

But as Eva went up to her room to unpack, it
occurred to her that this would leave her to dine alone
with Gus Blake – and the thought of that made her feel
even more nervous. It was ridiculous, really. She didn't
know the man and he'd been nothing but polite to her
so why did she feel like this?

Alice enjoyed another brief chat with Gus and Eva over
a cup of tea, but afterwards admitted she didn't really
feel up to joining them for dinner, so Gus carried her
upstairs. His being able to do that certainly made
things easier, Eva thought as she helped her friend
undress. Alice was very weak now and needed help
moving even a few paces.

'It was lovely to sit outside today,' she said wistfully.

'I do hope the good weather will continue, so that we can do it again.'

'I'm glad you enjoyed yourself. Shall I give you your medicine, now?'

'I suppose so. I hate feeling woozy, though.' Alice made herself comfortable then asked suddenly, 'Do you like Gus?'

'I don't know him.'

'His father used to tease me unmercifully when we were children – he was older than me – but Simon could be fun, too. He and his wife came to visit us once or twice before I went to live in Overdale, but I didn't see them again, though we exchanged letters and Christmas cards, of course, until they died.' She smiled reminiscently. 'Gus was a lively lad, always in trouble, but I did enjoy their visits. He's grown into a fine young man, hasn't he?'

As her friend yawned and drifted into sleep, Eva went into her bedroom next door and changed her crumpled travelling clothes ready for the evening meal. She wished she could eat in the kitchen with Jenny, as she usually did these days; wished most of all that Alice did not look so frail.

Jenny served the meal very formally, setting the table in the dining room and not attempting to chat as she brought the food in. She thought Eva was looking very stiff and correct tonight. Well, she was always stiff with young men because she hadn't known many. And actually Miss Blake had discouraged one or two fellows who'd taken a liking to Eva, which Jenny had thought unfair.

When the bell rang she went to clear away and was surprised at how little was left in the serving dishes.

Eva smiled at her. 'Thank you, Jenny. That was lovely.'

When their visitor said nothing, Jenny felt irritated. He had a hearty appetite but never bothered to say thank you or tell her he'd enjoyed something and she'd made a special effort since his arrival. She reckoned he was bone idle. When he wasn't with his aunt, he lounged around reading or strolled down the road to the local shop for cigarettes. If he'd had anything about him, he'd have gone out and tidied up the garden for them.

After she'd cleared up the kitchen, she walked across to her Grandad Gill's cottage opposite with the leftovers. She had been delighted to find a job so close to him after her grandmother died, because they were the only two Gills left now.

'I've got your tea here, Grandad,' she called as she walked in, then realised Wilfred Horrocks was sitting with him. 'Sorry. Didn't know you had visitors.' Her grandad looked at her basket and opened his mouth. She frowned at him, hoping he wasn't going to offer to share. He'd give his last egg away if someone looked hungry, her grandad would.

'I'm just leaving,' Wilf said abruptly.

She waited till he'd clumped off down the path to ask, 'What's wrong with him today? He looks like he's lost a pound and found a farthing.'

'He's out of work. His firm closed down a week or two ago and he can't find anything else. He's tried

everywhere. Says there are long queues if there's so
much as a sniff of a job.' John Gill sighed. 'And he's
running out of money. Can't even afford the bus fares
to seek work away from Heyshaw any more.'

'Oh, no. Poor thing!' She knew Wilf was an uphol-
sterer and had been working for a small furniture
manufacturer in Rochdale. Like quite a few people,
he had been on short time for a while, but unlike most
he had no family to fall back on. He was an outsider
who'd come to live in lodgings in North Hey after the
war. Everyone agreed he was a nice, polite fellow,
though he never said much about himself.

He'd helped her grandfather one day when the old
man had fallen over and since then had called in
regularly, which she thought kind of him. And it wasn't
out of pity, she'd seen that for herself, but because he
genuinely enjoyed the old man's company.

'His landlady's told Wilf he can stay on for a week or
two, but she can't feed him until he starts paying her
again, so he's managing as best he can,' Grandad said
with a sigh. 'He gets the odd night's work behind the
bar in the Dog and Duck, but that's all. He was hungry
today. I remember that look from when I was a lad.'

Jenny looked down at the plate, feeling guilty. 'Well,
there isn't enough for two tonight. That nephew of
Miss Blake's is a right greedy pig. I don't know how he
stays so thin. I'll try and bring a bit more tomorrow, so
tell Wilf to pop round in the evening.'

'He's a bit touchy about taking charity.'

'Then trick him into being here when I bring your
tea across.' She grinned at him. 'And don't tell me you

can't. You're a cunning old devil when you want something.'

He opened his eyes wide. 'Me? Eh, I never!'

While they chatted, Jenny cleared up the room quickly and efficiently. Grandad lived mainly in the kitchen since her grandma had died and recently he'd started sleeping in the front room because he found the stairs hard to manage. It was a good thing he owned this little cottage and had her to help out, because the old age pension didn't go very far. Those who had to pay rent as well as buy food found it impossible to manage on it without their families' help.

She sighed as she strolled back to Rose Villa. Grandad wasn't strong enough to do much work around his house now, though his spirit was undiminished and he was no one's fool. But he needed her help on a daily basis and she was beginning to worry about what would happen to her after Miss Blake died. She'd heard her mistress say everything would go to Eva, and her friend had assured her nothing would change, but would there be enough money to keep the big rambling house going? Would Eva really want to stay there on her own?

If Jenny had to look for work further afield, how ever would her grandad manage?

When they heard the kitchen door close behind Jenny, Gus jumped up and hurried out into the hall, opening the front door a crack and peering out.

Eva, who had followed him, could not imagine what he was looking at. 'Is something wrong?'

'That maid is taking advantage of my aunt, stealing food from her.'

Eva stared at him in amazement. '*Jenny?*'

'Yes. I saw her last night slipping out with leftover food in a basin and she's doing it again tonight.'

Anger nearly choked Eva. How dare he spy on them and jump to conclusions like this? 'You're absolutely wrong. Jenny is as honest as they come. She takes food to her grandfather *every* evening, sometimes leftovers and sometimes stuff she buys specially, because he's old and on his own. Alice knows all about it and is glad to share with him because Jenny does the work of two and always has.'

'Oh. Sorry. Just trying to keep an eye on things for my aunt.'

'Well, you can leave that sort of thing to me, thank you very much,' Eva snapped. 'I've been managing this house for the past two years and Alice hasn't complained. Now, I've got things to do so I'll leave you. We go to bed early, as I'm sure you've realised.'

He smiled, leaning against the wall, hands in pockets, not seeming in the least put out by the sharpness of her tone. 'So I gathered from your maid's disapproving manner last night. But your aunt's given me a front door key and I'm not at all tired, so I think I'll take a stroll down to the pub and sample the local brew. I'll try not to disturb you when I come back and you can trust me to lock up properly.'

When she heard the front door close behind him, Eva breathed a sigh of relief and went into her sitting room. Taking out her account book, she began to do last month's totals, but kept making mistakes, and in the end she pushed it away, knowing she was too upset to concentrate. For a time she sat staring into space, seeing Alice's body, so painfully thin except for the lumpy stomach where the growth was eating her away.

She didn't hear Jenny return because suddenly it all overwhelmed her and she started weeping. Putting her head down on her arms, she gave way to the grief she felt for Alice.

She didn't hear the knock or even the door opening, but suddenly Jenny was there beside her, hugging her and making comforting noises.

'I'm s-sorry.'

'Eh, Eva love, no one can be brave all the time and I bet you had to put a good face on things while you were away so as not to spoil your sister's wedding.'

Eva nodded, her breath catching on another sob.

'Why don't you come into the kitchen – I've got a lovely fire going there – and we'll have a nice cup of cocoa.' Jenny kept her arm round Eva's shoulders as they walked along the short passage, thinking that Miss Blake wasn't the only one who'd lost weight lately.

As she sat down in front of the kitchen fire, Eva gave a watery smile. 'What would we both do without you, Jenny dear? You're like a member of the family. I'm sorry Gus Blake speaks to you so arrogantly.'

'Eh, I don't let that sort of thing bother me. There's some as think you're stupid and below them because you're a maid. Well, they're the stupid ones, not me.' As they sat there waiting for the milk to boil, she hesitated then said bluntly, 'He's trouble, that one is.'

'Why do you say that? He's been very pleasant to me and Alice is delighted he's come.'

Jenny scowled as she poured the hot milk into their cups and stirred the cocoa in vigorously. 'Because of the way he stares at everything, so calculating and sly.'

'Well, I suggested he stay only for a day or two, because of my friend's condition, so he'll be leaving soon.'

'I'll believe that when I see it,' Jenny muttered. 'He's trying to worm his way in, if you ask me. Now, tell me more about the wedding . . .'

But although the chat with Jenny cheered her up, Eva felt her apprehension returning as she made her way upstairs. She looked in on Alice, who was sleeping soundly, thank goodness, then sought her own bed.

It was a while before she slept. She could not help wondering what Gus Blake wanted. It was one thing for a man like him to drop in and visit an elderly aunt, quite another for him to stay on for several days in a quiet village where nothing much ever happened. It just didn't make sense.

2

A few days before Eva arrived home, Sid Linney took possession of the family farm in North Hey. At last! he thought, looking round possessively. He'd been managing a smallholding the family also owned over near Rochdale while he waited for his bloody father to die, but the old man had lasted far longer than he had expected – or wanted.

Things were going to change now, Sid decided, wandering over to the window to stare out. His stupid father could have made far more money out of the place if he'd only pushed his workers a bit and not treated them so soft.

Angela moved to join him. 'We'll have to keep the housekeeper on, you know. Mrs Benton's been here for over ten years, ever since your mother died.'

'She's leaving.'

'What? Sid, you can't.'

'Just watch me tell her to get out.' He wasn't employing an uppity old hag like her out of sheer sentimentality, let alone keep someone around who had looked at him so scornfully whenever he'd visited.

He scowled as Angela went storming up to their bedroom. Didn't even stand by him. Just showed what sort of a wife he'd married.

'The house is your job,' he told her later, when Mrs Benton had gone weeping to pack her things. 'You can employ a scrubbing woman and a washer-woman, but I didn't marry you so that you could sit on your arse playing the fine lady.' He wished sometimes he'd never married the stupid bitch at all, because it had taken her seven years to give him a son and they did nothing but quarrel nowadays over the way she was spoiling the child.

That afternoon he called the three labourers together and gave it to them straight. 'I'm cutting your wages by two bob a week and you can like it or lump it. Times are hard and this farm's been let run down. At least you've still got jobs – and homes.' There was shuffling of feet and muttering, but no one said anything in protest. Sid caught a look of scorn on Aaron Brierley's face, however, and that angered him. He'd have preferred to sack that sod outright, because he didn't like the fellow's manner, but Lil Brierley was dying of TB and you couldn't throw her out in that condition, not unless you wanted to set your neighbours' backs up. In the meantime, he was going to insist on respect at all times.

'Oy, you! Brierley! Come back. What's wrong with your left leg?'

'I injured it in the war.'

'Is that why you're walking so stiffly?'

'I have to wear a leg brace.'

Sid stared at him assessingly. 'Then how the hell do you get down on your knees?'

'I manage. It just takes a bit longer.'

'Try managing without the contraption then, if you

want to keep your job. Time is money to me and I can't afford to employ someone who takes longer to do the work.' For a moment he thought the fellow was going to give him some lip, but he turned away without a word. 'Come back, you! When I give you an order, I expect you to show respect. Yes, *sir*.'

'Yes – sir.'

But for all the man's impassive expression, those bright blue eyes still held a trace of scorn. Sid watched him walk away and decided that if the work got done properly, with no nonsense about leg braces, he'd let Brierley stay on until Lil died before chucking him out. He'd been at school with Lil and had quite fancied her himself – till she'd had to marry Brierley. Then he'd found Angela, who had a bit of money but was older than him. He'd rather have had Lil, though. Angela was no bloody fun in bed.

But as soon as Lil died, that bugger was out. Sid preferred to employ a man who was properly grateful, who hadn't been his father's bloody pet, even if Brierley was good at fixing up the old tractor. He'd seen his father chatting and laughing with Brierley when they were working on the machinery and it'd made him sick. His father had never treated him so cosily. In fact, let's face it, he'd never got on with his father and was glad the old sod had died at last. And he'd drink to that tonight. A man deserved a drink or two after a hard day's work, whatever Angela said.

In the Dog and Duck, which was the only public house in North Hey, Gus Blake made his way to the Lounge

Bar and took his time removing his trilby and hanging it on the coat stand. He went to the counter and ordered himself a whisky, studying the other occupants: two men whose heads were so close they clearly wouldn't welcome an interruption, and another fellow sitting in one corner, fairly affluent judging from his clothing, but with a distinct resemblance to a pig, with his plump, jowly face and stubby bristles.

Gus carried his glass over and stopped, waiting by the table till the man looked up. 'The name's Blake – Gus to my friends. I'm a stranger to North Hey. Do you fancy a bit of company?' He indicated the empty chair, then said with a smile, 'If not, just tell me and I'll leave you in peace.'

'Aye, why not? Sit yourself down. I'm Sid Linney, just moved back here after my father's death. I'm a bit out of touch with folk round here myself.'

Gus set his glass on the table and shook hands, aware that the other was assessing his status. Well, let him. Gus's suit had been made by a top London tailor and you couldn't beat a dark suit for impressing people. Linney was wearing a nondescript tweedy jacket, which hadn't come cheap but had seen better days, and he had a reddened complexion that suggested an outdoor life. Probably a farmer.

'Visiting Heyshaw, are you?' Sid asked.

'Yes. I'm staying with my aunt at Rose Villa.'

'Ah, Miss Blake. My farm backs on to her garden.'

Gus oiled the conversation by mentioning the war and his own experiences. The fellow was impressed, as they all were, by his talk of the trenches and his fellow officers.

Another man came in, hesitated and joined them. Eric Beaman was a lawyer who had an office in the centre of Heyshaw. Gus made an effort to charm them both and soon had Sid laughing, but Beaman had no sense of humour and, after finishing his drink, took his leave.

'Funny old sod, Beaman,' Sid said. 'Comes in occasionally, but rarely stays for more than one drink. He also drinks at the Red Lion down in the centre of Heyshaw with the snobs from those big new houses down the road. War profiteers, that lot. Don't mix much with the locals.'

By the time Gus stood up to leave, the two men had agreed to meet the following evening for a drink. Sid made no bones about preferring to spend his evenings in the pub rather than at home with his wife and young son.

Gus smiled in satisfaction as he strolled slowly back to his aunt's house. A chap needed company when he was out for a drink and Gus wasn't fussy who he sat with as long as they shared his taste for dirty jokes and could contribute a few of their own. He'd often thought that he could have made a living as a comedian, but it'd have been an exhausting life travelling from one theatre to the other.

Things were starting to look quite promising here. He'd find a way to stay a bit longer. If he charmed the old lady, she might leave him something in her will. After all Eva Kershaw wasn't a relative, just an opportunist who'd battened on to an old lady and Gus intended to nudge her aside if he could.

The following morning, in his cottage across the fields behind Rose Villa, Aaron Brierley woke with a start and reached automatically for his rifle. Muffling a groan of relief as he realised he was no longer in the trenches, he fell back on the pillow. He should get up. There was always a lot to do before he left for the farm, but he felt tired before he started so lay there for a minute or two, wishing . . . wishing for a miracle. The more fool he!

After a minute or two he sighed and began to rub his aching left leg, feeling the ugly ridges of scar tissue beneath his fingers. He didn't know how he was going to manage at work today. He'd copped a Blighty back in 1917 at Passchendaele and without the brace his leg sometimes gave way. He shuddered even to remember those hours of agony before the stretcher bearers had managed to get him off the battlefield. He'd had to wait his turn because there were others worse off than him. He'd lain there helpless, hearing some poor bugger nearby screaming on and on, begging them to shoot him – and been glad when he heard a shot and the screams cut off abruptly. Fancy being glad when a man died! That was what war did to you.

The military doctors who'd treated him during the months he'd spent in hospitals and convalescent homes had kept telling him he was lucky to have the leg still and he knew he was just as lucky to have survived the carnage. So many hadn't. But whatever Lloyd George said about making Britain a country fit for heroes to live in, Aaron's life wasn't much cop.

He'd planned to leave Heyshaw after his discharge and find work as a mechanic. He'd only taken this lousy farm job so that Lil could have fresh moorland air in the hopes of a cure, because ordinary folk like him didn't have the money to send their invalids to a warm, dry climate to get over TB, did they? For a time she'd held her own, his return making life easier for her, but then she'd started getting worse again. Now she was too weak even to walk downstairs, so she lay there all day looking out through her bedroom window at the moors she loved so much.

There was no help for it: he would have to grit his teeth and take whatever Sid Linney dished out for a while, for her sake. She wasn't going to recover this time. They both knew that and even the girls realised what was happening. He worried about them, because his daughters were the light of his life. But ten-year-old Gracie had grown sullen lately, her eyes full of resentment, and Molly was far quieter than a child of six should be, playing games that disturbed no one, often sitting under the table whispering to her rag doll, or following her sister round like a lost puppy, her eyes huge with worry.

Old Mr Linney had been very understanding, letting Aaron nip home at lunchtime to check that Lil was all right. He wasn't even going to ask Sid if he could do that because he knew what the answer would be.

Rolling out of bed, he went to pull back the piece of sacking that curtained the tiny window. He'd made a sleeping space for himself in the attic to leave the front bedroom for Lil, and although it was all right up here in summer, it'd been bloody freezing last winter. Time to get started. The girls went back to school today.

He edged carefully down the rickety loft ladder and found Lil tossing and turning, absolutely drenched in sweat. Automatically he went to find one of the bits of old sheeting they put under her and touched her gently on the shoulder.

'Let me change that sheet for you, Lil.'

She jerked in shock and blinked at him. 'Eh, is it morning? Sorry, love. Had a bad night. And Mrs Harrop doesn't know whether she'll be able to make it today. Can you manage to get the girls off to school? If you bring me up some water I'll wash myself, an' you can leave me a few pieces of bread and butter for later. I'm not hungry now. Tell Gracie to order a couple of loaves on her way to school and get some ham when she picks them up on the way home. There's money in my purse.'

'All right.' He went to wake his daughters, chatting to them as they all got ready, but time ran out and in the end he had to leave Gracie to take Molly to school.

He smiled mirthlessly as he made his way down the lane to the farm. 'Well, Lieutenant Brierley,' he muttered, 'was it for this you trained as a mechanic, then went to Officers' Training School and learned how to send men to their deaths?' He let out a mirthless snort. Fat lot of good any of it did! He had been a fool to hope for anything better after the war.

The following morning Alice sat outside in the back garden for an hour with Gus, thinking how lovely it was that he could carry her around so easily. She turned her face up to the sun, enjoying the warmth, the buzzing of insects and the feel of life surging around her. Her nephew sat nearby, saying nothing, just smiling at her from time to time.

As Eva came out of the house with their morning tea, he looked up and smiled as if he liked what he saw. It was then that Alice realised what she should do. She'd been so worried about how Eva would manage on her own, knowing better than anyone how shy her dear girl was under that reserved exterior.

But what if Eva wasn't on her own?

'Won't you come and join us, my dear?' she asked.

'Er – not just now, if you don't mind. I want to go through the accounts and then I have some letters to write.'

When Eva had gone back into the house, Alice looked at Gus and sighed. 'I'd really hoped she'd meet someone and get married, but she's a little shy.'

He chose his words carefully to please her. 'She's pretty.'

She smiled at him and a minute or two later asked suddenly, 'You're not – you don't have a girl friend, do you, Gus?'

He hesitated, wondering if this was leading where he thought. 'No. Since the war I've been quite busy, not had time to think of girls, really.'

She nodded as if this pleased her. 'Do you have any idea what you want to do with yourself?'

He shrugged. 'See if I can rustle up some capital and start a business, I suppose. I thought there'd be more from Dad, but he wasn't much good at handling money so there's only the house left now, really. When I go back to London, I shall have to buckle down to something.' He reached out to squeeze her hand. 'But I'm so glad I came to see you before . . .'

She finished the sentence for him. '. . . before I die.'

'I don't like even to think of it. It'll make me the last of the Blakes, the only male left out of my whole generation.' He let that sink in for a while, before giving her a fond smile and asking, 'Would you mind if I came to visit you again? Eva suggested I leave soon, because she doesn't want me to tire you. And I don't want to impose, definitely not. But I could come back in a week or two – just for a couple of days – if that's all right with you?'

'You don't have any pressing reason to leave?'

'Well, only the need to start earning a living.'

She frowned. 'I could help out, pay you an allowance – if you'd stay on – if you're *interested* in staying on and – and getting to know Eva better.'

He looked at her thoughtfully, choosing his words with care. 'I'd love to stay and do that, Aunt Alice, but I can't sponge on you. It wouldn't be right. And anyway, I do have some money of my own. No need to pay me anything.'

'I insist. You'd be a big help. The way you can carry me around makes things so much easier. Please stay, at least for a few more days. We'll discuss your future again later, when we've given things a chance.'

After he'd carried his aunt in for a nap, he went for a walk into Heyshaw to consider his options. Hell, what a golden opportunity! He'd only stopped off here hoping for a night or two's free lodgings while he did a little business in the neighbourhood, but it might be even more profitable to stay on and charm the two ladies. At one point he stopped walking, threw his head back and laughed. He always had been lucky.

Eva Kershaw wasn't bad-looking, though he preferred livelier women if he had the choice. But she was Alice Blake's heir and that made a *huge* difference.

The next day, when Eva went to help Alice settle down for her afternoon rest, her friend said, 'Sit down a minute, dear. I have something to tell you . . . It's good news. Gus has agreed to stay on for a while.'

Eva stiffened. 'But, Alice, you're in no fit state to be entertaining a guest, and Jenny and I haven't the—

Alice laid one hand on hers. 'Hear me out. Apart from the fact that Gus is my closest relative now, I've been able to do all sorts of things because he can carry me around.' She looked wistfully towards the window. 'It's been lovely to go out into the garden any time I want. He's very strong, a fine young man, don't you think?'

'Yes.'

'And if we don't have some help, I'll soon be confined to my bedroom, shut away from everything.'

'We'd agreed to make this room into your bedroom. You'd not be shut away down here.'

Alice sighed and looked round. 'It's much nicer to have a separate room during the daytime, makes me feel more normal.'

'Then we'll use my sitting room as your bedroom and—'

'Eva dear, let me finish. I really like having Gus here. He makes me laugh.' She watched her protégée carefully. 'Aren't you enjoying his company?'

'I – um – don't really know him.' Actually, she

continued to find him unsettling and was looking forward to his leaving, to having the house to themselves again, all quiet and cosy like before – but of course she couldn't say that because it was Alice's house and Alice's nephew.

'You're too shy for your own good, my dear girl. It's not fair on you, being tied to a dying woman like this.'

'I *want* to be with you. Oh, Alice, don't ever think I grudge you the time. You've done so much for me and now I can do this for you. Besides, I do have company my own age. There's Jenny and my sisters and—'

Alice pulled a wry face. 'Jenny is the maid. She calls you "Miss Kershaw". Hardly a friend.'

Eva didn't contradict her, because Alice had old-fashioned views about some things, but *she* considered Jenny a friend.

'And you don't see your family very often, do you? I know you're very fond of your sisters, but Overdale's a bit far away for frequent visits and the Fylde Coast is even further. Besides, if you do regard me as a mother, as you've often said you do,' Alice blinked her eyes rapidly, but a tear still rolled down her cheek, 'you'll let me advise you while I can. It's not good for a young woman to be alone in the world, especially a troubled world like this. We thought winning the war would solve all our problems, didn't we? But it hasn't. There's so much unemployment and there's a rough tone in society now, which I mistrust. Things are changing too quickly. Even clothes. Look at how short skirts are getting. You'd never catch me showing my knees in public like those women in the magazines do. I dread to think where it'll all end.'

Eva tried desperately to find the words to avert what Alice was clearly leading up to, but somehow they eluded her.

'I've no time to do anything but speak bluntly, dear child. If Gus stays on for a while, it'll not only make my life easier, but you two young people can get to know each other better – and who knows what will come of it?'

Eva swallowed hard and stared down at the pattern on the carpet. Nothing would come of it. She was quite, quite sure of that. At least on her side. She had seen her sisters' love for their husbands and knew instinctively she could never feel the same way about Gus, pleasant though he was. There had to be some spark of attraction between a man and a woman, surely, if they were to spend their lives together?

Alice continued speaking, her tone persuasive. 'I wish you were truly my daughter. My main regret is that I didn't marry and have children, so I won't be leaving anything of myself behind when I die.' She stared blindly into the distance then looked at Eva and smiled. 'But maybe that won't happen to you.'

Eva could not bear to take the happy expression from Alice's face by voicing her doubts or objecting to these tenuous plans. There was nothing she wouldn't do for her friend, nothing. 'If you want Gus to stay, then of course I'll make him welcome,' she managed as the silence dragged on.

'I knew you'd see it my way. He's suggested taking you out for a drive. He has a lovely motor car. I might even go out in it myself one day.'

Eva wasn't in the least bit interested in going for drives with Gus Blake. 'I don't th –' Her protest tailed away as she saw Alice's expression turn steely. It reminded her suddenly of the days when her friend had been a Deputy Headmistress, the terror of young wrongdoers.

'Do it for me, dear.'

What could Eva do but agree?

When she left Alice, she hurried along to the kitchen. Closing the door, she leaned against it, giving vent to her feelings with a strangled groan.

Jenny looked up and paused in chopping the carrots. 'What's wrong, love?'

'*He* is! He's got round Alice and she's invited him to stay on here indefinitely.' No need to say who *he* was. Jenny's face showed instant understanding.

'Oh, no! What's she thinking of?'

'And that's not all, Jenny. She's trying to match-make. She's made me promise to go out for a drive with him.'

'You should have said no to that!'

'I tried, but Alice believes she's ruining my life and wants to see me enjoying myself.' She looked at Jenny. 'What am I going to *do*? I'm not at all attracted to Gus Blake.'

'You should definitely have refused, then. It's not fair to build up her hopes.' Jenny shook her head ruefully. 'But I know you, Eva Kershaw. You've never refused her anything since she's been ill. She's lucky to have you.'

'I'm even luckier to have her. Without her, I'd be working in a factory or shop. My mother turned really strange after Dad died and she didn't want me to become a teacher. It was Alice who paid my way when I was training. You're not supposed to hate your mother, but I did. All us girls suffered from her bullying, Lizzie most of all.' Eva sighed. 'So I'll go out with Gus this once, for Alice's sake, but I'm definitely not doing it again.'

That evening Jenny took enough food to her grandad's for two people, but Wilf wasn't there. The next day, by skimping on her own meal, she again managed to find enough for both men. It had set in to rain, so she put on a raincoat and headscarf before carrying the food across the road in her shopping basket. She found John Gill alone, sitting staring into the fire.

'Eh, is it that time already?' he asked, looking up.

'Yes. And I've got enough food for Wilf again.'

'I haven't seen him all day, though he usually pops in for a minute or two.' He hesitated. 'Look, love, will you go and see if he's all right? I'm not walking so well these days, but I know he's upset at being out of work and too proud for his own good, and I'm that worried about him!'

'All right. I know where his lodgings are. But you start eating your food while it's still warm.'

She dished up his meal, standing the rest to keep warm on the hearth, then put her outdoor clothes on again. As she hurried along to the other end of North Hey she kept her head down to avoid the rain, so when someone grabbed her arm just as she was about to turn into the street where Wilf's lodgings were, she let out a shriek.

'It's only me.'

'Eh, you nearly made me jump out of my skin, Wilfred Horrocks. I was just coming to see you.'

As the rain beat down on them, Wilf pulled her under the partial shelter of a tree. 'Is your grandad all right?'

'He's fine but worried about you. You haven't been to see him for two days.'

He avoided her eyes and muttered, 'I didn't want to take advantage.'

She noticed he was shivering and looked at him more closely. His clothes were as wet as if they'd just been pulled out of the washtub and his usually fluffy light brown hair was plastered flat to his narrow skull, looking almost black. 'Eh, lad, you're soaked to the skin. Whatever have you been doing, staying out in this weather?'

He shrugged. 'The landlady doesn't want me round the house during the daytime. There's a few of us from the village out of work and we'd been sheltering in the church, only Mr Morton said we made it smell bad with our damp clothes, so we had to leave. That new minister's a toffee-nosed snot! You'd think the church was only for him and his posh friends, wouldn't you?'

Jenny stared at him, aghast, then took his cold hand in both hers and said gently, 'Come back to Grandad's with me. He's really worried about you and if you don't get warm, you'll catch your death of cold.'

He pulled away angrily. 'I saw how you looked at me the other day. I'm *not* trying to take advantage of him.'

'I realise that. Of course I do. You've been good to him. Oh, Wilf, I didn't know you'd lost your job. I'm sorry I upset you.' She could feel him still resisting her, but as he shivered, she gave him a sudden shove in the direction of her grandad's cottage. 'Get moving, will you! What do you think friends are for if not to help one another?'

A minute longer he resisted, then sighed. 'All reet, lass.' He shoved his hands into his pockets and strode along beside her with a squelching sound that said how wet his boots must be.

Once back at her grandfather's, she pushed Wilf over to stand near the fire, saying cheerfully, 'I've found him for you, Grandad. The silly fool's been walking about in the rain all day because that landlady of his won't let him stay there in the daytime and that new minister wouldn't let them stay in the church. Can you believe that? And Mr Morton calls himself a Christian. I'd like to give him a piece of my mind, I would that!' She looked at Wilf, who was trying to stop shivering and failing. He had such a bleached, weary look to him she wondered when he'd last eaten.

She took charge again because it seemed the only way to get him to be sensible. 'No use you sitting around in those wet things, Wilf. You'll come down with pneumonia if you don't get warm. I'll go and look out some of Grandad's old things for you. By the time you've changed, I'll have a cup of tea and some nice hot food waiting for you.' She could see tears of shame welling in his eyes so bustled off quickly to give him time to recover.

When she came down again, Wilf was standing by the fire with his back to the room, steam rising from his clothes. 'Come on, my lad! Up you go and get out of those things! Back bedroom. And don't drip all over the rug. Bring your wet things down with you and we'll hang them near the fire.'

When he'd gone she looked at her grandfather and said in a low voice, 'Eh, what's the world coming to when men who've fought for our country are denied shelter in the church?'

He gave her a wry smile. 'The world's as uncaring as it's allus been where ordinary folk are concerned. You didn't think the war would change that, did you?' He glanced upstairs. 'Thanks for fetching him. Eh, you're a grand lass, our Jenny.'

She flushed and shrugged.

'Look, before he comes down – I thought I'd ask Wilf to come and live with me. Would you mind? I'd enjoy the company and I need the help. There's a lot of things need fixing round the place, things I can't manage any more, so it'll not be just charity.' He sighed and stared blindly into the fire. 'It's a bugger getting old. No teeth, no strength and no wife. I miss our Janey – and her apple pies.'

Jenny bent to give him a big hug. 'I'll make you an apple pie tomorrow. And why should I mind you asking Wilf to live here? It's your cottage. Lucky you own it and no one can throw you out.'

'As long as I pay my council rates.' He fiddled with

his cup, then shrugged. 'If things get bad, I can allus sell my dad's watch, though. Silver, it is.'

'I've got money in the bank, so you won't have to.'

He gave her a crooked smile. 'You allus were careful with your pennies.'

When Wilf came down carrying his wet things, she took them off him and laid them next to the sink, then thrust the cup of tea she had ready into his hands, noting that they were still blue-white with cold. 'Come and sit down at the table and let's get some food into you. Then me an' Grandad have a favour to ask of you.'

Wilf gulped some tea, cradling his hands round the cup and sighing in pleasure. 'Eh, that's so good.'

'Plenty more in the pot.'

The food was a rather mixed plate of leftovers from lunch and tea at Miss Blake's – half-dried mashed potato, a bit of roast lamb, the gristly end, some cabbage and a stale sandwich from Miss Blake's lunch – but Wilf ate it with an expression of such bliss that Jenny wondered again how long it was since he'd had anything decent to fill his belly.

When he left the sandwich, she urged, 'Eat it all up, lad. No sense in wasting owt.'

He looked at her, naked shame in his eyes. 'I thought I'd save the sandwich for tomorrow, if that's all right with you?'

Grandad cleared his throat. 'If you'll do a bit of shopping for me tomorrow, lad, there'll be a bit of bread and scrape for you afterwards, so you eat that now. You need to keep up your strength.'

Wilf nodded and bent his head over the plate again, avoiding their eyes.

Jenny's heart went out to him. That a man so willing to work should come to this, needing the charity of his friends – and a man who had fought for his King and country at that! But she said nothing, merely busied herself tidying up the kitchen. When he'd finished eating, she cleared the table and sat down opposite him, folding her arms and turning to nod encouragingly to her grandad.

He took out his pipe and began to fiddle with it. 'Jenny and me were wondering if you'd like to come and live with me here, lad? I'm noan so spry these days and it'd be champion to have a bit of help around the place, loath as I am to admit it.'

Wilf looked at him, mouth working with emotion, then pressed the back of his hand against his lips for a moment before asking, 'Do you mean that?'

Grandad shot him a quick glance, then concentrated on the pipe again. 'Aye. 'Course I do.'

'I can't pay you any rent,' Wilf said hoarsely.

'I don't want money, I want help. Our Jenny does her best, but the back garden's in a right old mess an' there's things need fixing all over the house.'

Wilf interrupted in a harsh tone, 'Let's not pretend about this. I'm grateful for your charity, but—'

Jenny got up and went to lay one hand on his shoulder. 'Me an' Grandad aren't letting your stupid pride stand in the way. You went an' fought for us in France, Wilf Horrocks, put your life at risk, an' if we can't help you now in return there's something wrong with the world. Besides, Grandad's not fibbing about the garden, it does need digging over and tidying. And it'll take a load off my mind to know he isn't on his own, especially with Miss Blake getting so near the end. I worry that he'll have a fall an' just lie here for hours without anyone knowing an'—'

She stopped aghast for Wilf was sobbing, harsh, racking noises, his whole body shaking with the vehemence of them. She couldn't bear to see it, so took him in her arms. 'Eh, lad. Eh, lad.' She began to rock him to and fro, as if he were a child, making shushing noises and letting him weep out his shame and misery against her breast.

Grandad sat with his back to them, staring into the fire.

When the storm of weeping had died down, Jenny held Wilf away from her and smoothed his hair back tenderly with her fingertips. 'You've been on your own too long, my lad! Don't you have any family at all?'

He shook his head. 'My brother was killed on the Somme. There were only ever the two of us. We were brought up in an orphanage, but they kept us together at least. We even joined up together. Since I got out of the Army, I've managed, but I've missed Clem so much –' His voice broke again but he took a deep breath and looked from her to John, saying huskily, 'You'll not regret this, I promise you, Mr Gill, or you, Jenny lass. I still get odd bits of work here and there, so I won't be too much of a burden, I hope.'

Grandad cackled suddenly and broke the tension. As the other two turned to stare at him in puzzlement, he chortled again. 'Well, I intend to be a burden, because I've just realised that with you to help me, I can go and have a sup of ale now and then. Our Jenny won't go into the pub, but I don't reckon you'd mind taking me, eh, lad? I'm not so steady on me pins these days, you see. I can't hold my drink like I used to, either, but a glass of ale still tastes good.'

Wilf gave him a watery grin. 'I'll not mind at all taking you to the pub, or anywhere else you need to go, Mr Gill.' He looked at Jenny, still sitting beside him. She wasn't beautiful, but she was trim and wholesome in her simple print dress, and he'd been wishing for a while he could afford to court her. But he couldn't. His Army gratuity was all gone now and he was losing hope of getting a permanent job.

Jenny was studying him openly, too, and when their eyes met, she nodded and gave him a quick smile before standing up. 'Right, then. You can move in tomorrow. I'll go and make the bed up, but see you put a hot water bottle in it tomorrow to air it out properly. After I've done that I'll have to get back. Eva will be wondering what's happened to me.'

When she came down she washed the plates, then took off her pinny and went to hang it up behind the cupboard door.

Once she'd gone Wilf stared down at his clenched fists and said gruffly, 'You must think me a right old mardy-face, crying like that.'

'I think you've had a lot to bear an' we all of us have a weep now an' then, whether we let on about it or not,' Grandad said gently. 'Now, lad, you can help me down to the pub this very night if you don't mind being seen in those old clothes of mine. I've a right thirst on me for a glass of ale, by hell I have.'

Once at the Dog and Duck, the old man counted out some coins and pushed them into his companion's hand. 'Two halves of best bitter.'

'I can't take your—'

'Nay, lad, I'm noan sitting here on me own. But we'll have to make one glass last till closing time.'

Wilf brought back two glasses of beer and sat down with a sigh of pleasure, raising his glass to his companion. 'Thanks, Mr Gill.'

'*Mr* Gill!' Grandad pulled a face. 'I'm not Mr Gill to anyone 'cept that bloody doctor. Call me Grandad. That's more friendly, like.'

'Grandad it is, then.'

They sat chatting for a while, then the old man hissed suddenly, 'Look at that sod!'

Wilf turned to follow the pointing finger and stare through the open area of the bar at a man in a dark suit standing by the counter at the other side, haw-hawing with laughter. 'Who is he?'

'Miss Blake's nephew. My Jenny can't stand him.'

'Then there must be summat wrong with him.'

'That's what I reckon. She's a good judge of character, my Jenny is.'

Grandad looked down wistfully at his glass, but resisted gulping the beer. 'I worry about what's to happen to her when Miss Blake's gone. There aren't any other jobs like that in Heyshaw, so she'll have to find work away from here. Eh, I'd miss her something shocking.' He took another infinitesimal sip then nodded in the direction of the lounge, where the posher folk congregated. 'Jenny reckons Master Gus bloody Blake is after his aunt's money. By rights everything should go to that schoolteacher lass as has been looking after Miss Blake the past year or two – real nice lass Eva Kershaw is, too, treats our Jenny decently. But dying folk don't always do the right thing. If they did there'd not be so many falling-outs over wills.'

'Well, there's nowt we can do about that.'

Grandad sighed. 'No. But it won't hurt to keep an eye on what that chap gets up to.' He squinted sideways. 'If you get any more work behind the bar here, you could try to listen to what he's saying, couldn't you? An' watch who he's spending time with?'

Wilf nodded. 'Aye.' Though he couldn't see what good it'd do.

They made their half pints last for an hour, which didn't improve the taste of the beer, but gave them the right to stay there till closing time. A lot of fellows were doing the same thing these days, which made the landlord Charlie Featherstone grumpy.

Wilf got the old man home again, helped John to bed then went back to his lodgings for the last time. He was lucky to have a friend like Grandad. Not many people would open their homes to an out-of-work chap who wasn't a relative. He wished suddenly that he'd known his own grandfather. Or his father. It was hard having no one to call family.

3

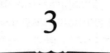

The following day after lunch Alice smiled at Eva and said coaxingly, 'Gus has offered to take you out for a little drive today. He was hoping to catch you when you got back from the shop to ask you himself, but he must have missed you. Why don't you go out with him, dear? The fresh air will do you good.'

Eva swallowed hard. Gus was always very pleasant, but her feelings about him hadn't changed. However, Alice was looking at her so anxiously she forced a smile. 'Well, all right. If you're sure you won't need me.'

'I shall have Jenny, shan't I?'

As soon as she'd heard the car drive away, Alice took the next step she and her nephew had planned together when he'd agreed to help with her little plan. She rang the bell. 'Ah, Jenny. Why don't you go and visit your grandfather for an hour or two this afternoon? I'm feeling very sleepy and I'm sure I shan't need anything.'

'I don't think I should leave you on your own, miss.'

Alice fixed her with a stern glance. 'Sometimes, Jenny, I long to be on my own – just for a little while.'

'Well, if you're sure . . .'

'I'm very sure.'

Alice listened to Jenny running up and down the stairs. As the kitchen door banged and the maid's footsteps faded away into the distance, she nodded in satisfaction that her stratagem had worked, though she felt rather guilty at deceiving Eva. Still, it was all for the best, it really was. She had to secure her girl's future. Times were hard and only likely to get harder, judging by what the newspapers said. A young woman with a private income would be easy prey for all sorts of scoundrels. She'd sent one or two young men packing over the years, because they weren't good enough for her Eva.

Five minutes later there was a tap on the front door and Miss Blake's lawyer and neighbour, Eric Beaman, walked straight in, as instructed. He was most helpful, explaining various ways of achieving her goal and helping her work out the details, though they disagreed over one or two points. However, she got her way by reminding him that she was the client and this was what she wished.

After he'd left, Alice lay quietly, not attempting to read her newspaper. She had a lot to think about and it was lovely to have the house to herself. One of the worst aspects of her illness was being so dependent on others. She hated that.

When Eva went to get ready for her outing she put on her coat, stared at herself in the mirror and on a sudden impulse pulled her soft felt hat down to a distinctly unflattering angle. She didn't intend to give Gus Blake any encouragement whatsoever.

He was waiting in the hall, leaning against the wall as usual.

She deliberately spoke in her most schoolmistressy tone. 'Could you please not lean on the walls, Mr Blake? It marks the wallpaper.'

He breathed deeply but said nothing as he straightened up. 'Rightie-ho. You ready now?'

'Yes. I'll just look in on Alice before we leave.'

'She's asleep.'

He put an arm under Eva's elbow and she had no option but to go with him to the front door. The car was waiting for them there, its black paintwork gleaming, its hood down. It was a large car, so he must have plenty of money. But if he wasn't here to get Alice's money, as Jenny suspected, what was he staying on for?

Gus started the car and looked at her. 'Where shall we go?'

She couldn't think properly with him so close. 'Um – over the moors?'

'Yes. Should be pretty up there on a sunny day like this, though there's a nip in the air now. There's a rug in the back if you're not warm enough.'

'I shall be fine. After all, we won't be out for long, will we? I don't like to leave Alice on her own.'

'Well, I thought if we found somewhere that sold teas, we could stop and have something to eat.'

'We can have tea when we get back. No use wasting your money.'

He grinned. 'I'm not short of the price of a meal, Eva.'

'Oh, well, whatever you want.' She was feeling flustered again.

'My aunt's given me strict orders to give you a treat. So tea and cream cakes it is.'

She sat stiffly as the big car throbbed into motion and fairly flew through the village, going much faster than she felt was safe. Clutching the leather strap on the door, she prayed they wouldn't knock someone down. People turned to stare, because motor cars were not all that common, and once a dog ran after them, barking furiously.

Half an hour later the car slowed down markedly on an uphill bit of road. Gus frowned. 'She isn't pulling properly and the engine sounds a bit rough.'

Eva listened. At first she could hear no difference, then, as the car slowed right down and jerked once or twice, she heard the engine falter. 'Is it breaking down?' she asked, wondering if they would have to walk back.

He flashed her a quick smile. 'Let's hope not.' But the smile soon faded.

At the top of the hill he let the car run off the road and come to a halt on some level, grassy ground. 'Better take a look, I think.' He went to lift the bonnet and peer under it, then came back. 'The engine's overheated, though I don't know why. I'm no mechanic. I'm afraid we'll have to turn back once it's cooled down so you won't get your cream cakes after all.'

She shrugged.

'Well, at least we've stopped somewhere with a nice view.' He waved one hand at the slopes below them, and in the distance Heyshaw itself. 'I hadn't realised how beautiful the moors can be. Do you ever go walking across them?'

'I used to. Before . . .' Her throat tightened with sorrow and she couldn't speak for a moment.

'It's been hard on you, hasn't it?'

She was surprised at the gentleness in his voice. Hadn't expected that from him.

'I've been through it myself, so I do understand. You keep a stiff upper lip because you don't want to upset them, but it's a strain.'

His sympathy made her want to weep and she had a struggle to keep control of her emotions.

Gus left her in peace for a few minutes, drumming his fingers absent-mindedly on the steering wheel. 'I know my aunt made you come out with me today. If you don't want to do it again, you don't have to. I just thought the odd outing might cheer you up, help you relax a bit. And it pleased her greatly.'

She liked him better for speaking openly. 'I think I've forgotten how to relax. I worry about Alice all the time. She's often in pain, you know, but she doesn't give in to it, so how can I give in to my own worries?'

'How long does the doctor think she's got?'

'A few weeks at most. She's already lived for longer than they'd expected.'

'You poor thing.'

Eva struggled to hold back the tears, but this time she couldn't and found herself sobbing against his chest. He didn't take advantage, just let her weep. When she pulled away and fumbled for her handkerchief, he held out his own, then stared across the moors as she wiped her eyes and composed herself.

'I don't know what came over me. I'm sorry to – to spoil your outing like this.'

'It's *our* outing. And you didn't spoil it. Gertie did.' He slapped the car affectionately. 'She doesn't usually let me down. Now, are you ready to go?' When she nodded, he got out and started the car up again, listening with a frown. 'There's definitely something wrong. Is there a mechanic in Heyshaw or am I going to have to go further afield to get help?'

'There's a big garage in South Heyshaw, about a mile away from home, and there's a man who repairs things for people sometimes in North Hey. Aaron Brierley, he's called, he lives just behind us. People speak well of his work – better than they do of the garage, actually. He works for Mr Linney on the farm and lives in one of the cottages there.' She knew him by sight because she had seen him with his daughter, Gracie, whom she'd taught briefly, but she had never spoken to him. He had dark hair, his clothes were shabby, and since the war he walked with a limp. Jenny said his wife was dying slowly of tuberculosis. If so, Eva's heart went out to him. She knew what it was like to watch somebody failing day by day.

'I'd better get in touch with this Brierley chappie, then, and see if he can sort out Gertie here.' Gus didn't speak for a few minutes, then looked sideways at her. 'I'd like to take you out again to make up for this. Will you come?'

He'd been so understanding about her weeping she didn't like to turn his offer down. 'All right.'

'I'll look forward to it.' He hid a smile at her tone. She was a funny, prim little thing, quite pretty but a real fusspot. Not the sort he'd usually have gone out with.

Eva concentrated on the road ahead and was relieved when he didn't say anything else. He was more tactful than she'd expected, but fancy weeping all over him like that! She often felt close to tears nowadays. She really must pull herself together.

When they got back, Gus parked the car and helped her out. 'I'll just have another look at old Gertie.'

But he didn't touch the car until he'd watched her walk into the house. Hell, she even walked primly and that damned hat made her look dowdy. What's more, she wasn't showing the slightest interest in him, which piqued him a little. Usually the ladies were all over him. Bit of a surprise, her weeping like that. Useful, though. He'd played the sympathetic friend rather well, he thought. She'd been much less stiff with him afterwards.

He chuckled and patted the car. 'Thanks, Gertie my love. You chose your moment well.'

Then he walked inside whistling, ready to turn his attention to Miss Alice Blake. He was a dab hand at soft-soaping old ladies, if he said so himself. And this one wasn't a bad old stick.

He hoped Beaman had kept the appointment and that Alice had got rid of that nosy maid of hers, as they'd planned.

He'd ask Sid Linney about this Brierley chap. Couldn't have Gertie breaking down on him again. He had several places he needed to visit. He chuckled. Always good to move to a new part of the country in his line of business. He'd soon be flush with money again. And maybe he'd let the old lady persuade him to accept a small allowance as well. Why look a gift horse in the mouth?

The following afternoon, Sid beckoned to Aaron. 'Friend of mine's having a bit of trouble with his car. I told him you'd look at it for him.'

'I will if he pays me there and then,' Aaron said bluntly. 'I can't afford the time to go pestering folk for payment, not with Lil so bad.'

Sid scowled at him. 'No friend of mine would welsh on such a small sum. I'll let you go early to do it, since we're a bit ahead with the work today. See you do a good job on Mr Blake's car. He's staying with his aunt, Miss Blake. She lives at—'

'I know where she lives.' Aaron knew just about everyone in North Hey by sight, and every track and path around it, because at first after he'd got back there had been nights when he couldn't sleep and went out walking till he'd tired himself out.

He hurried home, explaining to Lil what he was doing then giving himself a quick sluice down at the kitchen sink. No sense turning up smelling of manure!

He loaded his tools into the sidecar, glad of an excuse to leave the tiny cottage and use his motor bike. Maybe he'd take the girls out for a ride next

Sunday. He'd be able to afford a bit of petrol after this job and they loved to cram into the sidecar and ride with him across the moors. He smiled at the thought of giving them a little treat.

Watching him out of the window, Lil saw his face soften and smiled in sympathy. Eh, her Aaron didn't smile much these days. He was a good-looking chap when he did, though, seeming more like the man she'd fallen in love with when she was eighteen. She loved him still, but she wasn't sure he realised it. And though he was unfailingly kind to her – she reckoned he must be one of the kindest fellows she'd ever met, though he tried to hide that – she knew he didn't love her and never had. But with Gracie on the way they'd had no choice except to marry, and give him his due he'd not hesitated when she'd told him but had gone straight to ask her father's permission.

She sighed. Maybe he'd find himself another wife after she'd gone, one more suited to him, one who understood the long words he used and who liked reading books. She could never be bothered with books and had always preferred to keep herself busy.

Now that she couldn't do much, she read magazines when they could afford them. Aaron sometimes bought her a copy of *Peg's Paper*, her favourite, which was only a penny-ha'penny. She liked looking at the pictures, especially the one on the front cover, but it was hard to keep up with the serials when you didn't get the magazine every week.

Once, Aaron had been in a funny mood and had bought her *Homes and Gardens* for a change. That had made her laugh! It was meant for rich women and talked about the problems of 'the servantless home'. She'd never had any help until she got so ill and Aaron had had to bring in Mrs Harrop. She'd far rather do her own housework and couldn't imagine how rich women filled their days.

Homes and Gardens had had another long article asking, 'Is polished brass worthwhile?' which had also made Lil chuckle. But she had been interested in reading about that modern marvel, electricity in the home. She'd like to see that, eh, she would indeed! Imagine being able to get a good light simply by turning on a switch. The Brierleys had to make do with oil lamps and candles, and cook on an old-fashioned coal range, because they didn't even have gas out here at the farm.

She picked up the latest *Peg's Paper* and began to flip through it, but soon grew tired and drifted into an uneasy sleep, waking to a chilly room with the fire nearly gone out. By the time she'd hauled herself out of bed and mended the fire she was exhausted, so she snuggled down under the covers and snoozed on.

When the two children came back from school they entered the house quietly, tip-toeing upstairs to see if their mother was all right, then creeping down again when they saw that she was sleeping.

'Where's Dad, do you think?' Gracie asked.

Molly shook her head and took the earliest opportunity to go and sit under the table and play house. In her imaginary home there was a mother who sang and

cooked lovely meals for them, and who polished everything and made it look shiny. She took out her box of
treasures and pulled out the handkerchief the kind lady
had given her. Gracie said she was called Miss Kershaw and was a teacher, but she wasn't like Molly's
teacher. Miss Deevers hit you with a ruler and Molly
hated school.

Putting the soft, slightly scented handkerchief
against her cheek, she rocked to and fro, dreaming
her quiet little dreams.

The front gardens of Rose Villa looked beautiful,
though they could have done with a bit of tidying
up. When Aaron stopped his bike he sat there for a
minute or two enjoying the sight and smell of the roses
which had given the place its name. They were past
their best now, but still beautiful. Old Mr Blake had
been mad for roses, always begging cuttings of new
ones off people. Nothing looked quite as trim as it had
before the war, however. He gave a snort of sympathy.
How could it? Here was another household struck by
illness, and flower gardens weren't nearly as important
as caring for the dying.

He looked at the car. A Riley. He'd driven one of
those once in London while chauffeuring an officer
around. Nice cars. This one had an unloved air to it,
however, with rust beginning to show in a place or two.
And it needed polishing. Probably needed a few other
things doing, too. Wise men got to know their vehicles
and kept an eye on the mechanical details. His motor
bike was always in tip-top order.

He went to knock on the side door.

Jenny Gill opened the door. 'Eh, Aaron, I'm that glad to see you.' She lowered her voice. 'Mr Blake's been as bad-tempered as a wasp in a bottle today because he can't drive out in his precious car.'

'Well, we'll see if we can fix it.'

Her voice grew gentle. 'How's Lil? I'd have come up to see her, but they said she didn't want visitors.'

He shrugged, not wanting to talk about his wife. 'She's not so good. And she doesn't like visitors, I'm afraid. Doesn't want them to see how she's changed. Look, if you fetch out your Mr Blake, Jenny lass, I'll get on with his repairs while it's still light. I've got to get back to the children as quickly as I can.'

'All right.'

She went inside, thinking how worn down Aaron was looking. Before the war he'd been a fine figure of a man. Now, he not only looked unhappy, but as if he never got a square meal, either.

Aaron looked up to see the loud-voiced stranger he'd seen in the pub coming out of the house. Oh, hell, it was *his* car!

'Ah, you must be the chappie Linney told me about. Come and take a look at my Gertie.'

He didn't stay with Aaron, just left him to work on the vehicle. It was only a fuel blockage, which wouldn't take long to sort out, but the car needed some other attention as well so Aaron went to make sure Mr snooty bugger Blake was willing to pay for that.

'It'll be ten shillings if I go through everything, cash on the nail,' he said bluntly, having explained.

'Are you qualified to do all that?'

Aaron deliberately let his accent thicken. 'Aye. They trained me as a mechanic in th'Army.'

'Yes, there were some good chaps in the ranks.' Blake waved one hand in permission. 'Go ahead and fix her up, then.' He wandered off inside again.

Aaron didn't bother to tell him he'd been a lieutenant by the time he got invalided out. He hated rich snobs.

A little later Miss Kershaw came out. 'Jenny wants to know if you'd like a cup of tea?'

'I'd love one, thanks.'

'And a scone, maybe?'

He nodded, liking her quiet voice. He didn't know her first name and wanted to, for some reason. He'd ask Jenny later. 'My Gracie told me you'd saved our Molly from bullying the other day. I've been wanting to thank you for that.'

Eva flushed. 'I couldn't just walk past and let them hurt her, could I? How is she?' She had not been able to forget the little girl's unhappy face.

He shrugged. 'She's all right. It's a difficult time for us all, with my wife so ill.'

'Yes. I can understand that.'

Her face lost its cool, distant look and filled with compassion, suddenly looking soft and attractive. Which surprised him, because she was known as a confirmed old maid in the village.

'You could come into the kitchen and sit down for a few minutes while you drink your tea,' she added. 'Jenny and I are just taking a break.'

He looked down at himself. 'Better not. I might get oil on something.'

'I'll bring it out to you, then.'

He watched her walk back into the house. Neat and slightly plump like a pet hen Mrs Linney had brought to the farm with her. It was a bonny little thing with bright eyes. This young woman's eyes were bright and interested in the world, too, though there was a sadness to them as well. Her clothes looked as if they'd been freshly ironed and every hair was in place; her shoes gleaming with fresh polish. He'd never liked scrawny women.

Lil had been plump once, but she'd never looked like this. She'd been born untidy. Well, so had he until the Army trained him as a mechanic and taught him to be very tidy indeed, so that he knew instinctively where every single tool was. He still kept his tools in good order, but in the house you never knew where Mrs Harrop had shoved things. He'd given up trying to sort the kitchen out, because he was always too tired by the time he got the girls to bed and knew Mrs Harrop would only grumble that she couldn't find anything and mess it up again next time she came.

Miss Kershaw came out with a tray. The last time a woman had fed him so elegantly had been in London, when he'd been staying with a friend while on a short leave. James's mother had spoiled them both rotten, which had made it even harder to go back to the muck and blood. James had been killed soon after, poor sod. He'd been a good mate.

'Are you all right, Mr Brierley?'

'What?' He blinked and realised he'd become lost in his thoughts. 'Just wool gathering, remembering the last time someone served me tea on a tray with a fancy cloth on it.' He touched it with his little finger, which was still fairly clean. 'It looks lovely.'

There was the sound of footsteps on gravel and the owner of the car returned.

'Excuse me.' Eva hurried off into the house.

'How's it going, then?' Blake asked.

'Fine.' Aaron picked up the tea cup and drank. The other man looked at him sourly, as if he had no right to stop for refreshments, then walked back towards the house. Did he have a personal interest in Miss Kershaw? Aaron wondered. Surely not? Anyway, she'd hurried away, which a lass didn't do if she was interested in a fellow.

He enjoyed the scones enormously, picking up the crumbs with a dampened fingertip. There was nothing like home cooking. He and the girls lived mainly on bought bread and cheese or ham now, with the odd apple and sometimes vegetables from the garden.

When he'd finished he carried the tray across to the house and knocked on the door. Jenny opened it this time. 'Thanks, love. It was grand. Haven't had home-baked scones for a long time.' He lowered his voice. 'I know I'm being nosy, but what's Miss Kershaw's first name? I keep feeling I've heard it somewhere, but I can't remember it.'

'Eva.'

'That's it! Thanks.' Eva. It suited her, as neat as she was. It was amazing how the simple kindness shown by her and Jenny had made the day seem brighter. He found himself whistling as he went on with his work, methodically checking everything.

By the time he'd finished, it was getting dark and the sky was clouding over with a chill, damp wind blowing. He went to knock on the door again. 'Can you tell Mr Blake I've finished, please, Jenny love?'

The big chap came out and pretended he knew what he was looking at. He didn't, but he found a very small greasy fingermark, which Aaron wiped off and polished. There was no offer of payment, so he had to ask for his money. The rotten sod had done that on purpose for the sheer pleasure of exercising a little power.

But he did produce ten shillings when asked.

As Aaron was putting his tools back into his sidecar, Jenny came out with something wrapped in a brown paper bag. 'We thought your girls might enjoy a little treat. There are a few scones here. We've just done a big bake and we've plenty to spare.'

'Thanks. That's really kind of you.'

'It was Eva's idea. She loves children.' Raindrops began to fall and Jenny looked up at the lowering sky. 'You'd better get away quick or you'll be soaked. Give my regards to Lil.'

He watched Jenny as she walked back to the house and turned at the door to wave, her plain face lit by the warmth of her personality. As he looked down at the paper bag, a lump came into his throat. Sometimes a small kindness could make you feel like weeping. Daft, that was.

He pulled himself together and drove home, glad of the extra money, determined to give his lasses a treat with it, but hoping he wouldn't have to work for that plummy-voiced sod again.

That evening Sid Linney asked Gus, 'How did Brierley go?'

'Oh, he took care of the car very nicely, but he's a surly brute. I don't know how you put up with him.'

'With great difficulty, believe me, and only because his wife is dying of TB. The minute she dies, out he goes.' Sid smiled reflectively. 'In the meantime I keep him on his toes.'

'That's the ticket.'

A little later, Sid said thoughtfully, 'I can see Brierley managed to annoy you. How about getting your own back?'

Gus leaned back, smiling. 'What do you suggest?'

The following afternoon Sid came stumping across the field to where Aaron was digging up the potatoes old Mr Linney had always grown for his own use. He stopped work and stared at his employer, wondering what was wrong now.

Sid stopped a few feet away. 'Haven't got much done, have you? My father let you get lazy.'

Aaron said nothing.

'Didn't do your job properly yesterday, either. Blake's not best pleased with how you finished the job and says you pestered that nice young woman for food while you were there.'

Aaron gaped at him. 'I beg your pardon?'

'Don't you talk fancy at me. While you were playing at being an officer in France, others were here working their guts out to feed this country, which was equally important and don't you forget it.' Sid glared at his employee. 'I tell you frankly, if it weren't for that poor wife of yours, I'd not have you working here. My dad was daft to take you on with that gammy leg. I can get better help and more respectful workers, any day. Blake's quite right. You *don't* know your place.'

Stunned at this unexpected attack, Aaron kept his expression calm and his breathing even while he frantically tried to work out what Blake could possibly have to complain about. 'I don't understand what he's accusing me of,' he said at last, as Sid stood waiting, arms folded. 'I was *offered* a cup of tea and a scone. I didn't ask for anything. Why should I have said no?'

'Because you were there to repair my friend's car, that's why, not sit around guzzling cups of tea.'

It was a good thing Aaron had had practice during the war at dealing with unreasonable men who had power over him because he felt a strong urge to punch this ugly, red-faced brute in the face. 'I'll remember that next time and refuse any offers of refreshment. But I did a good job for Mr Blake. That motor's running sweetly now and will as long as he takes care of it.'

'Yes, well, that's one thing. No one denies you picked up a bit of mechanicking in the Army. But he says you left greasy finger marks all over the car. What sort of mechanic doesn't clear up after himself?'

'I didn't leave any marks on that car.' He was utterly certain of that.

Sid's face took on a dusky red hue. 'Are you calling my friend a liar?'

'I'm not calling him anything, just saying I didn't leave any greasy fingerprints on that car. If you think a man trained by the Army would do that,' Aaron bit off more angry words and finished lamely, 'then you're far and out.'

'Well, I happen to believe Mr Blake, who is an officer and a gentleman, so you can just go round there after work tonight – *in your own time* – and give that car a good wash and polish for him.'

'I have a sick wife and two children to look after once I finish work.'

'Should have remembered that and done the job properly the first time.' Sid gave him a sneering smile. 'I'll not employ men who don't finish jobs properly.'

The implied threat made Aaron so angry he could not hold back, 'So the children have to wait for their tea?'

'They must be used to that by now. And if you spent less money in the pub, you'd be able to afford proper help at home.'

Aaron took refuge behind his poker face while trying to work out what was happening, which usually helped in bad situations. It was clear that Sid and Blake had hatched up this plot together. What he couldn't understand was *why*? At that moment he'd have given all he owned to have been able to tell the other man to keep his rotten job. But he was as helpless as a chained convict because of Lil and that damned tied cottage.

'Now, get on with your work and less of your lip, Brierley. And see that you do a good job for my friend this time.'

Aaron turned away without a word.

After work he went home quickly, glad the evenings hadn't started to draw in too much yet. Lil seemed drowsy and only half-aware of what he was saying, so he explained what had happened to Gracie as he strapped on his leg brace.

'You always leave us. You don't love us!' she shouted at him, then turned her back on him and began to fill the kettle.

He stopped to stare at her. 'That's not true. Gracie, are you listening to me?'

She did not turn round.

He went to lay one hand on her shoulder. 'It's *because* I love you that I'm doing this. If I don't, I'll lose my job and then we'll all lose our home. And I thought I told you I didn't want you lifting that heavy kettle! Half full and no more, my girl, till you're bigger.'

She shrugged his hand off and kept her back turned to him.

He hesitated, wishing he could get through to her, but time was ticking on and he needed daylight to work in. Sighing he went to get his motorbike out of the shed.

When he arrived at Rose Villa, Blake came out, his expression very similar to Sid Linney's. 'I'll keep a better eye on you this time, fellow. I can't take my young lady out in a car that's covered in greasy fingerprints.'

There were indeed some greasy marks on the car, but Aaron was utterly certain he hadn't put them there.

In the kitchen Jenny stopped what she was doing to listen carefully through the open window. She couldn't understand what Mr Blake was going on about. She had seen Aaron Brierley polishing the car when he'd finished the other day and she'd seen the car, too. There had definitely been no greasy fingerprints on it. She would have noticed something like that because she had an eye for detail.

Someone came into the kitchen behind her and she spun round, putting one finger to her lips when she saw Eva.

'What's wrong, Jenny?'

'I'll tell you after. Shh.'

So they both listened to Gus berating Aaron, who stood there stolidly, his eyes blank and his expression wooden.

Jenny said nothing. For her the scene brought back unhappy memories of working as maid for an employer who was never satisfied. Her grandad had taken one look at her face when she came to visit him at the end of her first quarter and had told her roundly not to go back. She hadn't done that, but she'd given her notice for the next quarter and that had caused her a lot more trouble. She'd often wished she'd listened to Grandad. It'd have made such a difference to her life.

For Eva the angry, unreasonable man outside was a stark reminder of her mother and how she'd scolded or slapped them for imaginary wrongs. No one should have to put up with that and she thought less of Gus for behaving so unreasonably.

When the tirade ended Aaron picked up the bucket Gus had dropped at his feet and moved towards the kitchen door, not hurrying, not looking sideways.

Eva slipped out into the corridor, not wanting to embarrass him by her presence.

Jenny answered the knock with a cheerful, 'Hello, Aaron. What can I do for you, lad?'

'Can I have a bucket of hot water, please? Mr Blake wants the car washing.'

'It's only dirty because he drove it today,' she said in a low voice. 'Why do *you* have to clean it? Is he paying you extra for this?'

In an equally low voice, he replied, 'He told Sid Linney I'd left it in a state. If I don't do as he wants I'll lose my job.'

'Eh, he never! Shh! He's coming.' She raised her voice. 'You'll need a couple of soft cloths too.' As Gus came to stand near the door, she turned to busy herself at the sink, filling the bucket with hot water and sorting out some old rags, as well as the wash leather she used on the windows.

'Thank you.' Aaron moved back towards the car.

Gus Blake looked at her through narrowed eyes as if he suspected her of doing something wrong. Jenny tossed her head and let out an angry sniff. She wasn't answerable to him. Going back to her duties, she chose jobs which allowed her to watch what was happening outside, glad they had a modern kitchen with the sink under the window, not a narrow, old-fashioned scullery and shallow slop stone. Eh, those old stone sinks were a devil to keep clean, unlike this white ceramic one.

Mr Blake was pointing, snapping out orders, standing over Aaron. She had never seen such an example of a grown man bullying another in her whole life, though she had often seen kids doing it in a school playground. Just let Mr Blake try to treat her like that! She'd give him what for.

A creaking overhead betrayed the fact that someone was in the spare bedroom at that side of the house. It could only be Eva, who must be watching what was happening as well.

'You're not doing yourself any good, Mr Toffee-Nose Blake,' Jenny muttered. 'There's no one with a stronger sense of fair play than our Eva. If you want to get in well with her, you're going exactly the wrong way about it. She doesn't like show-offs and bullies. And neither do I!'

Upstairs Eva pressed one hand against her breast, aghast at what she was seeing. Why was Gus bullying Mr Brierley like this? To her knowledge he had only met the man once before. She would not have thought it of a nephew of Alice.

When he had finished and knew the car to be immaculate, Aaron turned to his tormentor and looked at him questioningly.

'This bit needs an extra polishing,' Gus said, pointing.

Mutely, Aaron wielded the soft cloth Jenny Gill had

given him. He heard footsteps on the gravel behind him, but didn't turn round.

'How splendid the car is looking!' Eva said.

Gus turned to smile at her. 'Ready for our ride tomorrow.'

Watching covertly, Aaron saw her press her lips together and her smile go a bit glassy. Then she turned to him. 'Your poor children must be waiting for their tea, Mr Brierley. Surely he's finished now, Gus?'

He pretended to scrutinise the car. 'Yes. That's better. You can go now, Brierley. And see you do a better job first time from now on.'

Aaron did not turn round or answer.

Gus stood and watched as the other man started his motor bike, thinking how Sid would enjoy hearing about this. As the sound of the engine throbbed away into the distance, he turned to see Eva looking at him disapprovingly.

'Mr Brierley's wife is dying of tuberculosis,' she said quietly. 'He has to get home from work as quickly as he can in the evenings to look after her and their two children. He doesn't usually accept any jobs after he's finished at the farm.'

'He didn't exactly accept this one. He was sent back to finish what he should have done last time. He'd left greasy finger marks all over the paintwork. These chappies have to be taught to toe the line. It was the same in the Army. You had to make sure the ranks did their work properly.'

Eva was growing a little tired of the way he kept harking back to the war, almost as if he had enjoyed it.

Her sister Lizzie's husband Peter didn't speak about the men under his command in this scornful way, nor did Polly's Richard. In fact, they didn't speak about the war much at all when the women were around, though Richard had started up a home at Stenton for those so badly injured they would need care for the rest of their lives.

No one could forget the war, even three years later, not with men passing you in the street on crutches or with empty sleeves pinned neatly to their jackets. Some of those missing both legs used pieces of wood to scoot themselves along on home-made wheeled trolleys, and she never knew whether to be sad for them or to admire their cheerful acceptance of their disability. There were artificial limbs, of course, provided by the Government, but not everyone could get on with them.

'I'm sure Mr Brierley understands that just as well as you do,' she said sharply. 'He was an officer too and they gave him two medals when he was invalided out after Passchendaele, Jenny tells me.'

As she walked back into the house Gus glared after her. He had not known that. Why hadn't Sid told him that when he'd asked for help in making his stiff-necked and insubordinate employee toe the line?

He was also furious with Eva for interfering and it took him a moment or two to calm down and pin a smile back on his face before following her inside. She was going to make an uncomfortable wife if she got up on her high horse about things that were none of her business.

Indoors Gus found no sign of her in the sitting room

and noticed that the dining table was set for only one person. He went into the kitchen to demand, 'Where's Eva? Is she going out tonight?'

Jenny turned a bland face towards him. 'Miss Kershaw's tired, sir. She's having a tray in her room tonight.'

Gus glared at her. He would not employ a cheeky maid in his house. That one would be dismissed straight away when he took over here.

4

When Gus began pressing Eva to go out for another ride in his car, she demurred. He could be good company, but she was still annoyed about him bullying Aaron Brierley. Besides, he seemed to regard the whole world with cynical amusement and that irritated her, as did the feeling that he was treating her like a child to be humoured rather than a woman who attracted him. She was twenty-four and had been earning her own living for years, managing classes of fifty children, noted for her efficiency and good results when the school inspectors came round.

She missed teaching dreadfully at times. Not that she begrudged giving it up for Alice – never that! – but they had been so happy and busy together before her friend's illness that she couldn't help wanting that back. Nowadays time could hang very heavily.

Jenny said Aaron Brierley's wife was dying, too, of TB. That must be awful for him, and the thought of those two children facing the loss of their mother wrung Eva's heart. Her own father had died when she was eleven so she knew how it felt to lose a parent, but for her it had happened with brutal suddenness in an accident. She didn't know how a child would cope with watching a parent die slowly day by day.

She remembered Aaron's face very clearly, for some reason. There was a shadowed unhappiness on it and pain, too. She and Jenny had watched him from the kitchen window. He had favoured his left leg every now and then, wincing sometimes if he moved incautiously. But he had a gentle smile that lightened his whole face and when she'd taken the tea and scones out to him, that smile had warmed her.

Alice's bell rang and Eva forgot everything as she hurried off to see what her friend wanted.

'I wonder if you'd bring me a cup of tea, dear, if you don't mind? And won't you join me for a while? I'm feeling very refreshed after my nap and I'd love to have a little chat.'

As Alice smiled brightly at her Eva felt a shiver of anxiety run through her. The older woman didn't look at all refreshed, but white and drawn as if she were in pain. 'Is it hurting?' Shall I bring your medicine?'

'No, dear. I'd rather keep that for the night time. It makes me sleepy and I don't want to waste my last few weeks on this earth.'

Eva bit her lip. Alice didn't like to be pitied and always spoke matter-of-factly about her coming death, but it was hard on others sometimes and it would have been a relief to weep.

'Just a cup of tea,' Alice prompted. 'I'm not hungry.'

As they sat and chatted, Eva couldn't help hoping Gus would leave them to enjoy their tête-à-tête. She'd had so little time alone with Alice since his arrival. But he did join them, of course he did. He seemed able to sense when his aunt was awake.

Or perhaps, she thought suddenly, he kept watch. Could he really be doing that, acting in such a calculating manner?

As he settled down into an armchair, some sort of message seemed to pass between him and his aunt.

Jenny was right, Eva decided. He *was* worming his way into Alice's good books. The trouble was, he made his aunt laugh, too, something no one else could do now and he seemed to enjoy her company as much as she enjoyed his. Surely that wasn't all pretence?

'Well, when are you two young things going to go out for another drive?' Alice asked during a lull in the conversation. 'I can't tell you how much good it does me to see you with a bit of colour in your cheeks, Eva dear.'

'I'm a bit busy this week, I'm afraid.'

Alice frowned at her. 'Nonsense. There's nothing that can't wait. Why don't you go out tomorrow? They say it's going to fine up. *Carpe diem*, my dear girl, where our Lancashire weather is concerned.'

'I'm sorry, but I–'

'*Please*, Eva. For me!'

Eva could no more hold out against her in this than she could in anything else. 'Very well, then. But just a short ride. I really do have a lot to do.'

'I'll look forward to it.' Gus smiled and turned the conversation neatly towards a book he'd been reading.

Alice grew quite animated because the book was one of her favourites and Eva forgave him a great deal for bringing that happy, interested expression to her friend's face.

But she'd never met a man before who lolled around all day smoking and reading. It didn't seem right, somehow, to fritter away one's life.

When Eva went out with Gus for the drive, Miss Blake again told the maid she could go and spend an hour or two with her grandfather.

Jenny was thoughtful as she got ready. She had to wonder if her employer was plotting something, and if so, what?

She found her grandfather dozing in front of the fire, heard a sound from outside at the back and went to see what was going on. Wilf was there, shirtless, wearing a ragged old vest with smears of damp earth on it. He was turning over the soil of the rear vegetable patch, whistling softly to himself, and he'd mowed the little square of lawn where her grandmother used to hang her washing out.

'I told you there was a lot to do round the place,' Jenny teased.

He looked up with a smile.

For a moment they stood there, not saying anything, and it seemed to her that something changed as the seconds ticked slowly past – something important. *I'm going to marry that fellow one day*, she thought, then blushed and went to brush a cobweb off the windowsill to try to hide her embarrassment at her own thoughts.

She was nearly thirty and had never been really

bothered about getting married because she'd enjoyed her work as a maid, not to mention having her own money and doing what she wanted on her days off. During the war she'd started walking out with a fellow, but he'd been killed and that had been that. His death had not devastated her and she had decided somewhat guiltily that she could not really have loved him. Looking back, she supposed she'd agreed to marry him because it was what *he* had wanted so badly and he was going back to France once he recovered from his injuries. Eh, the poor lad had been so happy when she'd said yes, she'd always been glad of bringing him that joy.

Whatever had got her thinking about marriage now? And with a man a year or two younger than herself as well, one who had no way of supporting a wife?

Only – the thought of marrying him would not go away. Ever since he had wept against her breast she'd kept thinking about Wilf Horrocks – as she worked, as she did the shopping and especially as she lay in her bed at night. His thin body had felt hard and manly against hers, while his shame at something which wasn't his fault had touched her to the core. It was silly to keep thinking about his eyes, but they were quite beautiful in a narrow face that was unremarkable otherwise, eyes of a very dark blue fringed with sooty lashes.

'Shall I make us all a cup of tea?' she offered. As he nodded, she turned to go inside and as she glanced down the side of the house, her eye was caught by someone walking past in the street. Sheer curiosity made her nip into the front room to see who it was, because not many people walked past into the nearby countryside.

It was the lawyer who lived in the big house next door. What was Mr Beaman doing at home at this time of day when his office was in the village?

'What are you–?'

'Shh!' She flapped her hand at Wilf and he shut up, joining her by the window in time to see Beaman cross the road and turn into the garden of Rose Villa. And he didn't come out, either, even though there was no one there to open the door to him.

Jenny gasped as she suddenly guessed that he must have been expected and told to walk straight in. 'The only reason that lawyer fellow's ever visited Miss Blake before,' she said slowly, 'was after she got sick, to make her will. Eh, do you think that rotten nephew of hers has got round her to change it?'

'I wouldn't be surprised, love.'

She turned to go back to the kitchen, automatically straightening the covers on her grandad's bed as she passed it.

'There's nothing you can do,' Wilf murmured.

'I can let Eva know what's going on, can't I?'

'Only if you're sure of it. Otherwise you may just make things worse. And any road, Miss Blake can do what she likes with her own possessions.'

Shaking her head, Jenny went to move the kettle to the hottest part of the hob, but could not stop thinking about Eva. Her friend was going to be the loser, she was quite sure. But she would never have expected it of her mistress, never in this world! Miss Blake usually dealt fairly with everyone.

Inside the sitting room at Rose Villa Eric Beaman discussed the new will with Alice Blake, watching her surreptitiously beneath lowered eyelids as he explained each clause. She kept nodding and then sitting lost in thought. He didn't interrupt her. It was best to give clients time to assimilate ideas.

'Yes, that's how I want it,' she said in the end, 'or as close as your legal language will allow. You must think it a strange will, Mr Beaman, but Eva is so shy. If I don't push her a little, she'll stay in her shell and waste her whole life.'

'My dear lady, you have every right to leave things as you please. It is not my place to pass judgement on your wishes.'

She nodded, then asked with a frown, 'It'll stand up in law? You're quite sure of that?'

'Of course. But it wouldn't hurt for the doctor to witness your signature, just in case anyone – um – tries to contest it. Shall I arrange to have it written up as you've specified?'

Alice smiled, lying back with a weary sigh. 'Please hurry with it. I tire so easily now I doubt I have much longer to live. You'd better arrange for two witnesses to come with you next time. You and Gus can sort that out.'

When he'd gone she lay wondering if she was doing the right thing. It was a bit – well, drastic. Then she thought of Gus, such a fine figure of a man – Simon's son, too, though he didn't really resemble her half-brother apart from being dark-haired – and her dear Eva, so shy and reserved. No, if she didn't do this, Eva would miss out on the important things in life, family and marriage, as Alice had herself. It might be too late for her now, but it was not too late for her dear girl.

When Aaron got home on the Tuesday night, he caught Gracie slapping Molly and saw the new loaf standing uncovered on the table getting hard, instead of being put away in the bread bin. He pushed his annoyance to the back of his mind as he asked his usual question: 'How's your mother?'

'Still sleeping. She said she'd had a bad day an' talking made her cough.'

So it did, but Lil could have listened to their childish tales for a little while, couldn't she? He made an effort to chat to his daughters as he got the eggs out and saw them begin to look a bit brighter for the attention. 'Anyone want a boiled egg and soldiers for tea?' he asked.

Molly nodded, but didn't speak.

'I didn't hear that,' he said, frowning at her.

'Please.' The child's voice was still only a whisper.

'Speak louder, love.'

'She can't,' Gracie announced. 'Even at school, she'll only whisper. Miss Deevers smacked her hand with the ruler yesterday, but she still wouldn't speak properly.'

'Why didn't you tell me that before?' Why hadn't he noticed? Guilt shot through him as he crouched down to look Molly in the eyes. 'Does your throat hurt, love?'

She shook her head.

'Then what is it, sweetheart? Why can't you speak properly?'

She shook her head and took a step backwards, her lips trembling as if she was going to cry.

He turned to look questioningly at Gracie, who shrugged. She'd crept back into the classroom after school yesterday because Molly had been hit and had poured ink into the teacher's desk, so she considered the affair settled now. No one knew who had done the damage, though the headmaster had made the whole school assemble in the hall and had ordered the culprit to confess. Miss Deevers suspected her, she knew, from the looks the teacher kept giving her, but couldn't prove anything.

Well, any time the teacher picked on Molly from now on, Gracie intended to do something about it. She didn't care if she got smacked herself, but Molly was only six and sobbed herself to sleep every time it happened, stifling the sobs in her pillow for fear of disturbing her mother. She didn't really understand what was going on, only knew that she had to keep quiet.

Aaron sighed, boiled a couple of eggs for himself and one for each of the girls, and cut some more slices of bread. 'Tell me about school. What did you do today? Did you have singing?'

'Molly can't sing any more. They're boring old songs anyway. I got all my spellings right, though. And Molly drew a nice picture in art.'

He served the simple meal, teasing and chatting, and

gradually the two girls cheered up. When he put them to bed, he started a tickling match and had the pleasure of seeing them snuggle down contentedly afterwards.

He cleared up the kitchen then tiptoed up to his wife's room with a cup of tea and a fresh jug of water. She opened her eyes then sighed and shielded her face against the light from the oil lamp.

'Thanks, love. Help me sit up and drink it, then I'll get some more sleep. I'm a bit tired today.'

He helped her drink, then emptied the chamber pot, rinsed it out and brought it back, hesitating in the doorway. It had been a rotten day from start to finish. Would it hurt anyone if he took a little time for himself? 'Mind if I nip down to the pub for the last hour? I'll only have half a pint, but I could do with a bit of company.'

'You go. But Aaron . . .' She hesitated, then said in a rush, 'We need to discuss what you're going to do after I'm gone. Maybe we could send the girls out to play and have a talk at the weekend?'

There was silence and she looked up to see him standing there with shoulders hunched.

'Not yet, love,' he said at last in that quiet, kind voice he often used with her, as if she was a child to be humoured. 'I reckon you'll be pestering us for a good while yet.'

She knew better but didn't press the point. She was tired today because she had coughed up blood this morning. She had got Mrs Harrop to burn the rags so he wouldn't know. Amy Harrop was a lazy old devil, but she could keep a secret. 'Ah, get off with you for your drink, Aaron Brierley,' she said. 'I need my beauty sleep.'

When he had gone she lay there with tears in her eyes until sleep overtook her again. Eh, he was lovely with the children. She had listened to them joking and laughing over their meal, and it had brightened her day, too. It was all she could do now, listen to others getting on with their lives – and try not to be too much trouble.

Inside the Dog and Duck everything was bright and cheerful. Sighing with relief at how normal it all looked, Aaron stood in the doorway, searching for a friendly face.

From across the room Wilf waved to him and pointed to an empty chair. Nodding, Aaron went up to the bar and got himself a half of best.

'How are you, Wilf lad?' he asked as he sat down. 'Mr Gill, you're looking well.'

'I'm feeling well, lad. All except me legs. Damned things won't work properly any more.' John sipped his beer, doing no more than wet his lips. Bloody stuff was lukewarm by now and Charlie Featherstone had been scowling across at them for the past half-hour, but he could only afford a half each. Once again, Wilf had protested about taking even that, not liking to be beholden, but it was no fun drinking on your own.

The three men knew each other well enough not to force conversation, so they sat in a companionable silence, letting the noise and warmth eddy round them. Aaron's leg was aching furiously, as it always did by evening now that he wasn't wearing the brace, but it was holding up, at least. He enjoyed the feeling of life and laughter here, so different from home where there was always the sense of something hovering, something dark and very final. Well, so it seemed to him.

A figure loomed over the table. The landlord. 'Why don't you come across and join us for a chat, Charlie lad?' Grandad asked before he could speak.

'Nay, I'd get nowhere if I sat drinking my own ale.' Charlie looked at Wilf. 'Want to earn a bob? Our Judy's got a headache an' I need someone to help with the clearing up.'

'Any time,' Wilf drained his glass and stood up. 'Can you see Grandad home for me, Aaron?'

'Yes, of course.'

As they walked back along the road, John Gill asked quietly, 'What's up, lad?'

'Nothing. I'm just a bit tired, that's all.'

'There's more nor that.'

'Well . . .' With the old man clinging to him and hobbling slowly along, Aaron found himself explaining how he'd been humiliated in front of Jenny and Eva Kershaw, and how rotten it was to work for Sid Linney.

'You're doing the right thing, son,' that creaky old voice said in the darkness. 'You have to think of your family at the moment. How is Lil?'

'Not good.'

The bony old hand patted his arm and brought with it a sense of comfort. 'Bear up, lad. It's all anyone can do. Life's a bugger sometimes, but it usually gives you pleasures as well as pain if you keep going.'

At home Aaron got things ready for morning then went straight to bed, letting the tiredness take him drifting towards sleep. Grandad Gill was a wise old fellow and kind with it. That's what it had been like in the war. Friends had helped you get through the horrors by offering their moral and physical support. He missed that, but at least he had met up with one or two lads in Heyshaw who had seen service in the trenches and they all looked out for one another when they could. Wilf had become a close friend.

Once Lil had died, Aaron intended to find a way to change his life. If his parents had still been alive, he'd have taken the girls to them and gone looking for work in the south, where there were more jobs, then brought the girls to join him. But he had no close relatives now, so he'd have to find some other solution.

What he'd really like would be his own little garage. There weren't many of these yet, but he could see the need so clearly. With more and more cars being built, people were going to need good mechanics close to where they lived. He could repair bikes and other equipment as well, and sell petrol. No reason to let the ironmongers do all the selling of that. In his garage, cars would be able to drive up and buy petrol from a roadside pump without having to lug a great big can into the ironmonger's shop, then pour it through a funnel and . . .

He fell asleep to his favourite dream and for once nothing happened to disturb him during the night.

5

The following day Eva reluctantly got ready to go out with Gus again. She was worried about how pale Alice was and as she turned to look back at the house felt so uneasy she had a sudden urge to shout 'Stop!' and jump out of the car. But she didn't, because she'd promised to go out with him.

'Penny for them,' Gus teased as they drove along.

Eva realised she'd been lost in her thoughts. 'Sorry. I'm not very good company today. I'm worried about Alice. Do you think she looks – worse?'

His smile faded. 'Yes. Even in these few days I can see a difference. But it won't do her any good if you hover over her, will it? She hates being a burden and feels you need a break.' After a slight pause he added, 'Whether you're chatty or not doesn't matter to me. I enjoy just being with you.'

He gave her such an understanding smile she couldn't help returning it, though she was still annoyed with him for the way he'd treated Aaron Brierley the previous day, and puzzled as to why. She'd learned as a teacher that there were usually two sides to a problem, only she didn't know Gus well enough to ask his side of it – or Aaron, either.

'Let's find somewhere and have those cream cakes I've been promising you,' Gus suggested as they bowled along. 'Then we can come straight back if you like. A fellow at the pub suggested some tearooms in Littleborough.'

'But that's –' She flushed as she realised how rude she was being.

'Too far?' he finished for her. 'Well, you won't fool Alice that you've had a real outing if we go back within half an hour, though we can do that if you insist.'

She gave him a rueful glance. 'You're right. Littleborough it is, then.' She set her worries determinedly aside and tried to take pleasure from the scenery. She also stole a few glances at the man beside her. He was definitely good-looking, so why was she not attracted to him? Perhaps she wasn't the sort to be attracted to any man. It was a secret worry of hers, that there was something wrong with her. Was Alice right that she wasn't giving Gus a chance? Would he really make someone a good husband? A good father? It would be nice to have children of her own . . .

Her thoughts went round in circles and all she could decide in the end was that she didn't know him well enough to come to any firm conclusions.

But it *was* nice to get out. She had been feeling very down lately and was annoyed with herself, because she usually coped better than this.

Relieved that his bluff had paid off, Gus stopped trying to make conversation and began to whistle. With the hood down, the wind stung their faces, but he liked the feeling of freedom that gave and the way people stared at them as they passed. He was doing well for himself and he hadn't finished yet.

He glanced sideways. Eva had some colour in her cheeks now and looked better for it, but she ought to have her hair bobbed. It looked so old-fashioned dragged back like that, and it was so soft it kept pulling out of the bun. He'd seen her several times tucking back an unruly strand. As if men liked women to look *neat!*

He looked at the bleak moorland scenery, so different from Kent. If he married Eva, he'd have to stay here in the north, because it would be safest, but it wasn't really where he wanted to be. Only how many people got everything they wanted out of life? He certainly hadn't.

Still, if you had money you could enjoy yourself anywhere, and the old lady sounded to have a nice pot stashed away. He grinned. He'd always told himself he'd been born to be an idle rich man, not a worker.

When the car had driven away, Alice rang for Jenny. 'You can go and see your grandfather now, dear.'

'I think I'd better stay here, Miss Blake. You're not looking at all well today.'

'I thought I'd already made it clear that even a dying woman enjoys a little privacy from time to time. Run along now and don't come back until four.'

You didn't argue with Miss Blake when she got that expression on her face, so Jenny slipped on a cardigan and walked across to her grandad's cottage.

Once there she explained that she was worried about

her mistress and wanted to keep an eye on the house, then went to stand in the front room. Safely hidden behind the net curtains she could watch the comings and goings at Rose Villa.

Sure enough, a few minutes later the gate of the big house next door clanged open and shut, and Mr Beaman walked past accompanied by his housekeeper. They crossed the road and both turned into Rose Villa.

'Spying again?' asked a cheery voice behind Jenny.

'Shhh!' She flapped one hand at Wilf and he came to stand beside her.

'What are you watching for?'

'Something's going on, I'm sure. Mr Beaman's just gone into Miss Blake's with his housekeeper. And *he* doesn't usually stay at home in Heyshaw during the week, let alone go out visiting.'

A few minutes later the doctor drove up in his neat little Singer Ten motor car and turned into the drive of Rose Villa.

'That settles it. She must have made a new will and they're signing it today,' Jenny said, blowing out her anger in a whoosh of air. 'Two witnesses, you need, for a will.'

'Aren't you jumping to conclusions?'

'What other explanation is there for that housekeeper going to call on Miss Blake? Mrs Pannell's never done that before so why should she start now? And anyway, she wouldn't go out with Mr Beaman. He always makes sure his servants know their place.' She'd seen a few maids come and go there over the past few years, chatted to them too and heard their views on their employer's finicky ways. They reckoned it was more like working for an old spinster lady than for a man, though he treated them fairly enough.

'They don't usually get the doctor in as a witness,' Wilf said, still unconvinced. 'Anyone would do for that. No, Dr Stott must be there for some other reason.'

After thinking it through, Jenny said slowly, 'They might get the doctor if they're afraid of the will being contested afterwards and want someone who can swear she was in her right mind.'

'They'd only be afraid of that if it contains something upsetting or unusual.' Wilf frowned at her. 'Is Miss Blake the sort to do that?'

Jenny didn't answer. She was trying to work it out. Gus Blake might not be there with them today, but he must have organised it all, yes, and taken Eva out of the way while the deed was done, just as he had before. She stayed in the front room, drawing up a chair close to the window, determined not to miss anything. Wilf kept her company, not pestering her with conversation. After a few minutes he went out without a word, returning with a cup of tea.

'You're a fellow after my own heart,' she said when he handed it her. 'I was just feeling like a nice sup of tea.'

'Glad to be of use.'

They exchanged smiles and sat on in silence. When she'd finished the tea, he took the cup away again.

'Someone's coming out!' she exclaimed suddenly, jumping to her feet. Wilf came hurrying back to join her.

The doctor emerged from the house, accompanied by the housekeeper, who nodded farewell to him and hurried back to Mr Beaman's house. Dr Stott stood beside his car for a few minutes, frowning and staring into space, then studied his pocket watch and suddenly jerked into action, turning the crank handle to start the motor and driving off quickly.

Jenny folded her arms across her chest, because she was feeling chilly now. 'This can't mean anything good for Eva, I know it can't. If only there was something we could *do*.'

'Well, there isn't, love, and you know it. Miss Blake can make any sort of will she wants.'

'Even if she's being unfairly influenced by another person?'

He nodded. 'Yes. You still can't do owt about it.'

'I can keep my eyes open, though,' Jenny muttered.

Once Mr Beaman had driven off, she went back into the kitchen but knew she was poor company. She couldn't settle to anything and kept looking at the clock, whose hands seemed to be crawling round. When they at last showed five to four she said goodbye and hurried back to Rose Villa.

Wilf looked at Grandad. 'Do you think she's right? About the will, I mean?'

'I reckon so. She's not stupid, our Jenny isn't.'

'She seems very fond of Eva Kershaw.'

'Yes. Them two have allus got on well. Jenny has to call her "Miss Kershaw" in public, but they're good friends in private. Help one another a lot.' Grandad sat frowning into the fire. 'Our Jenny's worried about her job, you know, whether she'll still have one after Miss Blake dies.' He shook his head regretfully. 'It must be grand to be rich an' not have to worry about putting bread on the table.'

Wilf sighed. 'Aye, it must.'

Grandad looked up quickly. 'You'll get some proper work eventually, lad. And in the meantime, I'm happy to have you here. It were a bit lonely on my own, sithee.'

'Ah, you're good company for an old codger,' Wilf said with a grin, enjoying the way Grandad cackled at his teasing words. He loved living there, had not felt so at home anywhere before, but he would rather have paid his way. Far rather.

Jenny tapped on the sitting-room door and found her employer lying on the sofa looking exhausted. 'Just to let you know I'm back, miss. Would you like anything? A cup of tea perhaps?'

'I think – some of my medicine. It's upstairs in the bathroom. The pain's quite bad today. I thought if I lay here quietly it'd pass, but it hasn't.'

'You should have let me stay with you, miss.'

'I wanted to be on my own.' Alice's face twisted with pain.

Jenny's expression was grim as she ran up to get the medicine. Did Miss Blake think she was deaf as well as stupid? That she hadn't noticed the comings and goings? But the poor lady was in pain and not thinking straight. Eh, she never used to be secretive about anything.

When Eva got home, Alice was half-asleep and roused herself only to ask if Gus would carry her up to her bedroom.

Jenny didn't manage to catch Eva on her own until they were laying the table for dinner. It was like the old days, when the two ladies had dined together every night, with the table nicely set and the best crockery, because Miss Blake said it was a waste not to use it. They'd had some good times together, the two of them, laughing and chatting over shared tasks. Eva wasn't one to stand on her dignity, unlike some people Jenny could mention.

In whispers, keeping an eye out for anyone approaching, she described what she had seen that afternoon.

Eva stood lost in thought for quite a long time, then said slowly, 'Even if you're right, I don't stay with Alice so that I'll inherit her money but because I love her.'

'I know that and so does she, but don't you care if *he* gets his hands on it?'

Eva shrugged. 'All I really care about at the moment is that my dearest friend is dying.' Her voice broke on the word and it was a minute before she could continue. 'I don't know how I'll cope without her, Jenny. I'm not strong and independent like you.'

Jenny could remember when her own mother had died, how lost she'd felt, how upset her grandad had been. She had had to pull herself together to comfort him. 'You'll cope because you have to, love. We all do.'

'Will I?' Eva sighed and went to fetch the cruet off the sideboard, then smoothed the tablecloth absent-mindedly. She felt less sure of herself and her own feelings with each day that passed.

After dinner Gus led Eva into the sitting room, took her hand and said simply, 'I think you know how fond I've become of you. And I think you also know how much my aunt would like to see us married. We've been getting on so well. Do you think you could become my wife?'

She listened in shock, trying in vain to tug her hand away from his. 'It's very kind of you to offer for me, but . . .'

He put one finger over her lips. 'Don't say anything. It's too important a decision to be taken lightly. I've been thinking about it for a couple of days, since my aunt made her feelings plain, and I really like the idea. But she warned me you were shy, so I made up my mind to tell you how I felt and then leave you to think about it. I know I'm rushing things, but the circumstances are a bit – well, they're difficult, aren't they?'

When she would have spoken, he shook his head and pretended to cover his ears with his hands. 'I'm not letting you answer rashly, my dear, so I'm going out to the pub and that'll give you time to start considering my proposal. But I will say this: apart from my own wishes, I can't think of anything which would make my aunt happier than to see us married.'

'But we hardly—'

'She's really worried about what will happen to you after she dies and longs to see you settled.'

Eva sat on alone after she'd heard the front door

close quietly behind him. She didn't really want to marry him. Well, she thought she didn't.

Or was it just that she didn't want to marry anyone?

She was facing such a great loss that it had taken over everything else in her life and she found it hard to think past that. Seeing Alice tonight looking so bone-white and limp had really upset her. She tried to brush away the tears with her fingers, but more followed.

When Jenny came in to ask if she'd like a cup of tea, Eva said baldly, 'Gus Blake has just asked me to marry him.'

'Eh, he's a quick worker, that one is. I hope you told him no.'

She shook her head. 'He didn't want an answer yet. Said I should think about it.'

'Cunning devil! Did he also tell you how it would please Miss Blake?'

Eva nodded. 'He's right. It would.'

Jenny took her hand and began to pat it. 'Don't do it, love. There's something – I don't know – *wrong* about him. Oh, he's good with your aunt, I won't deny that. He can cheer her up even now. But marriage is for life. Do you really want to spend the rest of your life with him?'

'What I really want is to continue living here with Alice, and I can't do that, can I? I don't know what I shall want to do – afterwards. And my wishes seem rather unimportant at the moment.' Eva stood up. 'I think I must be very stupid not to know my own mind. Maybe Alice is right. Maybe I do need a little push.

She's always been right about me before and she wants this so much.'

Jenny stared after her in horror. If she was certain of one thing, it was that Gus Blake wasn't right for Eva, who was shy under that cool exterior and needed a much kinder man. Surely her friend wouldn't let them push her into it?

You didn't marry a man out of gratitude to his aunt!

The following morning Alice decided to spend the day in bed, which was not like her. When Eva asked if they should send for the doctor, she shook her head. 'There's nothing he can do for me now.'

'Oh, darling!' Eva's eyes filled with tears and she knelt by the bed.

Alice reached out to stroke the soft, dark hair. 'Dearest girl, did Gus ask you to marry him last night?'

Eva nodded.

'And are you going to say yes?'

'I – don't think so.' She'd thought about it a lot and somehow couldn't bring herself to the sticking point.

'Then what *are* you going to do with yourself after I die?'

All Eva could do was shake her head, feeling numb and disoriented. 'Stay on here if I can and get another teaching job, I suppose.'

'Will that be enough to fill your life?'

A shrug was her only answer.

'Do you know what my biggest regret is as I die?' Alice said softly. 'It's that I've never had children. I don't want you to make the same mistake.' Her voice was low and fierce. 'If you like Gus and believe you could live comfortably with him, never mind about falling in love and that sort of nonsense. Think about the children you could have and say yes.'

As Eva still remained silent, she added, 'I've seen you with your sister Lizzie's children and with Polly's boy, seen you with your pupils, too. You'd make a wonderful mother.' She opened her mouth to continue speaking, grimaced and closed her eyes for a moment, saying faintly, 'I think I'd better have some more medicine. The pain is quite bad today.'

Eva looked at her in alarm, then hurried to fetch it.

Three days later Eva was woken by Alice's bell in the middle of the night. She found her friend tossing and turning, clearly in great pain.

'I'll get your medicine,' she said quietly.

When she got back Alice was weeping.

'Darling, what is it?'

'It's so humiliating.' Another sob escaped Alice's control, then she confessed in a whisper, 'I've wet the bed.'

'Is that all?' Eva said soothingly. But she knew how this would upset such a proud woman so tried to make light of it. 'That's nothing to do with you, just part of the illness. I'll soon change your sheets and no one need know except Jenny. And she won't say a word about it.'

'Don't – let Gus know.'

'Of course not,' Eva soothed. Working quickly, she stripped the bed, doing half at a time and rolling her friend gently to and fro. But Alice continued to weep silently.

When everything was neat and tidy, Eva sat on the edge of the bed, rubbing her friend's shoulder gently. 'Oh, dearest, please don't. It doesn't matter.'

'It does to me,' Alice said brokenly when at last the tears stopped. 'I've tried to be brave, to accept it, and you've been a wonderful comfort to me, my darling girl, but I'm ready to go now.' After a pause, she murmured, 'If only I could know you'd be looked after . . .' Then her eyes closed and the lines of pain faded gradually from her face as the medicine took hold.

Eva switched off the light, but went back to sit by the window of her bedroom in the moonlight, watching the patterns made by the branches of the sycamore tree for a long time, lost in thought.

In the morning she dressed carefully and went down to breakfast, waiting for Gus, who always rose later than she did. She fidgeted about the dining room, feeling hollow with apprehension, but utterly determined to fulfil her friend's last wish.

'Hello. Sorry I'm late,' he said, sitting next to her. 'Didn't sleep well.'

She poured him some tea then waited till he'd taken a piece of toast before saying carefully, 'About what you asked me the other day . . .'

He looked up quickly, his head cocked enquiringly.

When he didn't rush her, she felt grateful and a little more hopeful that if he continued to be so understanding they might rub along quite well together. 'I've been thinking about – things.' After a pause she forced herself to say the words. 'I'd – um – like to accept your proposal of marriage.'

'My dear girl, I'm delighted! Absolutely delighted.' He took her hand and raised it to his lips.

She could feel herself flushing and pulled it back, continuing as she had planned, determined to be open with him. 'I can't pretend I'm in love with you, Gus. I'm not. I don't think I'm the sort to fall in love, actually. But I think we could make a – a decent life together, and that's what counts, isn't it?'

'I'm sure it is. I won't pretend to have fallen madly in love, either, but I do like you immensely and I feel we're very well suited.' After a pause he asked, 'Shall we go and tell my aunt together? She'll be so pleased.'

'Yes. Later in the morning, perhaps. She had a rather restless night and is still asleep.'

He nodded, let go of her hand and continued to eat, wondering exactly what had happened during the night to make her change her mind. Whatever it was, he was pleased about it.

Perhaps he should get a special licence and marry Eva quickly before she could change her mind? No, that might seem too pushy. He'd better wait, do things the usual way.

When Eva went to tell Jenny that she was going to marry Gus, the maid's face crumpled in dismay and she clutched her friend's arm. 'Don't do it! *Please* don't. You know you don't love him.'

'I don't think I'm capable of loving anyone. I'm rather a – a cool person, really. But I would like a family of my own. Alice is right about that. And she'll be so happy when we tell her.' As the other would have spoken, she said firmly, 'Let's just leave it at that, shall we? My mind is quite made up.'

Jenny hesitated, then gave her head a little shake, because there was nothing she could think of to stop Eva from making this dreadful mistake. She felt really down in the dumps as she got on with her chores. Gus Blake was the sort of man to make a woman very unhappy, she was sure of that. Look how he'd bullied poor Aaron the other day. And how he treated Jenny because she was only the maid. He'd probably bully a wife, too, once he'd got her trapped. And he was so lazy he never picked anything up after himself, even, let alone helping them out a bit. The Blakes were minor gentry, really, but this one was no gentleman, that was sure.

Alice slept the whole morning, during which time Gus seemed restless, pacing up and down the garden. When there was a sudden shower, he came inside to stand in the doorway of Eva's sitting room. 'What are you doing?'

'Writing to tell my sisters about us.'

'Ah. Right. Carry on, then. Give them my best wishes.' He wandered round the ground floor, then began pacing up and down the garden room as the rain continued.

Just before lunch Eva went to tell him that his aunt had woken up, but was staying in bed.

'Good. Let's go and tell her.' He took Eva's hand and pulled her towards the stairs.

As they walked into the bedroom hand in hand, Alice looked at them. 'Does this mean what I think?' she asked in a voice which wobbled.

'It means Eva has made me very happy by accepting my proposal of marriage,' Gus said, smiling. 'So we've come to ask your blessing, my dear aunt.'

Alice burst into tears and they looked at one another in consternation, then Eva ran over to crouch by the bed.

'What's wrong?'

'Nothing's wrong. I'm just so happy,' she managed, patting Eva's cheek. 'Gus dear, come and give me a kiss.'

After he had complied with her request, she asked, 'Would you mind very much getting married at once? I'd love to see it.'

'Of course we will,' Gus said smoothly, not even looking at his fiancée.

'Whatever you want.' But Eva felt a shiver of apprehension run down her spine as she spoke. She would far rather have waited until she and Gus had got to know one another better. She simply wasn't the sort to rush into things.

But if Alice wanted the marriage so much, then she should have her final wish, Eva was quite determined about that.

The following morning she and Gus went to see the minister at the local church and arranged to be married in three weeks' time.

'Do you think we ought to have bought a special licence, or whatever it is you need, so that we could get married sooner?' Eva asked as they strolled home, because Alice looked so much worse today.

'No. Too much fuss and bother. I'm sure my aunt will last another three weeks. And anyway,' he smiled down at her, 'this will give me time to buy you a ring, and for you to get a pretty wedding dress.'

'I thought I'd wear the one I wore when I was Polly's bridesmaid. It's really nice.'

'Show me.'

'No, it's bad luck.'

But here again Alice took a hand and insisted on Eva going into Manchester to buy a 'proper' white wedding dress, a journey which necessitated a bus ride into Littleborough then a train journey into the city.

'I don't want to leave you,' Eva protested, 'and anyway, I shan't know what to buy. I'm hopeless at shopping for clothes.'

'Hmm.' After some thought, Alice suggested getting a woman from the village to come and sit with her, one who'd helped out while Eva was at her sister's wedding, so that Jenny could go with Eva.

Gus protested that a maid wouldn't know what sort of dress was right and that he'd be perfectly happy to take Eva into Manchester himself, but Alice grew agitated, insisting it was bad luck for the groom to see the dress before the wedding. He bit back further arguments and walked the two young women to the bus stop in Heyshaw.

'Make sure you get something tasteful,' he told Eva,

with a scornful glance at the maid. 'Tomorrow we'll go into Rochdale and see if we can find you an engagement ring.'

'He doesn't trust me, does he?' Jenny asked once he'd walked away.

'Pay him no attention. *I* trust you and that's what matters.'

They said very little as the bus chugged into Littleborough and were equally silent in the train. The rows of terraced houses gave way to countryside, then there were houses, shops, mills and warehouses as the train entered Manchester.

It quickly became obvious that Eva's heart wasn't in the search and they went from one shop to another without finding anything she liked.

'You don't really want to marry him, do you?' Jenny asked as they left another shop without buying anything, although there had been several pretty dresses.

'It's not Gus. I don't want to marry anyone.'

Jenny knew what she thought of that. Fooling herself, Eva was. 'Then you shouldn't do it, even for Miss Blake. It's your whole life that's going to be affected.'

'I've said I'll do it and I'll keep my word. You've seen how happy it's made her, Jenny. After all she's done for me, if I can't do this one thing for her . . .'

'It's not just one thing! It'll affect the whole of your life. Why don't you stay engaged till after she's passed on, then think again, see if you still—'

'If you don't stop talking like that you can just go home and I'll finish the shopping on my own.'

It wasn't like Eva to snap so Jenny breathed in deeply

a few times, then said, 'Let's go back to the first shop. I think they had the prettiest dresses, since you don't want the trouble of having one specially made.'

They bought a lace dress with a scalloped hemline and a dropped waist, which came with a matching coat of white satin.

'That's an older woman's outfit,' Jenny whispered. 'The dress with frilled panels down the sides is much younger-looking.'

'That one needs a flatter chest than I've got. This one suits me best,' Eva insisted. If truth be told, she didn't like any of the fussy creations they were being shown and did not care tuppence about having a fancy white wedding.

'You'll need a veil, too,' Jenny said.

The assistant brightened and began to bring out some of the fashionable, oblong, gossamer-like veils, which were held on by a wreath of artificial flowers.

As she set one on Eva's head, Jenny looked at it dubiously. 'That style doesn't flatter you, love. Maybe a hat?'

Eva looked at her face in the mirror. The veil definitely didn't enhance her looks. She had too low a forehead. 'I'd prefer a hat anyway.'

'You ought to get your hair bobbed while we're here,' Jenny urged. 'It'd make you look more modern. You can't fit half these hats on with that bun of yours.'

'I don't want to look modern. He'll have to take me as I am.' The words *or not at all* seemed to echo in the air between them and Eva added hastily, 'But I will buy some material for new underclothes and a new brassiere, perhaps.'

In the lingerie department of Affleck and Brown's, the lady assistant insisted on showing her the new 'bandeaux' that the younger women were wearing nowadays, whispering that they were designed specially to flatten generous bosoms like hers. Eva shook her head at them. How stupid! Flatten her breasts indeed! What a silly fashion that was!

However, she did buy some white silk stockings to go with the white kid shoes she had worn to her sister Polly's wedding. She also bought some peach-coloured Charmeuse material, liking its soft silky feel, and some lace to go with it. She would make herself some French-style knickers with this. But she blushed as she paid for it, not liking the idea that Gus would see her underclothing. She had read that some men liked to see their wives without any clothing on at all. She didn't think she could bear to be so immodest.

As they travelled back she said thoughtfully, 'Some people must have plenty of money, however hard the times are. Those shops looked to be doing well, don't you think, and they had plenty of stock?' She still had quite a lot of money left from the roll of banknotes Alice had given her because spending extravagantly simply wasn't in her nature. She had been too poor as a child ever to do that.

Jenny nodded. It had upset her, actually, to see the prices and to think of women spending that much money on tiny scraps of material while poor Wilf was unable to earn more than a shilling or two a week.

And until he had got a job she couldn't do anything about nudging him towards marriage. She knew that. But she did think he was attracted to her. He had a way of smiling when he saw her that lit up his whole face. She sighed. Gus Blake didn't smile when he saw Eva, for all his smarmy ways.

When they got home, Alice insisted Eva try on the dress for her. She lay in bed, smiling dreamily as Eva paraded up and down the large sunny bedroom with its chintz curtains. 'You'll make a lovely bride. But I do wish you'd bought a proper veil.'

'They didn't suit me.' She was, Eva had decided, a very ordinary sort of person, not suited to fancy clothing. A typical schoolteacher really.

And thinking about underclothing had made her worry about how she would cope with being a wife. She jumped nervously if Gus touched her; had tried to stop herself, but couldn't. She was obviously intended by nature to be a spinster and it was no use pretending otherwise. She should resign herself to that and break it to him gently that she'd changed her mind.

But Alice was beaming at her from the bed and telling her to keep the rest of the money in case she needed any more bits and pieces. She couldn't bring herself to upset her friend. Not now.

She would just have to go through with it and then make the best of things. After all, it would be nice to have children of her own. Alice was right about that. Even the church service said it was the main purpose of marriage.

*   *   *

On the Sunday Eva's brother and sister turned up. Jenny, who'd seen them out of the kitchen window, called out to her to come quickly. As Lizzie bounced out of the front passenger seat of Dearden's van, Percy got out of the back, where he'd been sitting on some cushions, and Lizzie's husband Peter got out of the driving seat, stretching and smiling down at his wife so tenderly that it brought tears to Jenny's eyes to see it. That was how people who loved one another should look, how she wanted Wilf to look at her.

Eva rushed out of the house, flung her arms round her sister and burst into tears.

'We can go back home again if it upsets you to see us,' Lizzie teased. 'Here, you daft ha'porth, stop that. You're supposed to be a happy bride, not a watering can.'

Gus came out to stand on the front doorstep. 'Aren't you going to introduce me to your family, darling?'

'Pushy devil!' muttered Jenny, who was watching and listening from the kitchen.

Eva wiped away her tears then turned to make the introductions.

'Peter said we should write and ask if it was all right to come and see you,' Lizzie said. 'But I couldn't wait, so we just came. I don't know why you don't get a telephone put in.' She lowered her voice. 'Especially now.'

'Because Alice hates them.'

'How is she?'

'Bad. Really bad.'

'Oh, Eva love, you poor thing. Maybe you should postpone your wedding?'

Gus frowned at Lizzie and said with an edge to his voice, 'My aunt wants very much to see us married. That's the whole purpose of doing things so quickly.'

Lizzie gave him a long, level look. 'There's also the question of what my sister wants, don't you think?'

For a moment tension crackled between them, then Peter stepped in and made some mild remark which defused the situation.

Eva linked her arm with her sister's and led the way into the house, talking with such determined cheerfulness that she seemed quite unlike her usual quiet self. If you asked Lizzie, Eva wasn't happy. Well, Lizzie wasn't, either. She didn't like the look of this Gus Blake or the way in which he talked to her.

As they settled down in the sitting room, Lizzie continued to study the engaged couple unobtrusively. Her sister looked strained and Gus was over-hearty, yet extremely watchful. When her eyes met his again, his face went very still with no expression showing. She'd rather know what a man was thinking, rather quarrel with someone outright than hide behind polite masks like this.

Jenny came in with the trolley laden with tea and sandwiches, plus slices of a fruit cake she'd made the previous day – though there was not as much as she'd have wished, because *he* had had three slices last night, the greedy pig.

'I'll just nip upstairs and see if Alice wants anything,' Eva said, but Gus stretched out a hand to prevent her. 'I'll go. You'll want to spend time with your sister.'

When he'd left there was silence, then Lizzie said with the bluntness for which she was famous in the family, 'He reminds me of Sam.'

'He's not at all like Sam,' Eva protested. 'He's very kind and – and considerate.'

'So was Sam before the wedding.'

Peter murmured, 'Lizzie love, you haven't exactly given him a fair chance,' in a warning tone and she shrugged her shoulders.

And although they chatted for another hour, it was that remark which stuck in Eva's mind. *So was Sam before the wedding.* Lizzie's first husband had been a wife-beater, so bad that they'd all been glad when he got killed.

'Shall I go up and say hello to Alice before we leave?' Lizzie asked.

'I'll take you,' said Eva.

But Alice was drowsy and although she smiled at Lizzie, she only seemed half aware of what they were saying to her.

'Let's go into your bedroom for a minute,' Lizzie suggested and dragged her sister next door before she could protest. 'What's up?' she asked immediately. 'For someone who's just got engaged, you've a face as long as a fiddle.'

'I – it's Alice, so ill and . . .'

'It's more than Alice, my girl. And I'm not letting you out of this bedroom till you've told me why you're marrying that man.'

'You don't like Gus?'

'I don't know him. And he does remind me of Sam – not in looks, I admit, but in the way he speaks and holds himself. That's bound to affect me, so I'm trying to be fair to him, but . . .' Lizzie let the words trail away, then gave Eva another hug. 'Why are you rushing into this?'

'For Alice. I owe her so much.'

'You don't owe her the rest of your life.'

Eva sighed. 'I know. Jenny says the same thing. But I've never felt particularly attracted to anyone, so I don't think I'm the sort to fall in love, like you and Peter. I would like to have a family of my own, though, so it seemed a good thing to marry Gus.'

'Well, it isn't. I've had one unhappy marriage and believe me, it's not worth it. Nothing is ever worth that.'

'It's all arranged now and it's making Alice happy, so I'm not changing it.' Eva stood up, her expression determined. 'We really should go down again.'

Lizzie followed, shaking her head in annoyance. When Eva got that look on her face you could talk yourself blue and you'd not budge her. She seemed gentle and biddable, but she wasn't, not when she set her mind on something.

After another half an hour of careful conversation in which they tried to include Gus, who showed no signs of leaving them alone, Peter said regretfully that they'd have to set off back because Emma, Percy's wife, and her sister were looking after their children. 'Our Matt is a rare handful at the moment, into everything.'

'And Emma's expecting,' Percy said in his usual quiet way. 'She's been a bit sickly.'

'Oh, how lovely for you!' Eva beamed at her brother. She knew that Emma's first child, although born after their marriage, was not his, its father having been killed in the war.

She walked outside with them and watched in silence as the maroon-and-gold-painted van chugged away. When she turned, Gus was standing on the doorstep and she had to force herself to walk across to him and smile.

What she really wanted was to be on her own and think about what Lizzie had said. Was her sister right? Was she making a terrible mistake? Was that why she could not feel easy about rushing into marriage?

And why had Lizzie taken such a rapid dislike to Gus when he had gone out of his way to be pleasant? Her sister usually got on well with people. As for Percy, he'd hardly said a word. What had he been thinking?

She wished she could talk to them on their own.

Oh, she didn't know what she wished! She was becoming quite silly.

6

Gus didn't say much about the visit from Eva's sister and brother, and neither did she. The first meeting hadn't gone very well, which had upset her, but least said soonest mended. Perhaps Gus had been nervous, meeting her family for the first time.

She paused in what she was doing with a wry smile. No! He wasn't the nervous sort. If anything, he was too confident for her comfort – or was he just too lazy to worry? She tried to understand what had gone wrong. She'd have expected him to have plenty in common with Peter Dearden, with their both having been in the Army, but the two men had hardly said a word to one another, standing stiffly polite and glassy-eyed. Gus had not talked about his war experiences at all, which had surprised her because he did talk about them sometimes to her and Alice, and Wilf said he talked about them all the time in the Dog and Duck.

As for Lizzie, she'd positively bristled with hostility towards him, almost from the beginning, and whatever she said, Gus wasn't like Sam Thoxby, not at all. He was a gentleman.

But best of all, he was Alice's nephew, so in marrying

him Eva would still feel connected to her friend. She really liked the thought of becoming a Blake.

A few nights later she woke suddenly to hear a faint sound coming from Alice's bedroom and rushed next door to find her friend lying in a shaft of moonlight, for she would never allow the curtains to be closed these days. Alice was turning her head restlessly from side to side as if distressed and the sound she was making brought tears to Eva's eyes, it was so helpless and sad.

'Alice, I'm here.' When there was no answer, she asked, 'Are you in pain? Shall I fetch some more of your medicine?' Though actually Eva had given her a large dose before she went to bed, which usually lasted through the night.

Oh, God, she prayed, *don't let her suffer any more. She doesn't deserve it.*

Alice fumbled for her hand and sighed in relief as she clutched it. 'No more medicine.' Her voice was the merest thread. 'But I wanted you – and I couldn't reach the bell – or call out. I thought,' another whimper, 'I was going to die alone.'

'You're not going to die yet—'

The ghostly whisper continued. 'I am, dearest. I can feel it – hovering very near. And it'll be – such a relief.'

'I'll fetch help,' Eva whispered, stroking Alice's forehead.

'No. Just you, now.'

She gave Eva a smile of such sweetness and joy that the young woman never forgot it. As Alice's hand tightened almost imperceptibly around hers, she sank down again on the edge of the bed. 'Can I do anything to help you?'

'Just stay with me. Do you – mind?'

'Of course not, darling. I *want* to be with you.' She looked down through a blur of tears at the hand which felt so limp in hers and then at the face she loved so much.

'You've been – like a daughter. And so kind – since this happened. I wanted to – thank you for that.'

Tears were rolling down Eva's cheeks now as the faint voice continued and she had to watch her friend fighting for breath.

'I wanted – to ask you – not to be angry with me.'

'Why should I be angry?'

'The will. It's for your own good. But I . . .'

But although Alice struggled desperately to finish what she was saying, she was unable to form another word. Eva leaned over her and kissed her cheek and for a last time their eyes met, with such love shining in Alice's that Eva could only hope her own love showed as clearly.

Then, after the softest of sighs, all breath left Alice's body and every movement stopped.

For a moment Eva could only sit there and weep silently. She looked towards the door, wondering if she should call someone, then shook her head and reached out to close her friend's eyes before taking hold of her hand again. As her tears dried up she said quietly, needing to say the words aloud to break that dreadful silence, 'I'm glad you went easily, Alice. You deserved that. And whatever is in your will, I promise you I won't be angry with you.'

After a while she stood up and laid the soft white hands across Alice's breast. She didn't cover her friend's face, though. It would have seemed wrong. She let the moonlight bathe it in silver one last time.

She went along to Jenny's bedroom, which was on the same floor, and slipped inside, not wanting to wake Gus yet.

Jenny woke as soon as the door opened, sitting up in bed to ask, 'What's wrong?'

'Alice has just died. Can you come and help me?'

And that started up a train of necessary activities that kept them both busy for the rest of the night.

When they woke him, Gus was very helpful, driving off to fetch the doctor and summon the undertaker Alice had chosen. But he didn't weep or even look particularly sad most of the time, just thoughtful.

As the funeral arrangements, which had been made in advance, fell into place very smoothly – when had Alice ever done anything inefficiently? – Eva did what was expected of her, feeling numb and tired more than anything else.

On the day before the funeral she asked Gus to join her in the sitting room before lunch. She had come to a decision and wanted to tell him first.

'You're very formal,' he said. 'What's so important it can't wait until lunchtime?'

'I – we need to talk. About our marriage.'

'Why? I thought everything was arranged. No need to change things, is there? My aunt wouldn't like that.'

Eva noticed how watchful he had suddenly grown and lowered her lids to veil her eyes from that sharp gaze. 'I want to postpone our wedding, Gus. It doesn't seem right to rush into it so soon after Alice's death. We were doing that for her, but now we can take our time, get to know one another better and make proper plans for the future. We never have sat down to work out what we're going to do with ourselves.'

'It all seems pretty obvious to me,' he said, getting out a cigarette and tapping it on his gold case before using his shiny gold lighter.

She watched, thinking he had some beautiful things, and then, guiltily, how glad she was to postpone the marriage.

He drew deeply on the cigarette, making the end glow bright red, then puffed the smoke out with a sigh of satisfaction. 'We'll go on living here, of course.'

'But don't you have a job or a business to sort out? Don't you want to go back to London to live?'

'Not really. If the old girl has left us enough money, there should be no need for me to find work. And this house will do us fine.'

She was puzzled. She had never met a man who didn't have an occupation of some sort and suddenly had a vision of what their marriage would be like if Gus were around all the time. It would be even more difficult than she had expected. 'I think every man should do something worthwhile with his life,' she ventured.

He threw back his head and let out a peal of laughter. 'Only if he has to, Eva. Don't be so naïve, my pet. People work because they need the money. Those who have money enjoy themselves instead and that's what I intend to do. There's a new spirit in the air now that the war is behind us. Enjoy yourself and devil take the hindmost.'

'Well, I still don't like the idea of your being idle. It seems wrong.'

'You'll have to get out of this working-class mentality,' he said scornfully. 'My dear girl, I can assure you that—'

Suddenly something snapped inside her. She had had enough, more than enough, of his attitude towards her. She might never have left Lancashire, and yes, she had been poor as a child, but she was well read and felt she had a reasonable understanding of the world. 'Don't call me "my dear girl" in that patronising tone!'

'Now, look here—'

'No, *you* look here, Gus Blake! I'm not a child and I'm not stupid, so I'll thank you to show me some respect.'

He took another drag on the cigarette and now his gaze was cold and assessing. 'You're taking offence where none is intended, Eva, so I suggest we postpone this discussion until after the funeral. You're too upset at the moment to think clearly.'

'Indeed I'm not. I never liked the thought of rushing into marriage and was only doing that for Alice's sake. Now that I don't have to, I won't.'

Outside the door, shamelessly eavesdropping, Jenny waved her hands in the air in triumph and did a little dance.

Gus stood up. 'We'll see what you have to say after the will's been read. In the meantime I've got things to do.'

'I shan't change my mind,' Eva flung at his back.

He turned round, smiling again. 'Don't be so sure of that.' He sauntered out of the room.

She sank down on the sofa, upset and puzzled by his behaviour, his certainty that they would marry as arranged. What had Alice put in the new will to make him so confident?

Later that day Eva walked down to the centre of Heyshaw to ring up her older sister from the post office and let her know that Alice was dead. She hadn't wanted to face this, knowing she'd weep. She saw no sign of Gus's car anywhere and wondered where he'd gone.

Lizzie was warmly sympathetic, but couldn't come to the funeral because both her children were down with measles. 'Will you be all right, love?' she asked anxiously. 'Shall I send Peter over?'

'Of course I'll be all right. And you'll need Peter to run the shop.' She knew that takings were down and the Deardens were both working extra hard to make ends meet in these precarious times.

'You'll have Gus to help you through the day, though.'

'Yes, I suppose so.'

There was dead silence from the other end, then, 'Eva?'

'What?'

'Is something wrong between you and Gus?'

'I want to postpone our wedding – I *am* going to postpone it – and he's being a bit awkward about it all.'

There was silence, then Lizzie said earnestly, 'Look, love, if things aren't right between you, don't do it. I think you're absolutely right to wait.'

The sympathy reduced Eva to tears and she couldn't speak properly. 'Mmm,' she managed.

'Oh, Eva, don't cry. It'll all work out. You'll see.'

Since Lizzie's voice sounded as if she were near tears as well, Eva pulled herself together. 'I'm all right, really I am.' Her sister had enough on her plate with two sick children and measles was one of the worst of the childhood illnesses. Children died of it sometimes. 'You look after my niece and nephew, and I'll look after myself.'

'Yes, but I'll be thinking of you, love. And if you want to come and stay with us for a few days after it's all over, well, you know there's always a bed for you here.'

'Yes. Thank you. I must go now.'

Eva walked slowly back up to Rose Villa, trying to stem the tears and failing.

Jenny wasn't in, so she went up to her bedroom and allowed herself to weep for a while, then forced herself to stop. 'That's enough!' she told her red-eyed reflection in the mirror. Taking several deep breaths, she brushed her hair, washed her face, then went downstairs to make herself a cup of tea. She didn't need anyone's support, not really. She might be sad, but she hadn't lost her wits.

She knew it was right to postpone the wedding and no one was going to persuade her otherwise.

Whatever the will contained.

★　　★　　★

The funeral was a quiet affair with Jenny sitting in the front pew alongside them, to Gus's annoyance. He and Eva had had sharp words about that this morning and she was discovering that although he was usually easy-going to a fault, if he didn't get his own way he could turn nasty.

As she bowed her head, supposedly in prayer for the soul of Alice Leyton Blake, Eva decided it was lucky she had not already married Gus Blake – a godsend as Jenny would say. She didn't think she would now, and that decision made her feel a lot better. She had taken the engagement ring off her finger and left it in her dressing-table drawer. She would give it back to him later.

The doctor and his wife were there and Mr Beaman, as well as Jed Comper, the headmaster of the local primary school, who had known Alice for years. They were all suitably solemn and looked very unlike their usual selves, with their black ties and armbands. Well, Eva felt a bit strange herself today. She was dressed in black, which didn't suit her, and her eyes were reddened because she'd wept again in bed last night, for all her resolve not to give way to her grief. Jenny's eyes were swollen, too.

Gus showed no sign whatsoever of grief. His expression was calm and thoughtful. Well, he hadn't known his aunt for long, had he?

No, a voice answered inside Eva's head, he'd only known Alice for long enough to persuade her to change her will.

As they went outside to watch the coffin lowered into

the grave, she tried not to think of Alice, shut up inside that thing, cold, dead . . .

A sob welled up in her throat and she couldn't hold it back.

To her surprise it was Gus who stepped forward and put his arm round her shoulders. 'Steady on, old girl.'

She nodded and concentrated on the words the minister was intoning. To her surprise, Gus's support was comforting. But unsettling. She never knew where she stood with him. Hated that.

Rain was threatening, but it had held off so far. She looked at the grey skies, heavy with clouds, and shivered.

They were all looking at her. Why?

'Throw some earth on the coffin,' Gus whispered.

Numbly she did so. She also threw in the rose she'd picked from their own garden, noticing for the first time that her finger was bleeding. She must have caught it on one of the thorns.

It was with enormous relief that she turned away after the last words had been spoken. But she stumbled on the rough path and again it was Gus who prevented her from falling and then offered her his arm.

'Here. Hold on to me. You're not yourself.'

She was grateful when he didn't try to talk to her. She didn't think she could speak without bursting into tears.

She slid into his car and let him drive her home, but felt guilty when she realised they'd left Jenny to walk back on her own.

The house felt empty. Normally she'd have run upstairs to see how Alice was. She'd never need to do that again.

'I'll just go up and check that I'm tidy,' she said. Really, she'd have liked to spend the rest of the day alone, getting used to a world without Alice. But the mourners had been invited back for light refreshments, on Alice's instructions, and then Mr Beaman was to read the will.

Aaron saw the hearse pass by as he came out of the village shop after delivering the milk for his employer. Automatically he set down yesterday's empty milk churn and took his cap off, standing with head bowed till the funeral cortège had passed. With a shiver he realised that one day soon he'd be the one following a coffin to the cemetery – only he wouldn't be able to afford a fancy hearse like that for his wife. Even the cost of the simplest funeral would be hard to find and he'd have to rely on Wilf and the lads to lend a hand getting the coffin to church.

And after Lil died Aaron would not only be out of work but out of a home, too. He looked down the hill towards the village centre. Not a bad place to live, Heyshaw, if you didn't have to work on a farm. And North Hey would be a perfect place for his garage. There was a corner of Linney's farm next to Rose Villa, rough ground that was no use to man nor beast but would be just the right place for a garage, since it fronted the main road.

He shook his head in annoyance at himself for

clinging to this stupid dream. Fat lot of hope he'd ever have of achieving it!

In the big black car driving slowly along behind the hearse he had seen Eva Kershaw sitting very upright. She seemed a nice young woman. Even Gracie had liked having her as a teacher, which was the first time that had ever happened.

The arrogant sod sitting beside Eva Kershaw wasn't pleasant, though, and definitely hadn't been looking sad, just smug, as if the world was doing exactly what he wanted. Wilf said Jenny reckoned he'd got the old lady to change her will, and if that was true, it was a crying shame. The fellow might be family, but where had he been since the war?

The doctor's car drove slowly along behind the funeral car. The Stotts had been quite friendly with Miss Blake. Well, they stuck together, didn't they, the professional classes? The headmaster of the local primary school was riding with them. But Sid Linney and his wife weren't there. Sid was trying to edge his way in with the more affluent locals and now ignored the smallholders his father had called friends. It amused Aaron to see how little progress he was making.

Wilf said Eva Kershaw was going to marry Blake. Well, all Aaron could say to that was, she'd regret it, by hell she would! He didn't trust that fellow an inch. He must have been a lousy officer to serve under.

And if Aaron didn't get a move on, he'd be regretting things, too, because Sid would complain again about him being slow. He hoisted the big churn onto the cart, feeling the strain on his bad leg and wishing he dare wear the brace. He shook the reins to make old Dolly walk on, glad it wasn't raining yet. With a bit of luck he'd get back before the heavens opened up.

The Stotts brought Jenny back to Rose Villa with them, just beating the rain. She hurried in while they were parking the car, but when Eva moved automatically to follow her to the kitchen, Gus blocked her way.

'For heaven's sake, let the woman do her job. It's what she's paid for. You're not a damned skivvy!'

Eva drew back, shooting him an angry glance.

'I can manage fine, miss,' Jenny said in that flat, toneless voice she'd started using with Gus.

'Well, don't forget to come and join us for the will reading,' Eva said. 'Alice made me promise to include you.'

'Yes, miss.'

Gus gave a scornful sniff, but didn't say anything.

The doctor and his wife peered inside the open front door just then, so Eva gestured to them to enter and took their coats, before leading them into the sitting room. Mr Beaman and Mr Comper joined them, then everyone made careful conversation. It was a relief when Jenny brought the trolley in and Eva could busy herself with pouring cups of tea and offering sandwiches.

She didn't try to eat, couldn't, felt too drained. Even the tea tasted bitter and unpalatable today.

The Stotts stayed for one cup, nibbled a sandwich then left, murmuring condolences. They were followed soon after by the headmaster, who looked as indecisive as ever. Alice had virtually run the school for him and since she'd left the children were getting rowdy and out of hand, in Eva's opinion.

Mr Beaman looked round, saw that no one seemed to have any further interest in the refreshments and cleared his throat. 'Ahem. If these things could be cleared away, I think it might be appropriate for me to read the will now.'

Gus went to ring the bell and when Jenny appeared, said curtly, 'Clear away, please.' He then flung himself into an armchair.

Eva wished he wouldn't sprawl around like that. 'I'll help you, Jenny.' She ignored Gus's frown at that.

When they were settled, Jenny included, Mr Beaman took out a crackling set of papers and looked over his spectacles at the three of them. 'I shall, if you don't mind, summarise what my client wished, because the provisions and clauses as expressed in the will are couched in fairly complex legal terminology. After that I shall provide you, Miss Kershaw, and you, Mr Blake, with a copy each, of the will which you may peruse at leisure.'

'Get on with it, man,' Gus said.

Mr Beaman cast him a disapproving glance and shuffled the papers again before speaking. 'Miss Blake has left a bequest of one hundred pounds to Jenny Gill, and her gratitude for the years of loyal service. This money is not to be paid until the rest of the estate is settled, however. I also have a reference for you, Miss Gill, which will help you to gain other employment.' He handed over a sealed envelope.

'Miss Blake told me what a hard worker you are and how willing always.'

Jenny's eyes filled with tears and Eva squeezed her hand.

'And now to the main provisions of the will. In brief, Miss Blake leaves everything else of which she stands possessed to Eva Kershaw on condition that she marries within one year of the deceased's death. Until that happens Miss Kershaw and Mr Blake are to have joint tenancy of this house.'

Gus grinned triumphantly at Eva.

She gazed stonily back at him, unable to believe what she was hearing but determined not to show how angry she was feeling. Why had Alice felt the need for this coercion when they were already engaged to be married?

'There is no provision made for – um, housekeeping money – during that year, I'm afraid, though you are both free to continue living at Rose Villa.'

'Until we marry!' Gus said, lounging back in his chair with his long legs stretched out across the hearth rug.

'Well, yes. Until you marry, at which time Miss Kershaw will inherit all Miss Blake's money, which will allow you both to live very comfortably and will also allow the rest of the estate to be settled.'

Jenny looked sideways, her face full of sympathy and concern. In fact, they were all looking at her, so Eva took a deep breath and forced herself to stay calm, as she had done when dealing with difficult children. 'What happens if we don't marry, Mr Beaman?'

He blinked at her in surprise. 'I thought you had arranged to get married next week?'

'No,' she said firmly. 'I've decided to postpone the wedding. It's too soon after Alice's death. But I'd like to know what happens if we don't marry at all.'

The fury on Gus's face astonished her, but she paid no attention to that and concentrated on what Mr Beaman was saying.

'Well, um, in that case, the estate would be disposed of by me in accordance with Miss Blake's other instructions, which are set out in a codicil. I am to keep this information to myself in the meantime.'

Jenny gasped, then there was silence.

Eva felt as though everyone were miles away. This was what Alice had been worrying about. This will. This outrage. 'Don't be angry with me,' she had begged as she lay dying. Suddenly Eva was quite certain that her friend had already been regretting the conditions she had imposed. What had she put in the codicil? Had Alice left everything to charity if her protégée didn't do as she asked? Somehow Eva found it hard to believe this.

And she was not angry with Alice, of course she wasn't, but she *was* angry with Gus, furiously angry, because she was quite sure he had known about this – perhaps even suggested it. 'What about Jenny's wages?' she asked.

'There is no further provision made for Miss Gill, though you will have more than enough money to continue employing a maid once you've married Mr Blake.' Mr Beaman smiled reassuringly at her. 'The estate is a comfortable one and the money is prudently invested, because this is not a time for taking risks. It will provide you with a good living for the rest of your life, as long as you do not erode the capital.'

Eva was suddenly aware that Gus had come to crouch beside her, his hand possessively on hers.

'Look, darling,' he said, 'I know my aunt's death has upset you, but given the conditions of the will, it'd only be sensible to get married as arranged next Saturday.'

Eva moved her hand away. 'I've already told you that I don't want to rush into marriage. I need time to recover and to see how we get on with one another. If Alice hadn't been so ill, I'd never have agreed to marry you so quickly.'

His face darkened. 'Well, you still can't afford to wait, otherwise you'll be penniless.'

She stared at him, then said in a distant voice that didn't really sound like hers but was all she could produce at the moment if she were not to start weeping, 'I have a little money put by and if necessary I'll still be able to earn my living as a teacher. I love my work and I'd regret giving it up if I married. It's a ridiculous rule that women must resign upon marriage.'

'We'll discuss this in private afterwards, I think,' Gus snapped, turning back to the lawyer. 'Is there anything else, Mr Beaman?'

'Yes. I'll need my client's bank book and any account books or outstanding bills. These will have to stay in my charge until things are – um – settled. I do have some discretionary money to pay any household bills and Miss Gill's wages up to today.'

Eva stood up. 'I'll get them for you.'

She knew exactly where they were and was back within a couple of minutes, in time to hear Mr Beaman saying soothingly, '. . . upset. Give her time.' She tiptoed backwards a few paces then walked along the hall to the sitting room noisily enough to be heard.

'Here you are,' she said, holding the pile of books and papers out to the lawyer.

As he stretched out his hands for them, the top ones slipped off.

'I'll get you a bag from the kitchen, shall I?' Jenny offered.

'Yes. And then you can go and pack your things,' Gus said harshly. 'We can't afford to employ a maid until we're married, it seems.'

Ignoring him, Jenny turned to look at Eva questioningly.

She in turn looked across at Mr Beaman. 'Is there anything to prevent me from inviting friends to stay here?'

'Well, no, nothing at all.'

She turned back to the maid. 'Then would you come and stay with me for a few days, please, Jenny? Not as my maid, but as my friend.'

'I'd be happy to, Eva love.'

Gus glared at them both, opened his mouth to say something, caught Mr Beaman's eye and in response to another warning shake of the head, snapped his mouth shut again.

When the lawyer had taken his leave, Eva went up to her bedroom. She felt disoriented, bewildered, and though she was trying not to feel angry at Alice, she could not help feeling upset. Of all the awkward situations! It would have been nice to have some money behind her in troubled times like these, not because she was greedy but because ever since her father's death she had felt a great need for security. Leaving her penniless until she married was a cruel thing to do. 'Oh, Alice, why?' she whispered.

As for Gus, he had seemed like a total stranger both yesterday and today – and a nasty stranger at that, except for the moment by the grave. Was he, too, unsettled by Alice's death? Or was it Eva's postponement of their marriage that was making him so angry?

There was a knock on the door.

'Who is it?'

'Me, Gus. We need to talk.'

'Not now. I'm too upset to think straight.'

After a moment he said, 'We'll wait till later then, give you a little time to pull yourself together. But we *must* talk, and soon.'

She heard him go downstairs and went to sit by the bedroom window, looking out across the moors through the yellowing leaves of the old sycamore tree outside her window. They would soon be falling as the weather grew cooler, but she loved the stark winter landscape almost as much as the greener fields and trees of summer.

Gradually the calm sweep of the moors and the drifting patterns of clouds soothed her and she began to think more clearly. She definitely didn't want to marry Gus Blake – or anyone else – and no one could make her do it.

She had earned her own living before and could do so again. She had never been rich and would not mind too much about the money. But oh, she would miss this house, in which she had been so happy – miss it quite dreadfully! It felt as though she was losing everything she loved.

7

When Aaron got home that night he went up to see Lil, but found her asleep. Downstairs the mess sickened him and he made a sudden furious onslaught on the kitchen, wishing it was like the one at Rose Villa, which had been so clean and cosy.

Mrs Harrop had not turned up again today. What if Lil died here on her own? That was a constant worry to him now.

Gracie was out at the privy, avoiding him. She hardly spoke a word to him these days, and her expression was usually either sulky or angry.

Molly was under the table, hidden by the tablecloth, cuddling her doll. He could hear the faint whisper of her voice as she talked to it. He couldn't remember the last time he'd heard her speak properly, but couldn't think how to deal with that problem. Men weren't trained to look after children. He was doing his best, but knew it to be woefully inadequate.

When he had finished washing the dishes, he squatted down and lifted up one edge of the cloth. 'Knock, knock! Is Miss Molly Brierley at home, please?'

She nodded, solemn as ever, and he frowned. To-night she looked as if she'd been crying.

He let the cloth drop and turned as Gracie came in, looking hunched and miserable. 'What's wrong with Molly?' he whispered.

'Miss Deevers hit her again today.'

'What for?'

'Because she won't talk properly. She said she's going to hit Molly with her ruler every day till she learns to behave herself.'

He closed his eyes for a moment. Could nothing go right? Then the thought of his daughter's unhappy little face made the anger overflow and determination surge up in him to do something about it. No one was going to beat his daughters, especially not now. 'Right. That does it. I'm going down to your school tomorrow to see that teacher of hers.'

'It won't do any good. Miss Deevers *likes* hitting people. She's a nasty old witch.'

'We'll see about that.' He'd have to beg Sid Linney for the time off, but sod that. The anger felt good, warming his veins, and he turned it into action as he used to do in the Army when furious about the carnage. 'Now, what shall we have for tea? I think we deserve a treat, don't you?'

Gracie shrugged. 'There's nothin' much in. It'll have to be toast.'

'Wouldn't you rather have fish and chips?' There was a chip shop in the village set up just after the war.

Gracie brightened immediately.

He was delighted to see her smiling. His mother would have thought shame to go to a chip shop and had considered one neighbour a feckless slut because she did so regularly, but such places were getting more popular nowadays and he couldn't cook as well as work long hours. Besides, the kitchen range here was as old and cranky as the cottage itself.

He thought of another small treat for them. 'How about we go and get the fish and chips on the motor bike? You two can ride in the sidecar.'

He held his breath as Molly peeped out from under the tablecloth, her expression hopeful. To hell with being careful not to upset her, because that hadn't worked! He grabbed her arm, tugging her out of her hiding place and making her squeak in shock. 'Come here, you little monkey. I need a cuddle.' He swung her up into his arms and gave her a big hug, growling and pretending to nibble her ear. Then he advanced on Gracie and drew her towards him, including her in the hug, too. And it felt good, so very good.

'I may not be the best father in the world,' he said, hearing how thickened by emotion his voice was, 'and I'm definitely not the best housekeeper in the world,' he stared round at the still untidy kitchen, 'but I do love you two, you know.'

Gracie sobbed and tried to hide it. He could have sobbed with her if he'd let himself, but their need made him pull himself together. 'It's hard for us at the moment, with your mother ill,' he said, searching desperately for the right words, 'but if we all help one another, we'll cope with – things.'

Gracie had her head buried in his chest now and her shoulders were shaking with sobs. He looked down at her and tears welled in his own eyes.

Molly tugged at his arm. 'And then Mummy will get better,' she whispered in that strange voice that sounded more like the rustling of paper.

Gracie looked up then and as he met her pleading eyes, he shook his head. No use lying to them. Or to himself. It wouldn't be long now. 'No, love. Your mummy's not going to get better. She's going to go to Heaven soon, like your grandma and grandpa did.'

Molly stared at him blankly. 'But I've been good,' she whispered.

Gracie froze against him.

'Being good doesn't make any difference, love. Nothing does,' he went on, unable to prevent his voice from coming out harsh and angry. 'These things happen. So we must just look after your mother as best we can while we've still got her.' He set Molly down and gave them both a push towards the back door, where everyone's outdoor things hung on a peg, Lillian's as well, because it seemed wrong to put them away while she was still alive. 'Come on now, you two. Get your coats on. We're off to the chippie's. I'll just nip up and see if your mum wants anything.'

Lil looked at him as he came into her bedroom. 'I heard.'

'Oh, love, I—'

'It's about time you talked to them about it.' She gave him a wobbly smile. 'Gracie understands what's going to happen, has done for a while now, but she won't talk to me about it and it's best to prepare Molly. I was proud of you for doing that, Aaron. It can't have been easy.'

He went across to clasp her hand. 'I'm proud of you, too, Lil. You must be the bravest lass in the whole world.'

She sighed and stared at the ceiling for a minute. 'I don't have much choice, do I? I'd as soon get it over with now. I've had enough of this.' She waved one hand at the cluttered bedroom.

After a short silence he asked, 'Do you want something from the chippie?'

She looked at him in faint surprise. 'Aye, I do. I fancy a few chips and a bit of haddock. Eh, I can't remember the last time I felt hungry.'

'Right, then.' He ran downstairs again to sling on his old Army greatcoat, because it was still the warmest thing he owned and the torn bit where a bullet had zipped through had mended up pretty well. The nights were getting a bit nippy now, especially on the bike. He wrapped scarves around the girls' necks, making a game of it, then they all went outside. When Molly began to skip as she walked beside him, he felt he was getting somewhere. After fastening the top of the sidecar down over the girls' solemn faces, he kick-started the motor and put his cap and goggles on, grinning sideways at the two faces peering out at him and waving his hand to them. They were both small for their age, he realised suddenly. About time he started feeding them up. And himself.

He chugged slowly along the muddy lane and down towards the village. The chip shop was a haven of light, with a short queue of people inside exchanging cheerful banter amid the smell of hot fat, frying batter and vinegar. He breathed it all in with relish as he opened the door.

Everyone turned round to look at them as he shepherded the girls inside and he nodded a greeting. 'Evening.'

Mr Haines, who had been a cab driver till he bought the shop, was just turning out a big net of freshly cooked chips into the metal tray. Mrs Haines was serving the customers. She looked up and beckoned the girls over, handing them a hot chip each. 'Here y'are, flowers. Keep you going till it's your turn.' She turned to Aaron and asked quietly, 'How's Lil?'

When he shrugged she didn't pursue the point. Everyone at North Hey knew about Lil. He had, he realised suddenly, been keeping them at a distance until now, acting as if everything was all right, refusing to acknowledge their concern. Why had he done that? 'It smells lovely in here,' he said, wanting to seem friendly.

Mrs Haines winked at him. 'Best chip shop in Lancashire, that's what.'

He recognised the man next to him in the queue and nodded. Another ex-soldier. There was a camaraderie between such men.

'That motor bike of yours sounds to be in right good nick,' Bob said. 'Eh, wish I had one of them. I'd take my lot out in it for rides.'

Aaron stared at him, struck by a sudden blinding thought. He needed more money, didn't he? Why not use his bike to earn it? 'I'll hire it out to you for five bob a day, as long as you take care of it an' buy your own petrol,' he offered. He knew the rates for hiring vehicles and asked for a little less, not charging mileage. This fellow had a good job, could afford a few bob.

'D'you really mean that?'

'You were a driver in the Army, weren't you?'

Bob sighed. 'Aye. Met some good lads in the Army. Lost a fair few, too.'

This was not the showing off of that arrogant sod Blake, but the quiet acknowledgement of a hard duty done, of dangers shared, of horrors you'd never tell civilians about.

Bob exchanged an understanding grimace with Aaron. 'A damned mess out there, weren't it?' Then he grinned down at his hand. 'Still, I don't miss them two fingers much. I were lucky. So were you.'

Aaron glanced down involuntarily at his leg. Yes, he was lucky to have come back. So many hadn't. But it had taken him a while to realise it. 'Well, I know you'll look after the bike.'

'I certainly shall. Next Sunday be all right, if it's fine? I had a bit of luck on the horses and the missus has been going on about us having an outing before the good weather ends.'

There was a chorus of good-natured jeers. 'Good weather for ducks, you mean!' someone called.

Aaron nodded. 'Yes. Sunday will be all right. I'll have the bike ready first thing.'

The two men shook hands solemnly, then Bob moved forward to receive his order.

Aaron stood waiting in the queue, delighted at the prospect of making some extra money. It would help greatly, as did his occasional job as a mechanic. 'If you hear about anyone else as wants to hire my bike,' he said loudly, 'just tell 'em to come and see me. I could do with a bit extra at the moment.' No need to explain why he needed it.

When it was his turn to be served, he found his daughters pressing against him, looking at the food gloatingly. The chips were golden, glistening with fat and tiny specks of salt, the batter on the chunks of fish was crispy and the mere sight of it made his mouth water. 'Put plenty of vinegar on!' he told Mrs Haines. 'Us Brierleys like our vinegar, don't we, girls?'

They nodded and Molly licked her lips.

He sang loudly all the way home, as Gracie cuddled the hot package to her chest while Molly beamed out of the sidecar at him.

He was still smiling as he climbed the ladder to his bedroom later that night. Funny how a trip to the chippie's had cheered him up so much. But it had. It was the warmth and light, the friendliness of the other folk in the queue. None of the ordinary folk in North Hey had much money to spare, but they were a kind lot – if you let them be. Which he would from now on.

You could cope better if you knew you weren't alone.

The following day he chose a moment when Mrs Linney was nearby and asked for an hour off to go and see Molly's teacher.

'Is something wrong with your little girl?' Angela asked at once.

'The teacher's hitting our Molly because she won't speak properly.' He looked at her miserably. 'She'll only whisper since her mother took to her bed. She thinks if she's good, it'll make a difference and I can't persuade her otherwise. I've not been making a fuss about it, but that teacher seems to be taking it as a personal insult and she's been hitting Molly with the ruler. Every day. Her poor little hand's that red and sore.'

'That's shameful. Picking on a child whose mother is . . .' She broke off in embarrassment.

He finished for her. 'Dying.'

Angela turned to her husband. 'He must go at once, mustn't he, Sid? It won't take him long to nip into the village and back.'

'I suppose so.' Her husband cast Aaron a darkling glance.

'I'll make up the time later,' he said.

'Aye, you bloody well will. I think the teacher's right and you're too soft with that child. You have to be firm with them or they get out of hand.'

'Not when they've got a mother who's so ill,' Angela said at once. 'How old's your Molly now?'

'Six.' He was annoyed that his own voice had thickened with emotion. He hated to betray his feelings to his new employer.

Sid shrugged and walked off with a sour expression.

Angela came to pat Aaron on the shoulder and sigh. 'He wasn't always so hard,' she said sadly. 'I don't know what's got into him since his dad died. I'll make it right with him.' She gave him a bleak smile. 'He won't want his fancy new friends to think him a harsh, unfeeling employer, will he?'

Aaron timed his arrival at the little school for morning playtime. The sounds of voices repeating a poem aloud and a piano tinkling out a tune cut off abruptly as the bell rang. He watched the children in Molly's class file out into the playground, winking at his daughter as she passed, but was upset by the traces of tears on her cheeks and the downturned corners of her soft little mouth.

Miss Deevers was still in the classroom, writing something on the blackboard. When he knocked on the open door to warn her of his presence she turned to stare at him. Her iron-grey hair was clamped into rigid waves along her broad head and her bearing was just as rigid. 'What can I do for you, Mr Brierley?'

He didn't intend to mince words. 'You can stop hitting my Molly.'

'Your child is refusing to speak, Mr Brierley. That cannot be allowed.'

'Her mother's dying and she's upset. This isn't the time to be harsh with her. So I'm asking you to stop hitting her for something she can't help.'

'She can help it. She must behave properly in my class and will grow up into a better person for the discipline. After forty years as a teacher, I think I understand these things rather better than you do.'

He could tell this woman didn't intend to change her behaviour in the slightest. 'We'll see about that.'

He strode along to the headmaster's room and

thumped on the door. She followed him and stood behind him, radiating anger.

When the door opened he spoke first. 'Aaron Brierley, Molly's father. Can I see you for a minute, Mr Comper?'

The headmaster nodded. 'Come in.'

As Molly's teacher stepped forward to join them, Mr Comper hesitated then said, 'Please allow me to deal with this, Miss Deevers. The bell is going to ring any moment now and your class will be coming back in.'

With an angry sniff she walked away.

The minute they were inside the office, Aaron said, 'That woman's been hitting my little lass and I'm not having any more of it. The child's deeply distressed because her mother is dying inch by inch in front of her. Molly's not being naughty, she just can't cope with it, that's why she won't speak above a whisper.'

'I can't tell my teachers how to maintain discipline and—'

'Well, this time I'd be grateful if you'd make an exception to that rule.' Aaron hadn't wanted to say it, because it wasn't really fair, but he'd use any means, fair or foul, to help his child. 'You lost your wife to the same scourge, man. Have you forgotten what it's like? Molly's six, that's all. And she's facing the same thing as you did.'

Jed Comper went very stiff for a moment, then shook his head and stared down at his desk for a minute before saying, 'Very well. I'll have a word with Miss Deevers. It can't be easy for any of you.'

Aaron shrugged. 'It isn't, but we cope. And I'm grateful to you. Very grateful indeed.'

'I hope we can show compassion at times like these.' Mr Comper cleared his throat, then added, 'The first time Miss Deevers smacked your little girl, someone poured ink into her desk afterwards. And there have been a couple of – incidents following further smackings. We think it's Gracie, but so far we've not managed to catch her out.'

'I'll have a word. If it's her, it'll stop at once.'

Jed inclined his head.

When he got clear of the school, Aaron could not help smiling. 'The young devil!' he muttered.

Aaron was not the only visitor to the school that day. In the afternoon, just as the monitor was about to ring the bell for the end of school, Eva walked across the playground. She stopped to smile at the sound of children's voices coming from one classroom. She knew what they'd look like – twitchy, dying to get off home. Oh, she did miss all this!

Pupils in the nearest classroom were now chorusing, 'Good afternoon, miss,' in that sing-song tone children used when speaking aloud together. She hurried on, anxious not to be caught up in the tide of young bodies, and reached the safety of the headmaster's doorway just as the pupils began to march out in their class lines: decorous, orderly until they got into the yard where the lines broke up and they were away, running, shouting, laughing, shoving one another, screeching for the sheer joy of their freedom.

Jed Comper was watching them from the main doorway, a half-smile on his face. He turned to Eva. 'Miss Kershaw, how nice to see you.'

'Could you spare me a few moments, Mr Comper?'

'Of course.'

When Eva was seated she said it before she lost her courage: 'I've come to see if I can have my old job back. I know Miss Deevers will be retiring at Christmas and you did say that if I ever wanted to come back to teaching, you'd be happy to employ me again.'

He looked down at his desk, then up again. 'I'm sorry. The position has already been filled.'

'Oh.'

'And I must confess to being surprised that you ask me that. I thought you were planning to marry?'

'No. I – we changed our minds. The engagement was mainly to please Alice and now she's gone, I find – well, I don't think Mr Blake and I really suit.'

He took a deep breath. 'The conditions of her will are being spoken of everywhere.' There had been a School Governors' meeting the night before and it had been the main topic of discussion, since Eva Kershaw had once been a teacher at the school.

She gazed at him in astonishment. 'But how can that be known?'

He shrugged. 'Alice wrote to me about it, asked me to talk to you if you tried to change your mind about marrying. She was extremely anxious to see you settled in a home of your own with a husband and children.' He watched her bent head and allowed his words a moment or two to sink in before adding more briskly, 'I can't say how the news got out to other people, but it is generating a great deal of interest in the village. You will, I gather, inherit a considerable sum if you marry?' When she nodded, he spread his hands helplessly. 'In times like these, with so many people lacking employment, I think you would be extremely foolish not to comply with the terms of the will.'

'I don't think the gentleman and I have enough in common to get married,' Eva said in a low voice, still avoiding his eyes.

He could not hide his amazement. 'You'll just let the money go, then?'

'Yes. I don't wish to marry Gus Blake.'

'Well, that's up to you, but even if the position here were not filled, I doubt the job would be given to you, not now people know about the will.'

She was surprised. 'Why ever not?'

'Because there are male teachers out of work, ex-soldiers some of them, like the man who will be joining us after Christmas. It is our policy to offer positions first to men who have served their country. They have earned that consideration, I believe. And secondly, in such troubled times, we offer positions to breadwinners, if we can.' As she looked at him in dismay, he hardened his heart and said bluntly, 'You'll find the same policy in operation everywhere else in the district.'

'Then I'll move away. They say things are better in the south.' But she didn't want to move away from Rose Villa.

He inclined his head. 'The choice is yours and of

course I shall be prepared to give you excellent refer-
ences if you require them. But, my dear, would it not
be easier to marry Mr Blake? He seems pleasant
enough. And it *was* Alice's final wish. Surely that
counts a little?'

Eva was fiddling with the fingers of her gloves,
smoothing them out assiduously in her lap. 'I just –
I don't think I'm the sort to marry.'

He clicked his tongue, more than half convinced that
she was simply feeling nervous about the prospect of
marriage. 'You are young, healthy and would make a
good mother. I really do think, Eva, that you should go
home and consider the matter further.'

She walked out, feeling bewildered. Was she being
foolish? Mr Comper clearly believed so. And would
she really not be able to get a job? How would she
manage if she didn't? It wasn't fair to consider only
males as breadwinners. There were many women who
had to support themselves. Surely they deserved some
consideration as well?

Oh, Alice! What have you done to me? she thought.
Could you not just have split the money between me
and your nephew if you wanted him to have a share? I
wouldn't have minded that. Well, she amended after a
moment, not as much anyway.

While Eva was speaking to the headmaster, Jenny was
carrying on with the housework. She might be nomin-
ally a guest in this house, but that didn't mean she
wanted to sit idle. As she was preparing a simple meal
for her and Eva's tea, humming to herself, she became

suddenly aware that she was not alone and broke off, turning to find Gus Blake standing in the doorway, staring at her.

'What's for tea?' he asked.

'You can get yourself what you like. This is for Eva and me.'

His expression darkened. 'You cheeky bitch! You don't know your place.'

She gasped at his words. Real gentlemen didn't speak to respectable women like that, whether they were maids or not.

He laughed, a sneering sound. 'And all this loyalty to a woman who is preventing you from receiving your own inheritance. You haven't the brains you were born with or you'd be trying to persuade Eva to see sense.'

'By that I suppose you mean she should marry you?'

'Naturally. As her aunt wished.'

'That's up to Eva, surely? None of my business.'

'Make sure it stays that way, then.' He smiled, but it wasn't a nice smile. 'She *will* marry me, you know. She'll have no choice if she wants to stay in Heyshaw. But *you* won't get your job back. I'll make damned sure of that.'

Such was the malevolence in his face and tone that when he had left the kitchen, she sank down on a chair, feeling quite shaky. He's bad, that one is, she thought, worse than I'd realised. He might hide it under a smiling face most of the time, but it's coming out now. Eh, I don't even like being in the house alone with him.

When Eva came back, Jenny could see that she had not had any luck in finding a job. 'Never mind, love. You'll just have to try in Rochdale.'

Eva flopped down on a chair. 'If Mr Comper is right, I'm not likely to find a job there, either. Let alone it's the start of a new school year and all the positions are filled, he says schools are all favouring men teachers, especially those who've served in the armed forces. "Breadwinners" he called them. Don't we single women need to win our bread, too?'

'They never think of that. It's why they pay women less than men.'

'And, oh, Jenny, the conditions of the will are known – Alice told Mr Comper about it herself, wrote and asked him to have a word with me if I tried to change my mind. He says people think I'm foolish for not marrying Gus Blake. Am I being foolish, Jenny? Should I reconsider?'

'Well, *I* wouldn't marry him. He gives me the shivers. He came in here asking what was for tea, and he spoke to me that roughly. Swore at me. I told him straight there's only enough for you and me.'

'Oh, Jenny, was that wise?'

'Eva love, we can't afford to feed him now. He eats more than both of us put together.'

Eva stared at her. 'I've got out of the habit of being poor,' she said, trying to smile, but failing.

'Well, you'll just have to get into the habit again, won't you?'

'Yes. We'll be all right for a while, though. There's quite a bit left from the wedding money Alice gave me.

But you're right, we had better be careful and Gus *will* have to pay his own way.'

In the passage outside the listener frowned. She had money left, did she? How much? Was it enough to allow her to hold out against him? He had better do something about that.

With a smile he pushed himself off the wall and went soft-footed into the sitting room, staring round it. A fussy woman's room, full of bloody ornaments. He'd change things round when it became his, get some bigger pieces of furniture that were comfortable to sit in. The house wasn't going to be kept as a shrine to Alice sodding Blake.

The following day Eva went by bus into Rochdale, still intent on finding a job. She could have written around to the various schools, but wanted to find something quickly. Surely someone would have a vacancy? She visited two schools and got the same answer at each. With the school year having just begun there were no jobs, and even if there had been, preference would be given to male applicants.

At the third school, the headmaster looked at her then snapped his fingers and exclaimed, 'You're Alice Blake's niece, aren't you?'

'Yes.' She didn't bother to contradict him. They'd often let people think Alice was her aunt.

'I was sorry to hear she'd died. She was an excellent teacher.' He frowned. 'But why are you looking for work? Surely she left you well provided for?'

'There are – conditions.' She saw comprehension

dawn in his eyes and wondered how he knew about the will. The previous headmaster definitely hadn't, though his answer to her inquiry about a position had been the same.

As if he'd read her mind, he said, 'I am acquainted with Mr Comper and he mentioned the will to me when I asked what would happen to you now. He said Miss Blake had told him about your reluctance to marry.'

She could feel herself flushing. Why had Alice done this to her? It was humiliating to have everyone knowing her business.

He looked over his glasses at her. 'My dear young woman, why are you wasting my time and your own like this? There are many people in Lancashire who don't have enough to eat, good people, more than willing to work. *Your* future will be quite secure, I gather, once you've married Miss Blake's nephew. I cannot believe you're being so ungrateful – or so utterly impractical – as to turn down such an opportunity to set yourself up for life.'

She stood up hastily, pushing her chair back. 'That's my concern, I think.'

'It's my concern if you're wasting my time. I had two children faint this morning from hunger. Go home and do your duty, Eva Kershaw. Marry the man your aunt chose for you. And be grateful for each good meal you eat thereafter.'

She left his office and walked out of the school. But when she had turned the corner of the street, she had to lean against the wall for a moment to pull herself together, because her legs felt shaky.

She had intended to have a cup of tea before returning, but it occurred to her that she should save her money and wait till she got home.

On the bus she sat thinking, staring blindly out of the window. Was she really being stupid about this? Everyone but Jenny seemed to think so anyway.

When Eva got home, Jenny wasn't in and Gus popped his head out of the kitchen. 'I've just got in myself and I'm making a cup of tea. Want one?'

She hesitated.

'I'm not going to try to browbeat you into marrying me, Eva.'

So, feeling unaccountably shy, she went into the kitchen and sat down at the table.

'I've been wanting to catch you on your own to apologise,' he said, pouring boiling water into the teapot and setting the tea cosy over it. He leaned against the wall with a wry expression on his face. 'I believe I treated you badly just after my aunt had died, spoke to you arrogantly. I apologise for that.'

It was the last thing she'd expected to hear and she stared at him.

'I was,' he said, fiddling with the tea cosy, 'looking forward to getting married. I desperately want a stable family life after the last few years. But the thought of facing another funeral – well, it reminded me of the war and latterly, of when my father died. Upset me. I'm sorry I took that pain out on you.'

She made a noncommittal sound in her throat.

'Couldn't you – think about it? Give me another go,

Eva? We could take our time, if you like. No need to rush into marriage, though as the church has been booked for next week, it seems a pity not to take advantage of that – it's your choice though, of course. But couldn't you reconsider?'

She shrugged, not wanting to upset him after such a generous apology.

He sighed. 'Well, let's leave it at that. In the meantime I'll pay my share of the housekeeping, but I'd be grateful if someone else could do the cooking. I wasn't thinking about how you were managing. Jenny could have put it more politely, but naturally I don't expect you two to pay for my food.' He gave her another of those wry smiles. 'It's an awkward situation, isn't it?'

'Yes. Very.'

'I didn't realise exactly what my aunt was planning, you know, just thought she wanted to see you married and intended to leave me a small legacy. After all, it is the family money and I am the last of the Blakes. I thought: there's plenty, so Eva won't begrudge me a share. That's why I helped arrange for Beaman to come while I took you out. But,' he held up one hand to stop her speaking, 'I didn't know exactly what she had in mind and I was never present at any of their discussions. I wanted to assure you of that.'

He turned back to the teapot and poured them out a cup each, bringing hers and then joining her at the kitchen table. 'I thought we could go and see the stonemason together tomorrow, talk about a headstone for my aunt.'

She took a sip of tea, then confessed, 'I can't afford a headstone yet.'

'Are you that short of money?'

She shrugged. 'I have a little. I shall need to make it last, though.'

'Then I'll pay for the headstone. It'll be my privilege. But you must come and help me choose the words and design. You knew her so well. It's strange that she didn't arrange that when she arranged everything else.'

'She felt the words should come from those who did the remembering, not from her.'

'Then you must complete that final task for her. Tomorrow?'

She nodded.

Which made her feel even more guilty as she walked up to her bedroom. Had she misjudged him? Certainly once or twice he had been very kind to her, as he had today. And no one was perfect, she least of all.

But she'd still rather not marry – him or anyone.

In her bedroom she stopped and stared round in horror because the room had been ransacked. She didn't realise she'd cried out until he came pounding up the stairs.

'What's wrong? Are you all right?'

She pointed mutely.

He came into the room and gasped in shock. 'My God! How can this have happened?'

'I don't know. Weren't you and Jenny at home today?'

'I was out for most of the morning. I don't know

about Jenny. She's probably across at her grandad's. Shall I fetch her?'

Eva nodded.

'Don't touch anything!' he warned. 'We'd better send for the police.'

But she didn't need to touch anything. The pot in which she'd kept the banknotes was lying shattered in the hearth. Whoever had ransacked her room had found her money.

What was she going to do now?

8

The following morning Eva stayed in bed much later than usual, sitting upright against the bedhead cushioned by pillows. Clasping her arms around her knees, she stared out through the leaves at the sky which changed from blue to cloudy, scattered a careless shower or two, then gradually turned blue again. She was trying to work out what to do, had to because she had lost everything now – adopted mother, job, money. Was she to lose her beloved home as well?

No mistaking the light footsteps running upstairs. When someone knocked on the door, she called, 'Come in, Jenny.'

'Fancy a cup of tea, love?'

'Yes. Um – would you mind bringing it up to me? I don't want to see anyone yet.'

Her friend nodded in immediate understanding that she meant Gus.

Within five minutes Jenny was back with a tray set out neatly: the teapot, two cups and a plate of biscuits. She set it down on the bedside table and turned to search Eva's face. 'You look peaky. How did you sleep?'

Eva shrugged. 'I didn't sleep at all well. I've been trying to think what to do, you see.'

'The burglar got the change in the kitchen pot as well,' Jenny said glumly. 'Good thing I took my purse with me or he'd have had my last couple of pounds as well.'

'Gus has lost some silver cufflinks and a tie pin, but he had his wallet with him.'

Jenny sniffed. 'Who cares about him? It's you who's the real loser.' She poured out a cup of tea, handed it to Eva, then poured one for herself, before coming to perch on the edge of the bed. After a couple of sips she asked, 'How are you going to manage now?'

'I don't know. I have a little money in the savings bank, but not much. I've been using my savings ever since I gave up work, you see.'

Jenny didn't say it, but she thought Miss Blake had been remiss, taking everything from Eva then trying to push her into marriage with her lanky lump of a nephew. 'Well, you've still got your sisters to turn to, at least. You could go and live with Lizzie, work in their shop for a while maybe, just till you get another teaching job.'

'And put someone else out of work?' Eva shook her head. 'That wouldn't be fair.'

'Well, you could just stay with them till you've found another job, then. There's bound to be one somewhere in England, if not as a teacher, then as a governess. I was reading in the paper the other day that things aren't half as bad in the south.'

'But I don't want to work just anywhere.' Eva waved one hand towards the window. 'I'm Lancashire born and this is where I want to stay.'

Jenny looked at her with narrowed eyes. 'You're not – you couldn't be thinking about marrying *him?*'

Eva avoided her eyes. 'It's one possibility, isn't it? I can't just dismiss it out of hand.'

'Don't do it! I wouldn't trust him an inch.'

'You and he don't get on. Neither of you can see the other clearly. He has some good points, you know. Even you must admit he was wonderful with Alice. And there have been a couple of times when he's been very kind to me, too.'

Jenny shrugged. 'I kept my mouth shut when I was just the maid, but now I'm here as your friend, I'll tell you straight: there's something about him that gives me the shivers. And you're not really comfortable with him, either. I've seen you jump when he touches you.'

Eva flushed. 'I never have liked people mauling me around.'

'Except children.' Jenny grinned suddenly. 'I've seen you cuddling them when you didn't think anyone was looking. And you fair used to get them eating out of your hand when you were a teacher. I've seen how they rush up to speak to you in the street still.'

Eva could not help smiling. After a moment she sighed. 'That's the main reason I'm considering marrying Gus, actually: I'd really like children of my own. Haven't you ever fancied getting married?' She let the words trail away.

'Not till recently,' Jenny admitted with a blush. 'I must say I'm getting a bit too fond of Wilf for my own good now, though.' She fingered the soft skin of her cheek, staring across the room into the dressing table mirror. 'I'm not pretty like you. I don't attract men. You do, or you would if you made a bit of an effort. You're too shy by half, my girl.' She snapped her fingers suddenly. 'Find another fellow, that's what to do. You don't need to marry *him* to get children nor do you need to inherit that money. You've a year to live here while you look around.'

'I don't know anyone else. I'm not – good with men. And how do I eat in the meantime?'

'You can manage for a bit, can't you? No need to make a decision today.'

'I can't manage for long. I only have a few shillings in my purse and a few pounds in the bank. Besides, there's another thing worrying me. Alice left you a hundred pounds, but you won't get it if I don't marry Gus. And if you have to move away from here, then who'll look after your grandad? If I marry Gus, you can go on working for us.'

They looked at one another. Jenny couldn't say the hundred pounds didn't matter, because it might make all the difference to her and Wilf.

'I don't think I have much choice,' Eva said, setting the cup down on the tray. 'I'll spend the morning in bed, if you don't mind, resting and setting my thoughts in order. If you see Gus, could you ask him if he'll be in this afternoon? I'll talk to him then.'

Jenny went downstairs and shed a few quiet tears in the kitchen, then sniffed and went to find Gus, who was reading the morning newspaper in the sitting room.

'Eva'd like to see you this afternoon, Mr Blake,' she said baldly.

His expression grew thoughtful. 'Ah. All right.'

Jenny decided it wouldn't hurt to mend a few bridges. She didn't want Eva's husband finding excuses to keep them apart. 'Would you like a cup of tea?'

His eyes narrowed, then he smiled. 'Yes, I'd love one. And a piece of cake if you have any.'

'I'll bring it through in a few minutes.'

Give him an inch and he takes a mile, she thought as she got it all ready. It's a wonder he's not fat, the amount he eats. Greedy in other ways, too, or he'd not have let his aunt do this. He'd told Eva he hadn't known what his aunt was planning, but Jenny didn't believe that for one second. Eva did, though. It was dangerous always to believe the best about people, Jenny decided darkly. She preferred to be wary until she knew a person really well.

Except with Wilf. A smile softened her face at the mere thought of him. He was looking after her grandad so well. He was a lovely fellow and as honest and hardworking as they came. She couldn't marry any other sort.

And she *would* find a way to marry him one day, if she had to do the proposing herself.

After lunch Eva got dressed slowly, making no attempt to look anything but her usual neat self. She wasn't going to pretend, not about anything. Jenny had brought her up some sandwiches, but she hadn't been able to eat them. When she was ready, she picked up the tray and carried it down. 'Here. You might as well take them across to your grandad and Wilfred. I think I'd feel better with just Gus and myself in the house, if you don't mind.'

'Oh, love!' Jenny came and gave her a hug.

Eva tried to smile and failed. 'Go on,' she said softly.

'All right. He's waiting in the sitting room.'

Not until the gate had clanged shut behind Jenny did Eva go to find Gus.

He looked up as she entered the room. 'You all right, old girl?'

She nodded and went to take a chair opposite him, wondering how to start.

'Jenny said you wanted to talk to me.'

She nodded again, then grew angry with herself. She had made her decision, hadn't she? Why was she acting so feebly now? She had even planned how she was going to say it so, taking a deep breath, she launched into her speech. 'I've been thinking about my – I mean, *our* – situation.' It was harder than she'd expected to say the words and when he started to get up, she waved one hand at him. 'I'd prefer it if you'd stay there till I've finished.'

He leaned back and folded his arms, his face expressionless.

She continued with her speech. 'As you know, I don't really want to get married. It's nothing to do with you, Gus, I just – I'm not the marrying sort, I think.'

He was watching her carefully and to his surprise he found himself feeling sorry for the poor little bitch. She was naïve and shy, very unlike other women he'd known. She'd probably be quite easy to live with, actually.

'But you still want to, we could get married. It'll – um – make life so much easier for us all.'

He smiled encouragingly. 'Of course I want to. I always did.'

'Yes. But there are things to settle first. I want children and I hope you do as well?'

He nodded, which seemed to satisfy her. He wasn't the slightest bit interested in children, but as he'd not have to look after them, it didn't much matter. Watching her fumble for words and flush as she spoke, he wondered what she'd be like in bed. Not much fun, he'd guess. She'd probably find it distasteful. Well, she'd learn to put up with it as most women did. He wasn't going to go without, not when he had a wife conveniently handy.

'I'd rather have separate bedrooms, though, if you don't mind. I've grown used to sleeping alone.'

He wouldn't mind that at all. It'd make it easier to come and go. 'Whatever makes you happy, Eva dear, though we can't get children without sharing a bed sometimes.' He smiled at the relief on her face. The pity he felt faded suddenly and impatience took its place. Stupid bitch! What a fuss to make about what was really only a sensible business arrangement! As the silence lengthened and she continued to fiddle with her skirt, he said in the gentlest tone he could summon up, 'I shall be delighted to marry you, Eva, and not just for the money. Like my aunt, I think we'll deal very well together. When a man decides to settle down, he needs a wife he can trust and respect.'

She looked up, smiling as if his words had pleased her, and he decided she'd be quite easy to manage. A few softly spoken phrases and she'd do exactly what he wanted. He had always enjoyed finding out the best ways to manage people. It made life so much easier than arguing and fighting.

'Yes. Yes, that's it exactly, Gus. If we respect one another, we can surely make a pleasant life together. And – there's one more thing. I want to keep Jenny on as our maid. She's a wonderful worker.'

'Whatever you like. The house is your concern.' Though the first time that damned maid answered back, she was out. He smiled at Eva, the smile which usually made women respond favourably to him, but she didn't bat an eyelid, the cold bitch. 'Am I allowed to move now?'

She nodded, but watched him nervously as he approached her. When he took her hand he could feel it trembling in his so changed his mind about kissing her and simply raised it to his lips, pressing a chaste little kiss on it, thinking, *Heaven protect me from frigid, virgin schoolteachers!*

'I'll go and see the minister tomorrow, if you like,' he said. 'See if he can still marry us on Saturday.'

'*Next Saturday?*'

Her voice sounded so full of panic, he could have shaken her. 'Why not? That's what we'd planned.'

'Please, Gus. Not next Saturday. Ask him for the week after. I really do need more time than that to – to get ready.'

'Whatever you wish, my dear.'

But he would ask for the soonest date possible, he decided, as he left the house. He didn't want her wriggling off the hook a second time.

Unfortunately, when he went to see Mr Morton, the man had gone away for the weekend, thinking the wedding cancelled, and there would only be the curate from the next parish for the next few days.

'Can't *he* marry us?' Gus demanded of the housekeeper.

'Mr Morton prefers to conduct the marriage ceremonies for members of this parish himself. The curate can read the banns for you, though.'

'Then why can't he marry us?'

'He wouldn't dare go against Mr Morton's orders. Mr Morton would not have gone away if he'd known you and Miss Kershaw were going to change your minds again, but his mother is ill and he took the opportunity to spend a few days with her.' She fixed him with the basilisk stare for which she was famous. 'It's probably as well to give you the extra time to make sure you're both absolutely certain of your own feelings.'

He bit back angry words. Stupid woman! Who did she think she was? God's ordained representative here? Thank goodness Eva wasn't the managing sort.

In the pub that night, he made a joke of his encounter with the 'dragon woman'.

Sid smiled sympathetically. 'She rules poor old Morton with a rod of iron. You'd better resign yourself to waiting till he gets back.'

Gus could wait for ever to marry Eva bloody Kershaw, but he didn't want to give her time to change her mind. There was money at stake, lots of it. However, he concealed his feelings and changed the subject.

When Jenny nipped across to see her grandad, he guessed at once that she was unhappy about something.

'What's up, love? You don't usually come across so early in the day.'

'Right this very minute Eva's telling that Gus Blake that she'll marry him, after all.'

'Eh, she's never! I thowt she had more sense nor that.'

'She says it's best for us all. But how can it be best for her to tie herself to a man like him?' She began to clatter around the kitchen, tidying up automatically. Her grandad seemed to go out of his way to leave things lying around. She'd never met such an untidy man. Wilf was much tidier, only he was out today, still looking for work.

'Well, it's probably for the best,' Grandad said in a comforting tone. 'I mean, it'd be a pity to throw away all that money, wouldn't it? And this means you'll get your legacy, too. Though I call it downright unfair to have left you money that depended on Eva getting married to that uppity southerner.'

Jenny was too loyal to Miss Blake's memory to agree with him openly.

'What are you going to do with the money?' he asked.

'Slap it straight into the savings bank. It'll feel good to have something behind me.'

He chuckled. 'Get away with you! You've been saving up ever since you were a little lass, and I've never seen you draw any of it out. You must have plenty tucked away by now.'

She scowled at him. 'That's my business. And in times like these, you can't have too much saved.'

His voice softened. 'Why haven't *you* ever got wed, lass? I wasn't sorry it didn't work out with that wet rag of a fellow you got engaged to during the war, but there have been others interested and you've never given them any encouragement.'

'I just – haven't felt like it until . . .' She broke off as she realised she'd been tricked into betraying her feelings.

He cackled and finished for her, '. . . until you met Wilf.' As she opened her mouth, he said quickly, 'Don't try to deny it. I've seen you looking at him, smiling when you see he's in.'

She swallowed. 'Grandad, I hope you haven't said anything to him!'

'Nay, what do you take me for? I'll leave that up to you, my lass. But I reckon you'll have to do the asking, because he's a proud sort, Wilf is. He knows you'll have this cottage and getting the money from Miss Blake will only make things worse. He doesn't feel he has owt to offer a woman at the moment.'

'He has himself. That'd be more than enough for me.'

As she spoke her expression grew soft and it seemed

to Grandad she looked almost pretty for once. 'Well, you'll have to think of a way to salvage his pride, if you want him, so put your thinking hat on.'

'You wouldn't mind, then, Grandad?'

'Lass, I'd be delighted. He's a fine young fellow, Wilf is.'

She gave one of her decisive little nods. 'Well, I can't do anything about it at the moment. Eva wants me to stay on as maid after she's married and I will – till I'm sure she's all right. But I'm not working for that fellow for too long. I can't stand him, to tell you the truth.'

'*He* may have other ideas. He looks the sort who'll want to rule the roost. What if he sacks you?'

'She won't let him sack me. She's shy, but she's got backbone when she needs it, never doubt that. But I still wish she wasn't marrying him. Any stranger off the street would be better than him.'

Aaron tried hard to make his daughters' life easier after the visit to the chip shop, but his employer seemed to get more cantankerous by the day and he came home exhausted most nights. It seemed as if he was always rushing to do something urgent, but at least that helped him sleep better. He was only having the nightmares about once a week these days.

Lil never came downstairs now and hardly ate enough to keep a sparrow alive, so he took the girls out to buy fish and chips again, and promised to take them every week, but that was the only treat he had time for. Well, at least Miss Deevers wasn't hitting Molly, though Gracie remained sullen. What was the matter with that girl?

One night he had had enough of his problems and abandoned everything once the girls were in bed to stroll down to the pub. He felt pleased when he saw Wilf and Grandad Gill sitting there.

Grandad greeted him with, 'You look tired, lad. And you're favouring that bad leg. Are you still not wearing the brace at work?'

Aaron shrugged. 'Not if I want to keep my job.' He'd fallen over yesterday when the leg let him down, but luckily Sid hadn't been around to see that.

Wilf stared into his glass. 'You hang on to that job, whatever it takes.'

Grandad's wrinkled old hand with its twisted fingers rested on Aaron's arm for a moment. 'This bad time won't last for ever.'

'It feels to been going on for a million years.'

'Mrs Harrop was talking to me. Seems your Lil's coughing up blood regularly now, an' a lot of it, too.'

Aaron stared at Grandad in shock. 'Mrs Harrop hasn't said anything to me. Why didn't she send for the doctor?'

Grandad squeezed his arm. 'Lil didn't want her to. And any road, what good would that do? Dr Stott can't do owt else to help her and you've done all you can for her, too.'

Aaron looked at him miserably. 'I haven't made her happy, though. I've never been able to love her and she knows it.' Only to Grandad could he have admitted this.

'No one can produce miracles to order. 'Specially when they have to get wed in a hurry. At least you did the right thing by her.'

After a minute or two Aaron said bitterly, 'When Lil dies, I'm not getting married again, not for anything. There'll just be me and the girls.'

Grandad grinned at him provocatively. 'Bet you do get wed again.'

'Never.'

'A quid says you do. Wilf, you're our witness.'

'You're on.' Aaron drank his beer and stood up. 'I'd better not stay too long. I don't like to think of anything happening with only the girls there.'

As he walked out, he passed the door of the lounge bar and bent to pick up a halfpenny someone had dropped. A voice the other side of the door was speaking and his attention was caught by a name.

'. . . Eva will learn to do as she's told once we're married. There's only going to be one master in my house.'

Aaron could see Sid nodding and taking a sup of beer, but not the speaker. He knew that voice, though. He didn't like to think of that nice lass married to such a lout and had been glad when Wilf told him the wedding was off. It must be on again. Eh, what was she thinking of? Couldn't she see what Blake was like?

Balancing a tray, Charlie Featherstone came along from the little snug bar patronised by the old women of the village. 'Still here, lad?'

Aaron offered him the halfpenny. 'Someone's dropped this.'

Charlie gave him a sneering glance. 'You keep it. A halfpenny's not much use to man nor beast.'

So Aaron put it in his pocket and left the pub. Whistling under his breath, feeling a little more relaxed after his talk with Grandad Gill, he walked briskly home. He didn't have any nightmares that night, but he did dream of Eva Kershaw with her soft, vulnerable face, for some strange reason. He kept trying to warn her not to marry Gus Blake, but she wouldn't listen.

Who was he to be offering anyone advice about marriage, anyway?

And Grandad Gill was wrong. He definitely wasn't going to marry again. Only there was no time limit, so he'd never be able to collect the quid bet, whereas if he ever re-married he'd have to pay up. He grinned. Trust that crafty old sod to look after himself. A real character, Mr Gill was, and the world would be a better place if there were more like him.

As Wilf escorted Grandad home a short time later, the old man chuckled softly. 'What's tickled you?' Wilf asked.

'Aaron Brierley saying he's never going to get wed again once his wife dies. He will, though. I've seen it time and again. He's a fine young fellow and some lass will tempt him to the altar, you'll see. Then you an' me will go out an' get drunk on the quid he owes me.' He cackled again.

Wilf shook his head, grinning. 'You're a cheeky old devil, you know that?'

'Aye. I allus have been an' I shan't change now. I'll

get drunk at your wedding, too.' The arm he was holding stiffened.

'Fat lot of chance there is of me getting wed. I can't even keep myself.'

'Not for lack of trying, lad. And you've done wonders with my garden. I'll start you on the inside of the cottage next. That's winter work. There's a lot we can do without spending much money, if we're careful.' He paused at the gate to his little front garden to look up at the young man whose bitter expression showed clearly in the moonlight. 'It's cheered me up to have you living with me. At my age companionship is a great gift.' He punched Wilf gently in the arm. 'Ah, stop fretting. Things will work out. You'll see.'

The dour expression softened slightly and Wilf said thickly, 'I'm grateful for your help, Grandad, more than I can say.'

'You don't need to say it. You show it every day. Now, take me out to the privy and then get me to bed safely. I shall need tucking up like a babby if I get any worse.'

But even that prospect didn't seem to upset him. Grandad had a capacity for making the most of any situation and Wilf admired that. He had grown to love the old man like the father he'd never known.

And to love Jenny Gill, too, heaven help him.

9

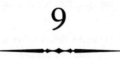

November

'We need to make the arrangements for our wedding,'
Eva said the next day. 'I'd better ring my family and—'

'Don't!' Gus said at once.

She blinked in shock. 'But I want them to be there.'

'Do you really? Look, they don't approve of me and
–' He held up one hand. 'Please let me finish. With my
aunt so recently dead, I'm sure they'll try to persuade
you to wait.' He saw by her expression that she thought
so too and smiled triumphantly. 'Do you really want
arguments and disagreements as we start our life
together? I don't. And yet I'd hate to come between
you and your family, especially your sisters. I know
how close you are. So it'll be better to present them
with a fait accompli then they'll just make the best of
things.'

She thought it over. No, she didn't want any disagreements and she was quite sure Lizzie would sense
her cool attitude towards this marriage and try to
persuade her to wait. She knew she was allowing
herself to be swept along by circumstances, but at
least Gus *wanted* to marry her! That meant a lot.

'Very well.'

But she was glad they could not get married until the following week. She needed a little time to herself first. Just a little.

She tried to persuade Gus to stay elsewhere until the wedding, but he simply laughed and refused in the most charming way possible.

'But don't you have things to settle in London?' she asked.

'No. I settled everything before I came here. I have a few bits and pieces which I'll have sent up, but that's all.'

'Were you planning to stay when you came here, then?'

'Only if my aunt wanted me and we got on well enough. Otherwise I'd have made a new start somewhere else. But she did want me to stay. I only wish I'd had more time with her.' He sighed and looked so mournful Eva let the matter drop.

The following day she did win from him a promise to spend the night before their wedding somewhere else, so that he wouldn't see the bride before they met in church.

'I didn't know you were superstitious,' he teased.

'Well, everyone says it's bad luck, so I don't want to – you know – risk anything.'

'Very well. How are you going to get to church, though, if I'm not to drive you?'

'Oh, it's not that far. Jenny and I can walk there.'

'In your full wedding regalia? It'll probably be raining. It seems to do that most of the time in Lancashire.

You'd arrive at the church looking like a drowned rat.' He looked at her and chuckled. 'No, a drowned kitten. All right. We'll get someone else to drive you there in my car. If I take a room in that lodging house opposite the church, I can easily walk across.'

'That'd be lovely. What about Mr Brierley? We could ask him.' She didn't know why she'd thought of him, but he'd seemed so competent when he was mending the car, as if he knew exactly what he was doing, and he'd had a kind face, too.

Gus made a scornful noise. 'Surely there's someone better than that surly devil?'

Only surly if you treated him badly, she thought, but didn't say that. 'Wilf Horrocks might do it, then. I think he knows how to drive. But we ought to pay him for his trouble.'

'I'll see to that. You go and ask the girl if he can drive.'

She frowned at him. 'Why do you keep calling Jenny "the girl"? She's thirty and a very competent woman.'

'It's just a way of speaking. She *is* a housemaid, after all.'

'She's still worthy of our respect. I don't like you calling her "the girl" so please don't do it again.'

He threw his hands up. 'All right, teacher. Now go and ask her.'

When she'd gone out he rolled his eyes to the ceiling. Stupid pernickety bitch! He was fed up of biting his tongue so as not to frighten her off. Not long now, though, and he could relax a bit.

*　　*　　*

One night Charlie Featherstone at the Dog and Duck received a phone call from London. A very pleasant-sounding man was asking if someone called Gus Blake was in Heyshaw.

'Yes. Staying at his aunt's house.'

'Ah. That's interesting.

'Can I give him a message? He's in here most nights.'

There was silence, then, 'No, I think I'd prefer to surprise him. We were in the Army together, you see. Has he been there for long?'

'A few weeks.'

'So he'd not planning to leave that you know of?'

Charlie chuckled. 'Not him. In fact he's getting married on Saturday.'

The man at the other end choked and began to cough. When he could speak again, he said, 'Sorry. You took me by surprise there. I never thought anyone would lead old Gus to the altar. You wouldn't know what time he's getting married, would you?'

'Early afternoon, not sure exactly.'

Silence, then, 'Fine. You will keep this to yourself, won't you?'

'Of course I will. It'll make a nice surprise for him to see an old friend. Er – you did know his aunt had died?'

'No, I didn't. Thanks for telling me. I'll see you on Saturday.'

The caller hung up before Charlie could get his name and he went back to the clearing up, smiling to think of how surprised Gus would be when an old friend turned up at the church.

*   *   *

In the middle of the night before her wedding Eva woke up in a panic. She couldn't do it. She just couldn't. Sitting up in bed, she felt her heart pounding madly and drew in a long shuddering sigh before lying down again.

She lay there trying to think of how she could tell Gus she had changed her mind again, but couldn't find any good reason, let alone tactful words. What she could imagine was how furious he'd be. And he'd have a right to be angry, too.

Besides, she'd still not have any money to live on and would have to move in with Lizzie. And Jenny wouldn't get her money, either.

After tossing and turning for a long time, Eva knew she couldn't face all the fuss it'd cause if she cancelled the wedding. It might be cowardly, but she just couldn't.

But she hoped Gus would be understanding the next night. Because she still didn't really like him touching her.

In the morning Eva got up early, feeling washed out. Relieved that Gus wasn't around, she went downstairs in her dressing gown and found Jenny in the kitchen, similarly attired, sipping a cup of tea.

'Like old times, isn't it?' Jenny said. 'The pot's still hot, not been made long.'

Eva poured herself a cup and sat down. 'Mmm, that's nice.' She sipped it slowly and felt the tension draining out of her. It had just been last-minute nerves, that was all. In the clearer light of morning it was obvious she was doing the sensible thing in marrying Gus. She'd be financially secure for the rest of her life and that wasn't to be sneezed at. 'I haven't felt so relaxed for ages,' she said as she poured herself another cup of tea.

'It's because *he* isn't here. Are you *sure* you're doing the right thing, love?' Jenny's eyes filled with tears. 'It's not too late to stop it, you know.'

Eva swallowed hard as her new-found confidence wavered, then told the truth. 'I'm not sure of anything. I just know it seems the best path to take *now*, for all our sakes.' She was relieved when Jenny did not press the point.

She stayed in her dressing gown, washing her hair and enjoying a lazy hour in Alice's sitting room as she dried it in front of the fire. That brought back memories of Alice brushing her hair for her in that motherly way she'd had, of the two of them chatting quietly together about this and that.

Surely, surely things would work out all right with Alice's nephew?

When it could no longer be delayed, she went upstairs and with Jenny's help put on the wedding dress. Jenny stood back to study her.

'Does it look all right?' Eva asked, twisting and turning in front of the mirror to examine herself from all angles.

'The dress is pretty, but it doesn't seem like you somehow. And it makes you look older.' Worst of all was Eva's expression, so sad and haunted. There was none of the usual excitement of a young woman marrying the man she loved, because Eva didn't love Gus Blake, and never would.

'Well, I shall be a mature married lady by this afternoon, shan't I?' Eva smoothed the lacy dress down and studied her feet in their soft kid shoes. It had started to spit with rain and she was glad Wilf was driving them to the church.

'Let me do your hair for you,' Jenny begged. 'You've flattened it down.'

'He must take me as I am.'

'But you're not usually like that.' Jenny stepped forward and took the comb out of Eva's hand. 'You have to look your best today,' she scolded softly as she arranged the soft, gleaming waves, so different from her own straight, fly-away hair. 'There. That's much nicer. You should do it like that more often, fluffing it out a bit.'

Eva stared at the stranger in the mirror. She didn't feel like herself at all, but she looked very smart, at least. 'Thank you. It does look better.' She turned to examine Jenny, who was wearing her best summer dress. 'You look nice, too. If this were a proper wedding, you could be my bridesmaid, not just my witness.'

'Why isn't it a proper wedding?' Jenny asked, eyebrows raised challengingly.

Before Eva could say anything, there was a knock on the front door.

'I'll go.' Jenny ran downstairs, then came up again, smiling. 'It's Wilf. But he's a bit early so we don't have to go for a few minutes yet.'

'We might as well.'

Jenny set her hands on her hips. 'Oh, no, we're not. We'll get there on time and not a minute before. Let *him* wait for you today.'

As they drove through the village towards the church, Eva looked down at the spray of flowers and greenery she was holding. Jenny had sent Wilf into Rochdale for them the previous day and had insisted on paying for them as her contribution to the wedding. Her friend was holding a much smaller, matching spray in her hand.

They had put them carefully into a bucket of water overnight, but the poor things were looking less than fresh. November wasn't a good time of year for flowers.

Eva breathed deeply, her heart already starting to thud nervously. After today she would be linked for life to Gus. *Mrs Augustus Blake.* It sounded – strange.

'We're here, love.'

Jenny's voice made Eva start. She hadn't even noticed their arriving at the church. As Wilf opened the door for her, another car drove past and stopped outside the public house. It was so rare for strange cars to stop in North Hey they all turned round to watch as a man and woman got out and went into the Dog and Duck.

'Don't look very happy, those two, do they?' Wilf said.

'Who cares about them?' Jenny began to fuss over Eva. 'Now, hold your flowers up, love. Just wait there while I go inside and check that everything's ready.' She bustled off.

'I wish you very happy, Eva,' Wilf said.

'Thank you.'

Jenny came back. 'Right. The minister's there and Mr Beaman is sitting next to your Gus ready to act as best man.' She patted the bride's shoulder and it felt so tense, she couldn't help asking, 'Still sure of what you're doing?'

Eva closed her eyes. No, she wasn't at all sure, felt like turning and running away. But she couldn't back out now – could she? No, no, of course she couldn't. What was she thinking of? She opened her eyes and stared at her friend. 'Yes.' But she couldn't manage a smile.

'Let's go, then.'

The two young women walked slowly down the aisle, keeping step instinctively. There was no organ playing, no crowd of guests, no displays of flowers, just the dusty old church they visited sometimes on Sundays. And since it was a dull day even the stained glass windows seemed less colourful than usual.

Gus stood up from the front pew and turned to watch Eva, smiling warmly at her.

From beside him Mr Beaman inclined his head in greeting.

She hesitated.

Jenny's voice was questioning. 'Eva?'

'I'm all right.' Taking a deep breath she moved on.

Mr Morton stepped forward. 'Are we all ready?' When they nodded he began to read the introduction to the wedding service, behaving exactly as if there was a crowd of guests to hear it.

It seemed so distant and unreal to Eva that she found it hard to follow the minister's words.

'Do you, Eva Kershaw, take—'

A voice from the back of the church yelled, '*Stop!*'

Eva jerked in shock and like the others swung round to see who had shouted.

The two strangers who'd gone into the pub were standing in the permanent twilight at the rear of the church.

'Oh, no, you don't, Gus Blake!' the woman called out in a strong London accent. 'Sorry, dearie, but he can't marry you because he's already married to me.'

She laughed. 'Missing presumed dead, indeed. I might have known the devil would protect his own.' She began to walk down the aisle, her male companion following just behind her.

Eva was too shocked to move. She heard Gus gasp and saw him turn away and begin to curse in a low voice as the two strangers came to a halt a few feet from the wedding party.

As he turned back to face them, the woman stared at him and opened her mouth as if startled by something. He stepped forward quickly and grabbed her arm. 'Don't say another word! It'll be to your advantage to discuss this in private.' He began to drag her back down the aisle, completely ignoring Eva.

At first the woman resisted, but then he whispered something and she stopped hanging back, walking by his side instead. The man with her looked round at

Eva, then towards Gus, frowning, before hurrying after the other two.

'I can't believe this is happening,' Eva said, clutching Jenny's hand. 'What shall I do? Can Gus really be married already?'

Jenny patted her hand. 'Eh, I don't know what to say. But if he already has a wife, he can't marry you, can he? And I for one shan't even pretend to be sorry. You know I don't think he's right for you.'

Mr Beaman was conferring with the minister and the two men seemed equally at a loss as to how to deal with the situation.

At the rear, a heated argument seemed to be raging. It was conducted in such low tones that the words did not carry to the main part of the church, but after a minute or two the woman who had claimed to be Gus's wife nodded. The man grabbed her arm, as if trying to make her change her mind, and they were off arguing again.

'Perhaps I should go and ask what is happening?' Mr Beaman muttered.

'I'd leave them to it,' Jenny said.

'Are you all right, Miss Kershaw?' Mr Morton asked. 'This must be very distressing for you. Perhaps you should sit down.'

'I'm fine,' Eva said. 'I'd rather watch them.' She frowned as she spoke. Surely she should be weeping? But she wasn't, didn't feel the slightest inclination to do so. In fact, she felt relieved, as if a heavy load had been taken from her shoulders.

In the end, Gus nodded and the woman who

claimed to be his wife grinned at him mockingly, then gestured towards the front of the church with one hand. He started walking back towards the altar, grim-faced.

Eva felt Jenny move closer to her and was glad of the unspoken support.

Gus stopped in front of them, but spoke only to Eva. 'I thought she was dead,' he said as mildly as if it were just a simple mix-up. 'They told me she was dead. I'm sorry, Eva, really sorry.'

'She *is* your wife, then?'

'Unfortunately, yes.'

Mr Morton began to splutter with indignation. 'I've never heard of anything like this in my life! I can't believe that you didn't even mention your first marriage, Mr Blake. You should have shown me a death certificate, at the very least, before arranging to re-marry.'

Gus cast an indifferent glance in his direction. 'A lot of people died during the war. I was told Clara was one of them. I had no reason to think the person who told me was lying.' He turned to scowl towards the rear of the church. 'Which made me very happy, I promise you.'

As if she did not trust him, his wife followed him down the aisle and came to stand with one hand on her hip, the other on his shoulder. 'Sorry to muck your wedding up, love,' she said to Eva. 'You've had a lucky escape, though you probably don't think so at the moment. You'll be a lot happier without this sly, scheming sod.'

As she linked her arm through Gus's, he tried to disentangle himself, but she clung tightly to him and he scowled down at her. 'I thought I asked you to wait for me near the door.'

'I'd rather have you where I can keep an eye on you, *Gus Blake.*'

For a moment, Eva could have sworn she saw fear in his eyes, but the expression was so fleeting she could not be certain.

'We're not exactly a loving couple,' Clara continued, speaking to Eva again, 'but he's all I've got. We thought he'd died in the war, then we heard he was up here visiting his auntie.' She glanced towards the man at the rear, a well-muscled fellow, who was watching them all very carefully indeed. 'My big brother came with me to look for you, *Gus dear* – though we didn't expect to find you getting married again, just soft-soaping the old lady.' She winked at Eva. 'He's good at winning folk over. Hope you didn't let him into your knickers.'

'Shut up, Clara!' He turned away from the woman and said in a low, urgent voice, 'Eva, I'm truly sorry.'

'I'm not sure I shouldn't send for the police,' Mr Morton muttered.

Gus swung round. 'There was no intention to deceive.'

Clara sniggered. 'Not if you say so, *dearest Gus.* And now, I think we'd better go. I can see that my brother is growing impatient and he can get a bit rough sometimes if anyone upsets him – or me.'

Gus growled something under his breath, grabbed her arm and strode off down the aisle, with her complaining, 'Slow down, you stupid bugger! I can't walk that fast in these new shoes.'

As the church door banged shut behind them, Mr Morton turned to Eva. 'Are you sure you're all right, my dear?'

'Yes.' She turned to Jenny. 'I think we'd better go home.' She looked down at herself. 'I want to get out of these clothes and into my own things.'

There was the sound of a car starting up outside, then driving away, then another one followed it.

'We'll need to discuss the will, Miss Kershaw,' Mr Beaman said. 'And I shall now have to make an inventory of Miss Blake's possessions and—'

'I can't discuss anything today.' Eva's voice wobbled suddenly and she began to walk quickly down the aisle towards the door, desperate to get away from this public humiliation. Jenny followed, not saying anything.

Outside the church Eva paused and looked down at the spray of flowers she was still carrying. 'I know *you* bought them, Jenny, but I can't stand the sight of them.' Without waiting for a reply, she threw them across the churchyard as hard as she could, then without even waiting to see where they landed said, 'Let's go home.'

Jenny followed suit with her own flowers and ran a few steps to catch her friend up. 'Here, link up with me.'

Eva shook her head. 'No. I can walk on my own. I'm not going to faint or have hysterics. I just want to go *home*.' Her voice broke on the last word.

As the two young women walked through the village, it began to rain, a fine, clinging drizzle. Eva lifted up her face to it, welcoming the chillness of the drops on her flushed and overheated skin.

Wilf must have seen them coming because he ran out of the cottage to ask, 'What's happened?'

Eva ignored him and continued walking.

Jenny paused for long enough to say, 'She didn't get married because Gus Blake's real wife turned up.' Then she ran after her friend, sure she would be needed.

They had barely got inside the house before Eva began taking her clothes off. The satin coat was discarded on the stairs. As she entered her bedroom, she began to fumble with the fastenings on the lacy dress.

'Here. Let me.' Jenny began to undo the pearl buttons down the back.

As the dress fell to the ground, Eva gave it a kick that sent it out of her bedroom on to the landing. 'I'd like to rip it to shreds!' she said through gritted teeth.

She opened her wardrobe and drew out one of her prim, everyday dresses, dragging it over her head with ruthless disregard for her carefully arranged hair. As the dark, wavy locks tumbled out of the bun, she pushed them back over her shoulders and gave her head a shake to loosen the rest.

She went to stare at herself in the dressing-table mirror for a minute, then turned to Jenny. 'I'm glad! More than anything else, I'm glad I haven't married him. If he'd do that, without being certain his wife was dead . . . what else might he have done?'

'Who knows?'

'Let's go down and get some food. I'm hungry now.'

On the landing she kicked the dress aside. 'You can throw that in the dustbin.'

Jenny picked it up. 'No, I won't. We'll press it up nicely and advertise it in the paper. We need the money.'

Only then did Eva's face crumple. 'Oh, Jenny, your money! You won't get it now. And how are we going to manage?'

'What you've never had, you never miss,' Jenny told her philosophically. 'And I have a bit put by for a rainy day, actually.' She looked at her friend and grinned suddenly. 'I bet that Clara is giving him what for at this very minute.'

A reluctant smile crept across Eva's face. 'He deserves it.' A few minutes later, as they sat down with some sandwiches, she said again, 'He can't have been sure she was dead, can he?'

'No.'

'Yet he was prepared to marry me for the money.'

'Yes.'

'Alice would be horrified to think of a nephew of hers behaving like that. I'm glad she wasn't alive to see it.'

They ate in silence for a while, then Eva said quietly, 'I don't want this talked about, not more than we can help, anyway. I'm sure I can rely on you to keep the details to yourself.'

'Of course you can, love.' Jenny hesitated. 'Look, I know it's early days, but what *are* you going to do now?'

'I don't know. I have a little money still in my savings bank. I'll try to pay you the wages that are owing and once I get some work, I'll pay you your hundred pounds gradually. Alice would want that.'

'You'll do no such thing! I won't accept a penny piece from you and you can't make me. But I will stay on here, if you'll let me, because I need somewhere to live. Grandad's got Wilf. You need someone, too.'

'Oh, Jenny, you're wonderful!' Eva gave her a big hug, then sniffed and said, 'I think I'll write to my sisters. I don't want them hearing a garbled version of all this.'

'And I'll go and pack his stuff.'

Eva turned in her tracks. 'I'd forgotten his things were still here. And he has a key to the front door, too.'

Jenny's face became grim. 'Then I'll nip across to Grandad's this very minute and get Wilf to put a good bolt inside all the doors, including our bedrooms. You can't be too careful.'

'How soon do you think he can do that?'

'This afternoon, probably. Grandad's got all sorts of bits and pieces in his shed. I'm not risking *him* coming back while we're asleep and murdering us in our beds.'

'I agree.'

Although she didn't think Gus would really harm them, Eva knew she would sleep better if she could lock the bedroom door.

Aaron heard about the wedding fiasco in the pub that night from Wilf and stared at him in shock. 'Blake was about to commit bigamy!'

'Aye.'

'And him so high and mighty. Is he in tonight?' He turned round to look towards the lounge bar.

'No. He drove off afterwards and no one's seen him since, but Jenny says his things are still at Rose Villa.'

'What's Eva going to do?'

As Wilf shook his head, Grandad took a sip of beer and said quietly, 'She'll be all right. Our Jenny wouldn't be so fond of her if she was spineless. My lass is a sound judge of folk.' His eyes rested on Wilf for a moment with fond approval.

'But didn't the will say Eva had to marry Blake?' Aaron wondered. 'Or could she just marry anyone?'

Grandad shrugged. 'I don't know. You'd have to ask yon Beaman chap.'

'It's none of my business, but I always think kindly of her for helping my Molly.'

'Most folk as know her do think well of her,' Grandad agreed tranquilly. 'And how's your Lil?'

Aaron shrugged. 'Hanging on by a thread. It's as if she's waiting for something before she goes.'

'Maybe she is,' said Grandad.

Well, if so, Aaron had no idea what it could be.

The Monday after her failed wedding, Eva went into the village to get a copy of the *Manchester Guardian*. As Jenny had suggested, she would try to find a job as a governess. She also intended to call in at Mr Beaman's office to discuss the will and how this new development would affect things, but as she walked into the village she saw him driving out of town in his little Singer Ten, so decided to postpone that. After all, there was no rush.

She ought to be unhappy about the wedding, but she wasn't. In fact, she felt as if she had awoken suddenly from a nightmare. For so long Alice's illness had dominated her life that she had lost direction for a while after her friend's death. But she was young enough and qualified to earn a decent living, and that was exactly what she intended to do.

Humming she strode round the curve in the road that led up to Rose Villa and stopped dead as she saw a car parked outside the house. Gus's car. He must have come back for his things.

When she got there he was sitting inside it, smoking a cigarette. He noticed her and got out, tossing the cigarette into the flowerbed. 'That damned maid of yours won't let me in. She's bolted the door on me.'

'I suppose you've come for your things.'

'No. I've come back to stay.'

She gaped at him. 'What do you mean?'

'My aunt's will gave me the right to live here for a year. That's not dependent on my marrying you.'

'*You can't possibly do that!*'

'I can, you know, and you can't stop me. What's more, if that *girl* of yours doesn't unbolt the front door and let me in, I'll break a window.'

'But why would you even want to stay here?'

'It's free and it's a long way from my dear wife. Two very useful attributes. And since I have some bits and pieces of business to finish off in the north, I might as well take advantage of the free accommodation.'

'But – what about your wife? Doesn't she want you back?'

'Not her. As long as I keep up the weekly payments we've agreed on, she's happier on her own. I enjoy your company much more than hers, believe me.'

His leer sent shivers down her spine, but Eva tried not to let him see her fear. 'I shall have to check this with Mr Beaman. And until then you're not coming in.' She tried to walk past him, but he grabbed her arm. 'Let go of me!'

'Not until you've let me into my home.'

'It's not your home now.' She tore herself from his grasp and backed away. 'And don't you *dare* touch me again!'

'Then don't deny me entrance.' He went across to the flower bed and picked up one of the stones that edged it. 'This should break the window of your little sitting-room without too much trouble.' He hefted it in his hand as if about to throw it.

'Stop!'

He paused, looking at her questioningly, but didn't drop it.

'Why are you doing this?' she demanded. 'Surely in common decency—'

'I'm doing it because it took most of my ready money to get rid of that damned witch I married. I need time to work out what I'm going to do next. Even a narrow-minded little provincial miss like you should be able to understand that.'

'Let me speak to Mr Beaman first and . . .'

His voice became softly meancing. 'Do you expect

me to sit out here in my car freezing to death until that old sod comes home from his office? Not likely!'

'If you were a gentleman—'

He threw back his head and laughed, a raucous, vulgar sound, then between chuckles told her, 'But I'm not a gentleman. It's a part I play when it suits me. It fooled my dear old auntie. It nearly bought me a comfortable life. And it will again, once I've sorted a few things out. Now, are you going to let me in or not?' He raised the stone again.

'Don't!' She could see Jenny watching them from the kitchen and went towards the side door with him following close behind. 'Let us in, please, Jenny.'

Jenny opened the door a crack. 'You're never going to let *him* into the house again?'

'I don't have much choice. The will allows him to live here, and anyway, he's going to smash in a window if I don't.' Spine very upright, Eva led the way inside.

He sauntered past her, winked at Jenny and looked round the kitchen. 'Any chance of some food?'

'No,' said Jenny. 'We can't afford to feed you.'

'Oh, well, there's always the fish and chip shop, isn't there?'

When he had gone upstairs, the two women looked at one another.

'What are we going to do?' Jenny asked in a whisper.

'I don't know.' Eva shivered. Gus seemed like a different person today, dangerous somehow.

10

As soon as she saw Mr Beaman return home from his office that evening, Eva hurried across the road to see him. His housekeeper opened the door but seemed reluctant to let her in.

'He doesn't see people at home,' Mrs Pannell insisted.

'This is an emergency and if you don't let me in, I shall stay here and bang on the door until he agrees to see me,' Eva insisted.

'Well, I never heard the like!'

The door was closed in her face, so Eva waited a couple of minutes, then banged the knocker hard. When no one answered, she banged again.

This time the door was opened by Mr Beaman himself. 'Surely this can wait until tomorrow, Miss Kershaw? I don't see clients at home.'

'Either you see me or I'll stay here and thump on your door all night long!' she shouted. 'This definitely can't wait.'

He drew himself up. 'Very well then. But how you can expect me to help you when all the papers relating to you and your inheritance are in my office, I don't know.'

'We don't need papers for this.' She followed him into a small study and when he gestured to a chair burst into speech before she'd even settled in it. 'Gus Blake came back this morning and says he's entitled to stay in Rose Villa for a year under the terms of the will, even though he and I can no longer be married. Surely that's not true?'

Mr Beaman sighed. 'I'm afraid it is. I did suggest to Miss Blake that the clause in question was rather – ambiguous. And had I suspected the true state of affairs, I would never have allowed her to include it. But you were at that stage engaged to Mr Blake and shortly to be married, so it didn't seem important.'

'How can I get him to leave, then?'

'You can't. He has a legal right to stay there.'

Eva stared at him in horror. 'But I can't live in the same house as him! Not now.'

Mr Beaman shook his head regretfully. 'There is nothing you can do about it, though I do see that it's awkward for you.'

She sagged against the hard back of the chair, which was as unyielding as Mr Beaman's expression, trying to think of a way to bribe Gus to leave. 'What about the furniture and Miss Blake's other possessions, then? Is he entitled to a share of them?'

He shook his head again. 'No, neither of you is. The contents of the house are to stay as they are until the end of the year, when the other provisions in the codicil come into force. Except for your own personal possessions, of course.'

'What are those provisions? Surely you can give me some idea?'

'I'm afraid I can't. My client insisted they remain secret until the year is over.'

'I suppose everything will go to one of Alice's favourite charities.' Eva swallowed hard. '*I* shall have to leave, then. I can't live with him, I simply can't.'

When he said nothing she looked up, but his face was completely expressionless. He was famous for that look. *Don't even give you a smile, that one don't, he's such a tight-arse*, Grandad Gill had once said in her hearing, which was very vulgar but true.

'What do you suggest I do?' she asked, feeling desperate.

'It's not for me to suggest a course of action.'

'But you were Alice's lawyer.'

'Miss Blake's lawyer, yes, but not yours. My first responsibility is to the estate. I shall send my head clerk to take an inventory as soon as it can be arranged. If you feel you need legal advice, you should find yourself a lawyer, someone other than myself.'

She stood up, suddenly sickened by his coldness. 'Send your clerk whenever you like. It makes no difference to me. I don't have the money to pay for a lawyer for myself. I don't even have enough to support myself for a year after the burglary.'

She left the house, banging the front door shut behind her and walking slowly back to Rose Villa, feeling furious as well as afraid. How pretty it looked in the setting sun – and how reluctant she was to go inside!

Eric Beaman watched her go, feeling very sorry for her. It did not do to get involved and of course he couldn't break client confidentiality, but he'd felt very tempted to help her. He had admired the way she'd looked after Miss Blake and knew she had been a capable and devoted teacher. He would never, he decided, agree to putting such outrageous terms into a will again, even if it lost him clients. The situation was giving him a great many worries.

If he could see a way to help Eva Kershaw without compromising his professional obligations, well, he would. But he did not intend to raise false hopes. It was not his way to speak until he was sure of something.

Jenny was in the kitchen and jumped in shock as Eva pushed the door open so abruptly it bounced off the door stop. 'Ooh, you gave me a start.' She lowered her voice. 'What did Beaman say?'

'He said he couldn't advise me because it was his job to act for the estate,' Eva said dully. 'But Gus does have the right to stay here. Where is he?'

'In the sitting room, smoking his head off. The place stinks of him already. He came in here looking for something to eat, but I made sure he didn't get anything. I told him straight I'd bought that food myself and if he took any of it, I'd report him to the police for stealing. Should have seen the look on his face.' She shivered and glanced over her shoulder as she added, 'I was frightened he was going to thump me.'

Eva went to sit at the kitchen table and rest her forehead on her hands. 'I don't know what to do.'

'Me neither. But I'm taking the rest of the food up to my room tonight and tomorrow we'll get Wilf to put a lock on that pantry door as well. Blake won't get anything to eat from me. Do you want something?'

Eva shook her head. 'Just a cup of tea, if you're having one.'

'You need to keep up your strength.'

'Food would choke me.'

As Jenny handed her a cup she said gruffly, 'Make sure you lock your bedroom door tonight, love.'

Eva looked up, horrified. 'He wouldn't!'

'He might. Just don't give him the chance.'

To their relief Gus went out soon after that, but he left his car behind and walked off down the road, whistling.

'Going to the pub, if you ask me,' Jenny said, peering out of the window and not turning round until their unwelcome visitor was out of sight, when she said loudly, 'Good riddance!' and began to gather the fresh food together in a couple of shopping bags, muttering to herself every now and then.

Wilfred was helping behind the bar that evening and when he saw Gus Blake come into the pub, he nudged Charlie, who whistled softly in surprise.

'Never thought I'd see that one in here again,' Charlie said. 'Still, a customer is a customer. See what he wants and make sure you're polite to him.'

So Wilfred moved along to where the bar opened into the lounge, ready to take an order. From there, he saw the whole thing.

Gus strolled across to where Eric Beaman and Sid Linney were sitting and made as if to pull out a chair.

'That place is occupied,' Beaman said frostily. 'In fact, all the places at this table are occupied.'

Sid stared from one to the other. He'd have let Blake sit there if only to hear his side of things – though how anyone could explain away a wife turning up just as he was about to marry another woman, it'd be hard to say. However, Beaman had *that look* on his face and Sid wasn't getting at outs with him. The lawyer was very rigid about right and wrong, and he knew too many useful people so on the rare occasions he came in here, Sid toned his language down and didn't tell any of his cruder jokes.

'They don't look occupied to me,' Gus said mildly.

Beaman simply turned his back and asked Sid how the effort to start a local football team was going.

Gus shrugged. 'Suit yourselves.' He went across to the bar and ordered a pint of best bitter.

Wilf obliged, but when offered a tip pushed the extra coppers back across the bar. 'No, thank you, sir.'

'You're as stupid as your sour-faced lady friend.' Gus sauntered across to an empty table where there was a newspaper lying on one seat and shook it open.

Charlie sidled along the bar to watch. 'What a nerve,' he breathed in Wilf's ear. 'Cool as a bloody cucumber, he is!'

'He's not happy, though. Look at that scowl.'

'Why did you turn down his tip?'

'Because I've not sunk low enough to accept money from someone like him.'

Charlie let out a sniff of amusement. 'Well, his money's good enough for me, so don't you go doing anything to upset him. Remember: the more customers we have, the more often you'll get work.'

'Yes, Mr Featherstone.' Wilf began to wipe the counter.

A little later, as he collected the empty glasses and wiped a few tables in the public bar, he quickly related to Grandad what had happened.

'Brassy sod, isn't he?' Grandad marvelled. 'Alice Blake must be turning in her grave.'

A little later, when Aaron popped in, Grandad passed the news on to him.

'Where's Blake staying now?'

Grandad eyed the scant inch of amber fluid in his glass with regret. 'He's back at Rose Villa.'

'Nay, surely not!'

'Jenny said the will allowed him and Eva Kershaw to live at the house for a year without marrying. That won't have changed.'

But although Grandad spoke phlegmatically, he was worried about his Jenny. He didn't trust that scheming sod one inch and he knew his lass was more vulnerable than she seemed.

At ten o'clock Gus still hadn't returned, so Eva went to bed, sliding the new bolt Wilf had fitted to her bedroom door and feeling better for its protection. She kept the bedside lamp on, trying to immerse herself in a book until she was ready for sleep. But tonight she couldn't seem to concentrate. She kept wondering what they were going to do and finding no hint of a solution, however hard she racked her brain.

At eleven o'clock she heard the front door open. It was slammed shut and Gus went into the kitchen. A few minutes later she heard the sound of cursing and concluded that Jenny had been right – he had been intending to take their food. Had he always been so predatory? His obvious anger at the situation made her feel more than nervous. Let's face it, she was rather afraid of him in this mood.

Slow footsteps sounded on the stairs and once they reached the top there was a pause. Eva listened intently. What was he standing there for?

Although she heard nothing, she suddenly gasped as she saw the door handle turn. 'What do you want?' she called.

'Some company.' He rattled the door handle, but the bolt was a sturdy one and held fast.

'Go away!' she called.

'Don't you want to see what you're missing?' he taunted through the door. 'Don't you get tired of your virginal bed?'

She didn't answer. His words were slurred. He must have drunk too much.

He thumped on the door. 'Sod you, you stupid bitch! What normal man would want a woman like you anyway? It was only the money I ever cared about, that's for sure.'

His footsteps sounded on the attic stairs, heavy, ominous. She was glad Jenny was sleeping on this floor now. She heard the door of his bedroom closing and almost immediately the creaking of the hard, narrow bed.

Shuddering, she slid down under the covers, leaving the lamp glowing beside her, glad they had electricity here, so that she didn't need to sleep in the darkness or set a candle by the bed and fill the room with flickering shadows. She'd be afraid every shadow was him, creeping up on her.

How could she *ever* have thought of marrying him? She must have been very naïve and stupid. Well, she was naïve where men were concerned, she knew, but she hadn't thought herself stupid before.

The next few days passed in an uneasy truce at Rose Villa. Mr Beaman's clerk came and went, a shrivelled elderly man who made long lists of every item in the house. Although he accepted cups of tea from Jenny, he did not allow himself to be drawn into casual conversation or make any comment on the situation.

Gus took over the big sitting room and they left him to it, hating to see the once-pretty room turned into a pigsty, but as Jenny said, if they tidied it up or waited on him in any way, he'd come to expect it.

However, he also used the kitchen and left that in a mess, too, which was of more immediate concern.

Sick of this, Jenny went to see him one day. 'We'd be grateful if you'd clear up the kitchen when you use it, Mr Blake.'

'Why should I when there are two women in the house to do that?'

'We're not your servants!'

He got up and came across the room to her, towering over her. She fumbled behind her for the door handle, feeling suddenly uneasy.

He set one hand on the door and prevented her from opening it, then used his body to pin her against it. Smiling, he whispered, 'I do believe there's a woman underneath that starched pinafore. Let's find out.'

She was so shocked she could not move, but when he began to make free with her body, touching her breasts and running his hands over her, she began to struggle. He was so strong she could not push him away.

'What you need is a man between your legs,' he growled in her face, and began to tug her skirt up.

She gave up trying to keep a brave face on it then and screamed for help, her voice sounding shrill and terrified, but she couldn't help it, couldn't stop screaming.

Dimly she heard footsteps come pounding down the stairs and then at last he moved away from her with a soft laugh. 'You can't prove a thing. But I'll make sure we're not interrupted next time.'

Jenny wrenched the door open and almost fell through it into Eva's arms, sobbing uncontrollably.

'What have you done to her?' Eva yelled over her shoulder at Gus.

He picked up his book. 'Nothing.'

'He took liberties,' Jenny sobbed. 'Touched me!'

'She's making it up. Another sour old spinster dreaming of a man.' Gus laughed and opened the book, ignoring them completely.

Eva stared at him for a moment, then pulled the door shut and put one arm round Jenny's shaking shoulders. 'Come into the kitchen, love. I'll make you a cup of tea and—'

Jenny stumbled along, looking so unlike her usual ebullient self that Eva was seriously worried about her. 'Is he – he didn't—'

'He just touched me.' Jenny scrubbed her eyes with her apron and collapsed into a chair, shuddering. 'I went in to ask him to clear up after himself in the kitchen. He shut the door and wouldn't let me leave, then pushed me against it and – touched me. All over.' She gulped and tried to hold the tears back, but couldn't – couldn't even keep her sobbing quiet.

Eva hovered next to her, patting her shoulder and trying to work out what to do. 'We should report him to the police.'

'He knows we won't,' Jenny sobbed. 'He knows they wouldn't believe us, and even if they did, they couldn't do anything, because there's no proof, only my word.' She looked at Eva then bowed her head. 'It happened to me once before, you see, only that time the fellow – he went all the way. And he hurt me, too.' Her voice trailed away and she bowed her head again to mumble, 'No one believed me. He was my employer, you see, well thought of. I was only nineteen and a newcomer to the town. Since then I've only worked for women.'

'Oh, Jenny, how dreadful.' Eva gave her a hug and for a moment the two women sat there in silence.

Jenny wiped her eyes, then whispered, 'I think he's trying to get rid of me.'

'But why?'

'I don't know. Maybe so he can go after you.'

'I'm no use to him now,' Eva said bitterly. 'All he wanted was the money and he can't get that if he's already married.'

'Well, there has to be some reason for this.' After a minute's frowning thought, she said, 'Maybe he wants the house to himself, then?'

'I can't see why. I can't even understand why he's come back, whatever he says about having business in the north.'

'No, I can't, either.' Jenny's lips quivered and her eyes refilled with tears. 'I thought I'd got over that, but this has brought it all back again.'

'We'll stick together from now on.'

Jenny looked at her. 'We can't. Not all the time. And it only takes a few minutes to attack someone.'

Eva sat lost in thought. 'Then we must each carry something around with us, something heavy to hit him with.'

'We're neither of us very big. He's tall and strong with it. Do you really think we'd stand a chance of fighting him off? He'd just take the weapon away from us and laugh while he did it.'

'I'm *not* giving in to this,' Eva said fiercely.

Jenny sighed. 'Well, we'll see how we go, but if you have to go out, let me know. I'm going to nip across to Grandad's from now on or ask Wilf to come over here. I'm *not* staying here on my own with *him*.'

And there they left it, except that Eva walked past him as if he didn't exist. 'If anything is broken or damaged,' she said loudly to Jenny when she knew Gus was within earshot, 'then I'm calling in Mr Beaman as well as the police. They did take an inventory, after all.' She heard a sound and spun round, grabbing a rolling pin when she saw that Gus had come through from the hall and was leaning against the door of the kitchen.

He chuckled. 'So fierce, aren't you? It might be fun getting to know you, after all, Eva Kershaw. Why didn't I realise there was passion inside that prim little schoolmistress?'

She continued to ignore him, but her heart thumped as he spoke. Jenny was right. It was frightening when a man looked at you like that and made suggestive comments.

But she would lose her self-respect if she let him drive her away.

And anyway, she had nowhere else to go, not yet. She had written off for two or three governessing jobs and the replies would be coming to this house, so she had to wait here till she heard. Surely, with her experience, she'd get one of them? She had to.

Aaron asked Angela Linney if he could nip home at lunchtime, since Sid had gone into Rochdale, and she readily gave him permission. He wanted to see if Lil was all right, because she'd looked like a ghost that morning. He was surprised to find Gracie there. 'Who said *you* could take time off school?'

'Mum was ill after you'd left this morning. She coughed up blood, a lot of it.' Gracie shuddered. 'Then just as we were leaving Mrs Harrop sent word she couldn't come. I didn't want to leave Mum on her own, so I took Molly along to school and then came home again.' She glanced upwards and lowered her voice. 'She's getting worse, isn't she? What are we going to *do?*'

'Try to make sure someone can look in each day.'

'You can't afford someone every day.'

He stared at her. 'How do you know that?'

She shrugged and stared down at her feet. 'I can't help hearing things. The walls are thin and there are cracks in the floorboards.'

He glanced up to the ceiling, which was also the floor of the room above. Talk about a hovel! This place had been built on the cheap by Sid Linney's grandfather and was falling down about their ears. 'Gracie, love, I –' He tried to put his arm round her, but she shoved him away.

'Why is it happening?' she demanded suddenly, hands on hips. 'Mum's not a wicked person. She doesn't *deserve* this!'

'I don't know why.' For once he let his guard down. 'It was the same in the war. Decent men getting killed, nasty men staying alive, things happening no human being should have to see, let alone experience.'

She looked at him with an expression too old for a child of ten. 'That's why you have the nightmares, isn't it?'

He nodded.

'Tom Luccan's dad's the same. Only he can't work at all now because he can't breathe properly.'

Aaron nodded again. Ben had been gassed. They all

saw him around the village, shuffling along, wheezing, more often than not just sitting outside his house watching what was going on. Aaron had even slipped him the odd tanner he could ill afford. The effects of the war would last for some people's whole lives – he glanced down at his leg – including his own. And he was one of the lucky ones. He realised his mind was wandering and pulled his thoughts together. 'That still doesn't mean you can stop going to school, love. Your mother and I want you both to get a decent education.'

There was a thumping on the floor. Lil's stick.

'I'll go,' he said hastily.

She was lying back against the pillows, looking nearly as white as them. 'I don't want either of them missing school for me,' she said in a thread of a voice. 'I told Gracie that but she wouldn't listen.'

'I don't want you left on your own all day, either, though.'

'I don't count now. But I want the best for my girls, the very best. You'll look after them, I know.'

He went across to hold her hand and pat it absent-mindedly. She raised the other one to run a finger down his cheek, then let it drop again, as if it were too heavy to hold up.

'You're a kind fellow, Aaron Brierley, even if you don't love me,' she said, with a shadow of her old grin. 'No, don't bother to deny it. This is no time for lies. If I can face the truth, so can you.'

She was gasping with the effort of talking, so he tried to take his hand away, but she clung on to it.

'See if you can find someone to come and sit with

me, if it makes you feel better. Anyone. Maybe that Wilf of yours would pop in sometimes. He's a nice fellow.'

'A man!'

'Well, we can't find a reliable woman, can we? They have their homes and families to look after. Wilf could come for an hour now and then, maybe.'

'You need a woman to look after you properly,' he said stubbornly. 'I'll see if I can find someone else. In the meantime it won't hurt Gracie to have a few days off school, just this week.'

Lil's face puckered and tears welled up in her eyes. 'No. Please, no. I don't want my daughters to see me die, Aaron. I'd *rather* die on my own than mark them for life.'

'You're a brave lass, Lillian Brierley.'

It pleased her, that compliment. He never gave compliments lightly, her Aaron didn't. Though what else you could do but be brave if you loved your family, she didn't know. She wasn't always brave during the dark hours of the night or when she was alone in her house. But she never let herself weep for long enough to redden her eyes.

Aaron could feel moisture welling in his own eyes as he went downstairs. He dashed the tears away and stared round, noting that Gracie had made an effort to tidy up. 'Good lass. It looks a lot better in here.' He hesitated, then asked, 'Did you hear what we were saying, your mother and I?'

She nodded.

'Then we'll let you stay off school for the rest of the

week, but you're going back on Monday whatever. Is that clear?'

'Yes, Dad. An' I've told Molly to come straight home tonight.' If her sister got out quick as soon as the bell rang, she'd be all right.

But Miss Deevers was in one of her moods and she kept the whole of Molly's class in for ten minutes, making them sit in absolute silence with their arms folded.

When Molly got out of school she could see her tormentors waiting for her, so she went the long way round. But they got to the end of her lane first, all three of them barring her way. She stood in the middle of the road transfixed by sheer terror.

Eva was in the kitchen when she saw the child weeping hysterically. Without even thinking, she ran out to see what was wrong and recognised Molly.

'You can't stand in the middle of the road, dear. Come and tell me what's wrong.'

Molly pointed with a shaking hand and Eva saw some heads bob back behind the wall that ran along the lane to Linney's farm.

'Are Christine Smart and her friends still bullying you?'

Molly nodded.

A gust of icy wind made Eva realise she wasn't wearing a coat, so she put an arm on the child's shoulders. 'Come into the house while I put a coat on and I'll walk you home.'

Molly sighed in obvious relief.

'Where's your sister?'

'At home.' It was so faint a whisper that Eva could only just hear the words.

'Is she poorly?'

'No, it's for Mum.'

Eva wondered why the child was speaking only in a whisper, but didn't press for an explanation. Children did strange things when they were upset and this poor child had more than enough to worry her.

She led Molly in through the kitchen. 'See who I found,' she said cheerfully to Jenny. 'Do we have a drink of milk and a biscuit for Molly? I'm going to walk home with her when I've got my coat on and I think I'd better take an umbrella too.'

Jenny pulled out a chair. 'Sit down, love. Won't be a minute.' Within seconds she had put a plate and a glass of milk in front of the child.

'Thank you.'

When Eva returned, Jenny said, 'I think she must have a sore throat, poor thing. She can only whisper. But she's still a polite little girl, aren't you, dear?'

Molly nodded, then took another drink of milk, leaving a white moustache as she started on the biscuit. When she'd finished she licked her lips, then looked from one to the other, as if uncertain what to do.

Eva finished tying on a headscarf and picked up the umbrella. 'Well, are we ready, Miss Molly Brierley?' She turned to Jenny. 'If *he* comes back you can nip across the road, can't you?'

'Yes. You get off.'

The wind was blowing more strongly now, gusting

so hard at times you had to lean into it. There was dampness in the air that said it would rain shortly. When they got to the lane, Eva saw three girls she recognised vaguely running away down it. Why were some children like that? Some adults too!

She felt a hand slip into hers and clasped it tightly, saying nothing. When they got to the far end of the lane, she turned left towards the farm cottage where the Brierleys lived. The wind was at their backs now, blowing them along.

'Goodness, what a wind.' She laughed down at the child. 'It'll not blow us away, though.'

Molly looked up at her and smiled.

Aaron saw them from where he was working in the nearby field. He hardly recognised the prim teacher in this glowing, wind-swept woman. Why was she bringing Molly home? He ran across to the wall and shouted, 'Is something wrong?'

They stopped to look up at him. 'Nothing's wrong,' Eva said lightly, shaking her head to warn him not to pursue the matter. She was relieved that he seemed to understand quickly and said nothing else. 'I'm just bringing Molly home. Well, it's the wind that's bringing us, really.'

As another gust howled around them, he stepped back. 'You'd better hurry up. It's trying to rain.'

At the cottage Eva would have let go of the little girl's hand and set off home again, but the door opened and Gracie rushed out.

'What's wrong? Why didn't you come home straight away, our Molly?'

A whispered explanation had her scowling again.

'I didn't catch that,' Eva said. 'Is it something I can help with?'

'Only if you can stop Miss Deevers picking on Molly. She kept the whole class in because of her, so they were mad at her.'

'Why does she do that?'

After a moment's hesitation, Gracie pushed Molly inside, then said in a low voice, 'Because she can't speak any more, only whisper. I wasn't at school today to look after her, you see.' She glanced over her shoulder and muttered, 'Mum's ill again, so I stayed home. Molly will have to stay at home with me tomorrow. She can walk to school safely in the morning if she's careful and once she gets inside the yard she's pretty safe, but they wait for her afterwards when they know I'm not there.'

Eva knew Geraldine Deevers of old. She always did manage to find a victim or two in her class and make their lives a misery for a whole year. And she had a particular aptitude for turning the whole class against those victims. 'Why don't I go and meet Molly tomorrow afternoon, then? I'm not busy at the moment.'

'Would you?'

'Of course.'

'You won't be late?'

'No, I won't be late.'

Eva walked back lost in thought. Those two poor little girls! As if they hadn't enough problems with their mother dying. She didn't at all mind helping them. It took her mind off her own troubles.

II

On the Wednesday of that same week Gus came into the kitchen where Eva and Jenny were washing up their breakfast things. 'I'm going away for the night.' He grinned and for a moment his expression lost its nastiness and reflected the genial man he might have been in other circumstances, the role he acted at times, the phantom Eva had thought she was marrying. But he only looked like that for a moment, then leered and added, 'Didn't want you to worry about me, girls. I'll be back tomorrow or the next day. Don't wait up for me.'

He went out, leaving his unwashed breakfast things still sitting at the end of the table.

Jenny and Eva exchanged glances.

'No,' Eva said. 'We're not doing them.'

'I hate having his dirty things lying about,' Jenny admitted. 'Makes me feel ashamed, as if *I'm* doing something wrong.'

'Forget about him. It's going to be wonderful not to have him around.'

At quarter to four the next day, Eva came into the kitchen in her outdoor things. 'I'm going to pick up Molly from school.'

'I'll just nip across to Grandad's, then, in case *he* comes back. Can't be too careful,' Jenny said with a wobbly smile.

Eva hesitated, scarf in hand. 'If it weren't for me, you'd leave, wouldn't you?'

Jenny also hesitated, then nodded.

'I'm grateful to you for staying on, I really am,' she wrapped the scarf slowly round her neck, 'but we can't go on like this for ever. I wrote for another governess's job from the newspaper today.' She brandished an envelope. 'I'm bound to get one of them soon and then we'll both leave here together.'

'I've decided not to look for another job yet. I've got a bit saved and I don't want to leave Grandad. I'll see if anything turns up in the neighbourhood. You never know.'

Eva nodded and went to find her everyday hat, the one that made Gus laugh every time he saw it, because he said it made her look like a schoolmarm. Well, let it. That's what she was. Or would be if they'd let her.

She arrived at the little red-brick school with its pointed gothic windows and walled asphalt playground just before the bell rang, nodding to a mother she knew and waiting for Molly, who came hurtling across the yard as if all the fiends were after her.

Miss Deevers stood at the door and shouted, 'Molly Brierley, come back this minute and walk out properly.' She saw Eva and frowned.

The child hesitated, then walked slowly back.

Eva could see three girls hovering nearby. She didn't

wait, but entered the gates and marched across towards the entrance.

'Parents are to wait outside the gates,' Miss Deevers said stiffly.

'I'm here to stop those girls bullying this child,' Eva said loudly. '*You* should be doing that but you're not.' She held out one hand to Molly. 'Come along, dear. I'll see you home.' Then she called across the playground, 'And you, Christine Smart, had better watch out. I've a good mind to go and see your mother about this, I have indeed.'

Colour high, Geraldine Deevers went back into the school.

The headmaster was waiting there. 'Miss Kershaw was right,' he said in a low, angry voice. 'You should be preventing them from bullying the child.'

Miss Deevers glared at him and walked past, knowing he would not do anything more about it. Stupid man! If she were running this school, things would get done *properly*. She'd be glad to stop teaching at the end of the year. She was too old to put up with the lax modern attitudes towards children.

Eva walked along holding Molly's hand and chatting brightly about what the little girl might have done at school, asking if she liked this or that and accepting nods or shakes of the head as answers. When they got to the far end of the lane, she smiled. 'I'll see you tomorrow, dear.'

Molly let go of her hand and went skipping across to her home.

Eva watched with a fond smile on her face.

And from the upper window of the cottage Lil watched too.

Gus returned on the Friday afternoon with some wooden boxes and a bulging suitcase in his car. Whistling under his breath, he carried the suitcase into the house and then went out to the garden shed.

Jenny squeaked in shock as he suddenly appeared in the kitchen doorway. 'What do *you* want?'

'Just to ask whether either of you minds me keeping a few things in the old shed? Since I'm going to be staying for a while, I thought I might as well bring the rest of my possessions with me.'

'Ask Eva. It's her house.'

'*Our* house,' he corrected. 'She and I share it – for the time being.' He took a sudden pace forward and as Jenny instinctively jerked away, he burst into loud, raucous laughter. 'Oh, dear, your nerves are getting very bad!'

Eva came hurrying along from her sitting room in time to see this and guilt shot through her as she realised how afraid her friend was of him since that incident. She had thought Jenny feared nothing, which just went to show. But if Jenny had been raped – a word Eva hated even to think, but it was the correct term for what had happened – she supposed it must have left a dreadful mental scar and Gus's behaviour had reawakened the bad memories.

She went through to face him from Jenny's side. 'You're pitiful!' she said. 'You probably pull butterflies' wings off for fun, too.'

'I never even touched her.'

'You don't have to touch someone to threaten them, so I'm telling you now, and I mean it: if you hurt Jenny in any way there are people in the village who will make sure you regret it.'

He breathed deeply and his look boded ill for her, but she had had enough of him and his bullying ways. Poor little Molly couldn't stand up to her tormenters, but Eva was going to stand up to hers from now on.

'He wants to store some things in the garden shed,' Jenny said as the silence lengthened and Eva for once did not lower her eyes.

'I wish he'd stay out there as well,' Eva snapped.

'My, my! The pair of you are so bad-tempered,' he mocked. 'Mind you don't bite your own tongues off. I'll put a new padlock on the shed door while I'm at it.' He waved a rusted piece of metal at them. 'This one fell off in my hand. Oh, and there are some more things coming by rail. If I'm not in, tell them to leave the boxes next to the shed.'

He went out and spent the rest of the afternoon fitting the hasp for a large new padlock on the shed door and sorting through his things.

Eva kept an eye on what he was doing from her bedroom window but didn't interfere. If he wanted to take possession of the shed, let him. It only held gardening tools and there wasn't much to do outside at this time of the year. Their old gardener had moved away to live with his son and she couldn't afford to hire anyone else.

Besides, Alice wasn't here now to see how untidy things were getting.

When Gus came back indoors he retired to the sitting room, where he lounged around smoking and reading the newspaper until opening time, upon which he made his way down to the pub.

'I'm sorry, Eva,' Jenny said after he'd left, 'but I can only stand another few days of this.'

'You can leave now if you want. I'll understand.'

'Not till you've worked something out for yourself. I wouldn't leave you on your own with him.'

Jenny turned away to busy herself stirring the stew for their evening meal and Eva did not pursue the matter further.

During the night Eva woke up, thinking she heard a noise. Yes, there it was again. Someone was creeping down the stairs. It could only be Gus. She waited a moment then opened her bedroom door cautiously. There was a light on in the kitchen.

He probably couldn't sleep, she decided, and was making himself a cup of cocoa. She went back to her room and lay awake waiting for him to come back upstairs, but he didn't. Although he was moving very quietly, she recognised the sound of the sitting-room door clicking shut, because she had closed it carefully herself so many times during Alice's illness.

A short time later she heard the french windows in the sitting room below open. Sliding out of bed, she crept across to the window and lifted one corner of the curtain cautiously, but it was a moonless night and she couldn't see anything. Funny, that. She'd have thought the light from the sitting room would have shown the part of the garden near the house. Then she realised it wasn't on.

What was he doing out there in the dark?

She thought she heard a motor vehicle in the distance, but it didn't pass the front of the house. And although she continued to watch till she was chilled through, it was too dark to see what was happening in the back garden, though she heard small sounds as if someone were moving about and smelled cigarette smoke. In the end she decided that Gus must have been out getting a breath of fresh air and having a smoke.

She fell asleep before he came upstairs and didn't worry again about what had happened. Everyone suffered from sleepless nights from time to time, and he had more cause to have an uneasy conscience than most.

If only he'd go away and leave them alone!

Things went from bad to worse during the days which followed. Whenever Gus passed either of the women, he would make suggestive remarks, laughing to see them both blush. They never left one another alone in the house now and Eva had once threatened him with the rolling pin when he got too close to her in the kitchen – would have hit him, too, if he hadn't backed away, hands raised in mock surrender.

In fact, she, who had never been violent in all her life, was shocked to realise that she would have loved to hit him with it. Hard.

The only explanation for his behaviour was that he was trying to drive them away. Well, she refused to go, absolutely and utterly refused. She had as much right to be here as him. More. Alice had spoken well of her half-brother, said what a gentleman he had always been, but his son was a scoundrel. Thank goodness Alice had never known that.

He went away again a few days later and during those two days the house felt different and both women relaxed a little.

Eva received a letter thanking her for her application for one of the governess's positions but saying the post had been filled by an applicant who lived nearby. There were a couple of jobs advertised in the south, but she didn't want to go so far away from her family. Indeed, she hated the thought of living anywhere else than Heyshaw, but she had only five pounds ten shillings left in the savings bank and was getting very worried about how she was going to manage if she didn't find work. Sighing, she wrote more letters of application.

She had enjoyed meeting Molly after school, but Gracie was back this week so Eva was not needed. She wondered about going to see if the girls' mother was all right, but Jenny said Lil didn't want any visitors.

So the time hung very heavily on Eva's hands and the weather had set in cold and rainy, making it too unpleasant to go for walks.

If she didn't find a job soon she would just have to go to her sister Lizzie's.

★   ★   ★

When Gus returned, their troubles recommenced. He had taken to rattling their bedroom doorknobs now when he returned from the pub, usually somewhat inebriated. Neither she nor Jenny wanted to make a public fuss about his behaviour, though Eva was beginning to think she would have to because they couldn't go on like this. But Jenny pleaded with her not to, saying that if they did, Wilf would probably take a hand and she didn't want to get him in trouble with the authorities or do anything which might stop Charlie Featherstone offering him casual work.

However, Wilf was more aware that there was something wrong than either of the young women realised. He had discussed it with Grandad, who was worried about how jumpy Jenny had been for the past week or so, not to mention the dark circles under her eyes. Wilf decided to ask her straight out on the Saturday evening what was wrong, but Charlie sent a message from the pub to say that he wasn't feeling the best and asking if Wilf could come and help out for the whole evening, so he didn't get the chance to see her before he left.

That night a stranger came into the pub, standing at the bar sipping a whisky and surveying the room. 'Quiet here, isn't it?' he remarked.

'It'll get busy later,' Wilf said. 'Not from round here, are you?'

'No. Been visiting relatives over Burnley way, but I had a bit of trouble with my car so I'm looking for a room for the night. I'd rather not push on in the dark and risk being stranded out on the moors. Is there anywhere round here I can stay?'

'There's the Red Lion in the centre of Heyshaw. They have a couple of rooms.'

'I've tried there. They're full. I suppose I'd better press on and hope for the best. I'll have another drink first, though, to keep me warm. Make it a double this time.'

Gus Blake came in just then. Wilf wondered for a moment whether he knew the stranger, because he thought he saw a look of recognition in each man's eyes. But he must have been wrong because they held the sort of conversation strangers hold when looking for company. He'd heard it many a time. In the end they introduced themselves properly and went to sit at the table in the corner.

When he looked up half an hour later, Gus waggled one finger imperatively at him so he went across. 'Can I help you, sir?'

'Two more whiskies. And look smart about it.'

Wilf went back, seething at his tone. He was never anything but speedy in his service because he needed this job too much. When he took the drinks back, Blake didn't offer him a tip, which saved him the trouble of refusing.

As he wiped down a nearby table, he heard the stranger telling his tale of woe.

Blake gave one of his over-hearty laughs. 'If you don't mind the lack of service, there's a spare bed at my place. It's good to meet someone who was in the war and have a yarn. Civilians never understand, do they? I can only offer you toast and marmalade for breakfast. And for a late tea,' he pulled out a large gold pocket watch and consulted it, 'how about fish and chips? We can just catch the village shop before it closes if we go now.'

'Do you mean it about the bed?'

'Why not? It's rare that I get such good company in this benighted spot.'

'That's dashed civil of you. But you must let me bring along some extra refreshments as a thank you.'

Another of those annoying flicks of the finger summoned Wilf and a bottle of whisky was ordered. When the stranger tipped him, he hesitated, then kept the money.

Blake watched him, with one of those sneering smiles. One day, Wilf promised himself, he was going to punch that arrogant sod and wipe the smile right off his face.

The two men went out together, then there was a rush of orders so Wilf dismissed the incident from his mind and concentrated on the customers in the public side of the bar, who didn't look down their noses at you and who said please and thank you when you served them.

When Gus came into the house carrying two newspaper bundles of fish and chips and bringing a stranger with him, Eva was angry. The kitchen was in a tip, because they'd pushed his dirty things to one half of the table and now kept their clean crockery locked in the pantry. Didn't he care if anyone saw the mess? Apparently not.

He waved one hand in her direction. 'Sorry about the mess. She refuses to clean up.'

'We refuse to clean up *your* things,' she stated loudly and clearly, 'because we are not your servants.'

'We've been left the joint tenancy in a will,' Gus told his companion. 'It's like living with a bloody wasp. As well as her slovenly ways.' Jenny came in at that moment, and he added, 'Which they both have.'

The stranger was eyeing them up and down in a leering way that was every bit as bad as Gus's.

Eva then turned to Jenny. 'We'll come back when his friend has left.'

'Oh, Mac's not leaving till tomorrow,' Gus said. 'Met him in the pub, offered him a room for the night, going to rehash the war. If you can have friends to stay, so can I.'

She stared at him in shock, hating the idea of two men of that type staying in the house. And Gus's speech was slurred, so he must have been drinking hard again. He was always at his worst then. 'In that case we'll leave you to it.'

Gus opened up the newspaper parcels and a strong smell of vinegar filled the kitchen. He waved one hand at his companion. 'We'll eat rough and ready. Like it was in the war, eh?'

They started eating with their fingers.

Eva and Jenny retired to her sitting room because it was far too early to go to bed.

Ten minutes later the two men started singing loudly and not at all tunefully. The words brought a blush to Eva's cheeks.

'Let's go to bed and leave them to it,' she said.

'We need our hot water bottles.'

'Then we'll go and fill them.'

Jenny hesitated, then nodded and accompanied her to the kitchen. As they left it with their stone hot water bottles, wrapped in their double flannel covers, they were followed by ribald comments about 'beds being warmed up more quickly by a man'.

'Perhaps we should sleep together tonight,' Jenny whispered.

'I was thinking about that. Only how can you lock up your room if we do that?'

Jenny stared at her, fear in her eyes. 'I can't.'

Eva tried to speak bracingly. 'We'll be all right. We have bolts on our doors, after all. And your room is at the front of the house, so if there's any trouble, you can open the window and scream for Wilf. The pub will soon be closing.'

Jenny nodded and looked relieved. 'Yes. Yes, I can, can't I?'

On the landing they paused, each reluctant to leave the other.

'It's getting worse rapidly, isn't it?' Eva whispered. 'I don't think I can face much more of this, either, but I *hate* to let him win.'

Maybe if she went to stay with Lizzie she could find some sort of work in Overdale. It wouldn't matter what it was.

On Sunday the stranger left at first light. Gus saw him off then retired to his bedroom again.

Just after lunch the Deardens' van turned up.

'It's our Lizzie!' Eva exclaimed and rushed outside

to fling herself into her sister's arms, surprising them both by bursting into tears. She'd had letters from all her family, commiserating with her on the wedding fiasco and its attendant problems, but Polly was too far away to visit her easily and Lizzie's children had been ill, while Percy's wife was feeling very sickly due to her pregnancy.

Lizzie hugged Eva, then held her at arm's length. 'I wanted to come and see you before, but those little devils of mine had the measles bad. Are you all right? You look dreadful.' Then she glanced sideways and frowned 'Whose car is that?'

'Gus's.'

'He's never dared show his face here again? What does he want?'

'He's living here.'

Lizzie gaped at her. 'How can he be? You surely haven't let him into your life again?'

'Alice's will allows him to live here for a year, so I can't stop him. She didn't know what he was like when she wrote it, and there's nothing we can do about it.'

'Is his wife with him?'

'No. There's no love lost between them and he apparently paid her to go away again. He says he's got nowhere else to go and might as well use the free accommodation while he's working in the north.' If you could call his occasional trips working. She still hadn't quite figured out what he did on them.

Peter got out of the van and Lizzie repeated the information for his benefit, ending, 'I'd like to give him a piece of my mind, the villain!'

Her husband grinned at her. 'You keep your thoughts to yourself, my girl. No starting fights on Sundays. Can we go inside, Eva, or do you intend to keep us out here all day? There's a real bite in the air and I could murder a cup of tea.' He shepherded his wife and sister-in-law into the house, nodding to Jenny who had come to the kitchen door.

'I'll bring you some tea,' Jenny said and retreated into the kitchen.

Lizzie and Peter followed Eva into her sitting room which, thank goodness, Gus hadn't tried to invade.

'Now, tell us everything,' he said. 'Don't leave a single detail out.'

Suddenly she could see what he must have been like as an officer, brisk but fair, concentrating on the task at hand, not letting his emotions rule his head as Lizzie did. He was a good foil for her impulsive sister. No wonder the two of them were so happy together.

Eva explained it all, including the fact that Gus had taken liberties with Jenny and was annoying both of them with his suggestive remarks.

No one said anything when she stopped speaking. Lizzie looked stunned and Peter sternly thoughtful.

There was a knock on the door and Jenny brought in the tea trolley.

'You should stay here with us as well, Jenny,' Eva said. 'He might come downstairs.'

'If you can stand us Kershaws,' Lizzie said with one of her warm smiles.

Peter pretended to scowl at her. 'You're a Dearden now, wife, and don't you forget it!'

She was unrepentant. 'I'm a Kershaw, too. Especially when I'm with my sisters.' Her smile faded. 'We three went through a lot together when we were girls.' She turned back to Eva. 'If you want to come and live with us, love, there's always room for you.'

'I'm not giving in to his bullying. I've been writing away for jobs and if I don't get anything, well, maybe I'll come for a visit. See if I can find anything in Overdale.'

Lizzie gave her a smile. 'That sounds more like the old Eva. You'd got very quiet while you were nursing Alice.'

Jenny shivered. 'Well, I'm not as brave as she is, I'm afraid. I'll stay as long as I can, but I'm not risking him trying to – force himself on us, and neither should you, Eva.'

'Do you think he'd go that far?' Peter asked in astonishment. 'Surely not?'

'He's already tried it on.' At Jenny's nod of permission Eva explained what had happened.

After another silence Peter cleared his throat. 'How about another cup of tea while we make our plans?'

'I'll see to that. You carry on talking.' Jenny began to pour milk into the cups.

'Do you have the will, Eva?' Peter asked. 'I think you said you had a copy. I'd like to read it myself.'

She nodded. 'Yes, I do.' She went to the desk and unlocked it, searching in the middle pigeon hole. It wasn't there. She hunted quickly through the other pigeon holes, then the drawers. 'It's gone! But I know I left it there.'

'You're sure of that?' he asked gently. 'When one is upset one can sometimes mislay things.'

'Not our Eva,' Jenny and Lizzie said together.

Lizzie finished it with what the family sometimes said in joke, 'She's the tidiest female in all Lancashire, if not all England.'

'Then we have to presume someone took it.' Peter went across to examine the desk lock but found no signs of anyone forcing it.

'It's got to be *him*,' Jenny said. 'Only the three of us have been in the house since the wedding. Oh, and that drinking friend of his.'

'Why would Gus want to take it?' Eva asked. 'He has his own copy.'

Jenny could only shrug.

'Have you ever studied it carefully?' Peter asked.

'No. I couldn't bear to see it all spelled out in black and white and Mr Beaman explained the main provisions.' Eva grimaced. 'I suppose I should have done, but at the time it was just another reminder of Alice and since then I've had a few other things on my mind.'

'You should definitely read it.'

Eva frowned at the desk. 'I still can't work out why Gus would do that, take the will, I mean. He has his own copy.'

There was silence, then Peter said slowly, 'Perhaps it contains some information which may be of use to you? Have you ever left the desk open?' When she shook her head, he examined the lock. 'There are no signs of it being forced, but it's a very simple lock. I could pick it myself with a hairpin.'

She shivered, feeling relieved that she had a good sound bolt on the inside of her bedroom door. You couldn't pick one of those with a hairpin.

'You'd better get another copy of the will, then,' Lizzie said. 'And keep it somewhere safe this time.'

'I'll go and see Mr Beaman first thing on Monday morning.' Eva stared down into her half-empty cup. She did not feel nearly as brave as she pretended, but she was determined not to be a burden on her family, except as a very last resort.

'Well, let's finish our tea,' Lizzie said. 'Then I'll tell you all about my two little monsters and what they've been up to.'

There was the sound of footsteps on the stairs.

'He's up,' Jenny said at once.

'Good.' Peter stood up. 'I'll just go and have a word with him.'

Lizzie's eyes followed him anxiously, but she didn't try to stop him. There was the sound of voices, then the door of Alice's old sitting room closed and they could not hear anything else. 'Do you mind if we just – listen carefully?' she asked. 'If there's a fight I'm going in and bashing that Gus on the head. I'm not letting anyone hurt my husband.'

Her sister's attitude was another lesson for her, Eva decided. You had to be braver about life than she had been. She'd just let things drift while Alice was ill. And she shouldn't have. She should have made more effort to secure her own future, stood firm against Gus.

*   *   *

In the other room, Gus went to lean against the mantelpiece. 'What do you want?'

Peter looked round in disgust. The place was like a pigsty and stank of stale tobacco fumes. He studied the other man who was actually smiling at him. 'Don't you think you should leave Heyshaw now?'

'None of your bloody business. I have a right to stay here and as I need a place to live, I intend to exercise that right.'

'Then I'd better make it very clear that if anything happens to Eva, if she's hurt in any way, she has two brothers and a brother-in-law who will make sure you regret it.'

Gus puffed on his cigarette and waved it airily. 'She's imagining things. It's that maid of hers. I've been teasing Jenny and I probably went too far. But the woman's a born troublemaker.'

'I don't think so. In fact, I believe everything Jenny has told me.'

Gus avoided his eyes, bending forward to toss his cigarette stub into the heart of the fire. 'You're a fool to trust a woman.'

'I would trust any of the Kershaw girls or their friends with my life.' Peter looked at him scornfully. 'Just remember what I've said about Eva.'

'And you just remember that I have a right to be here.' Gus waved towards the door. 'Now, I'd like some privacy if you don't mind.'

Peter rejoined the others. 'I've warned him to leave you alone, Eva. If he doesn't, I'll come back and prove that you have relatives who care about your welfare.'

'Percy can't be involved, not with his heart,' she said hastily. Their brother's heart problem had prevented him from being conscripted and she didn't want anything to happen to him.

'He doesn't need to be. I'm quite fit and able,' Peter said gently. 'And Johnny's twenty-one now, don't forget. Your younger brother's grown into a fine young man.' He frowned. 'What regiment did Blake say he belonged to?'

Eva tried to remember. 'I don't think he ever did.'

Peter pursed his lips. 'Hmm. One is normally rather proud of one's regiment, especially if one has been an officer. It's all a bit suspicious, so if you're worried don't hesitate to ring me and I'll come straight over.'

To her relief Peter didn't ask her whether she had enough money to live on until this year was up. Both he and Lizzie seemed to assume that Alice had left her provided for and that was the way Eva wanted it. For now, at least.

Even after they'd left she felt a warmth, knowing how her family cared, knowing she was not really alone.

But she'd take Peter's advice. Tomorrow she'd go into Heyshaw and ask Mr Beaman for another copy of the will, then she'd study it very carefully, though she couldn't see it offering a way out of this dilemma.

12

———◆———

Eva went into Heyshaw the following morning. It seemed silly to do this when Mr Beaman lived just across the road from her, but since he preferred not to be disturbed at home she didn't want to start off badly with this new request. It was sunny, but ice still silvered the edges of the fallen leaves that were lying in the shade and as she got into the village clouds began to cover the sky.

The elderly male clerk looked down his nose at her. 'Mr Beaman does not see people without an appointment.'

Anger surged up inside Eva. 'It'll take only two minutes for me to tell him something he needs to know as Miss Blake's lawyer. Please ask him.'

He hesitated then murmured, 'Just a moment, if you please, miss.'

When he came back he wore a sour expression. 'Mr Beaman will see you for precisely five minutes.'

Eva followed him into the lawyer's office, plonked herself down on a chair without being invited and got straight to the point. 'Someone has stolen my copy of Miss Blake's will, so I'd like another one, please.'

Eric Beaman frowned at her. 'Is this the important

news? You're wasting my time, young woman. You've probably mislaid it.'

'If I have one fault it's being *too* tidy. I've been teased about it all my life. I never, ever mislay things.' She saw he was looking dubious and added firmly, 'And anyway, the will was kept in my desk, which was locked. I haven't taken it out since the funeral.'

'Are there any signs of the lock being forced?'

'No. But my brother-in-law says it's a simple one and he could open it with a hairpin.'

'Has anyone else been in the house?'

'Apart from my sister and her husband, who came to visit me yesterday afternoon, only Gus Blake and an acquaintance of his who stayed overnight on Saturday, some stranger he met in the pub.'

Mr Beaman stared down at his papers for so long she opened her mouth to say something, but at that moment he looked up again and said in his thin, fussy voice, 'You were right to inform me of this, though it may or may not be important. I'll have another copy of the will prepared for you and will deliver it myself tomorrow after work, at which time I'll take a quick look round the house to see that everything is in order, if that's all right with you?'

'Yes, of course.'

As she walked briskly up the slope home she decided not to mention the lawyer's coming visit to Gus. Let Mr Beaman see for himself the state things were in.

Lil leaned back in bed and watched Aaron tidying the room. 'Once I'm gone, you should marry again.'

He swung round and stared at her open-mouthed. 'What the hell brought this on?'

'I'm thinking of the girls. They'll need a mother.'

He went to rest his arms on the high wooden bed foot and laid his chin on them, noting the dust at the bottom of each slat. Mrs Harrop seemed to get more slovenly by the week and Lil no longer noticed such details. 'I doubt I ever shall marry again, love. But you know you can trust me to look after the girls, if that's what's worrying you.'

'I'm certain you'll do your best, but girls of their age need a woman. You remember that.' She smiled, a ghost of her old cheeky grin. 'And remarrying might have a few other advantages for you. You always did like your bed rations, Aaron Brierley.'

'You, too, Lil.'

'Mmm.' She snuggled down and smiled sleepily at him. 'That was good between us at least, wasn't it?' She yawned hugely, then murmured, 'Leave the rest of the tidying for now. I'm so tired.'

He nodded and went downstairs. She was sleeping more and more, and the best he could wish for her was that she'd die in one of those sleeps, peacefully. She had never hurt anyone in her life, Lil hadn't, had always been generous to a fault. She didn't deserve a hard death.

But he wasn't marrying again. Not him! Once bitten, twice shy.

Anyway, he couldn't afford to start another family. Sid Linney would chuck him out of here as soon as Lil died and he still hadn't worked out where he was going to take the girls. That was beginning to prey on his mind.

Mr Beaman arrived at Rose Villa at five o'clock the following afternoon, carrying his briefcase and looking tired. When Eva opened the door, he raised his bowler hat to her, then allowed her to take it from him and hang it on the hall stand.

She showed him into her sitting room. 'Mr Blake uses the main sitting room and I spend my time in here or in the kitchen with Jenny.'

Before she could close the door, Gus peered in. 'Thought I recognised that voice. Is something wrong, Beaman?'

The lawyer looked down his nose at him. 'I'm here to do an inspection of the property.'

The smile vanished abruptly from Gus's face. 'What the hell for?'

'As executor of Miss Blake's estate, it's my responsibility to see that things are kept in good order.'

'Well, Eva keeps this room in good order, but you should see the rest of the house,' Gus said sourly. 'She and that so-called friend of hers are bone idle. They're letting everything go to rack and ruin.'

Mr Beaman gave Eva a level, considering look, then picked up his briefcase and walked towards the door. 'I'd better check that.'

Gus smirked at her and followed him out.

Furious, she followed them into the large sitting room, watching Mr Beaman look round, his face wrinkling in disgust.

'I can see no sign of Miss Kershaw's things in here,' he said.

Sudden hope filled her.

'What's that got to do with it?' Gus demanded. 'She's the woman of the house so it's her responsibility to keep things in order.'

Without a word Mr Beaman, who clearly knew his way around, moved on to the garden room, which looked unused and neglected. From there he went into the kitchen, half of which was immaculately clean. However, there was a pile of dirty dishes on one end of the table, one of them with cigarette ends stubbed out in the remains of the food.

'Whose are those?' Mr Beaman asked, pointing.

'Hers,' Gus said quickly, indicating Jenny.

'I don't smoke,' she snapped. 'Nor do Eva and I leave our crockery lying around. Every single thing at that end of the table is yours and well you know it, Gus Blake.'

Eva watched Mr Beaman's face anxiously, but his expression revealed nothing.

'Shall we go upstairs now?' he asked. There he peered into the bedrooms on the first floor after which he went up to the attics.

The two young women exchanged glances then Jenny went down to the kitchen and Eva lingered on the landing to listen to what was happening.

Gus's voice came down to her. 'That's *my* room and I'm damned if I'm having you going through my things.'

'A glance into the room will suffice.' As the other

man did not stir, Mr Beaman added sharply, 'If you remember, your aunt's will specifies that the house shall be kept in good order.'

Eva smiled and could not resist going up a few steps to peer through the banisters. Neither of the men even noticed her.

Gus moved back and Mr Beaman went into his room, standing in the doorway and staring round. 'Do you pay Miss Kershaw and Miss Gill to do housework for you?'

Gus spluttered with indignation. 'Of course I don't! Why should I?'

'Then I see no reason why they should clean and cook for you.'

As he started to turn round, Eva ran quickly down a few stairs, standing near the corner, where she was out of sight of Gus but in full view of Mr Beaman if he turned round. He didn't. He remained where he was at the top with his back to her.

'I'm satisfied that Miss Kershaw and her friend keep their things in order,' he said, 'but it's clear you don't, Mr Blake. I shall therefore request you to do something about that and shall return tomorrow night for a further inspection. If your part of the house is not clean and tidy by then, I shall take steps to ensure that you leave the property.'

Eva heard Gus mutter something. There was a moment's silence then he stepped backwards again. She thought it prudent to creep downstairs and wait for them in the kitchen.

★　　★　　★

Eric Beaman managed not to flinch, but he thought for a moment Blake was going to thump him. This was a different side to the jovial young man with whom he had shared an occasional drink in the lounge bar of the pub. And this sort of behaviour set the situation in a whole new light. He didn't like to think of two young women dealing with a violent man.

'I shall see you tomorrow,' he reiterated and walked slowly down the stairs, relieved when Blake didn't follow him.

In the kitchen he opened his briefcase and took out the new copy of the will, handing it to Eva. 'I advise you to find somewhere safer than your desk to keep this, Miss Kershaw. Your brother-in-law is right. Locks like that are flimsy.'

He realigned the papers inside the briefcase and closed it before adding, 'I suggest you study the will carefully and ask me if there's anything you don't understand. I shall return tomorrow afternoon to check Mr Blake's part of the house and make sure it's been cleaned up. I have informed him that I expect everything to be in order by then.' He hesitated, then lowered his voice and added, 'If you have any other sort of trouble, please let me know.'

With an inclination of his head, he went out into the hall, set his hat precisely upon his narrow head and left.

As the front door closed behind him, Eva and Jenny both said, 'Phew!' at the same time then smiled at one another.

'It'll be interesting to see what *he* does about clearing up,' Jenny said, jerking her head towards the stairs.

'Now, I've got some fresh buns and you've hardly eaten a thing these past few days . . .'

Before she could get the food out, footsteps thumped down the stairs and came towards them. Eva shoved the big envelope into the pantry and by the time Gus Blake appeared in the doorway she was filling the kettle.

He looked at them. 'Who brought old fussy-breeches in to check the house?'

'It must have been his own idea,' Eva said frostily.

'You were in the village yesterday morning. Maybe you went in to see him and suggested he do an inspection?'

'I went in to see him, yes, but on my own behalf. I said nothing whatsoever about inspecting the house or even about how messy your areas are. But I should think Mr Beaman will be coming in regularly to check things out.'

He stared at her. 'What did you go to see him for?'

'That's none of your business.'

'I'll find out,' he said. 'Be sure of that. And if I find you did tell him to come and check the house, you'll be sorry.'

Eva did not let her own anger overflow, because she had decided to have as little as possible to do with him and was certainly not going to descend to quarrelling.

He waited and when she did not speak, he turned to Jenny. 'I'll pay you to clean up my part of the house, though by rights you should be doing it free in return for your keep.'

She stared at him, then folded her arms. 'I'm not interested. You can clear up your own stuff.'

He took a step towards her, looking even angrier.

Eva stepped between them. 'If you touch her I'll go outside and scream for help. We'll bring all the neighbours running and Mr Beaman is one of them.'

For a moment all hung in the balance, then Gus stepped back. 'I'll bring someone else in to clean, then. They'll probably do it better than she would anyway.'

'Do that,' Eva invited him.

He flung out of the house and she sat down quickly on one of the hard kitchen chairs before her legs gave way beneath her.

'Thanks,' said Jenny.

'What for?'

'Standing between us. I thought he was going to hit me.'

'Well, he didn't.' But Eva had thought the same thing and now that she looked back she was surprised at her own rashness in standing up to him – but pleased with herself, too.

Blake came back an hour later with the woman who cleaned the Dog and Duck trotting nervously behind him. He stood in the doorway of the kitchen and waved one hand. 'You may as well start here. Those things need washing up. Pile them on this end of the table when you've finished.' He glared at Jenny. 'And it'd help if *you* got out of the way.'

She shook her head. 'I'm keeping an eye on my own things.'

As antagonism crackled between them, Mary looked uneasily from him to Jenny, who was standing with her arms folded and her back to the pantry door.

Eva saw and heard it all from the doorway of her sitting room but said nothing.

Not until he had taken Mary along to show her the sitting room and his bedroom did Eva go out to join Jenny, who was looking angry.

'You all right?' Eva asked.

Jenny shrugged. She wasn't all right, not really. Nor was her friend, for all her brave words. They were both feeling the strain of sharing a house with Gus Blake.

Eva took the will up to her bedroom and locked the door. Taking it out of the envelope, she unfolded it and read it carefully from beginning to end, then sat frowning at it, wishing she had someone with whom to discuss exactly what one or two of the clauses meant. Fond as she was of Jenny, she knew her friend would understand even less than she did.

It was only when she was doggedly reading it through a second time that she stopped and gasped, suddenly realising the most important thing of all: *the will didn't say she had to marry Gus Blake!* She read the relevant clauses twice more with feverish concentration. No, she hadn't misunderstood them. As far as she could understand from the legal jargon, all it said was that Alice *hoped* Eva would marry her nephew. The will required her to get married, but it did not specify to whom. And once married, she would inherit everything.

She began to pace up and down her bedroom, staring blindly out of the window as the implications churned around her brain. Coming back to where the will lay on her dressing table, she picked it up and read the clause again.

She could marry *anyone* and still inherit Alice's house and investments. Was that why Gus had taken her copy, to prevent her from realising? And why was he staying on here now that they couldn't marry? He didn't even like the north, often spoke of it disparagingly, and his wife knew where he was so he could no longer be hiding from her. It just didn't make sense.

Unless . . . unless he was hiding from someone else. No, surely not?

In the end she settled in her chintz-covered armchair by the window with a shawl round her shoulders, her feet on the matching footstool and her hands clasped loosely around her knees, watching the rain march inexorably across the moors towards her. The branches of the old sycamore tree creaked and groaned outside, lashing against the wall and window, shedding a few more leaves each time. She knew all the sounds that tree made, knew and loved them. Jenny said it'd give her the creeps to have branches tapping against her window panes in the night, and insisted the tree was far too near the house for safety, but neither Eva nor Alice had wanted to cut it down. It was so beautiful in spring, filling Eva's bedroom and the rear sitting room below with soft green light.

This was her favourite place for thinking things through. She let her thoughts drift where they would and stayed there until she was shivering. The sounds of cleaning seemed to have ended now. Time to go back downstairs and check that Jenny was all right.

When she tried to pick up the will, her hands were so cold she dropped some of the pages. Holding them clasped against her chest, she looked round the room. Where could she hide it? Better if Gus didn't know she had another copy or that she now understood the true situation. She was, she realised, rather nervous of pushing him too far. He was a man of many contradictions, but when he was drunk or angry he could be frightening.

She looked at the bed. No, not under the mattress. Not in her wardrobe, either.

Everywhere her eyes fell seemed too obvious. She was sure he came in here when she was out. A couple of times she had found her things slightly displaced. Only slightly, but enough for someone like her to notice. Sometimes it paid to be pernickety.

In the end she slid the will behind the wardrobe, balancing it on a slat bracing the back panel. It was the best she could manage.

Did this new understanding of her situation really do her any good? she wondered as she sat down again. Who else was there to marry? She mentally listed all the single men in the district, a list which included Mr Beaman, and smiled at the mere idea of approaching him. *By the way, would you like to marry me, Mr Beaman, so that I can inherit Alice's money?*

She could advertise for a stranger in the personal columns of the newspaper. She let out a mirthless sniff at that thought. As if she would ever do anything so outrageous. Definitely not.

It was always good to know the facts, but she was still going to have to work out some way of earning her living. And sooner rather than later. She blinked away a tear, determined not to give in to her worries. By the following October she would have to leave Rose Villa, and that was that.

The following day, when Eva went into the village to buy some stewing meat, Jenny finished drying the dishes. She had decided to go across and wash some clothes for her grandad and hang them out while the fine spell continued. You couldn't beat a good blow for freshening things up.

As she turned round to wipe her hands she gasped in shock. Gus was standing in the doorway, eyeing her in *that way*, the way she hated men to look at her.

As his eyes raked her body and he took one step forward, she was suddenly filled with blind panic and lunged for the side door, thinking only to escape. But he was across the room before she could get it properly open and slammed it shut with one hand while grabbing her with the other. She opened her mouth to scream and he pushed her against the door.

'Shut up your squalling, you stupid woman, and listen!'

Instead she screamed as loudly as she could, until he shook her so hard she hiccupped into silence.

'What do you think I'm going to do, murder you?' he mocked.

As she froze, completely gripped by terror now and beyond thinking clearly, he smiled slowly. 'Or rape you? That's what you were thinking, isn't it? That I was going to rape you? *Weren't you?*'

She nodded.

'Why the hell would I do that? You've a face like the back of a tram.'

She tried to pull away, but he wouldn't let her. Though he did not look muscular, he was far stronger than she was. The panic rose and rose until suddenly she exploded into action, nails raking at his face and when she could not reach it, the hand that was holding her. She flailed with her arms, trying to hit him, and kicked as hard as she could with her right foot.

'Stupid bitch!' He shook her again and as she continued to kick and hit out, sobbing loudly, he twisted one of her arms behind her back and pinned her against the door again, this time face pressed against it. 'I told you to listen to me. And this time,' he banged her head against the wood, 'I don't want you to interrupt. Do you understand?' Another bang and, 'Do you?'

'Yes!' she screamed at him.

'You're going to pack your things and get out of this house. I don't like sharing it with an ugly gutter bitch like you. If you won't earn your keep by keeping things clean, you're worth nothing to me.' After another pause, he repeated, 'Do you understand?'

'Yes.' She sounded beaten, she thought, hearing her own whimper of a response. Shame flooded through her. She *was* beaten, for he had found her weak spot and if he did not let her go soon, she thought she might go mad with fear.

He jerked her round to face him. 'Go and pack your things, then get out. And don't try to pretend to anyone that I've assaulted you, because I haven't. The police wouldn't believe you, anyway – I'd tell them you were asking for it, leading me on, and turned on me when I refused you.'

She shuddered, could not help it, felt like vomiting now.

He laughed. 'But you wouldn't do that, would you, ask for it? You don't like a man to touch you. What happened? Were you born frigid or did someone hurt you?' He didn't wait for an answer but continued, 'You and that schoolmarm make a fine pair. Man-haters, both of you.'

Jenny knew she could not defy him any longer, even for Eva's sake. Her grandad would let her move in and she could have his old bedroom. Looking at Gus's face, flushed with both anger and triumph, she knew her friend would not be safe with him, either. She'd persuade Eva to come with her.

'Go up and start packing, and be quick about it,' he repeated, very softly now, but with as much menace as when he'd been shouting at her.

She edged past him, her head hurting where he had banged it against the door, her whole being sick with shame and self-loathing. She felt as if she had let Eva down, let herself down too.

Gus Blake had won.

*　　*　　*

When Eva came back from the village, Jenny was waiting for her in the road, arms clasped around herself, looking pale and with a new bruise on her forehead.

'What's wrong? How did you get that bruise?'

'I told Grandad I tripped and fell, but it wasn't an accident. It was him, Gus Blake.' Jenny had to stop to press her quivering lips together and swallow hard, or she'd have burst into tears. 'Leave your shopping in our porch and walk with me along the lane. I need to tell you what happened.'

'What has he done to you?' Eva asked, horrified by how upset her friend was looking. 'He hasn't . . .'

Jenny shuddered. 'No, only repeated what he did last time. I'm sorry, love, really sorry, but I can't take any more. Just after you'd left he came into the kitchen.' She bit back a sob. 'Eva, he was like a madman, like one of those villains you see at the cinema. I was terrified out of my wits.'

'Did he hit you?'

'Not exactly. But he,' she gulped loudly, 'touched me again and told me he wanted me out of the house – and Eva, I knew I had to go. His face . . . it was awful, all gloating. *You* have to leave too. You can stay at Grandad's with me till you decide what to do. If you wait there with me till Wilf gets back, we'll go and get your things together. It's not *safe* for you to be in the house with that man.'

Eva stopped walking to hug her friend, holding her close and patting her back till the shudders had stopped. 'Oh, Jenny, it's all my fault. I shouldn't even have asked you to stay with me after what you'd told me.' She felt in her pocket and pressed her clean, neatly folded handkerchief into Jenny's hand. 'Wipe your eyes and don't cry any more, love. You're free of him now.' They turned to walk on in silence for a moment or two, then Eva said, 'I'm not leaving the house to him, though. I can't bear to let him win.'

Jenny stopped and grabbed her arm, shaking it in her urgency to make Eva understand. 'He's not a naughty child in one of your classes. He's evil and clever with it. He even guessed why it upset me so much for him to touch me, laughed about it. He'll find a way to get rid of you, too, I know he will, and it'll be as nasty as it needs to be.'

'Come with me to the police, then,' Eva begged. 'Tell them what's happened. Set the law on him.'

Jenny shook her head. 'No. I tried that last time. It does no good at all. They always believe the man, especially a well-spoken man. And when people find out what's happened, they blame the woman, think you're no better than you ought to be. I'm not going to tell anyone – and that includes Grandad and Wilf.' She sniffed and wiped her eyes again. 'If I told them, Wilf would go after Blake and get himself in trouble.'

'But Jenny, you can't just let Gus get away with it.'

Her voice was weary. 'They always do, his sort.'

They were now within sight of the farm cottage where the Brierleys lived and by mutual accord turned to walk back, avoiding the muddy ruts, not speaking, both lost in their thoughts.

'I'm not leaving,' Eva said as they got back to the

main road. 'If Gus attacks me I'll run screaming across the road to Mr Beaman, and we'll see if he can wriggle out of that.'

'He will. He'll say you egged him on. That's what they always do.'

They stopped to argue but nothing Jenny said would dissuade Eva from staying on at Rose Villa.

'Change to my bedroom, then,' she said in the end. 'At least from there you can throw the window open and scream for help if he tries to get in during the night.'

Eva's lips pressed together into a thin line that her former pupils would have recognised and she gave a quick shake of the head. 'Not another inch do I give way. You can't let bullies go unchecked.'

'This is more than *bullying!*' Jenny exclaimed, her voice rising to a near shout.

'Nonetheless, I'm not leaving.' Eva picked up her shopping from Grandad Gill's porch, agreed to go inside for a cup of tea and, once there, divided the food she'd bought into two. 'Here, you take your share, Jenny.'

Grandad watched this without saying much. He knew that sod over the road had hurt his girl in some way today, even though she wouldn't tell him why she was upset. He was relieved that she was coming to stay with him and Wilf for a while.

'You could come and stay here at night,' he said to Eva as she brought him his cup of tea. 'Whatever that fellow's done to send my girl fleeing, he'll do to you sooner or later.'

Jenny paused with her cup halfway to her mouth. 'I told you, Grandad, he's done nothing to me.'

'And I told you I didn't come down in the last shower of rain. If you won't tell me, you won't, but don't lie to me, flower.'

He had called her that when she was little. She bent her head for a moment, blinking her eyes, but not managing to hold back the tears.

His voice was soft and understanding. 'Folk as talk posh like yon bugger can get away with things folk like us couldn't. I know that. But he'll get his comeuppance one day, for all his lah-de-dah ways. Folk are getting his measure and the only one as'll talk to him now when he goes down to the pub is Sid Linney. Otherwise he sits by hissen or talks to strangers. Someone told me he goes down into Heyshaw to drink at the Red Lion sometimes.' He sipped his tea slowly, careful not to burn himself but eager for the warmth inside him. 'How does he get his brass without toiling for it, tell me that? He don't do owt, as I can see, 'cept cause trouble for you and my lass.'

Which was a long speech for him.

Jenny had kept her face averted all the time he was talking. When he stopped, she said dully, 'Since there's nothing we can do about him, Grandad, I'm not admitting anything, an' that's flat.'

Eva looked at her friend's strained expression and anger rose again inside her, reinforcing her resolve. 'I can't let him get away with it. I won't.'

And though they both tried to persuade her to stay at the cottage for a while, she refused point-blank to follow their advice.

She had been weak with Gus Blake before, had let him persuade her into things she hadn't wanted, like marriage. Fortune, in the shape of his ex-wife, had saved her. She wasn't going to be weak again – with him or with anyone else – whatever Jenny said.

She caught sight of herself in the mirror over the fireplace. Lizzie and Polly would have recognised that stubborn expression on her face and nudged one another. Alice would have given her a wry smile and said, 'Go your own way, then, my dear. One only learns by experience.'

Well, she had no experience of men like Gus, she knew that. She would be on her own with him from now on at Rose Villa and was more afraid of that than she had admitted, but she wasn't going to give in to him. She'd never be able to live with herself if she did.

13

For two days nothing happened at Rose Villa, though the atmosphere was tense. Eva's nerves were on edge all the time, but she tried not to let Gus see that. Although he did nothing worse than make snide comments or give her those sneering smiles as they passed one another, a couple of times she thought she saw a calculating expression on his face, as if he were trying to work out how to deal with her.

All she wanted was to be rid of him, to have her home to herself while she still could! Was it so much to ask?

When a letter arrived for him, she had no compunction about examining the envelope, but there was no clue to the sender, just the untidy, scrawled address and a London postmark. Perhaps it was from his wife. If so, it was the first time she had written to him.

When Eva heard the sound of his car, her heart sank, because she'd had a blissfully peaceful day just pottering round the house while the rain beat against the windows outside. Sighing, she continued with the letter she was writing to apply for another job as governess.

He was whistling under his breath as he came in, but that stopped abruptly and she heard him cursing under his breath as he picked the letter up and ripped it open. He went into the sitting room, banging the door shut behind him, and a couple of minutes later she heard the sound of something smashing. She didn't dare go to find out what had happened. Perhaps breaking something would vent his rage. She hoped it wasn't one of Alice's delicate little figurines. She'd go and check next time he was out and report the loss of whatever it was to Mr Beaman.

Gus went upstairs and she heard nothing more from him, though at one point she vaguely noticed him coming down and going out to the shed. After a while she forgot even to listen because she was trying to draft the best letter of application possible. So far she hadn't even got as far as an interview for any of the positions she'd written for and was feeling very downhearted about it all.

By the time she'd sealed the envelope, she was hungry enough to risk cooking her tea, a simple boiled egg and toast. She felt on edge as she ate, missing Jenny's cheerful company greatly. While she was washing up Gus went out again in his car. She stood watching him from the kitchen window. Rain was beating against the panes and the wind was rising, moaning round the house and lashing the bare branches of the trees.

Realising this was her chance to do a bit of snooping, she hurried down to the sitting room to see what had been broken. Tears filled her eyes as she saw the pieces of Alice's favourite figurine lying scattered about the hearth. She didn't disturb them. As she stood up, she stared round at the room where she'd spent so many happy hours. It was in a mess again. Usually when Gus went out in his car it meant he was drinking in the Red Lion and would be home late, probably the worse for wear. She'd make sure she'd retired to her room by nine, she decided, to be out of his way.

Unfortunately he caught her by surprise by coming home within the hour, still in the foulest of moods from the way he started banging the cupboard doors in the kitchen. She decided to wait to fill her hot water bottle and tried to settle down with her book, but in vain. She felt nervous and made sure the rolling pin was to hand, propped against the side of her armchair out of sight of the door. This was a dreadful way to live and she was increasingly tempted to go across the road and take refuge with Jenny.

When he left the kitchen, instead of walking past her sitting room, he flung open the door. He was swaying on his feet and scowling at her. Apprehension turned to a heavy lump of fear in her belly.

'Not hiding in your bedroom yet, Miss Eva school-marm Kershaw?'

'I'm not hiding anywhere, merely sitting reading. And I'd be grateful if you'd leave me to do that in peace.'

He didn't move, just stood there, his gaze roaming round the room then coming back to linger on her. She did not like the way he was looking at her, in fact it frightened her, so she let her hand drop down to grasp the rolling pin. She'd use it if she had to.

'Or maybe,' his words came out a little slurred, 'you

fancied some company, for once. Maybe there's a real woman inside that prim shell of yours.'

'I don't fancy *your* company and you've been drinking. Go away and sleep it off! I can smell the booze on your breath from here.'

He laughed, a snarl of sound, and took a step towards her. 'We'll sleep it off together.'

'We certainly will not! Go away and –' But he kept on coming, so she jumped up and shoved the armchair between them.

He seized the arm of the chair and pushed it aside, laughing as it crashed into her desk and sent her little clock catapulting to the floor.

She had kept the rolling pin hidden behind her back and as he reached out to grab her, she whacked it sideways at his arm, taking him by surprise.

He clutched the arm, yelling, 'You bitch! You need a lesson in manners.'

She didn't wait for him to attack her again – she attacked him. She might have been Miss Kershaw, sedate schoolteacher, for the past eight years, but she had grown up in the terraced streets of Overdale, mixing with rough children and learning how to deal with them. She acted instinctively. You didn't stand and wait for someone to hit you, you hit them first, as fast and hard as you could, to make them more wary of you in future.

And with boys, you knew where they were most vulnerable. Her father had taught all the Kershaw girls that.

So she rushed at Gus, wielding the rolling pin again,

surprising him so much she got in a couple more good hits before he began to fight back, punching her on the upper arm. As he drew back his arm for another blow, she kicked him hard in the crotch and he folded up with a soft 'Oof', fighting for breath.

Seizing the opportunity, she darted round him and ran up the stairs, still clutching the rolling pin. Rushing into her bedroom, she slammed the door shut with a sob of relief, fumbling for the bolt, wishing now that she had changed to Jenny's room and could yell for help from the window.

But the bolt wasn't there any more!

She stared down at the door in horror, seeing the holes where the screws had been. He must have removed it! She moaned as she heard him start slowly up the stairs, muttering and cursing. As she glanced round in panic, her eye fell on the chair near her dressing table, and she grabbed it, jamming it under the door handle, breathing a sigh of relief as she wedged it into place. That would hold him, surely, till he came to his senses?

And if he didn't?

Think! she told herself. But her wits seemed to have gone begging. And anyway, what could she do if he broke the door down? He'd soon take the rolling pin off her and then heaven help her.

The footsteps stopped outside her bedroom door.

'Got it safely bolted, have you?' he jeered, yelling above the sound of the wind.

She didn't reply, just watched as he shook the door. The chair wouldn't hold him for long.

Dashing across the room she heaved the bottom window up and leaned out. Surely if she shouted loudly enough for help the neighbours would hear her? But the wind was howling round the house so loudly that her voice would be lost in the noise of the storm.

The branches of the big sycamore were swaying to and fro just beyond her face. She stared at them and swallowed hard. It was a sturdy old tree. Could she climb down it? Lizzie was the one who had always climbed trees. Eva never had, not once.

As Gus's body thumped against the door again, making it shake, she realised this was her only chance to escape. Anything was better than staying in her bedroom and letting Gus Blake hurt her. Anything at all.

Wind roared into the room, rain beat against her face, and behind her the door continued to shake and rattle as he threw himself against it. Thank heavens for sturdy, old-fashioned chairs made of solid mahogany! But how long would it hold?

She got into a sitting position on the window sill, holding on to the window frame as she looked for a foothold on the tree. There! Just beyond her foot. She eased herself forward until her right foot was nearly there, then forced herself to let go of the window frame and grab the nearest branch as she fumbled for a secure foothold. With a groan of relief she found it.

She did not dare delay, so reached out with her left foot for a lower branch. But it was further down than she had realised and she nearly missed it, shrieking as she scrabbled for a foothold, holding on desperately with her hands.

The rain was half-blinding her and she shook her hair out of her eyes as she searched for the next foothold down. *Quick! There had to be one.*

She was clinging to the trunk now, had no idea of how she had got there, but it felt solid at least. Part-way round it, a little further down, she saw another big branch. 'I can do it,' she muttered to give herself courage. 'I *can.*'

She twisted her body carefully round the trunk towards it but as she moved her foot into place, it slipped on the wet surface and she grazed her leg on a spur, clinging desperately with her arms and other foot until she'd managed to right herself.

Above her from the bedroom came another thud followed by the sound of a door splintering and a roar of triumph.

'Don't panic,' she muttered. 'Don't you dare panic, Eva Kershaw!' She felt as if she'd been climbing for ever, but she'd only got down a few branches.

'What the hell—'

She risked a quick glance upwards to see Gus Blake leaning out of the window, staring down at her. The moon showed his expression clearly, first astonishment then a gloating triumph.

'I'll be waiting for you at the bottom!' he called and the head vanished.

She had no time to climb down the rest of the way, so rolled over on to her stomach then eased her body downwards, hoping to dangle from her arms before dropping. But she hadn't enough strength to hold herself for more than a few seconds and fell the last few feet, hitting the ground with a jarring thud and falling forward on to her hands and knees.

Sobbing, she pushed herself upright and set off running, trying to get round to the front of the house where she could scream for help. She could only hope Gus had chosen to go round the other side.

But her luck was out. She nearly ran into a tall figure and with a wild shriek of dismay, echoed by the wind, she turned aside, fear lending speed to her feet. She knew the garden better than he did, so dodged through the rockery, hearing him trip over something behind her and roar in fury as he fell. That gained her a little precious time.

The moon went back behind the clouds, peered out briefly and vanished again. Rain was falling steadily, now coming straight down, now blown sideways by the wind. Clad only in her skirt, blouse and cardigan, wearing thin house shoes, Eva shivered uncontrollably as she forced herself to run on, weaving her way in and out of the bushes. She had never been so miserably uncomfortable or so terrified in her whole life.

In the darkness behind her he shouted, 'I'll get you, you bitch! You can't escape.'

Gus was still between her and the house! Even if she could have screamed more loudly than this rising storm, she didn't want to give away her exact position to him.

Panting hoarsely, she crept through the shrubbery to the far end of the garden, knowing just where to climb over the dry stone wall that ran all round the house, because she'd done it so often. Any further along and she'd fall into the stream. As she got to the top of the wall, the moon came out briefly and there was a yell of triumph from further up the garden.

He'd seen her!

Close to complete panic, she jumped down from the wall and set off across the field, stumbling on the uneven ploughed ground. As the moon went in again, she changed direction, moving further away from the house. He would expect her to circle round towards the road, she was sure – and she would, but not yet.

She fell and got up, stumbled and slowed down to right herself, panting and gasping. After running for what felt like hours, with her legs feeling more leaden by the minute, she reached the other side of the field and clambered over the wall into the lane, scraping her hands on the rough stones. For a moment she hesitated, shivering and wondering which way to go, then decided not to risk trying for the road yet. She would head for the farm and ask for asylum there.

The moon stayed hidden and she ricked her ankle in a muddy rut, pausing only to regain her balance before setting off again, limping now but pressing on as quickly as she could. As the moon began to sail out from the clouds again, it suddenly occurred to her that if she ran in a crouching position, the wall would hide her, though that would slow her down still further.

She rounded the curve, half-blinded by the rain, and ran straight into someone. A man. She screamed at the top of her voice and when he caught hold of her, began to struggle wildly.

'What the hell—'

She realised dimly that it wasn't Gus and stopped struggling, instead clutching the man's arms as great shudders of relief washed through her. 'Don't let him – get me.'

'Eva? Eva Kershaw?'

Her 'yes' came out on a sob.

'Who's after you, for heaven's sake?'

'Gus Blake.'

Aaron could feel her shivering, sense her terror. Whatever was going on, he was on her side instinctively. 'Come on. My house is nearby. You'll be safe there.'

He kept his arm round her shoulders and she clung to him as they stumbled along together. Beneath the wet, clinging clothes, her body felt warm and soft against his, its curves surprisingly feminine. Why the hell was Blake chasing her across the fields on a stormy night like this? Had the fellow run mad?

Aaron wished his damned leg would let him move more quickly, but it was too risky in these slippery conditions. When the cottage loomed in front of them he grunted in relief as he guided her round to the back, their feet crunching on the gravel he'd laid recently to cut down on the winter mud that got tramped inside. He opened the door, relieved to see a dim glow in the kitchen range, and helped her sit down on a chair because she didn't seem capable of standing on her own.

When he'd adjusted the damper to make the fire

burn up, he turned back to her and even in the dim light could see she was shivering violently, huddled down with her arms wrapped round herself.

She looked up. 'Have you locked the door?'

'He won't come in here.'

'Please!'

'All right.' He went to slide the bolt which was stiff because it was rarely used, then picked up the lamp from the table, intending to light it.

'Don't!' she begged. 'He'll guess I'm here if he sees a light.'

Aaron set the lamp down again unlit, amazed at how afraid of Blake she was. 'He won't be able to do anything to you with me here. You're quite safe.'

'I don't want him even to know where I am. Please!' She shivered again.

'All right. Let's get you warm then, shall we? I'll go and find a blanket to wrap round you.'

'Thank you.'

Her voice was low and pleasant in his ears, without the slow, heavy accent of most of his neighbours, but still distinctly northern in tone. Like him she had modified her speech a little, but unlike that silly bugger Sid Linney, who used words wrongly or exaggerated what he considered an upper-class accent in his quest for gentility, she didn't try to hide her northern origins.

He had longed for the sound of soft women's voices like hers sometimes in the trenches.

There was a sound outside as he got to the foot of the stairs and he swung round. Hell, that bugger really was pursuing her and the fire was burning up now! If anyone peered through the window, the two of them would show up as plainly as anything, because the kitchen curtains had fallen to pieces last year and he hadn't bothered to replace them. 'There's someone coming round the side of the house!' he whispered, moving back towards her. 'Get down!'

Quickly he tugged her to the floor, smiling wryly as he realised they were seeking Molly's refuge. 'We can hide under the table,' he breathed in her ear and she let him pull her under the edge of the table cover.

The footsteps sounded clearly in spite of the noise of the storm. Blake was making no attempt to hide his presence and was very close now.

Aaron could feel Eva shivering still and slid his arm round her shoulders in the hope of warming her a little. It was a bit like the trenches, but he much preferred holding a warm, living woman in his arms to an injured or dying man.

'You all right?' he whispered as the seconds ticked past.

'Yes. Thank you.' She laid her head on his shoulder, exhaling as if at the very end of her strength.

He hadn't heard the footsteps go away, so he lifted the edge of the chenille table cover enough to peer across the room. He could see a dark shape outlined by the moonlight against the window. Someone was peering in. The head vanished and a minute later the person tried the door handle.

It seemed a very long time until the intruder crunched away across the gravel.

'He's gone,' Aaron whispered at last.

She began to weep against him. 'What am I going to do?'

'Let's get you warm first, then you can tell me what's been happening.' He got up and limped across to the kitchen range, pushing the kettle on to the hottest part of the hob. 'I'll just nip upstairs and get you a blanket. Will you be all right?'

'Yes.'

He heard a muffled sob, saw her wipe away a tear with the back of her hand and pretended not to notice, but his heart went out to her. What had driven the prim little teacher out into a stormy night without even a coat? And why the hell was Blake pursuing her? Had the bastard tried to rape her?

After lighting a candle Aaron went upstairs, pausing on the landing because the spare blankets were kept in a chest in the main bedroom now occupied by Lil. But there was no help for it. He couldn't leave Eva Kershaw shivering in wet clothes.

As he pushed open the door, Lil said softly. 'I heard you come in with someone and then I heard footsteps outside. What's happening?'

He explained quickly and she was silent for so long he wondered if she'd drifted off to sleep again.

'Take her down some of my clothes as well as the blanket,' she said. 'Poor thing. Some men can be right buggers.'

With her whispering instructions, he sorted out clothes, underclothes, a couple of blankets and a towel. 'You all right?'

'Mmm. Just tired.'

Downstairs he found Eva crouched in front of the fire, holding out her hands to the glowing warmth.

As he set the candle down on the table, she looked towards him. 'I heard voices. Have we woken your wife? I'm sorry.'

'Lil was already awake. Night and day don't seem to mean much to her any more. She suggested I bring you some of her clothes. I think they'll fit.' They no longer fitted Lil, hanging on her emaciated body like borrowed garments. He offered Eva the bundle. The fire was sending out more heat now. The best thing about this damned hovel was that you could warm up the tiny rooms quickly and there was peat as well as coal to burn if you knew how to cut and dry the turfs. 'I'll take the candle into the scullery while you change in front of the fire. Don't worry. We'll hear him if he comes back. Call out when you're ready.'

'Thank you.'

It didn't occur to her that Aaron would try to spy on her. She trusted him instinctively. The clothes fitted her quite well, though they were meant for a taller woman, and she gave a long, shuddering sigh of relief when she was dressed before calling softly, 'You can come out now!'

He brought the candle back. 'Here, give me those wet things. I'll wring them out and we'll hang them over the clothes horse.' But she still looked cold, so he picked up one of the blankets and shook it out, wrapping it round her shoulders. 'This should help as well.' He drew up a chair to the fire for her and she huddled down on it, holding her hands out to the blaze.

He busied himself preparing some cocoa for them both, turning to smile at her and ask, 'Better now?'

'Yes. You're very kind.'

'Well, you've been kind to my Molly, Miss Kershaw. That's what friends are for. I hope you'll consider me your friend from now on?'

'Yes. And my name's Eva. To friends.'

'All right. Eva it is. My wife's Lil.' He looked at the window. 'We need to get some more curtains for this room. I'm not having anyone coming round staring through my window like that again.' He felt outraged that Blake should do that and even try his door. Who did that sod think he was? He looked down as he stirred too vigorously in his irritation and slopped hot cocoa on his fingers. After adding milk and sugar to her cup, he passed it to her. 'There, that'll warm you up inside.'

They sat sipping together. There was a feeling of intimacy in the shadowed room, lit by only one candle and the glowing fire.

To her relief he didn't push her to explain, but let her pull herself together in her own time. Suddenly she wanted to tell him, to see if he could make better sense of what had happened. 'I think Gus intended to – molest me. When he came back drunk, I hit him with the rolling pin and ran upstairs thinking I'd be safe, but he must have taken the bolt off my bedroom door this afternoon. He followed me up, so I pushed a chair under the door handle and climbed out of the window and down the tree.' She started sobbing suddenly. 'But he kept chasing me and no one could hear my cries for help in such a storm.'

It seemed very natural to Aaron to put his arm round her shoulders again to comfort her, and she didn't push him away.

'Why is he doing it?' she sobbed against him. 'Isn't it enough that I've lost Alice, can't get a job, have no money?'

He tried to digest this information, saying in surprise, 'I didn't think *you'd* be short of money.'

'Well, I am. Someone burgled our house – I think it must have been Gus – and I have only just over four pounds left. I try to be economical, but I have to eat and buy the newspapers to look for jobs! Though I haven't been able to get a job because they're giving them to men first.'

'So you've no idea why Blake did this?'

'He'd already driven Jenny away and I think he's been trying to get rid of me. Tonight he was drunk and I think it was just sheer – nastiness.' After a pause, she said raggedly, 'Jenny was right. No one's going to believe me if I accuse him of anything. Gus will just say he was worried about me and was out looking for me, not chasing me. What am I going to *do?*'

And suddenly it came to him. A stop-gap solution, but they were both pretty desperate. 'Why don't you stay here till you can work out something permanent? I desperately need someone to stay with Lil. I don't want her to die alone but I can't take time off work because Sid Linney is looking for an excuse to sack me.' As Eva turned towards him, her face was close enough for him to see the faint flush on her cheeks, the way her hair fell in soft waves around her face as it dried. Pretty hair, it was, and she was pretty, too, in a quiet sort of way.

'You're offering me a job?' she asked at last.

He grimaced. 'Sort of. I can't pay you more than a bob or two, but there's a roof to keep out the rain, a good lock on the door and food.' He hesitated. 'It'd not be easy, though. Lil coughs up blood and there's a lot of washing. She might even die on you.'

'That's why Gracie stayed home the other week, wasn't it? To look after her mother?'

'Aye. But it's not right for children to have to face all this and I work such long hours that I can't do much about the house. If you could cook us some simple meals as well . . .' He broke off. 'What am I thinking of, offering a job like this to someone like you?'

'You're thinking of your family. As you should. And offering me the only help you can.' Eva hesitated. 'I don't want to bring danger to you all, though.'

'I'm still man enough to deal with Blake.' He grinned suddenly. 'And I'll put the word out to the lads to keep an eye on us all.' He didn't usually ask for help, but now he needed it for his family – and for Eva. As she considered this, she wrinkled her brow in puzzlement and he thought again how pretty she was. Why had he not realised that before?

'What do you mean, "the lads"?'

'There are a few ex-servicemen in Heyshaw. We look out for one another when we can. Not only Wilf, but one or two others. If there was need, they'd rally round.' He grimaced. 'Once I'd have managed on my own, but I'm not much cop in fights with this leg.'

She could hear the pain and frustration in his voice, see how his disability upset him. 'You've saved me tonight, Aaron, and I'm so grateful.' She giggled suddenly, feeling almost light-headed with relief. 'That's the first time I've sat under a table since I was a little girl myself. I used to love it, dreaming and making up stories.'

With an unforced smile on her face and her hair loose about her shoulders she looked so pretty he felt a tug of attraction, immediately followed by a pang of guilt. How could he fancy another woman when his wife lay upstairs dying inch by inch? Well, there was an easy answer to that. Because Lil hadn't been a wife to him in that way for quite a while now and he had a man's normal needs.

'We could try it for a few days,' she offered.

'You don't mind? It'll be menial work to someone like you.'

She laughed. 'I'm no hothouse flower. After my father died, we were desperately short of money and if Alice hadn't helped me to become a teacher, I'd be working in a mill or as a housemaid. I'm not too proud to dirty my hands, I promise you, though I'm not the world's best cook, I'm afraid.'

He smiled. 'You can't be worse than me. I'm good at boiled eggs, though.'

She looked down at herself. 'Will your wife let me borrow her clothes? I – daren't go back for my own yet.'

'Of course she will. She doesn't use them any more.' He stared into the fire as he admitted, 'I can't tell you what a relief it'll be to have someone here. I hate leaving Lil alone, but neither of us wanted Gracie to stay home and maybe see her mother die. She's only ten. And that Mrs Harrop has only been coming in when she feels like it and short-changing me on what she did around the house, too. Yesterday she sent me a message to say she can't come any more. I can guess why. She'll have got a job at one of the big houses and I've no doubt they pay better than I can. And she's frightened of catching TB. Aren't you?'

Eva looked at him, her eyes very direct. 'I won't short-change you – Aaron.' For the first time she allowed herself to use his first name, saying it hesitantly. 'And actually, I'm far more frightened of Gus Blake than of catching TB.'

He liked the soft way she spoke his name, liked it too much so stood up with a jerk that hurt his knee. Grunting involuntarily in pain, he began to rub it.

'Are you all right?'

'Just a gammy leg, courtesy of the Hun.' The pain eased and he started moving again. 'Right, then. I'll make up a bed for you on the couch in the parlour for tonight. There are thick curtains in there and no one will be able to see in. And if you can still face staying after you've tried it tomorrow, we'll work out something more comfortable for you to sleep on.' He'd give her his own mattress if necessary. 'The privy's just outside at the back. If you like, I'll stand guard while you go, just in case he's still hanging around.' He smiled ruefully. 'Though I'd make a better toy soldier with this damned leg brace.'

'There'd be two of us to fight him,' she said quietly, then smiled and added, 'Though I'm afraid I dropped my rolling pin as I was climbing over the garden wall.'

'Oh, I think Lil has one somewhere if that's your preferred weapon.'

It was funny to think of prim Miss Kershaw hitting people with rolling pins, climbing down trees and clambering over walls, he thought as he climbed up to the attic a few minutes later, though from the sound of it she'd given a good account of herself. He couldn't abide women who just stood around looking helpless. Eva had rescued herself tonight. He'd only helped her after she'd got away. He admired that in her. And why did folk think she was stand-offish? He hadn't found her at all like that.

Gus continued searching for Eva for over an hour, getting colder, wetter and more angry by the minute. He didn't want that bitch going to the police or claiming he'd touched her. But he could find no sign of her, no sign even of lights in any of the neighbouring houses. He went to check every single place nearby, just to be sure.

He couldn't work out where she had gone. One minute she'd been running away and he'd been gaining on her, the next she'd vanished. Had she gone into that farm cottage, the first place he'd tried? There had been a fire still burning, but no lights or signs of people moving around. Or had she gone up to the farm itself? If she had, Sid's wife might have taken her in. But the place was dark.

If Eva didn't come back by morning, he'd ask round the village, saying he was worried about her. He grunted in amusement. Yes, and he'd hint that she'd been upset for a while and he was worried about her state of mind. He scowled in the darkness. If it hadn't been for Clara coming up to Heyshaw, he'd be in easy street now, married and with enough money to live in comfort as he planned his next moves, plus the extra from his sideline – not to mention Eva Kershaw to warm his bed.

It galled him that he had to keep paying Clara to keep quiet. He didn't dare stop because she was well aware that if certain people in London knew where he was, they would have been after him like a shot. But she knew her payments would stop if they found him, so he thought he could rely on her not to say anything.

He still had a lot of stuff to dispose of, but money was building up, safely hidden in one of his boxes, and since he'd lose his northern bolthole by the end of next year, after he'd sold everything he might head off to America where no one would know him. He'd been thinking about doing that for a while now. Or South Africa. Australia, even. Anywhere as long as it was far away and warmer than this bloody place.

14

In the morning Eva was woken by the sound of voices, one of them a child's. She could not at first work out where she was. Then the events of the previous night came rushing back, making her shudder and burrow under the covers until she realised she had a job to do and threw off the blankets. Some light filtered into the room under the door, though it was still dark outside. By opening the door a little she had enough light to find the clothes Lil had lent her and pull them on quickly.

As she opened the door fully, she saw that the clothes were crumpled and needed mending. She pulled a face at her reflection in the mirror. It didn't look like her. She didn't even have hairpins so had to leave her hair hanging down her back.

When she went out into the other room, Aaron and his daughters turned to stare at her and she hesitated in the doorway.

'Ah, here she is,' he said, smiling and gesturing to her to join them. 'I've just been telling these two that you've agreed to come and look after their mother for us.'

Molly gave her a quick, shy smile.

'But she's a teacher!' Gracie exclaimed, positively

bristling with suspicion. She yanked Molly closer to her, as if claiming possession of her sister.

'They don't need any more teachers at your school,' Eva told her, 'so I'm not a teacher any more. But you do need someone to look after your mother.'

'Maybe she won't want you to look after her,' Gracie muttered.

'You mind your manners, Gracie Brierley!' Aaron snapped. 'I don't know what's got into you lately.'

Eva went across to the cooking range, saying in as cheerful a tone as she could manage, 'If you tell me what you like for breakfast, I'll get it for you from now on.'

'*I* allus get Molly's breakfast.' Gracie rushed to grab the wire toasting fork which was lying on the hearth next to a poker. Spearing a slice of bread, she held it in front of the glowing coals. 'She likes how I do her toast, don't you?'

Molly hesitated, but when her sister jabbed an elbow into her side, she nodded.

Eva shook her head warningly at Aaron as he opened his mouth to reprimand the child again. 'Well, you'll be the best person to show me what to do then, won't you, Gracie? I'll just watch, shall I, for today?'

There was a thumping noise from upstairs.

Aaron looked up at the ceiling. 'That's Lil. She bangs on the floor with an old walking stick when she wants something, because shouting makes her cough.' He glanced at the clock with a sigh, but moved towards the stairs.

'I'll go,' Eva said quickly. 'You get on with your

breakfast.' Though as far as she could see all he had in front of him was a doorstep of buttered bread, not even toasted.

She went slowly up the dark, narrow stairs feeling rather nervous. If Lil Brierley didn't like her, this refuge wouldn't last long.

Lil was lying in bed, huddled under the covers, her lank hair straggling over the pillow. She studied the other woman openly. 'Aaron told me what happened last night. You all right now, love?'

'Yes, thanks to your husband.'

'He has a kind heart, our Aaron, for all he tries to hide it.'

'I hope you don't think I'm trying to take advantage of that?'

Lil waved one hand. 'No. 'Course not. Don't mind me. Always putting my foot in it, I am, when I don't mean to. Used to drive Aaron mad.'

As she paused to catch her breath, Eva could see how much of an effort it was for her to talk and pity filled her. Lil couldn't be more than thirty and her life was almost over.

'I wanted t'say I'm glad you're here. I'm feeling that weak I doubt I can last much longer. I don't want the kids t'see me die,' her face crumpled into sadness for a moment, 'but I'm only human and I don't want to be alone.' After a few more gasping breaths she added, 'Do you mind staying with me if – it happens?'

'No, of course not. I nursed my friend Alice and was with her when she died.'

'What's it like, dying?'

'It was quite peaceful for Alice. I was holding her all the time.' Eva's voice wobbled as she added, 'Even when she could no longer speak, I could see her love for me in her eyes and I hope she could see mine.'

After a short silence, Lil said gruffly, 'Thanks for tellin' me that. No one'll talk to me about it and I'm that scared. I lie here an' shiver sometimes. Don't you tell Aaron that, though, because I try not to let on. He has enough on his plate.'

'If it's any help to you, I don't think I'm as scared now of dying as I used to be. It wasn't as bad as I'd expected with Alice.'

Lil gave her a shaky smile. 'I think I'll be all right with you, love, if you carry on telling me the truth. I stopped seein' folk 'cause they kept pretending I were going to get better an' I couldn't do with that.'

Eva went across to grasp her hand. 'I'm very grateful to have somewhere to stay – and for the loan of these clothes.'

There were footsteps on the stairs and Aaron peered in, his eyes crinkling into a half-smile as he saw the two women holding hands. 'Everything all right, then?'

Lil beamed at him. 'Yes. She's as nice as you said.'

Eva blushed.

Aaron cleared his throat, avoiding her eyes. 'Um, yes. Well, I have to go to work now. I'll come back at lunchtime if I can – Sid's supposed to be going out. I'll nip into Heyshaw on my motor bike to do some shopping for you then if you'll make a list, Eva. We're a bit short of food, I'm afraid.'

As he went clattering back down the steep, uncarpeted stairs, Eva turned to the sick woman. 'I'll do my best to look after you,' she promised. 'And the children. I'm not too bad at housework.'

Lil chuckled, a breathy, rasping sound. 'Eh, you're bound to be better at it than me. Used to drive Aaron mad, it did, my untidiness. What I liked was being outside, gardening or just walking on the moors. I used to grow all our own vegetables an' have hens, too.' Her eyes strayed towards the window as she added bitterly, 'Now I'm stuck inside all day long.'

'I'm the other way round,' Eva said lightly. 'Too tidy for my own good. That drives people mad, too. Now, do you want anything?'

'A cup of tea'd be nice. But get the girls off to school first, eh? I'm not going anywhere.'

When the girls had left, with an unhappy Molly trailing behind Gracie, Eva stared round the kitchen, turning in a circle where she stood. It was in a dreadful mess and made her shudder to look at it closely. She'd bet there were cockroaches in the dark corners and crevices. She looked up and realised that the floorboards of Lil's bedroom also formed the ceiling of this one. She could see daylight shining through some of the cracks. There was rising damp in a patch near the door, which was the only entrance, it seemed, and the pale yellow distemper was flaking off the walls everywhere.

Even so it was better than sharing a house with Gus. Anything was better than that. She took a deep breath and squared her shoulders. No use feeling sorry for herself. If she didn't like what she found here, she could do something about it, couldn't she?

She marched into the scullery where dirty crockery from the previous night and from other meals too was piled on the wooden draining board, which itself was in need of a good scrub. There was an old-fashioned slopstone with a hand pump instead of a modern sink, and in it stood a battered enamel bowl with a patched hole in the bottom. It was rimmed with a dirty grease mark. The dishcloth made her wrinkle her nose in disgust.

Back in the kitchen she got the kettle, took it into the scullery to fill it then pushed it on to the hot part of the hob before making a closer inspection of the room. Tools and cheap ornaments were jumbled together on the mantelpiece, the tablecloth was stained and ragged, the cooking range was dull and in great need of black leading, while on the floor in front of it there were drifts of spilled coal dust and ashes. The wooden floors felt gritty beneath her feet wherever she walked, the windows were dull and smeary, and it didn't help her present bleak mood that all the rooms seemed dim, because it was a dull day, with lowering charcoal clouds massed in the grey sky.

She was missing the convenience of electricity already, not to mention proper indoor plumbing.

While she waited for the kettle to boil she slipped upstairs. 'Which crockery is yours?'

Lil blinked at her in puzzlement.

'Don't you have to have separate things? You know, crockery, towels and so on? I'm sure I read about that somewhere when people have TB.' Eva frowned, trying to remember the details.

Lil shrugged. 'Eh, they give us a list once of what we should do, but no one has time to fiddle around with things. I don't trouble Aaron and the girls more than I have to, an' that's the best I can manage.'

'Oh.' Eva began picking up pieces of clothing and magazines, automatically tidying the room as they spoke. 'Do you know where the list is?'

Lil shrugged. 'Long gone, love. It were years ago, that. I've lasted longer than they thought I would, at least.'

'Would you mind if I sorted out some separate things for you, then? It's supposed to prevent infection of others, from what I remember, and there are the girls to think of.'

'Do what you like, love.'

When Eva took her up a tray with a particularly pretty teacup on it and a matching plate with bread and butter, Lil brightened.

'That looks right nice. It were my mother's cup, that one, just the one I'd have chosen for myself.'

'Do you need help eating?'

Lil eased herself up in bed. 'No, I can still manage to hold a cup of tea. It's walking as tires me most an' makes me cough, an' I can't talk for long. If you can keep the fire burning up here, it'll help. Aaron brought up a bucket of coal before he left. He never forgets. But it nearly kills me to get out of bed and stoke the fire.'

Eva went to add some more coal to the tiny fireplace. 'You must knock for me whenever you need something. There's plenty more tea in the pot but I'm keeping it warm downstairs, so knock when you want another cup. I hate cold tea, don't you?'

Lil sipped the tea and sighed in pleasure. 'I like it boiling hot like this. You make a lovely cuppa.' She looked at the bread and butter and pulled a face. 'I'm never really hungry, though.'

'Just eat a little, then. There isn't any jam, but I can put some on the shopping list and then perhaps it'll tempt you more. Is there anything you specially like to eat, something else I could get you?'

'Apart from a new pair of lungs? Nay, love. Whatever suits you will suit me. Just look after my little lasses, that's the main thing. And Aaron.'

In the kitchen Eva began work, reminded of her childhood as she tackled the gargantuan task of cleaning up the mess. While she cleaned and swept, mopped and scrubbed, she made lists inside her head, as always, of the order in which to do things. She was determined to have this room shining clean by teatime, then she'd tackle the rest of the house over the next few days. But she hoped Aaron would be able to get home at midday because there was hardly anything to eat.

Jenny wrapped a shawl round herself and went to stand at the front door for the umpteenth time to stare across the road at Rose Villa. 'Eva said she'd come over every morning to let me know she was all right,' she worried when Wilf joined her on the step.

'Shall I go and knock on the door? I can ask to see her.'

'Would you? I'd go myself, only his car's still there.'

For a moment they looked at one another, her eyes warm, his guarded. She knew Wilf fancied her, you could usually tell, but he was acting as if she was ninety and untouchable. As he strode off across the road, she watched him go with one hand pressed to her chest, just below her throat. He was such a lovely fellow and somehow she had to make him realise she didn't care about money.

Wilf knocked on the front door of Rose Villa and when no one came to answer it, knocked again. Footsteps came towards him and Gus Blake opened it.

'What do *you* want?' he demanded.

'To see Miss Kershaw.'

'Tell that nosy bitch across the road to mind her own business and don't come knocking on my door again.'

For a moment it was touch and go whether Wilf punched him in the face, but he held himself back. 'I still want to see Miss Kershaw.'

'Well, you can't.' Gus slammed the door in his face.

As Wilf went back to the cottage, he looked over his shoulder to see if there was any movement at the upstairs windows, but there was nothing. He was beginning to think Jenny had good reason to feel concerned.

'If Eva'd been there, she'd have heard us talking, surely, and come to the door?' he said after explaining what had happened.

'If she could. Maybe he's got her locked up. Do you think we should tell anyone?'

'Not yet. It's too soon to call in the police.' Wilf

scowled across the road. 'If he goes out, I'll nip across again and try to see something through the windows.'

'You'll be careful?'

He nodded, his eyes still on the house opposite. Now Jenny had got him worried as well. If Eva had been in the house she *must* have heard the door knocker and he'd spoken really loudly when he asked for her. 'We'd better keep watch from the front room. We'll take it in turns if you like. I've nowt else to do today.'

She could hear the bitterness in his voice and her heart ached for him, but she just said calmly, 'Thanks. That'll be a big help, Wilf love.'

Their eyes met for a moment, then he shook his head and looked away.

Just before noon Gus Blake strolled along the road and called in at the local shop, a small place which sold mostly groceries but also everything else it could cram on its shelves or pile around the edges of the floor. When it was his turn he bought some cigarettes and asked casually, 'You haven't seen Miss Kershaw today, have you, by any chance?'

Mrs Arden looked at him warily. She hadn't taken to him because he always looked down his nose at you and had played a dirty trick on Miss Kershaw, who was as polite a young woman as you could hope to meet. Fancy trying to get married again without making certain your first wife really was dead. However, you couldn't afford to offend a customer who bought as many cigarettes as this one did, so she said curtly, 'Miss Kershaw hasn't been in this morning.'

'Oh, dear. She went out yesterday evening, you see, and I haven't seen her since.'

There was dead silence in the shop. Mr Arden peered round the doorway from the back room, two old ladies edged forward, all looking at Gus expectantly.

'Miss Kershaw stayed out *all night?*' one old lady said at last. 'Eh, that's not like her.'

'That's what I thought,' Gus said, playing to his audience. 'But I don't know where to start looking for her.'

'Where was she going last night?'

Stupid old halfwit! Hadn't he just said he didn't know? 'I don't have the slightest idea. She has her part of the house and I have mine. All I know is she didn't come back and when I checked this morning her bed hadn't been slept in, so I'm feeling rather worried about her safety.' He kept his face straight, amused at how they were all hanging on his words.

What he really hoped was that Eva Kershaw had fallen into a bog, broken her ankle and was now dying slowly and painfully of exposure, because it still hurt him to walk after that low blow to his privates. The bitch would pay for that one day. He never forgot a wrong.

As soon as they saw Gus walk down the road towards the village, Wilf ran across and banged on the front door of Rose Villa again. He waited, listening intently, but no one came to answer it and there was no sound of movement inside the house. He tried both front and side doors and the french windows at the back, peering into every room, but there was no sign of Eva.

If Blake had taken his car, Wilf would have found a ladder and climbed up to the first floor, because one of the bedroom windows was partly open. But he didn't dare risk it, so went back to tell Jenny that he'd discovered nothing.

Which only made them worry more.

'She'll be all right, Eva will,' Grandad said a couple of times as the morning passed. 'She's got her head screwed on properly, that one has.'

Jenny didn't say anything. She considered she had her head screwed on all right, too, but it hadn't stopped that man attacking her, had it? She shivered at the memory, then saw Wilf watching her in concern and forced a smile. But he didn't smile back.

'I'll go and keep watch in the front room,' he said a few minutes later. 'You get on with your housework, Jen.'

Only *he* ever shortened her name. And when he said it his eyes softened. She wasn't imagining that, she knew she wasn't. But she couldn't settle to the housework with Eva missing, so did the best thing she knew to work off her frustrations. She got out the flour she had bought the day before and began to make some bread, pummelling the dough viciously, wishing it were Gus Blake she had at her mercy.

Eva tackled the floor first, sweeping it and then scrubbing every inch of it with a stiff scrubbing brush, working on hands and knees, even though the scratches on her leg from the tree were very sore. She had to change the water several times, so dirty did it get, and wondered what Mrs Harrop had done with her time here. The work made her remember her mother scrubbing like this, or more often Lizzie doing it, for her mother had bullied poor Lizzie mercilessly after their father's death, using her like a servant.

Eva kept the door locked and wondered from time to time what Gus was doing, if he had any idea where she was. Jenny would be worried about her, she knew, and she'd have to find some way of letting her friend know what had happened. But she didn't dare go into the village on her own.

When the floor was clean but wet, she looked at her reddened hands, one of them grazed from climbing over the wall, and grimaced. She wasn't used to this, had been spoiled over the past few years with first a scrubbing woman employed, then Jenny coming to them full-time. Her hands felt sore and raw and she went to hold them out to the fire's comforting warmth as she waited for the floor to dry.

Noon came and went with no sign of Aaron nipping home to do the shopping. Lil was sleeping so Eva went to take stock of the pantry again, deciding to knock together some scones. She smiled. They wouldn't be as light as Jenny's, they never were, but she needed to get used to the oven if she was to cook the meals. There was a gas cooker in Rose Villa. How things had improved since her childhood! But she thought she could still remember how to deal with a coal-fired cooking range, well, more or less. You had to get to know each one's vagaries and that would take time. Pity this one didn't have a hot water tank as well, but it was the smallest size of range, little more than a fire behind an iron grill with a solid hob above it and a cast-iron oven to the right of it.

She found butter, milk and a few eggs in the pantry, plus a chunk of hard cheese that should have been wrapped up, but there were no fresh vegetables or fruit, not even a jar of jam. The girls had had plain toast with butter for their breakfast and had taken along bread and butter for dinner. Most children went home at midday, but those who came from further away were allowed to eat lunch in the school hall. Bread and butter was no way to feed a growing child, though! They should at least have made cheese sandwiches. But Gracie had insisted on making their lunch, putting the unevenly cut bread into a tin box, then into her worn leather satchel which had one buckle missing, so Eva had decided not to intervene, not this first day anyway.

The scones did not rise at all well, but they were edible and as she was ravenous after her morning's hard work, Eva melted some of the rubbery remains of the cheese on an enamel plate on top of the hob and scraped the gooey mess over two scones, eating it with relish. Then she rolled up her sleeves and went back to work.

The girls came home at four o'clock, rosy-cheeked from running. They stopped dead just inside the kitchen door.

'It looks different,' Gracie muttered.

'I've been cleaning up a bit.'

They edged round Eva towards the stairs.

'We allus go up to see Mum first when we get back,' Gracie said.

'Ask her if she wants a cup of tea, then, will you? She's been sleeping, but I heard her stirring a few minutes ago. She hasn't knocked yet.'

There was a murmur of voices from upstairs. Eva sat and waited for the girls to come down again, not wanting to intrude on their time with their mother. She suddenly remembered Alice saying the one thing she regretted was not having any children. At least Lil wouldn't have that bitterness festering within her.

Eventually the two girls clattered down again, still in their outdoor things.

'She wants a cup of tea,' Gracie said.

'I'll take her one. Can you hang your coats up, please?' Eva asked.

'We allus put them on this chair.' The older child looked defiantly at Eva as she did so and made no attempt to pick up their coats and scarves.

Molly gasped and stood there with one hand clasped to her mouth as if expecting trouble, her eyes wide and terrified.

'That's a pity, because I have some scones ready to eat when the coats are hung up. We're going to keep this house tidy from now on, so that we can look after your mother better and so that your father will feel comfortable after a hard day's work.' Eva went to get out a plate and started splitting and buttering the scones, not looking at the girls.

Molly glanced from one to the other, still looking anxious, then went to tug at her elder sister's sleeve and stare up at her pleadingly.

Eva frowned as she watched this scene out of the corner of her eye. She still hadn't heard Molly speak, not even in the security of her own home, and the child only whispered when forced to.

With a loud, aggrieved sigh Gracie hung up the coats.

Eva brewed a pot of tea, set the plate of scones on the table and poured out two glasses of milk. As the girls came to sit down, she looked at their hands and clicked her tongue in disapproval. 'You'll need to wash those hands first.'

'You're not our mother!' Gracie yelled at her. 'We don't have to do what *you* tell us.'

'Didn't your mother make you wash your hands before you came to table?'

There was silence, then Molly nodded and trotted off into the scullery.

'Why are you so angry with me?' Eva asked the stiff, scowling child left sitting alone.

Gracie muttered something and stamped off after her sister. But she didn't spurn the scones when she came back.

When Eva took the cup of tea up, Lil gave her a lop-sided grin. 'I heard it all from up here. I'll have a word with our Gracie. She didn't used to be so cheeky.'

'No need. I'm managing fine.' And it was early days

yet. She and Gracie still did not really know one another.

Aaron didn't get back till after dark, looking grim and angry. 'Sorry, Eva. Sid had to go into Littleborough with some sheep and took me with him to help. I couldn't even let you know and—'

He broke off to stare round, not speaking for a moment or two. Eva looked at him anxiously. Had she put something back wrong, something that mattered to him?

'This room hasn't looked as nice for a long time,' he said, his voice gruff with emotion. 'Thank you. You must have worked very hard today.' He looked down at her hands, which told their own story, and gave her a wry grin. 'Not a lady's hands any more, are they?'

She smiled, but was slightly surprised that he'd noticed such a detail. 'No. But it's much more important to get this place clean, don't you think, and to cook food for you all? Anyway, I'd be a fool to play the fine lady when I'm homeless. I was born in a house not much bigger than this, Aaron. It was Alice who had the money, not me.'

He was impressed by the way she spoke so matter-of-factly, with not a hint of self-pity. And the clean, tidy room pleased him enormously. He hated living in a mess. 'I'll just wash my hands, then I'll nip up and say hello to Lil. Afterwards, if you like, I'll run you into the village on the motor bike to buy some groceries. We'd better have ham for tea. It's quick and easy. I just hope they've got a loaf left at the shop, or I don't know what we'll do. Lil usually asks Gracie to order a loaf on her way to school.'

He kicked off his muddy shoes near the door, went to wash his hands and face, then ran upstairs in his stockinged feet. It was only a few minutes before he came down again to ask, 'Can you look after your mother for half an hour, Gracie love? If me and Eva don't go and buy something to eat there'll be no tea, let alone breakfast tomorrow.'

She nodded.

'And lock the door after we've gone.'

She looked at him in surprise.

'There's a nasty fellow living at Rose Villa now. He's the one who hurt Miss Kershaw yesterday. We don't want him hurting you two as well, do we? So don't let anyone into the house unless you know them.'

Molly shrank closer to her sister and Gracie put an arm round her, glancing at Eva, her brow knitted in a frown. 'Why?'

Aaron had been turning away, but he swung round. 'Why what?'

'Why did he try to hurt Miss Kershaw?'

'Because he's a nasty fellow,' her father said impatiently. 'And it's not polite to ask personal questions like that.'

'I don't mind,' Eva said. 'I think it was because he'd been drinking, Gracie. And because he wanted to drive me away. He's much stronger than me, so I ran away. I had to climb out of the bedroom window to do it and scramble down a tree.'

Gracie stared at her, this time with more surprise than hostility.

Molly came across to take the hand Eva had grazed when she fled and lift it briefly to her cheek, then, as if surprised at her own temerity, she dived under the table.

'She likes to sit there,' Aaron explained.

'It must feel safer.' Eva looked at Gracie. 'What sort of jam does your mother like best?'

'Strawberry.'

'Then we'll get her some of that. And do you like porridge with treacle on it for breakfast?'

Gracie shrugged, which Eva took to mean yes.

'You've no need to put up with cheekiness,' Aaron said as he settled her in the sidecar.

'At the moment Gracie's upset and angry at the whole world. I need to win her confidence, not fight with her.'

'You're a kind lass.'

As he smiled down at her, the moonlight made his eyes seem very dark and mysterious. He was a good-looking man, Eva decided, or would be if he wasn't so unhappy. Well, all the family looked unhappy. And no wonder. He had put his leg brace on as soon as he got home, which had puzzled her. Surely he needed it for work as well?

Anything she could do to help him, to help the whole family through this difficult time, she would. It was good to have a purpose in life again. She had been drifting since Alice's death, letting Gus Blake push her here and there.

Being outside in the fresh air felt like being released from prison after her day in the cramped interior of the cottage. It might be dark now, but the weather had fined up and the moon had risen in a clear sky full of stars. She looked up at them, experiencing her usual pleasure at the way they sparkled down at her.

She had been afraid all day that Gus might turn up looking for her and had kept the door locked, only going outside when necessity drove her. She was ashamed of that fear, but could do nothing about it. But with Aaron beside her she no longer felt afraid.

As he helped her out of the sidecar at the shop he said in a low voice, 'If you like, I'll get hold of Wilf and we'll take you to collect some of your clothes from Rose Villa.'

She felt shaky at the mere thought of confronting Gus. 'Perhaps tomorrow.'

Aaron looked at her, his eyes understanding. 'He frightened you, didn't he? Badly.'

She nodded, swallowing hard against a lump in her throat. She had been over-confident about her own capacity to deal with Gus Blake. Not until last night had she truly understood Jenny's fear of a man attacking her again.

'Then we'll wait till you can face him,' Aaron said gently. 'Lil won't mind you borrowing her clothes. I'm glad you two are getting on well. She needed a friend.'

As they walked into the only shop in North Hey, a place brightly lit by gas, Mrs Arden gaped at Eva. 'You're all right then, love? Only *he* said you were missing!'

'I'm looking after Mrs Brierley for a few days.'

'You'd better tell yon fellow at Rose Villa, then. He's been asking everyone if they've seen you. Said you've been a bit upset since Miss Blake died.'

She might have known Gus would have covered himself against any accusations, Eva thought angrily. 'He can't have found my note, then,' she said as lightly as she could. 'And anyway, it's none of his business what I do. Now, Mrs Brierley and I have made up a list of things we need to buy . . .'

But Aaron noticed that her hand shook as she passed the list across and once again anger rose in him that Blake looked like getting away with what he'd done to her, and to Jenny as well, from what Eva had told him. If he could ever do something to spike that fellow's guns, he damn well would.

As they came out, he loaded the shopping into the sidecar and said, 'I think we'd better pop in at Grandad Gill's before we go back to let Jenny know you're all right.'

'Yes. Thanks.'

She avoided even looking at Rose Villa as they stopped outside Grandad's cottage, hurrying up the path, hoping Gus wouldn't notice them. Even before she got to the front door there was a shriek from inside and Jenny flung it open, clipping Eva in her arms and bursting into tears as she hugged her and drew her inside. There she held her friend at arm's length and started scolding her for worrying them all so much.

'I had to leave suddenly last night. Gus was – being a nuisance.'

Jenny stilled. 'He didn't hurt you, did he?'

'No. But he tried. I got away, though. Climbed out of the window and down the tree. Only I can't – talk about what happened,' Eva said, feeling near to tears again. 'Not yet.'

Without thinking how it'd look, Aaron came to put his arm round her shoulders and say to Jenny, 'Eva just wanted to let you know she was all right. We haven't had our tea yet so we can't stay. Why don't you come over to see her tomorrow?'

Wilf had joined them but was hanging back, as if uncertain whether he should be part of the group.

Aaron looked at him. 'Can you meet me in the pub later, Wilf lad? I'll buy you a glass of ale and tell you what's been happening. I need to discuss something with you.'

Jenny hadn't missed his arm round Eva's shoulders or the way her friend was clinging on to her self-control by the merest thread. 'Tomorrow morning be all right to come visiting, love?'

Eva nodded.

As Aaron helped her into the sidecar she muttered, 'I'm sorry. I don't know why I'm being so stupid and weepy. It just – brought everything back.'

'You're only being human, Eva. Don't be ashamed of that.'

She smiled mistily at him. 'Lil's right. You *are* a kind man, Aaron Brierley.'

That made him feel good all the way home.

15

———◆———

Later that night, Aaron met Wilf in the pub and bought them both a glass of beer. They settled in a corner to discuss what had happened in low voices, after which they sat in thoughtful silence.

'I didn't risk life and limb in the war so that buggers like yon can prance around playing officers still, no, nor treat young women badly,' Wilf said in a low, angry voice. 'By hell, I didn't!'

'Me, neither.'

'What are we going to do about him, then?'

Aaron drew patterns in some spilled beer. 'Not much we can do – without evidence.'

'So how do we get evidence?'

'With difficulty. At the moment I'm working all the hours God sends for another arrogant sod, then when I come home there's Lil.' Aaron paused. 'I can't really do anything while I have her to care for, Wilf. But after she's gone . . .'

'Not an easy time for you.' It was as near as he dared get to offering sympathy.

Aaron shrugged. 'I'm not the first and I won't be the last.' His expression lightened a little. 'But there's Eva now, looking after Lil and the girls. She says she'll stay as long as we need her. Eh, you should see how she's cleaned the place up.' He paused then offered a rare confidence: 'I've been worried sick about Lil dying on her own, but she likes Eva and having a bit of company's brightened her up.'

Wilf allowed himself another small sip of beer. 'Jenny thinks the world of Eva as well, says she's never really treated her like a maid, especially when they were alone together. She says Eva's a bit shy.'

His voice had grown warmer as he spoke of Jenny and Aaron looked sharply at him. 'Getting fond of Jenny Gill, aren't you?'

Wilf avoided his assessing gaze by staring down into his half-empty glass. When he spoke, his voice was low and bitter. 'I've no right to be fond of anyone, have I? I can't even support myself properly and if it weren't for Grandad, I'd be homeless – mind you, I really am helping him, so it's not all one way, but still . . .'

Aaron said no more. Times were hard round Heyshaw and getting harder rapidly. More and more men were being thrown out of work and he would soon be joining them. After another silence, he said casually, 'It wouldn't hurt to keep our eyes on what that bugger's doing, though. We could spread the word to some of the other lads as well, maybe.'

'Wouldn't hurt at all,' Wilf agreed. 'Bob and Stan have plenty of time on their hands. And even Ben notices things.'

'You might see what they can do, then?'

'Be a bit like being in the war again.'

'Yes. The comradeship was good. The rest . . .' He

shrugged. No need to tell Wilf what it had been like. A few minutes later he drained his glass and stood up. 'You stay on a bit, Wilf lad. I don't like to leave them alone for too long.'

The next day Jenny went round to see Eva, waiting impatiently until she thought the Brierley children would have left for school, anxious to find out exactly what had happened.

She looked round the small, dark cottage and studied Eva's face. To her surprise, her friend looked happier than she had since Alice's death. 'You look as if you're enjoying it,' she commented.

'Enjoying what?'

'Having a house and children to look after.'

Eva flushed. 'Well, it gives some point to my life, doesn't it? When I couldn't get a teaching job, I didn't quite know what to do with myself.'

'Miss Blake was right about one thing.' Jenny nodded her head several times for emphasis.

'What do you mean?'

'It is time you found yourself a husband and settled down. But she wasn't right about the man she chose for you. We'll have to look round for someone else, I reckon.'

Eva flushed bright scarlet. 'Don't be silly!'

Jenny didn't say any more, but she knew what she thought.

There was a thumping from upstairs and Eva jumped to her feet. 'I'll just nip up and see what she wants.'

In the bedroom Lil looked at her apologetically. 'I thought I'd better remind you that I can hear every word you say. I'm not trying to eavesdrop, I just can't help it.'

'Let me bring Jenny up, then you can be part of our conference.'

Lil's hand flew up to her hair. 'Oh, no. I look such a mess. I don't want folk to see me like this.'

'Jenny won't mind what you look like.' Then Eva realised how bad Lil's hair was and knew she would be ashamed to look like that, too. 'We could wash your hair for you afterwards, if you like?' she added casually. 'We used to do Alice's and we have it down to a fine art now.'

Lil looked at her with tears in her eyes. 'Eva Kershaw, it was a good day for me when you ran away from that fellow. I hate looking such a mess. *Hate it!* I only ever had my looks to attract Aaron, and now even they're gone.'

'Well, he'll love you again once we've finished with you,' Eva teased.

Lil gave her a look both sad and wise. 'Aaron never did love me. We got married because Gracie was on the way and he's been nothing but kind to me, but I know I'm not the wife he'd have chosen, however much he tries to hide it. I used to drive him batty sometimes with my slapdash ways.'

'Oh, Lil, no!' Eva clasped the other woman's hand.

'Me an' him both paid a high price for our pleasure, didn't we? But he's a good father and I'll not worry about the girls, at least. Sid Linney will sack him after

I'm gone, but Aaron will find a way to look after them. He's a clever man. I wasn't surprised when they made him an officer. Eh, he looked so handsome in his uniform!'

'Why does Sid Linney want to sack him?'

'Because they've never got on and because old Mr Linney was fonder of Aaron than he was of his own son. And who could blame him? I was at school with Sid. He's a coward, allus has been, an' sly with it.'

These confidences gave Eva something else to think about. Poor Aaron! He seemed beset by worries. And she'd only added to them, though she knew she was a big help as well.

Jenny didn't leave till nearly lunchtime and by then Lil was looking clean and well cared for, if exhausted, with shining hair neatly tied back and a clean cardigan and nightdress. Humming to herself, Eva prepared some dainty ham sandwiches for the invalid, cutting off the crusts and trying to make the tray look as attractive as possible.

Just as she was about to carry it upstairs, the door opened and Gus Blake strolled in.

She stopped dead, horrified that she'd forgotten to lock up after Jenny left.

'I thought your stupid friend would lead me to you, and she did.' He glanced round scornfully. 'What the hell are you doing in a hovel like this?'

'Keeping away from you and helping some friends out.'

'You've found a fellow to cuddle up to, more like. I

wasn't wrong, was I? You're dying for it.' He moved forward, his whole attitude menacing.

Upstairs, Lil gasped and sat bolt upright in bed, then reached for her walking stick and thumped hard on the floor.

Gus jerked round. 'What's that?'

'It's Lil,' Eva said quietly, recovering a little of her confidence. 'Aaron's wife, one of my friends. She's ill but she can still hear everything that goes on down here and see some of it through the floorboards.' She glared at him and moved back to the foot of the stairs. 'If you touch me, I'll have a witness this time.'

He stood for a moment, his eyes narrowed in concentration. 'I don't know what you think she'll be a witness to. All I asked was why you've left a good home for this place.'

'And made a few nasty snide remarks. Now please leave the house at once.'

'Yes, do,' said a voice behind him.

Wilf stepped into the room, not as tall as Gus, but wiry and with that upright stance that seemed to mark out many former soldiers, though not Gus Blake, for some reason.

The latter glanced at Eva, his eyes promising that this encounter would not be their last, then walked out of the cottage without a word.

Wilf winked at Eva and followed him.

Gus glanced round as the other man walked after him along the lane. 'You can go back to her now, Horrocks. She was obviously waiting for you.'

'Eva wasn't waiting for anyone,' Wilf said mildly.

'She's looking after a dying woman and her children. Besides, I'm Jenny's friend, not hers.' It was the first open admission he'd made of that and it made him feel proud to say it aloud. He continued to follow, keeping about ten yards' distance between the two of them.

Gus stopped abruptly and turned to face him again. 'What the hell are you doing?'

'Following you to make sure you get back to the village safely.' Wilf's tone was amiable enough, but his expression was grim and determined. 'And while we're chatting so pleasantly, I'll just mention that if you pester Eva Kershaw again *in any way*, there are a few of us in the village who'll take it amiss.'

'Who'd want to touch a frigid bitch like her? I was just worried about her safety.' Gus turned round and walked on down the lane, not looking to see whether he was being followed or not.

Wilf continued to stroll behind him, whistling cheerfully and stopping only when he came to the gates of Rose Villa.

That chap was like no officer he had ever served under. And why was he going after Eva? It didn't make sense. Nothing made sense. Was Jenny right? Did Blake want the house to himself for something illegal? If so, what?

Wilf grinned. She had such a lurid imagination, his lass did, and had already turned the fellow into a murderer, thief, spy and gangster. It was all those films she'd seen. *The Cabinet of Dr Caligari* seemed to have left a particularly vivid impression on her imagination and she'd told him the story of it at least a dozen times.

Eh, he wished he had the money to take her to the pictures, go out walking with her on his arm, even go dancing maybe, though he wasn't so good at that.

Cutting off such thoughts firmly, Wilf went to let Jenny know where he was going and returned to the farm cottage to check that the two women were all right.

He found the door locked and had to knock for admittance. 'You all right now, love?' he asked Eva.

She nodded, but she looked worried.

'Me and the lads will keep an eye on Blake as much as we can,' Wilf offered. 'Just remember to keep the door locked in future.'

'I will. I can't think how I came to forget. But I do have to go out sometimes with the washing or, you know, to visit the outhouse.'

After he'd left she went back upstairs and sat on the end of Lil's bed. 'I don't know what to do about Gus,' she admitted.

'He wants gelding, that one does,' Lil said.

Eva blinked in shock at this frank speech, then gave a snort of laughter. 'Yes, but since we can't do that, I'm worried about bringing danger on you or the girls.'

'Eh, it doesn't matter about me and I doubt he'll even notice them two. You're letting it get to you. Unless . . .' She broke off to stare at Eva. 'He didn't succeed in what he started, did he, the other night?'

'No.'

'Then you'll live to fight another day. I don't believe in letting things get me down.' She glanced sideways into the dressing-table mirror, which had been angled so that she could see herself. 'Eh, I do feel better with my hair looking nice.'

Eva went downstairs again, amused by Lil's ability to dismiss unpleasant thoughts.

By the time the girls came clattering in from school, she had the table laid with scones and jam to keep them going till their father got back. She was touched to see that they again went up to see their mother before eating.

When they came down again Gracie said gruffly, 'Mum's pleased with her hair.' Then, as if afraid of saying anything else, she went to wash her hands without being told, dragging Molly with her as usual. Back at the table, she took a scone, buttering it carefully and then spreading jam to each edge with meticulous care before passing it to her little sister.

Molly took a bite and began chewing, offering Eva one of her quick, shy smiles, oblivious to a smear of jam beside her mouth. Gracie ate her own scone with relish and accepted a second one.

Looking at them only made Eva more determined to take control of her life again. Children gave you such hope for the future. She'd missed being with them.

When Aaron got back he stopped in the doorway, this time expecting to see a warm, firelit room, but still overwhelmed by the reality. It took him a minute to find his voice and keep it steady. 'It's lovely to come home and see everything shining clean like this. Thank you, Eva.'

'I made a start on Lil's room today. She says you sleep in the attic. I'm a bit nervous of that ladder, I'm afraid.'

'Leave the attic to me. I'll bring my dirty clothes and bedding down, though, if you tell me when you want to have a washday. The copper's not bad, actually, soon heats up the water. I can fill it for you the night before.'

As he carried his lunch tin through into the scullery, Eva followed and took it out of his hands. 'I'll wash that out for you and it's my job to pack your lunch in the mornings from now on. You go up and see Lil. She has a surprise for you.'

He took the girls up with him, giving Molly a piggy-back and pretending to chase Gracie, who squealed with laughter. More laughter floated down the stairs as he negotiated the low doorway and pretended to bump Molly's head.

A few minutes later the girls came down to sit expectantly at the table, leaving him alone with Lil. The murmur of voices went on for a while, then he came down with a grimness in his expression that had not been there before.

Eva guessed that Lil had told him what had happened, knew she'd have to talk to him about it later, but didn't say anything just then. She had cooked a hash using a tin of corned beef and with it was serving some dried peas that she'd soaked and boiled up. She only dared try simple things till she got the hang of this kitchen range and anyway, she wasn't the world's best cook.

As they ate, Gracie spoke about her day and Aaron encouraged Molly to tell him things with quiet questions.

When Eva got up to tidy up the kitchen, he looked at his daughters. 'Aren't you going to help?'

His tone was mild but both girls jumped to their feet at once and started carrying crockery into the scullery, though Gracie had a sulky expression on her face.

While they were doing that Aaron turned his chair round to sit staring into the fire. It looked as tidy as the rest of the room, no ashes spilling out. Eva was talking about black leading it to make it look better. This was a poor sort of place, but she'd already set her mark on it and made it feel more homelike. Not a word of complaint from her, just cheerful hard work. He sighed. He could get used to this all too easily, must keep reminding himself that Eva was only here for a short time.

There was always a serpent in Eden, though, wasn't there? In his case it was four of them: his leg, Lil's illness, Sid Linney and Gus Blake.

Lil had been so pathetically proud of her newly washed hair, as if that made her skeletal face look any more attractive. And she'd clearly loved the way Jenny and Eva had come up to chat to her. He'd wanted to weep as she'd told him about it. Instead he'd managed to praise her and even stroke her shining hair, forcing words past the lump choking his throat.

He realised Molly was bringing back some of the washed crockery and setting the table for morning, very self-important as she put each plate carefully in place.

'There's a good lass,' he told her, enjoying her proud smile.

Gracie came in with the knives and forks, still looking sulky. 'What's wrong with you?' he asked. 'You've got a face like a wet Friday.'

She shrugged and went to set them out on the table.

'What's wrong?' he insisted, catching hold of her arm as she came round to his side.

Her sulky expression dissolved into tears and she glanced towards the stairs. 'Mum should be doing the washing up, not *her*,' she said in a whisper. 'It's Mum's kitchen and I want her ba-a-ack.' She began to sob.

'Come here.' He patted his knee invitingly and when she didn't move, pulled her across to sit on his lap, though she had said she was too big to sit there any more. As she sobbed into his chest, trying desperately to keep her weeping quiet so that her mother wouldn't hear, he patted her back and made soothing noises.

Eva peered into the room, saw what was going on and tugged Molly back into the scullery. 'Let's give you a good wash and leave Gracie with your dad,' she whispered. 'I have a towel here and we can wrap you in it when you're finished so that you can put some clean clothes on tomorrow.' She hadn't mentioned it but both girls smelled sour.

'We haven't got any clean clothes,' Molly whispered.

'Then I'll give your dirty ones a quick wash through tonight and let them dry in front of the fire. Do you have another nightie?'

The child shook her head and her whisper grew even fainter. 'The only other things I have are my Sunday things. I tore my other skirt last week. There's an old skirt of Gracie's I can have but it's too big for me. Mrs Harrop said she'd cut it down, but she forgot an' Gracie says not to bother Mum about it.'

Eva wondered what Molly's proper voice sounded

like. So far she had only heard her whisper. She didn't comment on that, but finished washing the child. 'Right, let me wrap you in this towel and we'll go upstairs. You can show me exactly what clothes you've got, eh? Don't look at your father and Gracie as we go through the kitchen, though, or say anything to them.'

As Eva picked up the towel-wrapped child to give her a hug, enjoying the smell of newly washed skin, Molly leaned closer to whisper in her ear, 'Gracie cries in bed sometimes, when she thinks I'm asleep. I don't let on to Dad.'

Eva felt near to tears herself at the agony behind these confidences. She set Molly down again and said, 'Don't tell her I know, either. She'd be embarrassed.'

Molly nodded and leaned against her for a minute with a sigh.

They lit a candle and went upstairs by its flickering light. Gracie didn't even notice them passing through the kitchen, but Aaron looked up and his face softened at the sight of them, hand in hand.

Lil was asleep in the front bedroom, a half-smile on her face, so Eva put one finger to her lips and they crept past the doorway into the girls' room. She had tidied it a little, but had not yet had time to give it a thorough bottoming. There was a double bed and a chest of drawers, that was all. 'Where are your things, dear?'

Molly obligingly opened the bottom drawer. In it were a couple of pairs of ragged knickers, which had been worn already, and another vest and liberty bodice in the same condition as the ones she'd just taken off.

Over the back of a chair were a few pieces of outer clothing, most looking in need of repair.

'Which is the skirt that needs cutting down?' Eva asked.

Molly fished out a crumpled grey check skirt from underneath the pile on the chair.

'Let's measure it against you and I'll take it up. Now, find me some of Gracie's knickers, will you, and a pair of yours, so that I can wash them through?'

When the two of them went down again, Gracie was sitting on the rag rug leaning against her father's knees, looking exhausted.

'I'm just going to wash a few of the children's underthings,' Eva told Aaron, then looked at the child sitting beside him. 'Molly's sorted out some of yours, Gracie. Now, the kettle looks to be boiling, so why don't you come and wash yourself all over before you go to bed.'

The sulky look came back on Gracie's face. 'What's the use of washing ourselves when our nighties are dirty?'

'They won't be tomorrow night,' Eva said firmly. 'And anyway, your bodies will feel nicer when they're clean.'

'Go on, love,' Aaron said quietly.

With a loud, aggrieved sigh, Gracie went across the room into the scullery, with Molly trailing behind her.

Eva carried the hot water through and refilled the heavy kettle.

'I can wash myself,' Gracie said when she turned round.

'I know you can, dear.' She went back into the kitchen, set the kettle on the hob again and sat down opposite Aaron, saying in a low voice, 'I'm afraid they both need new clothes, especially Molly. Every single thing they've got is dirty and they haven't got much.'

'I thought Mrs Harrop was seeing to that sort of thing. I've been giving her money for new knickers and things.'

'There's nothing new in the girls' room.'

He scowled into the fire. 'She's been cheating me, then. I'll go and see her about that.' He hesitated then admitted in a gruff, embarrassed voice, 'I haven't got much spare money at the moment.'

'Oh.'

The girls came back. 'Will you fill our hot water piggy, Dad?' Gracie asked.

Eva watched him get up. The kettle was too heavy when it was full and the girls were forbidden to try to lift it. She approved of that. So many children were scalded in accidents.

By the time Aaron came down again from putting them to bed, she knew what she had to do. 'Can you come with me to Rose Villa after work tomorrow? I need to get my clothes and there are some of Alice's old things I can alter for the girls. We can bring them back in your sidecar, if that's all right.'

He was silent for so long she grew worried she'd said something to upset him.

He looked up and said with a rasp of scornful laughter, 'It's the lame helping the halt, isn't it, you and me?'

She decided that only frankness would serve. 'Well, you *are* helping me, perhaps more than you realise. And I'm glad to be helping you . . . all of you.' She swallowed hard as she admitted, 'I'm still frightened of going back and facing Gus, but it has to be done. Could we get Wilf to come along with us as well, do you think? Gus can be very – difficult. I'll feel better if there are two of you to keep an eye on him while I pack.'

'I'll nip along and ask Wilf later.' Aaron spoke matter-of-factly, but before his injuries he could have dealt with Gus Blake on his own, he knew, and that thought galled him.

'While you're gone I'll wash these things through for the girls, then tomorrow I'll do a proper wash. If you have some dirty things, could you bring them down tonight, please, so that I can put them to soak?'

'I should have noticed the girls were short of clothes, shouldn't I?' he asked as he came down with a pile of clothing.

'You've had a lot of other things on your mind.'

He shook his head. 'I should still have noticed. Look, tomorrow we'll get fish and chips for tea, because you'll be tired after a day's washing.' He hesitated then said, 'Don't try to do everything at once. I didn't mean to use you as a skivvy. Just wash a few things, eh?'

'Oh, I like to keep busy.'

'Eva –' He broke off and went to put on his outdoor things.

She didn't ask what he had been going to say. There were a lot of things she wished she could say, too.

He was out for half an hour and when he came back, sat down in front of the fire again. 'Wilf will help us tomorrow.'

'Good.' His expression was so sad that without thinking she leaned across to lay one hand on his shoulder. His hand came up to clasp hers for a moment, then he looked sideways at their hands and stiffened, before standing up abruptly and backing away from her. 'I'll – um – go and see if Lil's all right.' He hurried upstairs.

She shouldn't have touched him, she decided, putting some of the dirty clothes to soak in buckets of water in which she'd dissolved some washing soda. Then she turned the girls' knickers round, hoping they would dry overnight in front of the fire.

Aaron didn't come down again. She must have embarrassed him, though that was the last thing she'd intended. What had got into her? She didn't usually go round touching people. Only . . . he'd looked so very unhappy.

The following day Eva worked hard but made time for a few quiet chats with Lil in between the various tasks. She'd forgotten what heavy work washing was, because from Rose Villa they'd sent it out to a washerwoman. Before he'd left, Aaron had filled the small copper in the corner of the scullery, carrying buckets across from the slopstone pump and tipping them in. He'd then lit a fire under it.

While she was waiting for it to heat up, Eva sorted out the washing, then grated up some of the hard chunk of Sunlight soap which was all she could find. It was like the washdays of her childhood, gruellingly hard physical work.

After rubbing the clothes on the washing board, trying to get the worst of the stains out because she didn't have time to boil them today, she washed and rinsed them, then put them through the mangle. Gradually the wooden clothes horse in front of the fire filled with clothes and the cottage with steam as they dried.

It was well past midday before she'd finished and she looked ruefully at her reddened hands. She even rubbed in a little butter, trying to soften them, but it didn't seem to help much.

She felt increasingly apprehensive as the afternoon wore on because she was dreading confronting Gus, but she had to get some of her own possessions. And she knew it was even more important to confront her fear of him.

When the girls came home she automatically got them a snack then turned the washing round on the rickety wooden clothes horse. She had got most of their things dry, at least. She picked up some mending and took it to the table where the oil lamp was shedding a circle of clear light. Best to keep busy. She never quite knew when Aaron would come home.

Today he came back early. 'I thought we'd go and get your things before tea, then pick up the fish and chips on the way back.' His face was unsmiling, his manner distant. 'I'll just put on my leg brace then we'll be off.'

She'd noticed his limp was worse than usual but didn't comment. Putting on Lil's coat and a headscarf, she followed him outside.

'You might as well ride on the back. It'll be quicker. I'll not go too fast.' He kick-started the motor with his good leg and gestured to her.

So she clambered on behind him and put her hands hesitantly round his waist. His body felt firm and strong against hers, and the intimacy of the position made her flush.

He stopped outside Grandad Gill's cottage and Wilf came out, followed by Jenny.

'It'll be quicker if I come and help you, love,' she said to Eva, her expression grim.

'Are you sure?'

'Yes.'

Aaron chugged slowly across to Rose Villa and parked as near to the front door as he could, waiting for Wilf and Jenny to join them. Before he could knock, the door opened and Gus appeared.

'What do *you* want?'

Eva moved forward into the light that spilled from the hall. 'He's come to help me get my things.' To her enormous relief Gus fell back and let her in.

'Make sure you don't take anything that doesn't belong to you,' he threw at her.

'And you make sure you speak politely to Miss Kershaw!' Aaron snapped.

Wilf came in out of the darkness and stepped to Aaron's side, thumbs locked into his belt, eyes cold and steady.

Eva stared from one man to the other. The atmosphere felt charged with animosity. It made her truly understand the phrase 'if looks could kill'. Telling herself not to be so fanciful and just get on with it, she went into her sitting room. Her cry of shock brought the others rushing to her side. Someone had broken into her desk, leaving her papers scattered all over the place.

Aaron took charge and it wasn't till much later that Eva realised how instinctively they'd all obeyed him.

'Go and check your bedroom before we do anything else, Eva. Take Jenny with you and don't touch anything up there till you've reported back to me.'

Wilf grinned. This was how an officer should behave. He'd never seen Aaron Brierley quite like this before, but now he had, he would have bet a quid that during his Army days Aaron's men had jumped to it when he gave an order. Eh, it was strange how the war had brought out the best in some men – and the worst in others.

Eva and Jenny ran up the stairs and found the same story in her bedroom. Someone had ransacked it, tossing clothes around and making no attempt to hide what they'd been doing. It could only have been Gus.

'Someone's gone through my things up there as well,' Eva called down indignantly to Aaron.

He turned and yelled, 'Hoy! Blake. Get out here.'

Gus came storming out of the sitting room. 'Who do you think you're talking to?'

'You. The sod as ransacked Miss Kershaw's things.'

'I wasn't *ransacking* them but searching for clues as

to where she was.' He glared at Eva. 'If you will vanish without a word, you must expect people to worry.'

'You know why I left.'

He breathed in deeply and turned on his heel.

'Go and fetch Mr Beaman, Eva,' Aaron said. 'I think he should see this.'

Gus spun round. 'You mind your own business, Brierley!'

'Miss Kershaw is my business as long as she's living with us.'

'I bet she is.'

Eva left them standing bristling at one another, running across the road to bang on Mr Beaman's door, determined to tell him everything.

The housekeeper looked at her sourly. 'I told you last time, he doesn't like being disturbed at home.'

'I wouldn't have come unless it were an emergency.'

Mr Beaman appeared behind the housekeeper. 'It's all right, Mrs Pannell. I'll deal with this. Please come in, Miss Kershaw. I'm glad to see you're all right. Mr Blake was worried when you went missing.'

'I went missing because he tried to – to –' she could feel her face going scarlet, but was determined to say it – 'force his attentions on me. I had to climb out of the bedroom window to get away and he chased me across the field.'

The lawyer stared at her in shock. 'Have you reported this to the police?'

'What good would that do? I have no proof. I took refuge with Mr Brierley and his family and I'm going to stay there for a while. He has two little girls and his wife is ill, so they need help. I don't think Lil has long to live.'

Eric Beaman began to nibble at his forefinger. 'You're probably right,' he said in the end. 'The police could do nothing and in such cases they can be very harsh with a woman who complains. But I'm glad you've told me and I do believe you about why you left. In fact, I've been feeling concerned about your position ever since the wedding was stopped. Unfortunately the will is very explicit in allowing him to stay at the house for a year, so I can do nothing to prevent that.' He shook his head. 'Now, is that all or did you have some other reason for coming to see me tonight?'

'My rooms at Rose Villa have been ransacked. Before I collect my clothes, I'd like you to see them. Mr Brierley, Mr Horrocks and Miss Gill are at the house now, making sure nothing is touched. Will you come and take a look?'

'Very sensible of you. Yes, indeed I shall.'

'It was Mr Brierley's idea to fetch you.'

'That doesn't surprise me. He was, I'm told, a very able officer until he was injured.'

Funny, she thought as they walked across the road together, how each time she saw Mr Beaman he seemed to unbend a little more.

To her relief Gus had vanished again. She showed Mr Beaman round the house and he inspected her sitting room and bedroom in silence. The bolt had been screwed back to the inside of her bedroom door again, she noticed, as if to give the lie to her claims. She pointed it out to them, however, and told them it had been missing before.

Wilf went to examine it. 'There are scratch marks round it. I didn't make those when I fixed the bolt on for you. I'm not that bad a workman.'

Both Mr Beaman and Aaron examined it, exchanging frowns.

'You don't know whether anything is missing?' the lawyer asked Eva.

'It's hard to tell.'

'Jewellery?'

'I only have a locket and I always wear that.' She pulled it out to show him. 'Would it be all right for me to take my clothes now?'

'Yes. I think we've seen enough to assess the situation.'

'And can I take Alice's things as well? The will said they were mine and I don't have much money left now, so they'll come in useful.'

'You'd have plenty of money if you got married. Don't dismiss the possibility.'

'There is no one.' She led the way briskly downstairs, not wanting to pursue the point, but stopped as she saw Gus waiting at the foot of the stairs.

'What's she been saying about me?' he demanded. 'A pack of lies, I'm sure.'

Mr Beaman looked at him coldly. 'Miss Kershaw has merely been showing me the damage done to her part of the house, presumably by you?'

'I was trying to find some sign of where she'd gone. She could have been lying dead on the moors, for all I knew.' Gus's colour was high and he met the lawyer's gaze with a hard, angry stare.

'What you have done is for your own conscience. However, although I cannot ask you to leave the house, I can assure you that there will be weekly inspections of the premises and if anything is missing, you will be held liable. Some perfume has been broken in Miss Kershaw's room and a bottle of what I believe is skin lotion. You will, I am sure, wish to replace those. You may leave the new ones with me to pass on to her or give her the money to buy her own.'

With a snort of disgust Gus fumbled in his pocket. 'How much?'

Eva hesitated, not wanting his money, then reminded herself that she could not afford to refuse it and named the exact sum.

He tossed it on the floor in front of her so that the coins rolled here and there. That made her angry, so she turned to the lawyer before picking them up. 'He broke Alice's little china figurine as well, the Royal Doulton one she loved so much. Perhaps the rest of the ornaments should be packed away if he's so clumsy?'

'Excellent idea, Miss Kershaw. I shall send my clerk across to do that tomorrow. Perhaps you and Miss Gill would come and assist him? Shall we say ten o'clock? You will know which things are delicate. I can pay you hourly rates for the work.'

'I don't need –' Eva began, but Jenny elbowed her in the ribs. 'I mean, thank you very much, Mr Beaman. I –' Another dig of the elbow made her amend that to, 'I mean, *we* shall be happy to help your clerk.'

Gus growled something indistinguishable, swung on his heel and vanished into the sitting room, slamming the door behind him so hard the ornaments on the hall table rattled.

Wilf picked up the coins and handed them to Eva.

'Have you checked the kitchen?' Jenny asked suddenly.

They filed down and found it in a mess with the pantry door open and the padlock missing.

'The food in the pantry was mine,' Eva said angrily. 'He's taken the padlock off and stolen some of it.'

Mr Beaman studied it carefully. 'I fear it would not be worth calling in the police, though it is indeed stealing. But with such a small amount, you're better simply taking what's left.' He inclined his head to them all. 'I think you have enough helpers to keep you safe, Miss Kershaw, but don't hesitate to call me if you need my help again.' A wintry smile creased his features briefly. 'Even after hours.'

When he'd gone, the two women packed Eva's better clothes in a suitcase, then bundled everything else that might be useful into some sheets, including Alice's clothes and toiletries, which Gus hadn't touched, taking them down to Aaron and Wilf.

'The sidecar's full,' Aaron said an hour later. 'If you'll stay with the ladies, Wilf, I'll take the first load home and come back for anything else.'

'My pleasure.' Wilf had not stopped grinning since Mr Beaman left.

Eva felt deeply sad at how things had turned out, as well as relieved that Gus had remained in the sitting

room. But there were enough staples like flour, sugar
and currants left to supplement the Brierleys' food and
she was pleased to be able to make a contribution. She
could see how his lack of money was galling Aaron, but
you couldn't afford to be proud when you had so little,
as Jenny had just reminded her.

'I'll come to the cottage to collect you tomorrow
morning so you can do your shopping,' Jenny said as
she gave Eva a farewell hug. 'You don't want to walk
along that lane alone.'

'And I'll go and sit with Lil,' Wilf added.

Eva felt tears well in her eyes as they drove away
from Grandad's. It was wonderful having such good
friends.

Aaron stopped the motor bike outside the chip shop
and fumbled in his pocket, pressing some money into
her hand. 'Here. You go in and get fish and chips for us
all.'

She let him give it her, though she now had her
handbag back and a little money of her own, because
she knew it was important to him not to take any more
charity than he needed.

From the bright warmth of the chip shop she glanced
out of the window to see him sitting hunched up
against the cold on his motor bike. He looked very
alone. She did wish she could help him more.

With a click of her tongue at her own foolishness, she
cut that thought off abruptly and turned to pay for the
food. She was helping him as much as she could, as
much as he would allow.

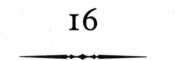

16

The following morning Eva got up early and began to unpack, relieved to have her own clothes back. Last night she'd put the food away carefully, but had been too tired to do anything about the other things.

She got breakfast, saw Aaron and the girls off, then hunted through the bundles. When she'd found what she was looking for, she smiled and took the garment upstairs. 'Here.' She held out one of Alice's dainty bed jackets to Lil. 'I brought this for you. Try it on.' She draped the pink and blue garment that Alice had knitted herself round Lil's thin shoulders.

'It's lovely!' Lil stroked it and then looked at Eva, tears in her eyes. 'You're so good to us.'

'We're helping one another.' She picked up the other things and laid them in Lil's lap. 'These were Alice's too. There's lavender water and face powder and hand cream.'

The thin hand was still caressing the fine wool as Lil stared down at the bottles. 'Oh, Eva, are you sure?' she asked with a catch in her voice.

'Of course I am. You enjoy them. Look, let me open the lavender water then you can put some on.'

Lil sniffed ecstatically then beamed at Eva and

patted the bed. 'Sit down a minute. Tell me again about that will of Miss Blake's, what it said you should do? I've been trying to get it straight in my head and I can't.'

'It doesn't matter.'

'Please. I hate it when I can't work things out. They fret at me.' She raised her wrist to her nostrils and sniffed again, still smiling gently. 'Go on. Tell me before you leave then I'll have something to think about today.'

So Eva explained the provisions of Alice's will once more.

There was a long silence, then Lil frowned. 'What happens to that nasty sod if you get married before the end of the year?'

'I don't know. As I'm not likely to—'

'You don't know about that. A year can be a long time. Eh, I wish I still had a year left. I'd give anything to see another spring.'

Eva took her hand. 'Oh, Lil.'

'Don't get soft on me.' She sniffed and swallowed hard. 'And don't change the subject, either. They call me stupid, but if my whole future depended on something, I'd check on every single detail till I understood. Can you find out what'd happen if you got wed sooner than the end of the year?'

'There's no need, surely?'

'For me,' Lil coaxed, with one of her wide grins. 'Go on. Humour a dying woman.'

Eva could not help smiling back at her. 'Humour a bossy woman, more like.'

But her questions had made Eva wonder so she decided to write a note to Mr Beaman while she was at Rose Villa. She'd give it to his clerk to deliver.

Jenny wasn't alone when she arrived to go shopping with Eva. 'Wilf said he'd look after Lil if she didn't mind having a man around the place. I know you'll feel better if she's not on her own.'

Eva gave her a hug then gave Wilf one too for good measure, before running up to tell Lil she'd got a gentleman visitor and help her straighten the bed.

'Good thing I've got my new bedjacket,' Lil said proudly. 'I could entertain the King in this, couldn't I?'

Jenny and Eva walked briskly along the lane to the main road. It was a fine day and even though it was chilly, the winter sunshine felt good on their faces. They stopped at the gates of Rose Villa, intending to wait for the clerk before going in.

'The car's gone!' Jenny exclaimed. 'It was here when we left to come and get you, because Wilf had a quick squiz. I wonder where he's gone?' She frowned and looked at Eva. 'He goes away quite a lot, doesn't he? Have you any idea what he does on these trips?'

'None at all and I don't care. I only wish he'd never come back!'

The clerk arrived and they all went inside. The place was in a mess, though there had been an attempt to tidy up the kitchen.

'Dear me!' said the clerk. 'My wife would think this very bad housekeeping.'

'So would we,' said Jenny, looking round in disgust. 'Where shall we start?'

'How about in Alice's sitting room?' Eva suggested. 'It'd be better to do that while Gus is away.'

The two women sorted out the ornaments and other bric-a-brac, taking them into the kitchen where the clerk sat at the table making detailed lists.

Not long afterwards a carter came up from Heyshaw to deliver a pile of tea chests filled with straw. He carried them inside, looking round curiously. 'There you are. I'll be back at four to pick them up as arranged.'

Eva watched him pat the patient horses, then swing up into the driving seat and shake the reins. As the cart moved off, she turned to Jenny. 'Aaron says in a few years everyone will be using motor lorries to transport things. It'll be a pity for the horses, won't it? Do you suppose one day there won't be any?'

'Eh, who knows? But it'll not be a pity about the droppings they leave everywhere. They may be good for the garden, but it's not much fun to step in a pile, is it?'

'Trust you to think of that, Jenny Gill!'

'I'm the practical one; you're the dreamer.'

'I'm not getting much dreaming done at the moment.' Eva spread out her reddened hands for inspection. 'I've only time for practical things.'

On the way back to the cottage Eva stopped to buy some pork chops and cabbage, waving at poor Ben Luccan, who was sitting outside the house as he did every fine day. Jenny had insisted on accompanying her, though there had been no sign of Gus returning to the village.

'Shall I send the bill to the house as usual, Miss Kershaw?' the butcher asked.

'No, I'll pay now. I'm looking after a sick friend and I'm buying everything as I need it, not running up any bills.'

'But Mr Blake said—'

'If he's been buying things you should send those bills to him personally.'

He frowned at her. 'My Blake said it was for the house. Been buying steaks and all sorts of stuff, he has. No cheap cuts for him.'

Eva exchanged disgusted glances with Jenny. 'You should tell Mr Beaman about that. I shall continue to pay for everything I buy.'

As they walked up the hill towards the lane, Jenny let out a little snort. 'Blake doesn't miss a trick, does he?'

'No. I wonder what other surprises he has up his sleeve for us.'

'Aaron and my Wilf will fettle him if he tries anything on us from now on,' Jenny said confidently.

'My Wilf?' Eva teased.

Jenny blushed, then tossed her head. 'There's nothing definite, but you can tell when a fellow's interested. And if he doesn't do something about it, I will.'

When her friend and Wilf had gone home again, Eva sighed. She envied Jenny. She only wished she had a fellow of her own. Oh, she was being stupid. What fellow had ever been interested in her?

She went up to see Lil who was looking pale but happy, and smelled of a fresh application of lavender water.

*   *   *

In the pub that night Sid Linney was sitting on his own looking bored. Gus hesitated by the table. 'Want some company?'

Sid grinned. 'Why not? Beaman won't be in tonight. He's attending some sort of fancy lawyers' dinner over in Rochdale.'

Gus slid into a chair. 'How are things going at the farm?'

'How'd you expect with a labourer who can't even walk properly?'

'Brierley?'

Sid nodded. 'If it weren't for his wife . . .'

'He's relying on that, isn't he? He's got Miss Kershaw looking after the poor woman now. He's a real expert at playing on folks' pity. I recognised his sort at once. We had one or two chaps like him in our company, but in the Army you could make them toe the line.'

Sid glanced sideways at Gus. 'I heard Miss Kershaw was staying with him. They said you drove her away from Rose Villa.'

Gus forced a laugh. 'I was just flirting, but she took it amiss. Talk about a cast-iron maiden! Now that I know my wife is alive, I'm a reformed character, but Eva won't believe me.'

'Is Mrs Blake coming up here to live with you, then?'

'No. I'll only be here for a few months. I have some temporary business in the north, so it's very convenient to have Rose Villa. My wife is staying down in London, but I visit her every now and then. A chap needs his rations, doesn't he? If it weren't for that, who'd want to marry?'

'You're right there, by heck you are. Bloody women! I caught my wife slipping Brierley some eggs today. What does she think I am, a bloody charity? As soon as Lil dies, he's out, whatever *she* says.'

'I don't believe in letting women rule the roost. Here, let me get you another one.'

Gus changed the topic when he brought the drinks back but was pleased to think of Brierley being thrown out of house and job. Pity his wife was taking so long to die. Before he wound up his business in this part of the country, he'd make sure he paid Brierley back – and Miss Tight Knickers, too. It took a lot to get him angry because it was a tiring emotion and he liked a quiet life, but those two had done it.

Two days later Wilf walked along the lane to take Mr Beaman's reply to Eva. A shower caught him halfway, but he hardly noticed it because he was feeling down in the dumps. Living with Jenny was becoming more and more of a strain. She wasn't pretty, but she had a comfortable face, especially when she laughed, as she did often, and she was really good company. Even playing draughts and halma with her was fun. She was just – well, right for him.

He wanted to tell her how he felt about her. Hell, he'd never wanted anything as much in his life. Surely soon he'd find a job? There had to be something a man like him could do apart from the odd night's work in the pub.

They said there was work still in the south, but like Jenny and Eva he didn't want to leave Heyshaw. It wasn't just her and Grandad. There was Aaron, a good friend now, and one or two other lads he saw at the pub. It was home, the only real home he'd ever known. After the war he'd missed his brother dreadfully and had spent a few weeks travelling aimlessly round the country, looking for somewhere to settle.

In Heyshaw he'd found it. You didn't leave that behind unless you were forced to.

Eva waited till Wilf had left before she opened Mr Beaman's letter. It was short and to the point:

> *Dear Miss Kershaw*
>
> *In response to your query: should you marry someone else before the year is up, Mr Blake will have to leave the house. You will not only have sole possession, but will inherit Alice Blake's entire estate. The will specifies only that you must marry in order to inherit; it doesn't say to whom.*
>
> *If I can help in any other way, please do not hesitate to contact me.*
>
> *Yours sincerely,*
> *Eric P. Beaman*

'Nothing wrong, is there?' Aaron asked from his chair by the fire, clicking his tongue in annoyance as he dropped his pincers on the worn rag rug and bent to pick them up. He was mending the heel of one of his boots, using an improvised last made from a chunk of wood and making a good job of it as far as Eva could tell. Was there nothing he couldn't fix?

She stuffed the letter hastily into her apron pocket. 'No, just some information from Mr Beaman about Alice's will.' She was tired but hauled herself to her feet. There was always something to do here, she'd found.

Aaron was up before her, putting one hand on her shoulder. 'Sit down. I don't like to see you looking so tired. I'll make the cocoa tonight. I'll just see if Lil wants a cup.'

So Eva stayed in the chair, rocking gently and staring into the fire. She could not stop thinking of the letter and wishing there were someone she could marry. It'd make life so much easier. Then she remembered how reluctant she had been to marry Gus and shook her head. How could she possibly marry a stranger?

Aaron came back down. 'She's asleep.' He set about making the cocoa, frowning. 'She never used to sleep so much.'

Eva didn't pretend. 'She's very weak now.'

He paused for a moment, eyes closed, pain on his face. 'Yes, I suppose so.' Then the kettle boiled and he lifted it carefully off the hob, pouring water into their cups, stirring carefully before adding milk. 'There you are.'

She began to sip the cocoa, feeling lazy and tired.

'I wanted to thank you for giving those things to Lil,' he said abruptly in a low voice. 'They've made her so happy. I should have remembered how much she liked pretty things and bought her something occasionally.'

'You did the best you could, I'm sure.'

'But it hasn't been good enough, has it? She got ill again, the children need your charity to clothe their bodies, and what we'll do when Sid Linney sacks me doesn't bear thinking of.'

They continued to sip the cocoa in companionable silence, then he finished repairing the shoe heel and they went on to chat more generally. Wilf brought over the occasional used newspaper from the pub and they would both devour these, hungry for news from the world outside the small, crowded cottage, discussing what had happened energetically.

Unemployment remained high, especially in the north, and both of them agreed that the government was doing too little for the people of Lancashire. The cotton industry seemed to have collapsed and although some said it would revive again, Aaron wasn't sure. They were behind the times in Lancashire now, he said. Their machinery was old while other countries like America had new equipment which could produce cotton goods more cheaply and efficiently.

A friend of Aaron's, who had lost his job, was entitled only to fifteen shillings a week for fifteen weeks, with one shilling per week for each child, and was worrying himself sick. The new National Insurance Act was hard on ordinary people. The money it provided was barely enough to survive on and after it had been used up, what then?

'Poor man!' Eva said softly.

Aaron nodded. It'd be his turn next, he was sure.

'Trade unions are trying to help their members,' he

said, 'but there's a limit to what they can afford to do.'

'They were saying in the shop that the church in Littleborough has set up a soup kitchen,' Eva commented.

'I should be shamed to feed my family that way,' he said gruffly. 'I'd pawn everything I owned first.'

Eva looked at him sympathetically. Everyone knew the pawnshops were doing a thriving trade, because Lancashire folk were proud and hated to ask for charity. Look at Wilf, how touchy he could get if you offered him anything.

'And yet,' Aaron added thoughtfully, 'down the road in Heyshaw lives a man who's made a small fortune in the brief post-war textile boom, before selling his mill and retiring in style. His former employees won't be able to retire in style, but at least Charles Manning and his wife provide work for a few people in their fine new home and garden.'

'It's never fair, is it?' Eva said. 'Some people have so much and others – well, they're struggling to put bread on the table.' She hesitated, then confided, 'I hated my mother, but I can understand now how afraid she was after my father was killed. She was left with four young children to feed and only my older brother Percy of working age. His wages were barely enough to manage on.'

Aaron leaned back in his chair, stretching tiredly. 'You're fond of your brothers and sisters, aren't you?'

'Yes, especially my sisters. Though we're all three as

different as chalk, cheese,' she hesitated and finished with a chuckle, 'and parkin.'

'Shall you go and live with one of them after Lil dies?'

'I might go to Lizzie, if I have to, but I hate the thought of being a burden on her and Peter.' She watched Aaron covertly. His face was partly hidden by the shadows, a strong face, with a firm chin and dark, steady eyes. Tonight his whole body looked weary. She knew his bad leg ached at night, because she'd seen him rubbing it when he thought no one was looking. 'What are *you* going to do, Aaron, you and the girls – afterwards?'

He shook his head. 'I don't know. I lie awake at night worrying about that. I don't have any family left, you see. Grandad Gill has offered to take us in temporarily if we're stuck, only how can I impose on him like that, let alone his cottage isn't really big enough? And the girls are a bit young to go on the tramp, don't you think?' A yawn caught him by surprise and he began to gather his things together. 'I think I'd better get up to bed now or I'll be fit for nothing in the morning. Goodnight, Eva. Thanks for all you're doing for us.'

'It's my pleasure.' And it was.

When he'd gone she sat on for a while, thinking about the quiet hour they'd enjoyed together. That was what it must be like to be married to someone with whom you got on well: sitting and chatting together, playing with the children, making a home. Quiet pleasures, the ones she enjoyed most.

Jenny was right. Eva did want a home of her own and

children. Why had she never met anyone she could marry? What was wrong with her that young men had never shown an interest?

Two days later Dr Stott turned up at the cottage in the afternoon. Lil said he came every few weeks, whenever he felt like it, but this time Eva had sent a message to him by Jenny, wanting to know what she should do for the best to help Lil.

'You're looking well, my dear,' he greeted her.

'I'm feeling well.'

He looked round with a grimace. 'I didn't think to find you living in such conditions. Alice would be very upset.'

'It's Alice's will that's made it necessary for me to find a home and work,' Eva said sharply, then tried to smile at him. She had always found him and his wife pleasant enough, though rather snobbish.

He harrumphed and cleared his throat. 'Well, I'd better examine my patient, had I not?'

He went upstairs and she couldn't help overhearing. He talked to Lil very differently from the way he talked to her, as if Lil were an ignorant child. Eva was surprised by that, wouldn't have thought it of him. Yet when he came down ten minutes later, looking grave, he was his old self with her again.

She put one finger to her lips and pointed upstairs to warn him to speak quietly, then whispered, 'Can you tell me how she is, what I should be doing to help her?'

'She's looking brighter than last time. I'm afraid the only thing you can do for her is what you've been doing already: keep her happy. It can't be long now – days, a week or two.'

Eva stared at him in horror. 'Are you sure? She's seemed so much better lately.'

'Her lungs are in very poor condition and she tells me you have to help her to do everything now. If she's lucky she'll die in her sleep. If not she'll get pneumonia and die more painfully. Are you sure you should be taking on this job, my dear? Didn't you do enough with Alice?'

Eva bowed her head. 'The Brierleys took me in when I had nowhere to go. I *want* to help them. Besides, I've grown fond of Lil and the girls.'

'But I thought you had Rose Villa for a year, whether you married or not?'

'Gus Blake is still living there. He was being . . . difficult.'

Dr Stott looked round with an expression of disgust, making no attempt to keep his voice down. 'But still, to come to this!'

She raised her chin. 'I feel privileged to be able to help Lil and her family. I'd forgotten what life can be like when you're short of money. It's done me good.'

When he'd gone, Lil knocked on the floor. She was lying in bed propped up with pillows and was, Eva thought sadly, looking more insubstantial by the day. 'What can I get you, dear? A nice cup of tea?'

Lil looked at her with frightened eyes. 'I heard what that old bugger was saying. It won't be long now, will it?'

Eva hesitated, but it didn't seem right to lie. 'No.'

'You will stay with me at the end, won't you? I shan't be nearly as afraid if you're with me.'

'Yes. Of course I will.'

Lil sighed and sagged back against the pillows. 'That's good, then. After the weekend I want to talk to you. Seriously. On Monday morning, when they're all out.'

'Very well.'

The weekend passed very slowly. Lil hardly stirred, but insisted Eva help her into a pretty bed jacket each morning. When the children visited her, she lay and smiled absent-mindedly at them, saying very little. After they came downstairs again, Molly usually vanished under the table with her rag doll.

Gracie would sit around looking sullen, helping with the housework if you asked her, but not volunteering.

'Can you sew?' Eva asked the day after the doctor's visit, hoping to distract her.

The child shrugged. 'We do it at school, but Miss Matcham makes us sew bloomers and combinations. When you can't afford the material, the school gives you some and it's horrid scratchy stuff. No one wants to wear them.'

'How about making some French knickers, then? They're very fashionable.'

There was a flicker of interest on Gracie's face and she began fiddling with the edge of the tablecloth. 'Might be all right.'

Eva went into the front room and came out with some of Alice's old underclothes. 'We can alter some of these for you. I know a good pattern for French knickers.' She ought to. She'd had to teach sewing at school, like all women teachers. 'You choose which colour you want.'

Gracie stared at the pretty material, in pink and cream as well as white, then reached out hesitantly to touch it. 'Don't you want them for yourself?'

'I have plenty. These are just going to waste. But you'll have to help me with the sewing.'

'That one's pretty.' The child touched a peach petticoat.

Eva looked at it, remembering the time she and Alice had gone shopping for that material. They'd each sewn some underclothes out of it, but Alice had hardly worn hers.

'Why are you crying?'

The child's voice brought Eva back to the present and she wiped away the tears with her fingertip. 'I was just remembering Alice.'

'What happens when people die?' Gracie asked suddenly.

'They stop breathing and then we wash their bodies and bury them. But we never forget them.'

'Does it hurt to die?'

'Sometimes. But Alice died peacefully in my arms.'

Tears were dripping down Gracie's cheeks. 'I don't want Mum to die,' she whispered. 'I don't, I don't.'

'No one does. But we can't always choose what happens to us. I didn't want Alice to die, either. So I made sure she knew I loved her – she was like a mother to me, you see – and then afterwards I managed the best I could, because I knew she wouldn't want me to mope.'

With a sob, Gracie slid down and vanished under the table. When Eva lifted the tablecloth she saw the two little girls hugging one another and weeping silently. After a moment's hesitation, she let the cloth fall again and spread out the underwear Gracie had chosen on the table, giving the children time to grieve.

Upstairs the sick woman was weeping too, tears of mingled anguish and relief: anguish at the thought of leaving her two little girls motherless and relief at having found someone to see them through the next few weeks, someone both kind and capable.

She had one more request to make of Eva and was not sure how best to word it. But surely her new friend would do as she asked? It seemed so obvious.

When Aaron and the girls had left on the Monday morning, Lil waited until the sounds of clearing up had finished, then banged on the floor to let Eva know she was awake. She was feeling clear-headed today and her idea seemed just as splendid after several days' thinking about it.

When Eva came in with a cup of tea, Lil let her straighten the bed then said, 'Sit down, love. We need to talk.' She looked at the other woman, so young and fresh and plump, and for a moment envy speared through her, knife-sharp. But she pushed it resolutely aside and started to speak, praying as she had never prayed before that for once she wouldn't put her foot in it by her blunt speaking. 'I want to ask you something – beg you.'

Eva took her hand and sat on the edge of the bed,

saying gently, 'You don't have to beg. If I can help you in any way – any way at all – you know I will.'

'Wait till you hear what I'm asking.' Lil took a deep breath. 'Aaron and the girls will be chucked out of here as soon as I'm buried. I know this house isn't much cop, but it's been home to us since soon after Molly was born and we've had some happy times here. Old Mr Linney was running the farm then and Aaron was fit and strong. It even seemed as if I'd get better again.' Her eyes strayed to the window. 'At least it has the best views of any cottage in Heyshaw. That's been a big comfort to me.'

She paused to sigh and stare blindly into space as memories flooded back. Eva sat quietly, waiting till she was ready to speak.

Lil pressed on, sounding a bit breathless. 'You'll be homeless, too, Eva. You've been happy here, though. I can hear everything that goes on through the chinks in the floorboards and you sing while you're working. Why, even Gracie has started to talk to you and she doesn't talk to many people these days, poor lamb.'

She began to pleat the bedcovers in her agitation. 'I can't go in peace knowing they'll be thrown out. I feel I have to hang on.' She let out a soft groan and when she looked back at Eva, her eyes were fierce. 'Only I don't want to hang on any more. I've had enough of this and I'm tired. I'd like to go to sleep and never have to wake up again. So please, Eva, will you marry Aaron after I'm dead? Will *you* look after my girls and let them live in your lovely house?'

17

Eva could not speak for shock, only stare open-mouthed at the sick woman. '*What did you say?*'

Lil gave her a faint smile. 'You heard me. I asked if you'd marry Aaron and look after the girls once I'm gone. I know it'll cause talk, but it'll solve everything.' She paused briefly to gasp in some air and continued full-tilt, 'It'll give *you* your home back – and my girls will not only have somewhere to live, but someone to look after them, someone who's fond of them.' Another desperate gasp for air and then, 'And Aaron would look after you if that nasty sod tried any more tricks.' She clasped Eva's hand. 'I've thought it all out, gone over and over it in my mind. It's the right thing to do, the only thing to do.'

When her companion didn't reply, Lil studied her face and said with less certainty, 'I've seen you with the girls. You're lovely with children. Surely you want some of your own? Surely you could find room in your heart for mine?'

Eva had been sitting frozen in shock but now she stood up abruptly. 'I do love your children, but you've taken me by surprise.' What terrified her most was that she found the idea instantly tempting, knew Lil was right: it really would solve all their problems. 'How could I even begin to discuss something like that with Aaron while you're still alive? It'd sound so heartless, as if I couldn't wait for you to die.' She looked earnestly at the invalid. 'And you know that isn't true.'

'I know.' Lil gave her hand a quick squeeze.

'And anyway, what about him? Would he even want to marry me?' Probably not.

Silence enfolded them for several long minutes, then Lil said, 'If you think you could do it, love, I'd talk to Aaron for you. I'm sure he'd take it better if it came from me.'

'I need to – to think about it first.'

'But you're not refusing? You're not, are you?'

Eva spread her hands wide, feeling helpless. No, she wasn't refusing. And she'd realised the reason. She wanted to marry Aaron Brierley because she really liked him, only she didn't want *him* to marry her for her money. Oh, she was being so stupid! She tried to focus on the girls and their needs. If she sought shelter with her sister Lizzie in Overdale, she would miss them dreadfully. She had barely begun to know them, poor whispering Molly and bewildered, angry Gracie.

But it was Aaron her thoughts kept coming back to. She liked being with him, it was as simple as that. She enjoyed their chats in the evenings, looked forward all day to that quiet hour in front of the fire, even after so short a time. Did he enjoy being with her?

She looked up and realised her companion was watching her intently.

'You've got quite fond of him, haven't you?' Lil asked. 'Not just the girls, but him too?'

Eva nodded, unable to pretend.

'And he likes you as well, so I reckon you could make something of a marriage if you both set your minds to it.' With a long sigh, Lil slumped back against the pillows and closed her eyes. 'Eh, I can't even talk for long an' I used to natter all day. Now I get that tired . . .' Her voice trailed away and her eyes flickered then closed.

That evening Aaron was late home, scowling as he entered the kitchen and even snapping at the girls. He nipped up to see Lil but came down almost immediately. 'She's asleep.' He ate his tea in silence, hardly saying a word apart from please and thanks. The girls ate quietly, too, seeming to understand that this wasn't the time to chatter.

After everything had been cleared up, Molly tried to retreat under the table, but Eva caught hold of her hand and whispered, 'Come and sit on my knee and I'll tell you a story.' As she settled the child on her lap, she turned to send a warning look at Gracie and gestured with her head in the direction of Aaron, who was sitting glowering into the fire. 'Come and join us. Leave your dad in peace, dear. He's tired.'

He looked up briefly, tried to smile and failed.

Gracie shrugged, scowled, but dragged a little wooden stool across.

Eva began to tell them a story, making it up as she went along, about a unicorn trapped in the woods which was rescued by two brave little girls. When she had finished she realised Molly had fallen asleep, lying peacefully against her breast. As she looked down at her and then sideways at the older girl, she knew she loved these children deeply and would feel happy and privileged to step into their mother's shoes.

Gracie, who was leaning against her thigh, turned to give her a half-smile, eyes filled with dreams. 'I saw a picture of a unicorn once in a book. It was lovely, all white and dainty.'

'I had a favourite book about a unicorn when I was a child. It's packed away in the attic at Rose Villa. When I next go back I'll get it out and give it to you. I've been wanting to find a girl who'd treasure it as I did when I was a child.'

'Really?'

'Yes, really.' Eva suddenly realised that Aaron was staring at her. His face didn't betray his thoughts but at least the dreadful scowl had gone.

'Time for bed, you two,' he said abruptly. 'Let me carry Molly up, Eva. She can have a wash in the morning.'

When he'd gone, Gracie whispered, 'His leg's hurting tonight. He allus gets that look on his face when it hurts bad. And Mum fell asleep when I was talking to her.' She slipped her hand into Eva's and scowled down at the floor as she asked, 'Will *you* tuck me up in bed tonight?'

Eva felt near tears at this further sign of Gracie accepting her. 'I'd love to, dear. Nip out to the back first and I'll wait for you.'

When they went up, she found that Aaron had put Molly into bed in her clothes. Gracie immediately demanded the same treat.

'All right, if you want to go to school with your skirt all crumpled tomorrow. I haven't finished making your new things yet.' It took so long to do them without a sewing machine and there was so much washing to do with Lil that she hadn't a lot of spare time.

Gracie hesitated, then with a sigh began to get undressed. When she had put on the ragged flannel nightdress, Eva tucked her in and she lay staring up by the flickering light of the candle, her eyes wide and unwinking.

'Are you all right, love?'

Gracie pulled Eva down and gave her a sudden hug, then twisted round and turned her back, as if afraid of having shown emotion.

Eva tucked the covers round her, stroked her hair and then realised Aaron was staring at her from the doorway.

Without a word he led the way downstairs. 'You're good with them,' he said abruptly as they settled down again in front of the kitchen fire.

'I like children. That's why I became a teacher. I miss it.' She heard him sigh and wriggle around as if his leg was hurting, but didn't dare show she'd noticed let alone offer him sympathy. Instead she got out her sewing and moved to sit at the table near the oil lamp, where she could see well enough to continue with the alterations to Molly's new skirt.

'Linney was on my back all day,' he confided

suddenly. 'I'm sorry if I was out of sorts when I came in. I nearly punched him. I think he wanted me to, then he could have sacked me. I've promised myself I'll put up with it till Lil doesn't need this place any longer, but it gets harder by the day.'

'It's not everyone who can hold their temper in,' she said. 'My sister Lizzie used to fizz with anger some-times.'

'And you?'

'I mostly keep my thoughts to myself. And anyway, I've never had as much to get angry about. I was the lucky one. Alice took me away, gave me so much and –' Her voice broke and she was unable to continue. It still hurt to think of her friend and mentor lying dead in the graveyard.

It was a while before he spoke again. 'About your wages – I can only offer you a couple of bob a week. I feel guilty about that.'

'I wouldn't take a penny from you.' She kept her gaze on her sewing. 'You lodge and feed me. That's enough.'

'But you're working so hard,' he burst out. 'I feel guilty every time I see how reddened your hands are.'

She laughed and spread them out to examine them before continuing with the sewing. 'Signs of honest toil. I'm proud of them.'

'I didn't know what to expect when you came here.' He hesitated, then said, 'I certainly didn't think I'd like you this much. You're a grand lass, Eva Kershaw, and I'm really grateful for your help. We all are.'

She smiled and bent her head again, feeling warmed

by what he had said. Peace and quiet wrapped around them. When a few minutes had passed she stole a glance at him and found him gazing into the flames again. Lil's suggestion came back to her and made her cheeks glow. Could she? Dare she?

But at least he had said he liked her. That made such a difference.

She liked him, too.

The next day Eva took Lil's morning cup of tea up and stood by the bed. 'I've been thinking about what you said and I'll marry Aaron if – if that's what *he* wants. Will you ask him? I could take the girls to visit Jenny this evening. That'd give you time alone with him.'

Lil's smile lit up her whole face but she didn't even lift her head from the pillow and her voice was a faint thread of sound. 'I'm so glad, love. I think – it's the right thing – to do. Eh, my girls – will be safe now. I'm that happy.'

She was fighting for breath today, Eva thought sadly as she walked back down the stairs to drink her own tea. Dr Stott was right: Lil was failing rapidly.

When Eva went up later to bring the cup down, she found the invalid lying across the pillow, her eyes staring blindly towards the moors she loved so much, and a big brown stain across the quilt where the tea had spilled.

'Oh, no! Lil, no!' She hurried to the bed, but could find no pulse. And besides, there was no mistaking the look of death. She closed the staring eyes, then rushed down to put on her coat and tie a scarf round her head.

She had to let Aaron know at once. It wasn't till she was halfway along the path to the farmhouse that she realised she was still wearing her slippers, but she gave a laugh that turned into a sob and continued flopping wetly through the mud.

By the time she got to the farmyard, her feet were soaked and icy cold. She could see no sign of where the men were working, so ran to the house and banged on the kitchen door.

Mrs Linney opened it, stared at her tear-stained face and said, 'Is something wrong?'

'Lil's just died.' Eva shivered. 'Do you know where Aaron is?'

'In the cowshed. I'll call him in for you.' Angela came outside and tugged on a rope that set a bell clanging loudly, then gestured. 'Come inside and wait.'

Eva looked down at her soaking, muddy feet. 'I'd better not.'

'You'll catch your death out here. I'll lend you some wellies to go back in.' She tugged Eva inside and said in a low voice, 'I'll try to keep Sid off your backs till it's all over, but he's been in a rotten mood all week and poor Aaron can't do anything right.' After a moment she added cryptically, as if thinking aloud, 'And to think I might have married Ernest Backworth.'

In the kitchen she presented Eva with a brimming cup of tea and got out some wellington boots. 'Here, try these for size.'

Sid Linney came in, rubbing his hands, his face ruddy with cold. He scowled when he saw Eva. 'What's *she* doing here?'

His wife gave him a shove. 'Don't be so rude, Sid.'

Aaron followed his employer inside, stopping dead at the sight of Eva. She could see from his face that he'd guessed why she was here. There might have been only the two of them in the room as she went across to lay one hand on his arm. 'I'm sorry, Aaron. Lil passed away a short time ago, so quietly I didn't realise till I went up to fetch her cup. She looked very peaceful I don't think she can have suffered at all.'

He closed his eyes for a minute, then nodded and turned towards the door.

With a look of immense satisfaction Sid opened his mouth, but his wife dug him in the ribs and hissed, 'Not now!'

Aaron didn't even seem to notice. Eva followed him outside, walking beside him as he limped along the path. He didn't say anything so she didn't either. The first flakes of snow began to fall as they reached the cottage.

He went straight upstairs and she hesitated, not knowing whether to join him or not. But she didn't want him to feel he was on his own so she went up, staying in the bedroom doorway.

He was smoothing the hair back from Lil's forehead, his face ravaged with sadness. After a minute or two, he turned to Eva. 'I didn't want her to go on her own.'

'And she didn't want to die in front of the girls,' Eva said. 'She can't have known what was happening. I was talking to her not long before.'

'Give me a few minutes alone with her, then I'll go and fetch Mrs Clay.'

Eva knew the midwife laid people out as well as bringing them into the world, but it didn't seem right to hand Lil over to a stranger. 'Just fetch the doctor. I can do the rest. I think Lil would prefer it.'

He looked at her and said in a tone of wonderment, 'Is there no end to your kindness?'

'I'd grown very fond of her. Um – what about the funeral? Can you afford it?'

He nodded. 'I've been saving up for a while now. I can't afford anything fancy, but we can manage something decent, at least.'

When Dr Stott had left, after providing them with a death certificate, Eva set to work to wash Lil's body and found Aaron beside her, ready to help.

'I've done this before,' he said. 'We saw a lot of death over in France.'

'Shall I fetch the girls home from school afterwards?' she asked.

'No. I'll do that. But thank you.'

It was only after he'd left to get his daughters that Eva realised Lil hadn't had a chance to tell him what she wanted him to do.

She took a deep, shuddering breath. Maybe she shouldn't think of that now. But she seemed to hear Lil's voice saying firmly, 'It'll solve all our problems.' She had seen the gloating expression on Sid Linney's face today and had no doubt whatsoever that the Brierleys would soon be homeless.

Could she ask Aaron to marry her?

And if she did, would he agree to it?

* * *

There was still snow heaped in odd corners when Lil's funeral took place. It was, like so many in these troubled times, a home-organised affair. Aaron took the top off the sidecar and used it to transport the coffin to church. He and Wilf carried the simple wooden box he had made himself down the narrow stairs, not without difficulty, and tied it in place on an improvised platform, then Aaron drove the motor bike very slowly down the lane while the others walked behind it to the church.

Molly clung to Eva's hand but Gracie walked on her own, hunched up, refusing to let anyone touch her. She had been like this ever since her mother's death. No one had seen her weep, but they could all feel her anger.

The little church felt icy and people's breath misted around them as the minister's booming voice sent the burial service echoing round the stone walls. Several people from the village had turned up to pay their last respects, some of them friends of Lil, others men who'd been in the Army. Even Ben Luccan was there, pushed by his wife in his basket chair.

Mr Morton spoke briefly about the sadness of a woman dying young, of the family's loss, then led the way briskly outside. By this time Molly was shivering violently, so Aaron let his friends carry the coffin and swung the child up into his arms. Eva tried to take Gracie's hand, but the girl shook her off and insisted on walking next to her father.

'She's taking it hard, poor thing,' Jenny whispered.

Eva nodded, her eyes on the stiff little figure scowling down at the hole in the ground where they were lowering her mother's coffin.

Afterwards Aaron asked Wilf to bring the motor bike home later and help him take off the improvised platform that had carried the coffin. He stayed to thank those who'd attended the funeral, then took his daughters' hands and started to walk home.

When Eva didn't join them, he stopped and turned to look inquiringly at her, gesturing with his head. She hurried to catch them up, feeling warmed that he had included her.

The wind had grown stronger while they were in the church and it was a miserable walk home along the half-frozen mud of the lane. When they got to the cottage they found Sid Linney waiting for them, hands on hips, a gloating expression on his face.

'He'll have come to give me notice,' Aaron muttered. 'The rotten sod couldn't even wait till tomorrow.'

As they got to the corner where Sid was standing, his smile broadened and they all stopped in shock. Two men were piling their furniture and personal possessions outside the cottage, heedless of where things landed.

Aaron let go of his daughters' hands and ran forward. 'What the hell do you think you're doing?'

'We're putting you out. You're sacked and I need my cottage for the new man.'

'You can't do that! You have to give me a week's notice.'

'Not if you're mistreating my property, I don't, and as Jack and Bill will testify the house was in a disgusting state when we arrived.'

Eva moved to join them. 'It wasn't! I left it immaculate.'

'You keep out of this,' Sid growled.

'I won't be silent if you continue to tell lies,' she answered hotly.

The two men doing Sid's dirty work avoided Aaron's eyes and went back inside again for another load. He followed them and barred the door. 'For pity's sake, we've just buried the children's mother!'

'Sorry, pal, but jobs are scarce,' one whispered, then raised his voice to say loudly, 'Get out of the way, please.'

Aaron hesitated, then went back to Eva and said in a low voice, 'Take the kids away. They shouldn't see this. Take them to Grandad's. You'll all be safe there.' When she didn't move he gave her a push. 'Go on!'

She hesitated, then pulled the two bewildered children back to where the lane began. As Molly began to sob, Eva took a sudden decision. 'Gracie, your father needs help. Take your sister to Grandad Gill's and tell Wilf what's happening. Ask him to bring the lads to help your father. Can you remember all that?'

'Yes. Aren't you coming with us?'

'No. I'm staying with your father. Be as quick as you can. I'm depending on you.'

Gracie grabbed her sister's hand and set off running down the lane. Eva watched them for a moment, seeing Molly fall over and Gracie drag her sister to her feet and pull her on. Then, taking a deep breath, Eva hurried back to the rear of the cottage. She wasn't leaving Aaron to face three men on his own.

As she rounded the corner she saw him struggling with the two farm hands while Sid Linney egged them on to 'give him a pasting'. Although he fought fiercely, he was no match for them, especially with his stiff leg. When they knocked him to the ground he fell awkwardly and from the way he lay there, half-curled with both hands on his leg, she knew it must have been injured.

To her horror Sid walked over and deliberately kicked him in the bad leg. As Aaron yelled in pain, the burly farmer smiled and put the boot in again. As he drew back his leg for another blow Eva reached him and shoved him so hard he staggered a few paces and had to struggle to regain his balance. By the time he'd turned round she had ranged herself protectively in front of Aaron, who was rocking to and fro, in so much pain he was in no state to defend himself.

'Don't you dare touch him again!'

'I reckon he's learned his lesson.' Sid laughed. 'See how your whore likes sleeping rough tonight, Brierley.'

Aaron had jerked into a sitting position and tried to push himself to his feet, but his face was bone white and he fell back with a groan. As Eva knelt beside him she thought Sid looked disappointed and guessed suddenly that he wanted his newly sacked employee to attack him. 'That man's trying to goad you,' she whispered. 'Don't respond.' She knew from the newspapers how punitive the law could be against men who attacked their employers.

'I can't – even stand. My leg is – easily damaged. And he knows it.' Aaron looked at her, shame warring with anger. 'Why didn't you go to Grandad's? I can't protect you if they turn on you next.'

'I'm not going anywhere. You need me as a witness.'

A mattress was suddenly tossed out of the door, its ragged blankets sliding off it into the mud. Sid trampled over the mattress in his muddy boots, laughing, but also watching Aaron carefully.

'Sweet Jesus!' Aaron muttered. 'The man's gone mad. But I think you're right. He does want me to attack him.'

Eva put her arm round him, crouching beside him, speaking in a low voice. 'I told Gracie to send Wilf. He'll be here soon.'

'How can I just do nothing? What's going to happen to the children?'

And suddenly it came to her how to start fulfilling Lil's wishes. 'You're going to move into Rose Villa with me.'

He stared at her and for a moment it was as if they were alone, as if the noises around them had faded into the distance. 'I can't do that.'

'Yes, you can. There's plenty of room and furniture. I have the right to live there until next October and Gus won't be able to attack me with you and the girls there.'

Sid strode over. 'That's right, you stupid bitch. Cuddle up to him. Gus Blake says you're like a bitch on heat, always wanting it.'

She had never seen such anger on a man's face as on Aaron's, but as he jerked forward, she pushed herself between the two men. 'Don't! He's not worth it. Think of the children.'

Aaron stopped mainly because he couldn't get up, but he looked at Sid and said slowly and distinctly, 'One day I'll make you sorry you said that.'

Sid laughed. 'You and whose army?' He continued laughing as his men tossed Lil's clothes and bed out into the mud.

Eva and Aaron said nothing, but she held his hand and he gripped hers tightly as the destruction continued. Then Wilf came into sight, pounding down the lane towards them, and she muttered, 'Thank goodness! Oh, thank goodness.'

Sid moved over to his two employees. 'Leave the rest of his things. He can clear them out himself. But you're to stay and make sure he doesn't try to move back in again. Don't come for your money until the place is empty and you've locked it up.' Then he walked quickly off towards the farm.

Wilf stopped in shock at the sight of Aaron and all the things scattered around them. 'What's the hell's going on?'

'We're being thrown out – literally,' Aaron said, his voice cracking on the words.

Before he could offer a fuller explanation, there was a whooshing sound and flames shot up from the shed.

'The bastard's fired the shed. It's got my tools in it.' Aaron got as far as standing upright before he fainted from the pain.

Wilf vanished in the direction of the shed and after a quick glance down at the still figure, Eva followed him, tears rolling down her cheeks but anger throbbing through her in a great, thumping tide. She could not believe that this was happening. Not in England. How did Sid think he'd get away with it?

She and Wilf scooped buckets of water up from the rain butt used to water the vegetable garden in the hot weather and tossed them at the flames. If the fire had been set in summer, their efforts would have done little good and everything would have been destroyed, but at this time of year the wooden walls were too damp to flare up quickly.

By the time they'd got the tools out Stan had joined them. Wilf explained quickly what had happened and Stan gaped at him. 'That bugger fired his own shed?'

'We'd have a hard job proving it. He's been in sight the whole time, striding across his field,' Eva said. 'And his men have been here as well. He must have paid someone else to do it.'

She went back to Aaron, who was just stirring, and sat down in the mud to cradle his head on her lap and murmur meaningless noises as she stroked the hair from his brow. She was beyond tears now, but the anger was lodged deep.

Wilf came up to stand beside her. 'I'll send Stan back for the motor bike. It's a good thing I hadn't brought it back yet or it'd have been damaged by the fire. The wooden platform is still on it, so we can take Aaron back to Grandad's without him bending that leg. What's the excuse for all this?' He gestured towards the mess of furniture and possessions.

'Sid Linney's claiming the cottage was in a mess and that gave him the right to sack Aaron and throw him out. When his men knocked Aaron down, Sid kicked him deliberately on the bad leg. I think he was trying to goad him into attacking him and I'm afraid he's really damaged that leg. He destroyed our possessions deliberately. I watched him go out of his way to trample over them.'

As Aaron moaned, she looked down. 'Never mind that now. He needs to see the doctor.'

'We'll get him back to Grandad's. He can have my bed.'

'No. We have somewhere else to go.' She saw the question in his eyes. 'Rose Villa. I have the right to live there till next October.'

'What about Gus Blake?'

A chill smile curved her lips. 'He's going to hate it.'

18

Wilf drove the motor bike slowly along the lane, with Eva sitting behind him keeping an eye on Aaron, who seemed to be holding on to consciousness by willpower alone. The lines of his face showed the pain he was experiencing, but no sound escaped his lips. Once, his eyes caught hers and she thought the expression in them softened a little, as if he would have liked to smile but could not.

Stan stayed to watch over the Brierleys' sodden, mangled possessions and as they were chugging down the lane another of 'the lads' appeared. Wilf slowed down even further to yell at him that Stan would explain what was going on and continued on his way.

At Rose Villa Eva breathed a sigh of relief when she saw that Gus's car was missing. She wanted to get Aaron settled before she faced Alice's nephew.

She went to look for the spare key, which they always kept under a plant pot near the front door, but it wasn't there. For a moment she couldn't think straight. 'The key's gone!' she exclaimed, turning to Wilf. Then she pulled herself together. 'We'll just have to break a window because my key's somewhere in that pile of things outside Aaron's cottage.'

'Let me check the windows first. There may be one open.'

He vanished round the side of the house and she was left to stand beside Aaron, who reached out for her hand then closed his eyes again.

Jenny came rushing across the road to join them. 'What's happened?' She saw the clasped hands and raised her eyebrows at Eva.

Gracie came pounding after her, dragging Molly with her, as usual, and Eva let go of Aaron, wishing the girls had stayed with Grandad.

'I'm all right, you two,' Aaron told them. 'Just hurt my bad leg, so I can't walk.'

They went to stand beside him, their eyes flicking from one adult to the other as they tried to understand what was going on.

'We need to get your father warm and fetch the doctor,' Eva told them, trying to sound reassuring, though the fear that Gus might return was fretting at her. 'I haven't got my key and Gus has taken the spare one, so Wilf's gone round the back to check whether he can get in anywhere.'

'I know where there's a back door key.' Jenny ran round the side, only to return shaking her head. 'He must have found that as well, the rotten beggar. Why did he move it?'

'To stop us getting in. Only he won't do that. We'll break in if we have to. A pane of glass is easily replaced.' Eva looked up at the sky, which was threatening more rain. 'Could you go and ask the doctor to come and see Aaron, Jenny? You've still got your bicycle, haven't you?'

Jenny nodded. 'All right. Won't be long.'

Eva was left to stand there, trying not to let the girls see how worried she felt, wishing she could still hold Aaron's hand, as Molly was doing. There was no sign of Wilf.

Behind the house Wilf had seen a partly open window and started to climb up the big sycamore tree that leaned towards it. As he got higher, moving carefully from one branch to the next, he looked back and noticed a line of footprints going across the bare earth of the vegetable garden to the wall, then crossing the ploughed land of the field behind the house. He stopped for a moment to frown and wonder who would be climbing over the back wall, and doing it more than once, to judge by the number of footprints. They seemed to lead to a big can standing next to the shed, the sort of can in which people brought home oil for their lamps. It was so shiny and new that it looked out of place in the dark mess of a winter garden and couldn't have been standing there for long.

Then he forgot about that as he hauled himself up to the branch beside the bedroom window and tried to open it further. But he couldn't move it, even though he thumped the sides in frustration. He'd guess the wood was swollen with damp and couldn't imagine why it had been left open like that. A child could have got through the gap, but he was too big. He climbed down, wondering which window to break, but when he got back to the front of the house and saw the two little girls standing next to their father, he stared at them through narrowed eyes. 'What are you like at climbing trees, Gracie?'

She blinked at him in surprise at this unexpected question.

'There's a window open upstairs at the back. I'm too big to get through it but you might manage. Do you want to come an' have a try?'

Eva stepped forward. 'I don't want to risk her safety.'

'I wouldn't do that, but it's a good climbing tree and we can easily get high enough for me to lift her through the window. Then she could go downstairs and open the front door for us. What do you think, flower?'

Gracie nodded. 'I could try. I like climbing trees.'

Aaron stretched out his hand towards her. 'Are you sure, love?'

'Yes, Daddy.'

'Can I help at all?' Eva asked.

'No. You stay with Aaron and the little 'un.'

As he vanished round the house with Gracie, Molly took hold of Eva's hand while still holding her father's.

Once again they could do nothing but wait – and hope. As the minutes ticked past, Eva kept an eye on Aaron and saw that he was beginning to shiver, in spite of the blankets piled on him.

Suddenly Wilf came running towards them, grinning. 'She got in all right. Eh, she's a grand little climber.'

They all stared at the front door as the seconds ticked by slowly. Then Gracie called, 'I'm here!'

But the door didn't open. Eva let go of Molly's

hand and went up to the house. 'Are you all right, dear?'

'Yes, but there isn't a key, so I still can't open it.'

'Try the kitchen door.' Eva ran round to it and peered through the kitchen window.

Gracie vanished, then reappeared. 'There's no key here, either.'

Eva tried to think. Surely Gus wouldn't have taken the kitchen key with him? It was a big one and would weigh his pockets down. He'd probably have put it somewhere close by. 'Look round, dear. See if he's hidden it somewhere nearby.' As more agonisingly slow seconds passed, she wondered why Gus was going to so much trouble to keep people out of the house.

Suddenly there was a yell from inside the kitchen. 'I've found some keys, but I don't know which one it is.'

'Try them all, dear. Just take your time.'

There was a noise of metal rattling, then, 'Not this one.' Another rattle. 'Not this one.' Then there was a shriek.

'What is it?' Eva called. 'Are you all right?' If she didn't get an answer soon she'd smash the window in herself.

The door swung open to show Gracie, beaming in triumph.

'Oh, you clever thing!' Eva swept the girl into her arms for a quick hug and for once Gracie didn't push her away.

Will came up behind her. 'Can you get the front door open or do we bring him in through here?'

'I know where there's a spare front door key. Alice always worried about losing keys.' Eva went along to her office and stood on a chair to pull some books off the highest shelf, one Gracie would not have been able to reach, even with the chair. Taking the key hidden behind them, she hurried along to the front door and within seconds had it wide open.

'Right, let's get him inside out of the cold,' Will said. 'You all right, lad?'

Aaron nodded. 'Yes. Sorry to be so useless. It knocked me sick for a while, but the pain's easing a bit now.'

'We'll carry you inside.'

'I can manage.'

'Not this time, lad. Can you carry his feet, Eva love?'

She nodded and together they lifted Aaron off the sidecar platform and carried him into the house.

'Where to?'

She hesitated. But there was only one room which would do. 'Alice's bedroom, the big one at the front.'

She wasn't a large woman, none of the Kershaws were except for the youngest, Johnny, but she summoned up the strength from somewhere to help manoeuvre Aaron up the stairs, round the bend and into Alice's room. The bed wasn't made, so they had to lay him on the floor while Eva hunted out some bedding. When at last they got him into bed, he was shivering again.

'Stupid,' he muttered. 'Don't know what's wrong with me.'

'I'll go and fill you a hot water bottle,' she said.

Downstairs she found the two girls standing in the hall, holding hands, pressed flat against a wall as if overwhelmed by their surroundings. 'Welcome to your new home, you two. Come into the kitchen and we'll fill a hot water bottle for your father. We need to get him warm.'

They followed her, wide-eyed, as she filled the kettle from the tap and lit the cooker with a match from a packet lying on the table next to an ashtray full of cigarette butts.

'You've got a gas cooker,' Gracie said. 'My friend's mother has one of those. And electricity. Can I switch the light on and off? They never let us touch the lights at school.'

Eva realised all over again how deprived their lives had been. 'Yes. Gas cookers are a lot easier than a kitchen range and you can each switch the light on and off once for practice. It's bad for the light bulbs to do it too often, though.'

Solemnly they each turned the light on and off.

'There. You'll be able to do the same thing in your bedroom.' She emptied the overflowing ash tray with a grimace. 'We don't need *that*, do we?' The whole house reeked of stale cigarettes. She knew it was fashionable to smoke, but she'd never liked the smell of it and could not blame housewives of the previous century for banishing gentlemen who wished to smoke to a separate room and giving them special smoking jackets and hats to absorb the smell.

The pantry shelves were empty, except for half a loaf, a jar of jam and a packet of butter. 'These belong to Mr Blake. We haven't got any food yet, but we'll go out and get some soon, or maybe Jenny will take you down to the shop when she gets back from the doctor's, then you can help her carry the things back.' She finished filling the earthenware hot water bottle and picked it up.

'Can we come up with you to see Dad?' Gracie asked.

'Of course you can, dear.' She led the way upstairs. It was wonderful to be back, even with the prospect of a confrontation with Gus looming. She closed her eyes for a moment as she got to the top of the stairs, relishing the simple luxury of a carpet runner beneath her feet, wallpaper, curtains . . . all the paraphernalia of an affluent life. She would never take any of it for granted again, that was certain. Guilt swept through her. How could she be so selfish as to think of that when Aaron needed her? 'Come and say hello to your father, then we'll sort out a bedroom for you two.'

Aaron was lying propped up against some pillows with Wilf standing beside him speaking in a low voice. They broke off as Eva entered the room and Aaron accepted the earthenware bottle gratefully, cuddling it to his chest for a moment with a sigh of relief. 'Eh, that feels good.'

'Is there anything else you need?' she asked.

'Just to say thank you, Eva. You've been wonderful today.'

She could feel herself flushing. 'Well, you looked after me when I needed help. Wilf, can you stay with Aaron while the girls and I sort a few things out?'

'We were just discussing it. I think I'd better sleep here till he's on his feet, if that's all right with you? I can bring my mattress across and kip down on the floor in here. He's going to need help and you don't want to be alone with Blake. We can bring Jenny in as well to share your room.'

'Won't Grandad need someone?'

'I can get the lads to stay with him in turns till I can move back across the road.'

Aaron spoke from the bed. 'We need to plan what to do. Properly.'

There was a pregnant silence as Eva looked from one to the other and the two men exchanged nods that were promises as well.

'Aaron's good at planning things,' Wilf said as one stating a simple fact. 'If he'd not been injured he'd have been a Captain at least by the end of the war.'

Then they heard it, a car turning into the drive and stopping in front of the house. She ran to the window and stared out. 'It's him.'

The front door slammed open and a voice roared up the stairs, 'What the hell is going on here?'

She moved towards the door. 'I'll go and tell him.'

'You go with her,' Aaron told Wilf. 'The girls can stay with me.'

He lay and listened to Wilf follow Eva downstairs, cursing his damned leg and Sid Linney too. What use was he to man or beast when he was incapacitated like this?

Eva's voice floated up the stairs. 'I've moved back in,

that's what's going on. And I've brought a few friends to stay with me so that I won't be lonely.'

Aaron grinned. He was glad she was standing up to that sod. 'Come and sit on the bed,' he whispered to his daughters. 'But keep quiet. I need to listen to this.'

Gus stared at Eva, then a nasty smile crept across his face. 'If you need company, you only have to ask.' He took a step towards her.

Wilf moved round the bend in the stairs to stand by her side. 'She won't need to trouble you. And you won't need to trouble us, either, I'm sure.'

Gus scowled at him then looked back at Eva. 'It's one man after another with you, you bitch.'

Wilf was down the stairs before anyone had realised what he was doing. He shoved Gus so hard he staggered back and fell over, then Wilf stood over him so incandescent with rage that even Eva was shaken by the sight.

'If I *ever* hear you talk to her like that again, I'll shove your filthy words back down your throat!' he roared. 'You're very brave when it comes to ill-treating women and bullying men with gammy legs, but let's see how you go with me. I'm fit and strong and I can get very angry indeed when people upset me.'

'I'll have you arrested for assault if you lay one finger on me.' Gus got to his feet again.

Eva stepped forward. 'And I'll bear witness that he was merely defending me.'

Gus brushed his hair back. 'Who'd believe *you?*'

'Mr Beaman did when I told him why I had moved out to live with the Brierleys.'

Breath whistled into Gus's open mouth but he caught Wilf's eye and shut it again. He walked across the hall to the sitting room, turning at the door to snap, 'Well, you'd better keep out of my way!' before slamming the door shut behind him.

The look in his eyes had been so malevolent that Eva felt worried. She hated to expose the children to this. Only what choice did they have but to come and live here?

Wilf sniffed and then looked down at his hands. He raised them to his nose and sniffed again.

Eva watched in puzzlement.

He put one finger to his lips and beckoned her up the stairs again. When they were in Aaron's bedroom he held his hands out first to her then to Aaron. 'What do they smell of?'

'Lamp oil,' she said instantly.

Aaron nodded agreement.

'It must have been on his jacket.' Remembering the oil can in the back garden he went into Eva's room to stare out of the window and see if he could spot it. He bobbed back so that the curtains hid him because Gus Blake was returning to the house, entering it through the french windows. Wilf could see the side of the shed clearly and the oil can had gone.

He turned to see Eva in the doorway and realised from her expression that she had guessed what he suspected.

'Did he use lamp oil to set fire to Aaron's shed, do you think?' she asked quietly.

'Could have done. He's a friend of Sid's, that's for

sure. I've seen them together in the pub many a time. They're as thick as thieves. Beaman doesn't sit with either of them any more, though. Look, don't say anything about this to the girls. I'll have a quiet word with Aaron when he's alone. I reckon we're going to have to be very careful. Blake's obviously prepared to do anything to get rid of us, legal or not. Well, the lads and I have plenty of time on our hands and maybe we'll enjoy having something to fill it.' He grinned at her and went back to Aaron's room, whistling cheerfully.

Wilf Horrocks had, she realised, come fully to life, his eyes sparkling, his face flushed, his whole body alert and eager. He must have been more depressed than anyone had realised by his jobless state. How would it affect Aaron, who was now in the same position?

Then she noticed the state of her bedroom and could not hold back a soft sound of pain. Gus must have left that window open deliberately and the weather had beaten in through it, staining the carpet and curtains. She went over to feel them and they were damp. There were dead leaves here and there, blown in off the tree, and the whole room felt clammy.

She hurried back into Aaron's bedroom, where the two men had their heads together and the girls were looking out of the window. 'I need some help closing the window in my bedroom, Wilf. Can you do something about it, do you think? I'll need to light a fire in there as well to dry the place out.'

He nodded. 'Come on, girls. We'll go and get some tools and I think Grandad might just give you a piece of

Jenny's cake if you ask nicely.' He looked across at Eva. 'Stay here with Aaron, love, till I get back.'

She nodded.

When Wilf had left she felt unaccountably shy. 'It's not exactly been a welcome for you, but I do hope you and the girls will be happy here.'

'It's a relief to have a roof over our heads. We'll be physically comfortable anyway. This is a lovely bed. Beats the straw-filled mattress I've been sleeping on in the attic.' His smile had the same alert quality as Will's.

'You're starting to look better,' she told him.

He nodded. 'Aye. I'll soon pull out of it again. But it's best to let the doctor check my leg. I think the skin was broken and we don't want it to get infected.'

'At least you'll be able to wear the leg brace all the time from now on.'

'Yes.' His expression was very serious now. 'I don't know what we'd have done without you today, Eva. Thank you.'

'Well, I couldn't have come back here on my own, so we're still helping one another.' She lowered her voice. 'I don't understand why Gus wants to stay on here. What can there be in the north for a man like him?'

'I don't know, but I'm damned well going to find out. I may be physically incapacitated, but there's nothing wrong with my mind. I think the first thing will be to see what's in that shed of his.'

'He's got it well padlocked.'

Aaron grinned. 'Wilf has a way with locks. But we'll have to wait till Blake's gone away on one of his little trips before we can investigate.'

Jenny came back just then, glowing with the exercise, and was soon followed by Dr Stott, so Eva had no more time to chat privately with Aaron. The two women went downstairs and began to unpack, taking stock of the food and deciding what to have for tea, which necessitated a quick trip down to the local shop. Jenny took the girls with her to 'help' and Eva gave her some of her precious remaining coins, trying not to think of how they were going to manage after the money ran out.

When Dr Stott came down, she took him into her own sitting room and asked, 'How is he?'

'I've painted the leg with iodine. As long as it doesn't get infected, he'll be all right. It must be very painful.' He looked at her in the fatherly way he had. 'He refused to tell me how he got the injuries. Do you know?'

She nodded. 'Sid Linney knocked him over and kicked him deliberately on that leg.'

He gaped at her. 'Who told you that?'

'No one. I saw it for myself. But the two men working for Sid will no doubt swear differently.'

'I don't know what the world is coming to.'

While she was doing the shopping Jenny met Angela Linney. She would have given her a wide berth, but Angela came up to her.

'I need the answers to a few questions, Jenny, need them desperately. Can you spare me a few minutes? Perhaps the girls could take some of the shopping home?' She waited until they had gone skipping along the road before asking. 'What happened today at the cottage? What really happened? Sid won't tell me, just says he sacked Aaron Brierley and Aaron attacked him.' She hugged herself against the bitter wind. 'I nipped down through the orchard when Sid had gone out and I could see two of Aaron's friends loading his furniture on the Ardens' handcart. And some of it had been badly damaged. How did that happen?'

'I don't think –' Jenny liked Angela Linney, but was afraid this was some ploy of Sid's to cause more trouble.

'I don't agree with a lot that Sid's done since we came here,' Angela said, as if she could read the other woman's mind. 'In fact, I don't like him very much. I made a big mistake marrying him and I thought I could live with it, but I'm not sure I can stay with a man who treats people so badly. *I need to know the truth, Jenny.*'

'All right.' Jenny explained what had happened.

Angela didn't say a word but bowed her head when the tale was over and let the tears run down her face. 'I'm not having my son growing up with a father like that.'

'Can you afford to leave Sid?'

'Yes. I have an old aunt who's never liked him. She knows I'm not happy and she said if ever I needed shelter I could go and live with her.' Angela brushed her tears away hastily as a woman she knew approached, nodded a greeting, then turned back to Jenny. 'I'll give you my address before I leave. Perhaps you'd be kind enough to keep me in touch with what happens?'

Jenny nodded, then watched her go, feeling sad for her. It must be dreadful to be married to a boor like that, but it was a drastic step to take to leave your husband.

Then she saw the cart of furniture turn from the lane on to the road and hurried the girls along to catch up with it. They'd all need to work together to unload it and even from here, she could see how many of the things were damaged.

Sid Linney had a lot to answer for.

So did Gus Blake.

But Aaron and Eva were both liked in the village. People would keep an eye on their interests from now on.

19

When Eva went to bed that night, weary as she was, she tipped the money in her purse on to the dressing table and counted it carefully. It wasn't much, just under two pounds. She knew Aaron could have little more than her and with four of them to feed, the situation would soon become desperate.

Jenny came in and cocked an eye at the neat little piles of coins. 'You all right for money, love?'

Eva shrugged. 'At the moment I am, but it won't last long, and I don't think Aaron is any better fixed.'

'I can lend you some if you need it.'

Eva shook her head, then took the plunge and tried out Lil's idea on her friend. 'If I married Aaron, we'd have plenty of money – and we'd be able to get rid of *him* as well.'

Jenny's mouth fell into an O of surprise, then slowly that turned into a smile. 'I didn't think you'd have the gumption to do something like that.'

That wasn't quite the reaction Eva had expected and she wasn't sure she liked her friend's comment and what it said about her. 'It was Lil who suggested it. She was going to ask Aaron, only she died.'

'So now you'll have to ask him yourself.'

'Yes.' Eva carefully picked up the coins and put them back in her purse. 'And the sooner the better. Will you take the girls across to Grandad's tomorrow morning to give me some time alone with him?'

'Yes, of course. And Eva—'

'What?'

'— I think you're doing the right thing.' She didn't say it but she also had the feeling that Eva had grown rather fond of Aaron. As she lay in bed, drifting towards sleep, Jenny realised how much she envied her friend. If she thought Wilf would agree to marry her, she'd ask him tomorrow, wouldn't hesitate for a second.

But although she knew he was fond of her, she also knew he'd say no.

The following morning Jenny and the girls went across the road to help Grandad and Wilf began work on the motor bike, taking the platform-like structure off the sidecar and replacing the top. There had been no sign of Gus, but his car was there so presumably he was still in bed.

Aaron was in his bedroom waiting for the doctor, but Wilf said he was dressed so Eva screwed up her courage and went in to see him.

He was lying on top of the bed under the quilt, staring out of the window, and didn't turn round to look at her immediately. 'Wilf—'

'It's not Wilf – it's me.'

He swung round then. 'Eva. How are you? The girls came in earlier, full of themselves after using your fancy bathroom, and I just watched them walk across the road with Jenny. They look happier again, thanks to you.'

'I'm glad. I thought you were going to stay in bed today.'

'No. I'm not one for lying around. I need to think, make plans. I'm only waiting here till the doctor has checked my dressing. I need to start looking for another job, and quickly too.' He flushed. 'I don't have much money left, you see, not after the funeral. Sid didn't pay me a week's wages in lieu of notice and I doubt he's going to.'

'I don't have much money left either. That's what I came about. I have a suggestion.' Avoiding his eyes, she took the plunge. 'This isn't the right time for what I'm going to say, I know that, but it *will* solve all our problems. It was Lil who suggested it, actually, and she was going to put it to you herself, only she died.'

When she risked a glance in his direction, she saw that he was looking puzzled. She could feel her cheeks glowing with embarrassment even before she said baldly, 'If I get married before the year is up, I'll inherit Alice's house and enough money to live on comfortably, so I thought we could . . .' Her voice faltered because he was sitting bolt upright glaring at her.

'Are you suggesting what I think?' Aaron demanded.

She swallowed hard, trying to find the words to soften his anger. 'Yes. I wouldn't have spoken yet, only we can't afford to wait.'

His anger didn't seem to abate in the slightest. 'You're telling me Lil suggested this – *my Lil?*'

She could only nod.

'I don't believe you.'

'What?' She began to get angry herself. 'Why should I lie to you?'

He opened his mouth then shut it again, shaking his head in bafflement. Finally he said very quietly, 'You can't mean it!'

'I do. If I don't get married I'll have to go and live with my sister Lizzie. I don't want to be a burden to them, not if I have some other choice. And anyway, I love this house. It's been my home for several years. I want to stay here.'

'But we only buried Lil yesterday.'

'I know, and I'm sorry about the haste, but she'd understand our need, *did* understand. If we wait till our money runs out, we'll not only be unable to buy food for the girls but we'll not be able to pay for a wedding.'

He heaved a sigh that was almost a groan. 'I'd thought to find work.'

'Wilf's been looking for months. He's tried everywhere round here. There is no work going. And anyway, you won't be fit for manual work for a while.' She watched him, trying to gauge his reactions.

When he did speak it was to say bitterly, 'Do you *really* want to marry a man who can't even earn the money to feed and house his children?'

'I have to marry someone. Alice's will made sure of that. And I'm in the same dilemma as you. I tried to find work myself before I agreed to Gus's proposal, but all the jobs were being given to men, particularly returned soldiers. Gus pretended he was fond of me and – and I was foolish enough to believe him.' She could feel her face flaming with the embarrassment of that. 'At least you aren't trying to fool me about anything. It's clear you don't want to marry me, even with the money as an inducement.' Her voice broke on the last word. Humiliation scalded through her.

He reached out to grasp her hand, holding it between both his, staring down at it as he said gruffly, 'I'm being selfish again, thinking only of myself. That man hurt you badly, didn't he?'

She nodded, watching his hands – strong yet gentle, shapely in spite of the cuts and grazes from the previous day's fight.

'It must have taken a lot of courage to ask me.'

She nodded, unable to meet his eyes.

'Look at me, Eva.'

She did as he asked.

'I'm half-crippled, I drink too much and I have bad nightmares. You could find a dozen more suitable husbands than me.'

She tried to pull away. 'If you can't face the thought of marrying me, just say so.' To her consternation a sob escaped her control.

'Oh, Eva, Eva.' He pulled her into his arms and gave her a cuddle. 'I'm trying to think of you, of how unfair it'd be for a man like me to take advantage of this stupid will and marry you.'

'I don't know anyone else to ask and anyway, I don't want to marry a stranger,' she muttered into his chest, her voice muffled. It was easier to speak when she didn't have to face the scorn in the eyes. 'And – and I enjoy your company, we've had some lovely chats in the evenings, so I thought . . .'

'There's more to marriage than chatting, Eva.'

'I know. But I also like the way you love your daughters, your kindness to everyone. Wilf thinks the world of you and so do the rest of the lads. Look how they rallied round to help you yesterday. I think you'd treat me right and I'd feel safe with you, Aaron. I never felt safe with Gus.'

He was silent for so long she looked up. He was staring into the distance, not at her, but he seemed to feel her eyes on him and looked her way again. 'You've just offered me a very big compliment.'

He was going to refuse, she knew he was! But she'd run out of arguments and could only sit there feeling stupid and ugly. This man was no different from the others. He didn't really want to marry her. She felt a tear run down her cheek, because that thought hurt so much. She hoped he hadn't noticed, but of course he had.

He raised one hand and wiped the tear away with his fingertip. 'I'm sorry I've made you cry. But, Eva, this is ridiculous! You *can't* want to marry an old crock like me.'

'I do. I already love your children. That was one of the reasons Lil thought it was a good idea. And I'd do my best to – to make a good life for us all. I don't think I'm hard to live with.'

'You shouldn't be saying those things to me. I should be saying them to you.' He pushed her to arm's length and looked at her very earnestly. 'Eva Kershaw, you must be the most generous person in the world.'

She met his eyes and waited numbly for him to dress up his refusal in more kind words. As if that'd make a difference.

Instead he said simply, 'All right.'

'*What?*'

He smiled. 'I said, all right. I'd be honoured to marry you – and given our circumstances, the sooner the better.'

She felt so dizzy with relief she clutched him to prevent herself from falling. 'You really mean that?'

'Would I joke about something so important?' He kissed her gently on the cheek. 'And I too shall do my best to help build a good life for us all.'

She didn't know what to say or do.

He didn't, either. He studied her face, trying to work out how she must be feeling. She had been expecting him to refuse, that was clear. Why did she have such a poor opinion of herself? Didn't she realise she was an attractive young woman? The fiasco with Blake must have destroyed her confidence – well, he knew she had always been shy. 'Was it really Lil who suggested we marry?'

'Yes.'

'That's typical of her. She always made the best of whatever life dished out to her.' He still couldn't believe he'd never see her again, grinning at him, teasing him into being more cheerful. 'Did she tell you we had to get married because Gracie was on the way?'

'Yes.'

He bowed his head. 'We got on all right, but it wasn't love between us. I don't think I'm the sort to fall in love.

I want you to understand that now, because I don't want you expecting what I can't give.'

'Friendship will be enough for me,' she offered.

'Yes. I can certainly give you that.' Though he and Lil had been friends and it hadn't really been enough. There had always been something lacking, some spark he had seen occasionally flying between youngsters who were courting – seen and envied. And Eva was very different from Lil, more fragile in some ways. He'd have to tread carefully with her. She was a mass of contradictions: gentle, intelligent and pretty, but when the chips were down she'd had enough backbone to stand up for herself and for him as well.

And the girls liked her, even Gracie.

But being together day after day without the sweetening of love could be – difficult. As she would find out.

It was a relief to both of them that the doctor arrived at that moment to check Aaron's leg.

When Eva had shown the doctor out she looked up to see Gus standing on the landing watching her. She shivered involuntarily and wished Jenny were around.

'All alone?' he asked, starting to walk down the stairs.

The way his eyes were raking her body was disgusting. She didn't want to give ground to him, yet she didn't want to stay here and face him alone.

A door banged upstairs and Aaron limped on to the landing. 'Ah, there you are, Eva.' He ignored the other man completely and began to make his way down the stairs, stiff-legged now he was wearing the brace.

Gus smiled at Eva and mouthed the word, 'Later.'

As he vanished in the direction of the kitchen, Eva ran to Aaron and clutched his arm. 'I'm so glad you came out just then,' she whispered. 'The way he was looking at me frightened me. I think he intends to start pestering me again.' Then she grew annoyed at her own fearful reaction and tried to smile at him. 'So we'd better make some plans quickly, hadn't we?'

Aaron put his arm round her shoulders, upset to think Blake could frighten her so easily. 'Let's go and tell Beaman our news and ask him what we have to do.'

'You shouldn't be out yet. Surely it can wait a day or two?'

He grinned. 'While I sit around and rest? I'd go mad. Besides, we have the motor bike. I shan't have to walk far. Will Jenny keep an eye on the girls for us? I don't want to send them back to school today.'

'I'm sure she will. Shall I nip across and ask her?'

'Get your coat and hat first. We'll leave as soon as you get back.' He followed her out, smiling as he watched her run across the road. Then he joined Wilf, who was polishing the motor bike. 'Thanks, lad. That bugger's been annoying Eva already. Keep an eye on things here, will you?'

'Aye.' Wilf gave a final last polish to the bike and as Eva returned, said, 'You shouldn't be starting this thing with that leg of yours.'

'We've got urgent business in Heyshaw.'

'Then let me drive you there.'

Eva looked anxiously from one to the other, wanting to add her persuasions to Wilf's but unsure of how Aaron would take any interference from her.

He sighed and looked down at himself. 'Happen you're right. Very well. You drive us in, lad. We'll stop at Stan's on our way, though, and ask him to come up and stay with Jenny and the girls.'

For once, Mr Beaman was not busy with a client and when the clerk saw Eva, he actually smiled at her as he said, 'I'll tell him you're here.'

'Leave this to me,' Aaron whispered.

Mr Beaman waved them to seats and looked at them across his desk. 'Did the move go well?'

'As well as could be expected.' Aaron took a deep breath. 'Eva and I came to tell you that we're going to get married. I know it's too soon after my wife's death, but we both have problems which will be solved by it.'

The lawyer looked from one to the other and nodded slowly. 'Very wise.'

'You aren't going to try to persuade her out of it?' Aaron burst out.

'Certainly not. As I've mentioned before to Miss Kershaw, I think getting married is the best thing she can do. And I know you by reputation, Mr Brierley.' He smiled deprecatingly. 'One cannot live in a village without hearing all the gossip. I'm sorry about your wife, and sorry you have to get married again so quickly, for it will inevitably cause talk. But I shall feel very happy about entrusting Miss Kershaw's future to you, and I'm sure Miss Blake would have agreed if she'd known all the facts about her nephew.'

Eva exchanged surprised glances with Aaron. 'You sound as if you know something about Gus.'

'I am looking into a few matters concerning Mr Blake. I have a good friend who is an Inspector of Police in London. He's helping me. When I have a fuller picture I'll share the information with you.' He frowned down at his desk. 'I think you should get married quickly, by special licence. That way we can ask Mr Blake to leave at once. I should feel much happier if you weren't sharing the house with him, Miss Kershaw.'

'I can't afford a special licence,' Aaron said with a scowl.

'Then allow me to lend you the money from the estate, which you can pay me back within hours of marrying. In fact, I'll send my clerk with you to help make the necessary arrangements. But I think you should keep the impending marriage secret until it's a *fait accompli*.'

'Is all this necessary?' Eva asked. 'I don't want it to look as if we're ashamed of what we're doing. There's going to be enough talk as it is.'

'We'll do what Mr Beaman advises,' Aaron said. 'Then after we're wed I'll get the lads in to throw Blake out.'

'It might be best if I return with you after the wedding and inform Mr Blake myself,' Eric Beaman said. 'And I should like to attend the ceremony, if that's all right with you?'

'I'm not afraid of him!' Aaron protested.

'I think perhaps you should be – if not afraid, at least extremely wary. I can't say more at this stage.'

Eva clutched Aaron's arm. 'I agree. Gus frightens me. He wasn't like this when my aunt was alive, but he seems to get more – *difficult* each time I see him. But we have Wilf and Jenny staying in the house tonight, so we should be safe enough.'

'Very sensible. Now, let's sort out the practicalities.'

When they eventually got out of the lawyer's office, Eva looked at Aaron. 'I can't wait to get rid of Gus.' She saw Wilf sitting on the motor bike, chatting to two men about it, because motor bikes and cars were still enough of a novelty in Heyshaw to attract spectators. 'Are we going to tell Wilf and Jenny? And what about the girls?'

'We won't tell the girls. In fact, they'll be safest at school tomorrow. But we will tell Wilf and Jenny. They can come and be witnesses for us.' He looked at her very seriously. 'If you change your mind, though—'

'I shan't!'

'But if you do, don't think I'll kick up a fuss. I want you to be very sure it's what you want.'

'And you? Are you sure?'

'No. I still feel it's unfair to take advantage of you like this.'

She wished he didn't always say that, wished just once he'd say he was happy to marry her. Oh, she was stupid! She wasn't a child and this wasn't a fairy tale. She should simply accept that it was a marriage of convenience, entered into reluctantly on his part, and then, like Lil, she should make the best of it.

When Sid Linney came home that night, after a day at the market, there were no lights showing in his house. 'What the hell's going on?' he muttered to himself.

He stopped the lorry and ran inside, wishing they had electricity here and vowing to get it installed soon, whatever it cost. 'Angela! Where the hell are you? *Angela!*'

But there was no sound from anywhere in the house. In the kitchen there was a red glow in the range, so he opened up the damper and fumbled for some matches to light the lamp. When he had it burning cleanly he held it up to scan the room and caught sight of an envelope propped up on the dresser. Setting the lamp down, he ripped open the envelope, muttering under his breath in annoyance as it tore the edge off the letter.

Dear Sid

By the time you read this, I'll have left you. The way you treated Aaron Brierley and his family – and on the very day he buried his wife – sickened me. In fact, I've been unhappy with your behaviour for a while now, because you treat me almost as badly as you treat others. We should never have married. I wasn't born to be a doormat.

Timmy and I are going to live with my Auntie Edna. There is no way you can ever persuade me to come back to you. If you even try, I'll reveal a few of your less savoury secrets to the police. Blackmarket profiteers can still be prosecuted, you know.

Angela

He re-read the letter in astonishment, then stood glaring at it, unable to believe that his wife could behave like this – or make such threats. How dare she do this to him? He wouldn't miss her company, but how would he manage without someone to run the house? And he hadn't treated her badly; he'd always put good food on the table, bought her new clothes every year. What more could a wife want?

Well, she wasn't keeping his son from him, definitely not. He'd get on to his lawyer tomorrow. Beaman would find a way to force her and the boy back.

Only – what exactly did she know that the police would be interested in? He hadn't involved her in certain wartime activities, thought he'd kept them secret. The bitch must have been spying on him.

Screwing up the letter, he hurled it into a corner and stormed out to the pub. On the way he picked up some fish and chips and sat eating them in the van, then washed his hands in the gents before he went to sit in the lounge bar and stare in bafflement at the world, which was not doing as he expected.

When Gus Blake came in Sid poured out his tale of woe immediately, without revealing Angela's threat. 'What do you think of that, eh? She's run mad. Giving women the vote after the war was stupid. It's gone to their heads. They think they're as good as men now.'

'Ah, you're well shut of her. Women are more trouble than they're worth.' Gus glared into his glass of whisky, then drained it. 'Want another?'

'Aye. Why not?'

They sat and drank damnation to all women, then

Gus ambled home, weaving from side to side as the chill night air hit him. As he stumbled down the drive of Rose Villa, he saw the motor bike sitting there, the symbol of that bastard Brierley who had dared to invade Gus's territory. Muttering a curse, he aimed a kick at it but missed, ramming his foot into the low wall beside it instead. He cursed even more loudly as he banged his toe.

As he was drawing back his leg for another kick the front door opened.

'I shouldn't do that if I were you,' Wilf said. 'I might feel tempted to do the same to your nice shiny car.'

Gus glared at him. 'Mind your own bloody business!'

'It is my business. Aaron's a friend of mine.' He stepped back as the other man pushed past him into the house, grimacing at the smell of booze that surrounded him. As Gus walked towards the kitchen, Wilf followed, leaning against the door jamb. He had put another padlock on the pantry door, though if what Aaron was doing worked out, he'd be able to pull it off again soon.

Gus glared at the locked door. 'Trusting lot, aren't you?' Not waiting for an answer he fumbled around among the litter piled at his end of the table, finding only a crumpled paper bag with a few stale biscuits in it. Taking that with him, he grumbled all the way up the stairs.

Wilf went back into Eva's sitting room. 'He's rotten drunk. Good thing we heard him coming along the drive. He was about to attack your bike, Aaron. I wonder what's upset him.'

'He got another of those letters today,' Eva said. 'From London. They always seem to put him in a bad mood. I think they must be from his wife.'

'Poor woman!' Jenny said feelingly. 'I don't envy her, married to that.'

Aaron had been yawning and trying desperately to stay awake. 'I think I'll go to bed now.' He pushed himself upright. 'Good night, Eva, everyone.'

Wilf stood up. 'I'll see you upstairs.'

'I can manage on my own.'

Aaron limped out and they heard him moving slowly up the stairs.

Eva sat on for a while longer, then said goodnight. She could not believe tomorrow was her wedding day. She was just going to dress neatly, she decided. No flowers, no fuss. She didn't want it to be anything like her previous attempt at getting married.

Wilf and Jenny sat on for another hour. Stan was staying with Grandad for a day or two, so for once they could take things a bit easy.

'Do you think Blake will go quietly tomorrow?' she asked.

'No. I think he'll kick up a fuss. Aaron wants me to ask a couple of the lads to come round while we're out to keep an eye on things. I think he's right. You can't trust that fellow. I'm glad I didn't serve under someone like that.' He frowned. There was no way he could picture Blake as a serving officer, somehow.

When Jenny went up to join Eva in the bedroom they were sharing, he checked all the doors and windows and made his way to the room he was sharing with

Aaron. From the attic the sound of gentle snoring drifted down. Well, sleep in peace, Gus Blake, he thought with a grin. It's your last night in this house.

As he lay down on the hard straw mattress beside Aaron's bed he envied his friend. What wouldn't he give to be marrying Jenny tomorrow!

20

Eva got the girls off to school in plenty of time the next day, sending a note to the headmaster to explain their absence and inform him that their mother had died. Though Jed Comper would know this already in a place as small as Heyshaw, she knew it helped the school records to have an official letter. But it upset her that the two girls looked thoroughly miserable as they sat and ate their breakfast.

Jenny had nipped across the road to help Grandad, but Wilf was within earshot so Eva didn't worry too much when Gus came into the kitchen. But both girls glanced at him fearfully and edged closer to one another. He noticed, of course, and pretended to lunge at them, which sent Molly sliding under the table with a squeak of terror.

'It's wonderful that a grown man finds pleasure in bullying two little girls,' Eva snapped and wondered if that was a fleeting look of shame on his face. 'Come on, dears, let's get you out of here.' She pulled Molly from under the table and gave her a cuddle, helping her into her outdoor things and straightening Gracie's woollen hat before kissing an unresponsive cheek. In spite of the cold wind she took them to the gate and waved goodbye.

When she got back Gus was eating the toast she had made for herself. 'That's stealing,' she said loudly.

He laughed and crunched up the last bit of crust, then picked up the cup of tea he had filched from her pot and wandered off to his sitting room.

Eva went upstairs and took a bath, luxuriating in the way she could do that without having to fill and empty a tin tub by hand, which had been the only way at Aaron's cottage.

When she went into her bedroom to get ready, Jenny was there.

'I saw the girls go off to school.' She smiled and lowered her voice. 'This is a bit better than last time, isn't it?'

'I hope so.'

'Hey, what's wrong?'

Eva stared down at her comb. 'I'm worried that I'm pushing Aaron into this, that he doesn't really want to marry me.' After a gulp, she added, 'I don't want him to grow to hate me.'

'He already likes you, if that's any help. His eyes go all warm when he watches you and the girls.'

She looked up, startled. 'Do you really think so?'

'I'm sure of it.'

A little heartened, Eva finished getting ready.

'Not that hat!' Jenny said firmly, taking the small felt cloche out of her hand. 'I don't know why you ever bought it. It makes you look about seventy. Wear this one today.' She produced a hat of her own, her Sunday best of navy felt. It had a broad brim, curved upwards at one side, and satin ribbons round the crown, tied in big loops. The ribbons had been changed to match Eva's blouse. 'There!' She adjusted the hat carefully and swung her friend round to face the mirror. 'You look lovely.'

Eva stared at herself. She did look better, but she also looked extremely nervous.

When they went down, Aaron was waiting for them in the hall. 'I'd like to speak to Eva on her own, if you don't mind,' he said to Jenny.

Fear clamped round Eva's heart. Surely he wasn't going to back out now? She followed him into her sitting room, hands clasped tightly on the handle of her handbag.

'Are you all right?' he asked, his eyes going to her hat.

She nodded, hoping he liked it.

Gently he unclamped her hands from her handbag and kept hold of them. 'I haven't changed my mind, if that's what's making you look so worried. I wouldn't do that to you, Eva. I just wanted to ask if we could leave a bit early so that I can buy you a ring.'

Relief coursed through her. 'Can you afford that?' She was sorry she'd said it the minute the words were out, because his expression became more distant.

'Yes. Jenny's lent me the money.' He looked at her. 'It'll be your money that pays her back tomorrow, but one day I'll earn the money for the ring, I promise you.'

'There's no need. It'll be *our* money once we're married.'

'I think there is a need. A man should buy the wedding ring.' He stood up and pulled her to her feet, his eyes crinkling into a smile. 'You look lovely. I like the hat.'

'It's Jenny's,' she confessed. 'I'm not very good at choosing clothes.'

'You've got a good friend there.'

He looked nice, too, she thought as she followed him into the kitchen. She had never seen him in his Sunday best, a dark suit with a white shirt and neatly knotted tie. But he had to put the old Army greatcoat on over it.

Two of his friends were waiting for them in the kitchen with Jenny and Wilf. 'Stan and Bob will keep an eye on things while we're out,' Aaron said, giving them a nod. 'We'll go into Heyshaw on the bike, because I don't think my leg's up to much walking yet. If you sit in the sidecar, it won't blow that pretty hat away.'

Jenny gave Eva a big hug. 'Me and Wilf will walk down and meet you there. Good thing it isn't raining, eh?'

Aaron parked the bike in the village centre and it attracted the usual stares and frowns. Some people were excited by the new forms of motor transport, others said they were smelly and insisted that nothing would ever replace the horse.

As he helped Eva out of the sidecar, he stepped back to study her, then reached out and adjusted her hat slightly.

His nearness made her breath catch in her throat, as did the intimacy of the gesture. She smiled at him uncertainly. 'Thank you.'

The jeweller's shop was small and known more for its clock and watch repairs than for its jewellery. But it had a tray of wedding rings which the lady assistant brought out and laid on the counter with a puzzled glance at Aaron, whom she clearly recognised. 'I was sorry to hear about Lil,' she murmured.

'Thanks.' He bent over the tray. 'Come and choose a ring, Eva.'

They both ignored the woman's gasp as they bent over the glass-topped tray together. With his warm body so close to hers and the woman's shocked stare on the other side of the tray, Eva had trouble concentrating.

'How about this one?' He put his arm round her shoulders and pointed to a simple gold band, with a pattern of little stars stamped in a circle round it.

She forgot her embarrassment. 'Oh, that's lovely.'

'I'll get it out for you, sir.'

The ring fitted Eva's hand perfectly and she looked at him with such a glowing smile that Aaron felt something move inside him, a warmth and protectiveness.

He paid for the ring, slipping the little box into his pocket and turning back to offer her his arm. 'We'd better get across to the church.'

There was another gasp from behind them, so he turned round and said, 'Yes, we are getting married and actually, it was Lil's idea so I don't feel at all guilty about it. There are some very good reasons for our haste.'

When they were outside he said a little grimly,

'Maisie Exton will soon spread the news for us. It'll be all over the village by tonight.' He knew gossip was inevitable, but he was dreading facing it.

They walked in silence for a couple of minutes then Eva said suddenly, 'Isn't it wonderful that the ring fitted me? It seems like an omen somehow.'

He stopped and as she looked up at him, said, 'I think I'll rely on my own efforts to make a happy life together, rather than omens. But I am glad we got you a nice ring, Eva.' Giving way to a sudden impulse he bent to kiss her cheek, breathing in a mixture of soap and freshly ironed blouse and a faint, teasing hint of eau de cologne. He'd forgotten how dainty a woman could smell.

Wilf and Jenny were waiting for them in the church porch and Mr Beaman came hurrying along the street soon afterwards.

As they moved towards the front of the church, Eva's heart began thumping and she felt a little light-headed, but she had Aaron's arm to hold on to, and Jenny beaming at her from the other side.

This time the wedding service went without a hitch. She heard her voice wobble slightly on her first response, but grew more confident as the ceremony progressed. Aaron spoke quietly but firmly, showing no sign of nerves except perhaps for a pulse beating rather quickly in his temple.

'I now pronounce you man and wife,' Mr Morton said, with a cool, disapproving expression on his face. 'You may kiss the bride.'

Aaron turned to give her a chaste salute on the

cheek. The soft warmth of his lips seemed to linger there as they made their way to sign the register.

'May I offer you both my congratulations,' Mr Beaman said as they came out of the church. 'I think you've done the sensible thing.'

Sensible, thought Eva with a sigh. What bride wanted to be called sensible on her wedding day?

'And now, perhaps you could come into my office and sign some papers, after which I'll accompany you back to Rose Villa. And if I may suggest it, you should have all the locks changed as soon as possible, just to be on the safe side.'

'We'll walk back and see you at Rose Villa,' Jenny said, giving her friend a hug then, after a moment's hesitation, hugging Aaron too.

In the lawyer's offices, Eva signed several papers, then Mr Beaman handed the newly-weds a summary of what the inheritance involved.

Aaron gasped as he glanced down the lines of figures. 'I hadn't realised it was so much!'

'It's carefully invested. I presume you and Mrs Brierley will not want to change that?'

Bitterness rang in Aaron's voice. 'What do I know about investing money?' He shoved the piece of paper away from him as if repudiating it.

'Did you look after the money for Alice, Mr Beaman?' Eva asked.

'Yes.'

'Then I think we'd like you to continue doing so. I don't know anything about investing money either.'

'I must warn you that incomes from shares and

stocks are declining, and will probably continue to decline, but if we continue to act conservatively, you should weather the current downturn, even if it goes on for years.'

'You think the bad times will continue, then?' Aaron asked.

'I'm afraid so. The country is still recovering from the war and will be for several years, in my opinion.'

There was silence in the comfortable room, broken only by the sound of the clock ticking and coals shifting in the fireplace.

Eva suddenly remembered something. 'What would have happened at the end of the year if I hadn't got married? I still find it hard to believe that Alice would have left her money to charity and let me go penniless.' She'd wondered about that a few times, especially as Alice had given her such a large sum of money, allegedly for her wedding clothes.

The lawyer looked at her and smiled. 'You're right. She wanted you to marry, but if you hadn't done so, you'd still have received half the estate and Gus the other half.'

'Oh.'

'I couldn't tell you that, or even hint until now, but I must say I think you've done the right thing in marrying Mr Brierley.' When neither said anything, he began to gather the papers together. 'And now, do you wish to ride back to North Hey in my car?'

'We have the motor bike. We'll meet you at the house.' Aaron stood up and led the way out. They walked across the road and as he helped Eva into the sidecar, he said accusingly, 'I doubt I'd have agreed to marry you if I'd known how much money was involved. And you didn't even *need* to marry me, it turns out.'

He tried to pull down the top of the sidecar over her, but she prevented him. 'I'm glad I married you, Aaron.'

Their eyes met in a long look that seemed to say more than words ever could.

'Well,' he said at last in a gentler voice, 'I'll try to make sure you don't regret it.' Then he closed the sidecar and went to kick start the bike, grimacing with pain.

At Rose Villa he helped her out in silence. She didn't know what to do or say, and was relieved when Mr Beaman drove up in his neat black Singer, and Will and Jenny walked across the road to join them.

Eva was definitely glad she'd married Aaron. She wanted to make a life with him and his children, wanted it more than anything in the world. The money was far less important.

Everyone waited to enter, looking at Aaron and Eva expectantly to lead the way.

With a slightly heightened colour he offered her his arm. 'I'm afraid I daren't risk carrying you across the threshold, Eva.'

She took his arm, trying to smile at him but feeling apprehensive, and together they led the way inside.

'Let me do the speaking.' Mr Beaman moved purposefully across the hall to knock on the sitting-room door. He didn't wait to be invited to enter but simply pushed it open and went inside. The others followed.

Gus was lounging in a chair reading a book and smoking a cigarette, but jerked upright as the lawyer entered. 'What do *you* want? It's a poor lookout if a man can't have a bit of privacy in his own home.'

'I've come to tell you that this is no longer your home.' Eric Beaman looked round in disgust. The place was in a disgraceful state again, with full ashtrays on every surface and newspapers scattered across the floor as if they had been simply tossed aside when finished.

'I'll get that woman back in to clean,' Gus said. 'She was ill last week or it wouldn't be so bad.'

'That would make no difference. Under the terms of Miss Blake's will, Miss Kershaw inherits the house and the rest of the estate if she marries. I have just witnessed her marriage to Mr Brierley and am here to ask you to vacate the premises immediately.'

Gus jumped to his feet, his face turning dark red with anger as he looked across at Eva. 'You conniving little bitch! What is it? Two days or three since his wife died?'

Aaron lunged forward but Eva dragged him back. 'Don't let him goad you. *Please!*'

Mr Beaman turned to them. 'It would be better if you left us now.' When the door had closed behind them he looked at Gus Blake, making no attempt to hide his distaste. 'I shall ask you to be out of this house in three hours' time.'

There was silence, broken only by Gus's deep breathing, then he shook his head 'I can't do it!'

'I see no reason why not.'

'I have some larger possessions in the shed. I'll need to find somewhere to keep them. I'm not leaving them here. Give me a week.'

'No. That would be most uncomfortable for all concerned, since you are not the most accommodating of guests. I suggest you take a room at the Red Lion and leave the boxes here until you can move them. I'm sure my clients will not be unreasonable about your keeping them in the shed.'

'And what if they decide to rifle through them, claiming someone broke in? I need to stay here to keep an eye on them, I'm afraid. All I own of value in the world is in those boxes.'

'Then I'm surprised you keep them in a garden shed.' Mr Beaman walked slowly round the room, thin, ageing and yet in no way afraid of the taller young man. 'I repeat: you have three hours to move out,' he took his watch out of its little pocket and looked at it, 'which will bring us to two o'clock this afternoon. If you don't do so, I'll be forced to bring in the bailiffs and we'll impound all your possessions – including the contents of the shed.'

He held up one hand to prevent Gus from speaking, 'What's more, if I hear you insulting Mrs Brierley like that again, I shall advise her to sue you for slander. And finally, because of Mr Brierley's injuries, gained in the defence of his country, I intend to stay on the premises myself until you are out of the house. I'm sure Mr

Horrocks will be happy to help you carry anything too large for one person to move.'

Gus opened his mouth, shut it again, then moved towards the door. 'I'm the only Blake left and I've been cheated out of my inheritance. I'm not going to leave it at that.'

'If you wish to waste your money suing, that's up to you. But I feel impelled to warn you that a case would not be likely to succeed. You may or may not be a Blake,' there was a moment's heavy silence as they stared at one another, 'but you only arrived in Heyshaw just before your aunt died. Some might say very opportunely.'

Gus slammed the door open and clumped up the stairs, muttering to himself as he went.

Mr Beaman moved at his usual sedate pace to the kitchen to tell his clients what had been arranged.

Within two hours Gus had filled the car with his possessions and was about to make one final check of his rooms.

Mr Beaman joined him just as he was staring round the sitting room. 'I would like to inspect the rooms with you before you leave,' he said.

The four people in the kitchen left the door open and when the two men went upstairs Jenny stood in the hall, shamelessly eavesdropping.

There was a burst of shouting from upstairs and Gus came clattering down. 'Anyone can make a mistake!' he yelled up the stairs. He turned to see Jenny standing in the doorway and gave her such a malevolent look she took an involuntary step backwards. 'I haven't finished with you,' he said, too softly to be heard from upstairs. 'Or your friend.' He marched out to his car and drove off.

Wilf put his arms round Jenny, who was visibly shaken by this parting shot. 'I don't know why you're getting so upset. There's nothing he can do to you because he won't be here.'

'He's the sort to find a way to get his own back, either by hurting me himself or by paying others to do it. I tell you straight out, Wilf Horrocks, I'm frightened of that man.'

'Nay, I won't let him hurt you, lass.'

'You can't be with me every hour of the day or escort me every time I go shopping in the village, can you? And you won't be with me in bed while I'm having nightmares about him.' She leaned against him for a moment. 'I've never seen such hatred on anyone's face. Never.' Was it her imagination, or did Wilf's arms tighten around her?

Mr Beaman came downstairs just then and she pulled herself together, stepping away from Wilf.

'I found a smouldering cigarette in the wardrobe,' he said. 'I'd guess Blake left it there deliberately, hoping to start a fire, but of course one cannot prove that. I think it would be wise to check all the other bedrooms for similar problems. He was, after all, alone up there for most of the time he was packing.'

'Jenny and I'll go and check,' Wilf said, taking her hand and tugging her with him.

Eva looked at the lawyer. 'We're really grateful for your help today, Mr Beaman. Aren't we, Aaron?'

He nodded.

'I like to think that I've played a small part in seeing justice prevail,' Mr Beaman said, then took out his watch. 'And now, I must return to my office. If you need anything, don't hesitate to call me.' A wry smile twisted his narrow lips. 'The two of you are, after all, among my most important clients now.'

When he'd gone Eva looked uncertainly at Aaron, who was staring out of the window.

He turned as if he felt her eyes on him and said bleakly, 'They're going to call me a fortune-hunter.'

'They'd have thought you that whatever the amount involved. I know you're not and that's what counts. And now I'm going to make a start on cleaning out that sitting room *he* used.' She hesitated, then said with her back to Aaron, 'Maybe you'd like to go and move your things into my bedroom while I'm doing that. If you don't mind, we'll use that room not the one you're occupying at the moment. It still reminds me too much of Alice.'

There was a long silence before he said, 'I don't think we should share a bedroom yet.'

She could feel tears welling in her eyes at this rejection, so didn't turn to face him. 'That's up to you.'

He didn't answer and when she turned round, he was gone.

Later that afternoon there was a tap on the kitchen door and Aaron, who had just come down, opened it to find his daughters standing there, looking unsure of their welcome.

'Is this the right door to use?' Gracie asked in a whisper.

Eva stepped forward, glad to have someone to break the awkward silence between her and Aaron. 'You can use any door you like, dear. This is your home now.' She settled them down at the table with a drink of milk and a jam butty. 'How was school?'

Gracie shrugged.

Molly stared down at her plate.

Eva didn't press them to tell her more but she was worried at the way they always clammed up when she asked them about school. Something was wrong, she knew it. But what? She turned back to continue the discussion she had just begun with Aaron. 'We need stocks of just about everything, foodwise. The girls will be all right with Jenny. Would you mind driving me to the shop and bringing the things back in your sidecar? There'll be too much to carry.'

He nodded. 'You girls stay here.'

'Is that man at home?' Gracie asked. 'He frightens Molly and me.'

'He's gone, moved right out, and he'll never be coming back.'

As they both sighed in patent relief, Eva looked at Aaron. They had decided to talk to the girls after tea to tell them about getting married.

Aaron had rested his hand on Gracie's shoulder and was smiling down at Molly. No one had ever offered Eva such casual, easy touches except her sisters and she could not help feeling jealous.

Then she chided herself for wishing for the moon.

She had married him, and it hadn't been for the usual reasons, so of course it'd take time for them to settle down together. Why could she not accept that?

As soon as they entered the shop Mrs Arden and her three customers fell silent. Aaron stood there with arms folded, scowling round. Eva hesitated then went up to the counter, nodding a greeting to everyone as she did so.

Mrs Arden broke the silence by moving forward with a smile. 'I believe we have to congratulate you two.'

Aaron only grunted so Eva tried to deal with it. 'Yes. It's sooner than we wanted but we all needed a home. You did know that Alice left me the house on condition I married within the year?' She tried to smile as if it was all perfectly normal, but couldn't because it definitely wasn't normal to marry within a couple of days of the first wife's death.

'I had heard something about that,' Mrs Arden allowed. 'What happens to Mr Blake, then?'

'He's moved out.'

'I see. And how can I help you today?'

'Oh, please serve the others first. We can wait our turn. We need rather a lot of things.'

Mrs Arden's eyes brightened. 'I'll call my Sal in to serve the others. If you're setting up your store cupboard, I'd best help you myself.

So Aaron stood there, his face expressionless, while the two women discussed at length what was needed and the pile of packets on the counter grew higher. He and Mr Arden eventually carried the results of this shopping expedition out to the motor bike, then he turned to Eva. 'You all right to ride on the back? There's no room in the sidecar now.'

'Yes, of course.'

'Tie your headscarf on tightly then.'

She clambered on to the bike, feeling the anger radiating from his rigid body. As he drove her back, the machine roared along the road as if it were voicing its owner's feelings, but once there he helped her carry the things indoors in the same grim silence as they had set off.

Like a stranger.

Like someone who bitterly regretted what he'd done.

The money was standing between them, she thought in despair. And she didn't know how to make Aaron realise that it didn't matter to her, that *he* was the one who mattered – he and his two daughters.

The money obviously mattered too much to him.

That night Sid Linney went and sat morosely in one corner of the Dog and Duck, his expression so forbidding no one attempted to join him.

Eric Beaman certainly didn't. He stayed quietly in a corner, consuming a glass of stout with great appreciation. The Red Lion might be a more congenial place, but the Dog and Duck's beers and ales were the best kept in the district.

When Gus Blake sauntered in and nodded to him in a friendly fashion, Eric choked on his drink, unable to believe his eyes. He did not return the nod but changed his mind about leaving, ordering a second glass of stout and edging his chair round a little, so that he could observe what was going on.

Gus approached Sid. 'Mind if I join you?'

Sid eyed him morosely and shrugged.

Gus didn't ask how Sid was managing without his wife, but related how he himself had been thrown out of Rose Villa and why.

'Never! And you the old lady's nephew an' all,' Sid muttered. 'What's the world coming to? And you say Eva Kershaw has married Brierley?'

'Yes. It surprised me, I must admit.'

'But he's only just buried t'other one!'

'Yes. It's amazing what some men will do for money. I don't envy you living in the same village. He'll be showing off now that he's got money, patronising you and causing trouble.'

'Just let the bugger try!'

'And the worst of it is, I have to find somewhere else to store my boxes. Do you know anywhere round here? I don't want to head back to London yet. Still got a few deals to tie up in the north.'

Sid frowned. 'I don't rightly understand what it is you're dealing in.'

'All sorts of bits and pieces. Stuff sold by folk who are short of money after the war. Antiques. Bits and pieces of jewellery. I buy cheap in the north and sell at a premium in the south, where prices are higher and there are more folk in work.'

'And that pays well?'

'Very well.'

'Well, it sounds a lot better than slaving on a farm. And for what? She's taken my son away now. What's the point of it all? Who's to inherit? The lad won't be brought up to farming, not with her and that interfering witch of an aunt.'

'Let me get you another drink.'

When Gus returned, Sid said slowly, 'I've got some space in the back of one of my barns. You can store your stuff in there if you want.'

Gus sipped his drink slowly. 'That's very generous of you. And you wouldn't mind me coming and going, packing and unpacking?'

'As long as you don't upset my cows!' He gave a bitter laugh.

'I need somewhere out of sight to keep the things, somewhere with a lock on the door. An open barn's no use to me.'

'How many boxes are there?'

'Seen that garden shed at Rose Villa?'

'Aye.'

'Enough to fill it.'

Sid pursed his lips. 'There's a room in the old part of the building, sort of store room, with stone walls and a door. Don't use it much nowadays. There's a key, though it'll be rusty, it's so long since anyone's used it.'

'Sounds ideal. I accept, and gratefully.' After another sip or two, Gus asked with feigned casualness, 'Would you mind if I brought some of the boxes in by night? I don't want people poking their noses into my business. I've worked hard for those things and it'd only take a burglar an hour or two to wipe out all my profit.'

'Ah, we don't have burglars here in Heyshaw.'

'You haven't been reading the newspapers. Burglary is on the increase now that so many folk are out of work. Would you not steal to see your kids fed?' He let that sink in before adding, 'Best not to risk it.'

Sid shrugged. 'Suit yourself.'

'I might even be able to cut you in on a deal or two if things go well.' Gus slapped him on the back. 'No use brooding on things, is there? If you haven't got a wife, there are plenty of other women around in times like these who'll do anything for a quid or two.'

Sid nearly choked on his beer. 'Get on with you!'

They walked out together an hour later to check the storage space at the farm. Sid was looking considerably brighter and Gus wore a smug air.

Eric Beaman, who had caught enough of the conversation to wonder what Blake was up to, waited till they'd had time to get right away, then folded up the newspaper he'd been pretending to read, tucked it under his arm and walked home thoughtfully. That fellow was brewing some mischief, he was sure, though he could not imagine what.

He'd better warn Brierley that his enemies were getting together, and suggest that if possible he and Horrocks inspect the boxes before Blake took them away.

That evening, after tea, Aaron and Eva took the girls into her sitting room. The adults sat down in the two armchairs and the girls sat on the rug in front of the fire.

'Eva and I have something to tell you,' Aaron began.

They looked up at him, sitting cross-legged, each cradling a cup of hot, milky tea, their faces flushed from the heat of the fire.

'Your mother and Eva had a chat before she died. Lil wanted to be sure you two would be looked after properly, you see, and she knew Mr Linney would throw us out. She said Eva and I ought to get married because if we do that, we can all stay here at Rose Villa, make it our home, and Eva will be able to look after you.'

There was silence as the girls tried to take this in.

He gave them a minute or two then pressed on, 'It's a bit soon after your mother's death, but when Miss Blake died, she left a will saying Eva could only inherit her house and money if she got married, so that's what we did this morning. Eva's now my wife and your new mother.'

Gracie stared from one adult to the other in shock as the information sank in. 'No! No one can take Mum's place. You said there'd just be us afterwards. You *said!*'

He cast an apologetic glance at Eva. 'That's not very kind of you, Gracie. Eva has given us a home and you like living in Rose Villa, you know you do.'

But Gracie was sobbing uncontrollably and Molly's face was quivering as if she was about to cry as well.

He looked at Eva apologetically. 'She doesn't understand what she's saying.'

Gracie broke off weeping to shout, 'I do so understand! We only buried Mum two days ago and already you're forgetting her. Well, I'm not having another mother.' She looked at Eva with intense loathing. 'You're *not* my mother and you never will be. I hate you!'

Although the words hurt, Eva said only, 'I know I'm not your mother, dear, but I hope I can be your friend.'

'I don't *need* another friend. I've got Molly.' Gracie flung one arm round her sister's shoulders and scowled at them.

'Can I talk to the girls on my own?' Aaron asked. 'Would you mind?'

So Eva walked out and stood in the hall. Gracie's reaction hurt and would colour how Molly regarded her, she had no doubt. She felt very much the outsider at the moment. She didn't want to join Jenny and Wilf in the kitchen so walked into the big sitting room. It still reeked of cigarettes and although she and Jenny had taken all the rubbish out, it felt alien. *His* room still.

So she went upstairs. But her room hadn't changed. Aaron's things were still in Alice's old bedroom. He couldn't even bear to share a bedroom with her. Tears welled in her eyes and she brushed them away quickly, not wanting anyone to see her weeping on her wedding day.

Aaron came looking for her a short time later. 'What are you doing up here in the cold?' he asked in that kind voice he used with the children.

She turned to look at him warily.

'The girls understand the situation now, I think,' he

said, 'but I can't get Gracie to apologise to you. She can be very stubborn, I'm afraid. So I'll apologise on her behalf for her unkind words.'

Eva shrugged. 'Only time will sort it all out and heal her anger. I can wait.'

'You're very understanding. They're getting ready for bed now. I think they feel safer in the kitchen. They're not used to having so many rooms. Jenny's made them some cocoa and when they've finished I'll see them to bed. Why don't you come down and join us?'

She nodded, but the minute she went into the kitchen, the girls stopped chatting to Jenny and scowled at her.

Nonetheless, Aaron insisted she and not Jenny put them to bed, and he went up with them to help. This made the girls fall silent, because they both knew their father would tolerate no cheekiness.

When Eva bent over to kiss Gracie good night, the girl turned away.

Molly allowed a kiss, but stared at her with frightened eyes and did not kiss her back.

As they went downstairs Eva saw how stiffly Aaron was walking and forgot her own worries. 'Your leg must be hurting. I'll help you change the dressing later.'

'I can manage, thank you.'

'It'll be easier, surely, if I—'

He stopped walking. 'Eva, just let me be for a while. If you leave us all to settle in gently, in our own time, it'll all work out, I'm sure.'

'Very well.' But she was hurt by what felt like a rejection by all three of them and when she lay in bed that night, she didn't try to hold back the tears. She didn't want to take things easily. She wanted Aaron to be her proper husband, wanted him in her bed, by her side. Wanted to stop being so alone.

21

Once he was sure Eva was asleep Aaron got up again and crept downstairs, not putting his leg brace on because he wanted to be able to move with more freedom, not to mention stealth. He hated deceiving her but didn't want her running into danger, and in her own quiet way she could be very determined. Wilf had gone back to stay with Grandad Gill, but they'd agreed that Aaron would signal when everyone was asleep, so he switched on the kitchen light, which could be seen from across the road, and waited for his friend to join him.

'I've brought my tools,' Wilf said as he came in. He indicated a roll of stained canvas slung across his body. 'Have you got a torch?'

'Yes. Look, are you sure you can do it without leaving any sign?'

Wilf grinned. 'Oh, yes.' He patted the roll with its strange bulging shapes. 'They taught me some useful tricks in the Army. I could blow up the shed, too, if you wanted.'

'I don't think we'll need to go that far. It could just be Blake's personal possessions in those boxes, after all.'

'But you don't think so?'

'No. There's something about him – I can't put my finger on it, but it makes me uneasy. And I don't want him coming near Eva again. Ever.'

The two men left the house quietly via the french windows of the big sitting room.

The muffled click of a door opening downstairs was enough to wake Eva. She sat up in bed, her heart thumping. Was someone trying to break in? Had Gus returned? Slipping out of bed, she moved the edge of the curtain so that she could peep through the window. As her eyes grew accustomed to the darkness she saw two male silhouettes below in the faint light of a half moon, but to her frustration the waving branches of the tree outside her window impeded her view. Then they moved on and she saw that one of them was limping. It must be Aaron.

What was he doing out there in the middle of the night? And who was the other man?

They were heading towards the shed where Gus's things were stored. So they were checking what was there, were they? Without even telling her! Well, she wasn't having that. Aaron might not want to share her bedroom, but he wasn't going to keep other things from her. She'd been too protected in her life with Alice, she knew that now, and intended to change it.

Snatching up her dressing gown she shrugged into it, then dragged her coat on over that, slipping her shoes on her bare feet in her haste to join Aaron and, she guessed, Wilf. Well, who else could the other man be?

A minute later she was passing through the french

windows of the big sitting room, following the two men. It was a very still night so she tried to move quietly, wanting to see exactly what they were doing before she revealed herself. Suddenly she tripped over a root and a few seconds later someone grabbed her, putting a hand across her mouth. She struggled wildly for a moment, then something about her captor made her realise who it was and she stopped struggling.

He fumbled across her face, feeling her hair, which was hanging loose down her back, then moved his head closer to whisper, 'Eva?'

'Yes, Aaron.'

'What the hell are you doing out here?'

'Finding out what *you're* doing.'

He chuckled and put his arm round her shoulders, leading her over to the shed where Wilf was working on the padlock by the light of a small torch dangling from a hook above the shed door.

'We have a visitor, lad.'

Wilf swung round, grabbing the torch to shine it on her face. He laughed and let it point downwards again, steadying its swing with one finger. 'You ought to keep your wife under better control and – ah!'

The loop of the padlock clicked open and with a murmur of satisfaction Wilf unhooked it, opened the hasp and hung the padlock back on the loop of metal. Eva expected him to open the shed, but he didn't. He took the torch and examined the edges of the door minutely, finding a small piece of wood wedged in one corner, something Eva wouldn't even have noticed. He laid that carefully on the nearby window sill.

She shivered, suddenly aware of her bare legs, and Aaron put his arm round her again.

'Go and wait for us inside,' he whispered. 'You'll catch your death of cold.'

'No. I want to see what Gus is keeping in there.'

As Wilf shone the torch to and fro, they could see that the shed was full of wooden boxes of various sizes, all with lids nailed firmly down. The piles reached nearly to the ceiling and the three people almost filled the small space left, body pressed against body, breath mingling to mist the chill air.

'Gus didn't bring this many things with him,' Eva said at last in puzzlement. 'I only saw him take half a dozen boxes in. Where have these all come from?'

'He brought them in over the back wall of the garden, I should think,' Wilf said, remembering the line of footprints he'd seen from Eva's bedroom window when he and Gracie broke in.

'But why?' Aaron asked thoughtfully.

'So no one would know how many boxes there were?' Eva offered.

'What would that matter if they were only his books and personal possessions?'

Aaron stared round. 'He'd not lay traps so that he'd know whether anyone got in if they weren't valuable. And no one nails down boxes of books like that.'

Wilf shone the torch carefully over the boxes nearest him. 'One or two of them have been opened recently. I can re-open those without leaving any traces of tampering. It'd be more of a risk with the others, which haven't been opened for a long time. We'll try this one first, I think. Come and hold it steady for me, Aaron lad.'

Eva watched him examine one of the boxes with the same meticulous care for markers or booby traps as he had with the door. It was a while before he even attempted to open it and by then she was shivering. But she wasn't going back to the house till the men did. Definitely not.

The box revealed pieces of monogrammed silverware, each carefully wrapped in black cloth. Wilf played his torch over them in silence.

'Stolen, I should think,' Aaron said. 'We need to make a sketch of that monogram if we're to trace the pieces. It's in Latin, so we can't be sure which country they're from. I think I can remember the design and words. Fasten up that box and we'll check the others.'

The next was smaller and contained jewellery, mostly gold, the rings set with precious stones. One brooch had *Ma bien aimée* set on it in diamonds.

'Remember as many of these pieces as you can, Eva,' Aaron said. 'Were the Blakes rich enough to own jewellery like this?'

'No. And Alice always said Gus's branch of the family was quite poor. His father was only her half-brother and Alice didn't get on with her step-mother, so she was brought up by an aunt.'

'Then who does this belong to? It looks like top-quality stuff.'

The air was suddenly so charged with animosity that Eva looked from one man to the other in puzzlement.

'He was in France and Belgium, from what he said in the pub.' Wilf's voice was a snarl.

'I think we're talking about looting here,' Aaron said, and looked at Eva. 'There were some who robbed the corpses on the battlefields. Bad enough taking "souvenirs" from the Germans, I never did it, but when it comes to stealing from our own lads and our Allies' homes . . . well, we knew what to do with sods like that when we caught them!' He looked round, frowning. 'What I don't understand is how the hell Blake got this much stuff home from the front without being noticed. And I can't actually see how one man could acquire so much.'

'Unless,' Wilf said slowly, 'it's not just one man's hoard. Unless it was an organised operation. There were one or two of those, sadly.' He re-fastened the box and turned to a third one. From this he brought out another piece of silver, again with a monogram on it, this time with a motto in French.

Aaron turned to Eva. 'I'm going to have trouble remembering the designs of these two monograms. Could you fetch us a pencil and paper, love? Will you be all right going back to the house on your own? I'll keep watch outside till you return.'

She was only a few yards away from the shed when she heard a sound from the foot of the garden. Turning to stare into the darkness, she realised someone was climbing over the wall. No, more than one person. There was a splashing noise and someone cursed loudly and emphatically until another voice clipped out a sharp order: Gus's voice.

She looked towards the shed and saw that Aaron had vanished inside, presumably to warn Wilf. She would be in full view when the newcomers reached the shed so edged back towards a garden seat, crouching down behind it partly hidden by a bush but still able to see what was happening. Her heart was pounding and she felt very alert.

The other man falling into the stream had delayed Gus, thank goodness. But she was on edge until two figures emerged from the shed. One clicked the padlock back on the door and reached up to fit the marker into the door frame, then they both slipped into the almost leafless shrubs nearby, sinking down and merging with the dark earth.

She couldn't move any further away in case she stumbled and alerted the intruders, but suddenly realised her pale skin would betray her so scraped her hand along the ground and rubbed it over her face. It was freezing cold and damp, and she was shivering. Was this how it had been in the trenches? She wanted so much to understand a little of what Aaron and Wilf had gone through.

Three figures appeared round the corner of the shed, the first one much taller than the others. He shone a torch briefly on the door, checking the telltale wooden marker before opening the padlock and going inside. The others waited outside. A minute later the door opened again and there was a murmur of voices. One of the men followed him inside, but as the two of them came out again, the moon went behind the clouds. Eva could only wait, unable to see, shivering in the biting cold and wondering what they were doing.

When the moon reappeared there were no men outside the shed, but the door was still open and an occasional flicker of light from inside suggested some-one was using a torch.

It was several minutes before two men returned, this time avoiding the stream. The moon was no longer obscured by clouds so Eva was able to watch them carrying away a large box. They came back for others.

The tall figure eventually came out of the shed and locked the door again. It was clearly Gus. He stopped to look up at the house, then turned towards the bottom of the garden. She saw his silhouette against the sky as he climbed over the wall, but forced herself to count up to a hundred before she moved. As she pushed herself to her feet, her limbs were so numb she moved awkwardly and nearly fell.

A shadowy figure appeared beside her, steadying her. She realised it was Aaron and collapsed into his arms with a low groan of relief.

'Thank God you're all right,' he whispered, holding her close to him.

'Just c-cold,' she managed through chattering teeth.

He kept his lips close to her ear. 'Let's get you inside and warm you up. Try to move quietly. Sounds seem to carry further at night.'

Even with his bad leg, he seemed more sure of himself in the darkness than she was and a couple of times prevented her from tripping.

Inside the house she reached automatically for the light switch and he grabbed her hand.

'Not yet, love. We'll go through into the kitchen and get something to warm you up. I don't think we should switch any lights on until Wilf gets back.'

'Where's he gone?'

'He's following them.'

'But that's dangerous. What if they see him?'

'Then he's in trouble.'

She looked at Aaron, but it was too dark to make out his expression. 'Shouldn't you go after him in case he needs help?'

His voice was harsh. 'With this damned leg, I'd probably trip and warn them.'

She heard the pain in his voice and wondered yet again what it was like for a strong man suddenly to find himself disabled. She watched, still shivering, as he worked in the dark kitchen to heat water, make cocoa and fill a hot water bottle. He left all the gas burners on and gradually the room got warm. The blue light from the flames gave it an eerie glow. In fact, everything seemed slightly unreal to Eva.

There was a faint click from the direction of the sitting room and Aaron swung round. A minute later the kitchen door opened and Wilf appeared.

As Aaron relaxed, Eva saw him put down the big chopping knife.

'They put the boxes in a lorry and drove off,' Wilf said, accepting a beaker of cocoa. 'Thanks, lad. My fingers are like icicles.'

'I wonder where he's going to store them now?'

'If it's anywhere round here we'll find out, and if he's been looting our own or our allies, me and the lads will make him very sorry for it before we hand him over to the authorities, I promise you.'

'Steady on,' Aaron said warningly.

Wilf's calm tone was chilling. 'You'll not stop us, Aaron. Scum like that should be taken out and shot, and no one will ever persuade me different.'

'I just want you to take it easy. We need to prove it first, don't we?' He turned to Eva. 'Do you have that pencil and paper, love? I think we can risk putting the light on now.'

She nodded and went to get them.

With swift, sure strokes Aaron sketched the crest and the words they had seen on the first piece of silver, then listed the individual items. 'Have I forgotten anything, Wilf?'

He picked up the paper and studied it. 'Sugar bowl.'

Aaron added it to the list, then took a second sheet of paper and made another sketch, this time hesitating over it. 'I think it went like this. Does either of you remember the details?'

Eva studied it, then took the pencil out of his hand and reshaped one of the lines. 'I think it was more like this.'

'Aye, that's right. Well done, lass. And the motto was here.'

'Yes. You're very good at drawing,' she said, leaning over his shoulder to look at the pieces of paper.

'You have to be able to sketch out machinery and parts,' he said absent-mindedly, still studying the second drawing and making adjustments to it. 'That's as close as we're likely to get, I think.' A yawn caught him by surprise and he stretched his arms above his head. 'I think we'll leave it for tonight. I'll make some better copies in the morning. Come on, lass. Time we got up to bed.' He grinned suddenly. 'And you'd better wash your face, too.'

Eva gasped as she realised she was still covered in black streaks of earth. 'Why didn't you tell me before?'

'It suits you. And anyway, it was very sensible of you. I knew you hadn't had time to get back to the house and was terrified they'd see you.'

The warm approval in his voice pleased her, as did the thought that he'd been afraid for her safety, but when she went into her bedroom and closed the door, loneliness seemed to descend on her like an icy cloud. For the past few years she had enjoyed her own company, or so she'd told herself, but she'd enjoyed the sense of camaraderie tonight far more. She felt she understood the bond between 'the lads' much better now.

As she got ready for bed, she almost went across the landing to ask Aaron if they could stay together. But she couldn't bring herself to do that. He was the one who had decided they were to sleep apart. It was for him to decide when he wanted to share her bed.

If he ever did.

In the morning there was no sign of him so Eva and Jenny got the girls ready for school. They left, protesting loudly that they hadn't seen their father. When

Jenny went across to see how Wilf and her grandad were, there was still no sign of Aaron and Eva wondered if he was still asleep.

She fidgeted about then gave in to temptation and crept up the stairs, relieved to hear him moving about in his room. She tapped on the door. 'Are you all right?'

He opened the door and smiled at her. 'I'm fine.'

'I was worried when you didn't get up at your usual time. Would you like me to bring you up a cup of tea?'

'I'll come down for it. I got up again last night, you see. I couldn't settle till I'd made proper copies of the sketches and fiddled around with that second crest. I think I've got it more or less right now. I didn't wake up till I heard you saying goodbye to the girls.' He gestured towards the door. 'I could murder for some food.'

'I'll cook you breakfast.'

It felt cosy and intimate to cook him fried eggs and toast, then sit with him while he ate. He finished the plateful of food quickly, eating with the neat economy of movement with which he did everything except walk. Pushing the plate away with a sigh of satisfaction, he stared round. 'This is luxury to me.'

'I – um – hope you're going to be happy here.'

He laid his hand over hers. 'Shh. Stop worrying. Let things happen. We'll all shake down together after a few weeks, even our Gracie.'

He didn't take his hand away but sat frowning in thought, so she sat quietly, enjoying his touch, enjoying having him to herself for once.

After a few minutes he looked up at her. 'I think we

need to send copies of those drawings to the relevant authorities. If you don't mind providing the money, I'd like to send Wilf down to London with them. He has some useful connections there still. He was well thought of, you know. They wanted him to become an officer, but he refused.'

'What did he do in the war?'

'Reconnaissance. Went behind enemy lines gathering information. Brave fellows, his lot.'

'Fools, more like,' Wilf said from behind them.

Eva turned round with an involuntary squeak of shock. 'I didn't hear you come in.'

He winked. 'Haven't lost my touch then.'

'I thought you'd know who in London to take these sketches to,' Aaron said. 'We've got enough money now to send you. You can tell folk from the village you're doing a job for an old friend somewhere nearby, and while you're away I'll leave the third set of sketches with Beaman and tell him what's been happening. He's nobody's fool and we need to make sure Blake doesn't wriggle off the hook, whatever happens to us.'

'You'd better be careful while I'm gone,' said Wilf. 'We can bring Stan in to stay with Grandad, but you'll need someone to keep watch here at night.'

'Bob will help.'

'We should pay them,' Eva said. 'We can say they're helping us with some renovations or sorting the garden out, if you like.' She paused, then said sadly, 'It's serious, isn't it? What Gus has been doing?'

'We think so. Not everyone would worry about it. There were some who were always on the fiddle. But I never could abide thieving, and this is on rather a large scale.'

'Alice couldn't stand thieving, either. She would have been so upset to think of her nephew doing something like that. And if you think there's danger, we'd better change the locks, hadn't we? Gus still has a key to these.'

Aaron gave her an approving nod and she felt warmed by it.

Maybe he was right, she thought as she went about her daily chores. Maybe they should get used to one another first before they slept together.

After all, what did she know about things like that?

Gus Blake got up early that same morning after a lousy night's sleep. The Red Lion was a noisy place, with people passing by under his window making their way to work from a ridiculously early hour. But the pub was sloppily run and no one had noticed him leaving or coming back during the night, at least.

He was furious that he'd had to move the boxes. They'd be nowhere near as safe at Sid Linney's. He'd hoped to have another few months at Rose Villa! Keeping his things in a private house in an isolated place like Heyshaw had been perfect, especially one with a back entrance across the fields. Now all that had been ruined by that stupid bitch and her clod of a lover.

He tried to keep his anger under control as he ate breakfast in the lounge bar, chatted to the waitress and nodded to the only other guest, who looked like a commercial traveller, and a seedy one at that.

When he had finished he drove out to the farm and

found Sid Linney standing scowling at two men who were repairing a section of dry stone wall.

'Oh, there you are,' Sid said glumly. 'Come over to the house, old chap. Sorry it's in such a mess.' He stared round angrily as they entered. 'I'll have to get myself a bloody housekeeper, I suppose.'

'Why don't you make your wife come back? If you got hold of your son, she'd soon fall into line.'

'I don't know as I want her.' Sid gave a scornful sniff. 'It's a bugger, isn't it? I don't miss her at all except for the housework. Can't think why I married the stupid bitch in the first place. It's a relief not to have her criticising what I do, always wanting to spoil the labourers with cups of tea, or giving them eggs and vegetables. She was too soft with them by half.'

Gus tried to keep an alert, interested look on his face until he could change the subject. 'Thanks for lending me your lorry. I didn't disturb you last night, did I?'

'Disturb me?'

'We brought the first lot of stuff across.' He grinned. 'You must be a sound sleeper. The dogs barked till they recognised me.' His smile faded. 'I couldn't find a key to that old store room. You sure you've got one? I don't like leaving it unlocked.'

'I'll go and fetch it in a minute. You look buggered.'

'Yes. You can't get a lie-in in a noisy hotel.' A thought suddenly struck him. 'You don't want a lodger here, do you?'

Sid looked at him in surprise, then nodded slowly. 'I do if you're going to pay half the expenses of the housekeeper and food.'

'I don't mind, as long as I get use of that space in the barn free.'

Sid stuck his hand out and they shook on it. 'We'll seal the bargain with a shot of whisky, eh? Then I'll lend you my cart to go and pick up the rest of your stuff from Rose Villa. One of the men has taken the lorry out on a job this morning. You can move in here today if you want. It's poor cheer sitting on your own at the end of the day an' you're a good drinking mate.'

'You'd better lend me your men as well as the cart. I'm no good with horses. It'll only take an hour.'

'Get the lads who helped you the other night. My men have enough to do on the farm since Brierley left.'

Gus breathed in deeply, but said nothing.

As they walked outside Sid stared at the big car. 'Whatever it is you're doing must pay a damn' sight better than farming. I couldn't afford to buy a posh car like that, that's for sure.' He was scowling as he went back to work.

Gus watched him go, then set off to find his two helpers again. Not his first choice of a companion, Sid Linney, but he'd put up with the fellow for the time being. A few more weeks at most should see nearly everything sold, then he'd settle his score with the Brierleys and leave the country.

When Jenny came back across the road, she said with an attempt at a smile, 'I'd better start packing my things now, hadn't I, Eva love?'

'Could you stay on for a day or two? I've got an idea

about the future, but I'll need to talk to Aaron about it first.'

Jenny hesitated, then asked, 'Why is he sleeping in Alice's old room? Don't you want to share his bed?'

Eva shook her head blindly, tears rising in spite of her efforts not to give way to her emotions. 'Yes, I do. I want a real marriage, but he said we should wait till we know one another better.'

Jenny gave her a hug. 'Well, maybe he's right. It's early days yet, isn't it? Lil's only been dead a few days. Give him time to recover.'

Eva sniffed. 'I know. I keep telling myself that. But sometimes I think no man will ever want me. Gus didn't, just the money, and – and I had to persuade Aaron to marry me.'

Her voice rang out so sharply that Aaron heard it in the hall and stopped dead. He hadn't realised how much to heart she'd taken his refusal to share her bedroom and it surprised him that such a pretty young woman should have such a low opinion of herself underneath that cool exterior. It was partly due to that nasty sod, but also Miss Blake's fault. They'd been joking in the village for years that the old lady guarded her young friend carefully, and had even warned off a couple of young men who'd shown an interest because she didn't want her protégée to marry and leave her. He wasn't sure how true the rumours were, but he'd heard them more than once.

He tiptoed back down the hall, then approached the kitchen more noisily. 'Have you –' he began then stopped as a horse and cart clopped into the drive, followed by Gus Blake in his big black car. 'Hide these! I'll go and keep an eye on Blake.' He thrust the sketches at Eva and flung open the kitchen door.

She shoved the papers into Jenny's hand and went out to join Aaron. 'You're not going on your own. I don't trust Gus.'

He turned to grin at her. 'Protecting me, are you, lass?'

She could feel her cheeks growing hot. 'Better safe than sorry.'

He put an arm round her shoulders and smiled at her before turning to watch Blake, who was ordering the two men around. They were the same ones who had thrown Aaron's possessions out of his house for Sid Linney and he recognised the cart as Sid's. Was that where Blake was storing his things now?

'You need to ask our permission before you go into the back garden,' he called as Gus started towards the side of the house without a word of greeting.

'Do you want those boxes taking away or not?' Gus demanded, expression thunderous.

'Yes. But on the other hand, we don't want folk walking in and out of our garden as if they own it.'

There was a pregnant silence, then Gus snapped, 'All right if I move my things, Eva?'

'As long as you're careful not to damage anything,' she replied.

She nipped inside for their coats, then she and Aaron went round the back and stood watching what was going on. That earned them a few more dirty looks from Gus.

It didn't take long to get the boxes loaded onto the

cart and when the horses had clopped away, followed
by a scowling Gus in his car, Eva looked at Aaron.
'Now what?'

'Now we send Wilf off on his little trip.'

None of them even considered speaking to the local
bobby, who was a placid fellow not noted for his
intelligence.

But before Wilf could set out, another of the London
letters arrived for Gus by the second post. Eva took it
to Aaron, who was mending a cupboard door in the
kitchen. 'What shall we do with this?'

He studied it. 'Steam it open and read it.'

'Are you sure?'

'Yes. Put the kettle on, will you?' When the water
was boiling he worked carefully and got the envelope
open without tearing it. After reading the letter, he
passed it to Eva. 'It's only a reminder from his wife
about the money.'

But the letter seemed a strange one to her, not at all
the sort of thing a wife would write to her husband,
even if the two of them didn't get on. 'Why has she
underlined "Mrs Blake" like that?'

He glanced indifferently at it. 'To remind him
they're still married, I suppose. I'll copy down her
address. Maybe it'll come in useful.' He resealed the
letter by moistening some gum on an unused envelope
and rubbing it on the flap of Gus's letter. 'There. Do
you think anyone will notice?'

'No. That's clever.'

He chuckled. 'Amazing what you learn to do in the
Army.'

'How shall we get it to him?'

'Leave it with Charlie Featherstone at the pub. He'll pass it on.'

Wilf and Jenny turned up just then. He was packed and ready to leave for London. He grimaced as Aaron passed him some money. 'I'll go carefully with it, I promise you.'

'Don't stint yourself, lad. It's money well spent if it helps catch thieves. And you need to eat and find decent lodgings while you're there, think on.'

'I'll walk with you into the village, Wilf,' Jenny said abruptly.

Eva sighed as she watched them set off. 'She's very fond of him.'

'He's fond of her, but he won't marry her unless he has a job. A man has his pride.'

She nodded and turned away, thinking he was speaking for himself as well.

He pulled her back, set his hands on her shoulders and looked her in the eyes. 'I heard what you were saying to Jenny about me not wanting you.'

'Oh.'

'I do want you, but I don't want to rush things. We're near strangers and you've never been married before. It really is best to take things easily, get to know one another.'

Her heart lightened a little. 'If that's what you wish.'

'It is. And there's another thing we need to talk about. I'm a bit like Wilf. Independent. I'll need to find a way to earn a living. I can't just live off your money, however much you have. It wouldn't sit right with me. I know jobs aren't easy to come by, but I'm a trained mechanic so surely someone will want me? With enough money for petrol it'd be no problem to travel into Littleborough or even Rochdale every day.'

This was an opportunity to share her thoughts. 'I've got an even better idea. You once said you'd like to open a garage.'

He shrugged. 'I still would. Only that takes money.'

'Well, we have money now. And what better way to spend it than on starting a business for you to run?'

He stared at her, his eyes very blue and serious. 'You'd trust me that much?'

'Of course I would.'

He had to turn away and she knew he was fighting for control of himself. How harrowing it was to see good men like him and Wilf so desperate for the dignity of work!

His voice was rough. 'I swear I'd pay you back, Eva. Every single penny.'

'Get on with you,' she said lightly. 'We're husband and wife. It'd be like paying yourself back.' During a long silence she watched a variety of expressions chase one another across his face, but the brighter look in his eyes pleased her.

He walked to the kitchen window to stare out. 'I could set it up in the front garden, you know. There's plenty of room and you – we – would still have the back garden. That'd keep the costs down quite a bit. Would you mind that? It'd make a mess of the front and there'd be folk coming and going all the time, so I'll understand if you don't want it.'

She saw hope hovering behind his wariness, as if he dare not trust in it yet. 'I think that's an excellent idea.' It was her turn to hesitate before asking, 'Could I help you with it, perhaps? Do the office work and accounts or something. They don't allow married women to teach, you see, and – well, I'm not used to being idle either.'

'Won't running the house keep you busy?'

'I want to talk to you about that as well. Could we keep Jenny on as maid, do you think? She needs work in the village so she can stay near Grandad, and we could get Wilf in to look after the garden as well. The man who used to do it has left the district and it's too big for me to manage on my own. And you'll be busy with your garage.'

'I can't get used to having so much money.' He saw her wince and gave her a rueful smile. 'You do what you want, love. I wish more rich folk used their money to help others. Maybe then this country wouldn't be in such a mess. I'll have to make plans, work out how best to open a garage.' He looked down at her solemnly, one hand on her shoulder. 'You don't think I'm stupid, wanting to work when I could sit idle on your money?'

'No. I don't think you're stupid in any way, Aaron.'

'You'd better start learning to type then, if you're going to be my secretary.'

He let go of her, smiling now. For a moment his eyes were so full of dreams that she could see what he must have looked like as a young man and she felt like weeping for what the war and its aftermath had done to him and others like him.

22

In London Wilf went to see his former major who was now working in an office job behind the scenes. Hugh Grimmond might be interested in what they had found in Heyshaw, but if not would at least be able to tell Wilf where to report it. He had no difficulty getting in to see the ex-officer with whom he had worked closely for the final year of the war and whose life he had once saved.

Hugh stood up to welcome him, beaming. 'Wilf Horrocks! What are *you* doing in London?'

'Come to see you.'

As Hugh gestured him to a chair, an alert expression replaced the smile. 'Something cropped up?'

'Could be.' Wilf explained the situation and handed over the sketches of the crests and the list of what they'd found. 'We thought it looked suspicious. Oh, and I also have a London address for Blake's wife.'

Hugh studied the papers and began chewing one thumb. Wilf knew better than to interrupt his thoughts.

When he looked up a short time later Hugh said only, 'Can you come back to see me tomorrow? I'll look into this and decide how to tackle it. Where are you staying?'

'I've still got to find somewhere.'

'We have a flat for people who are helping us. You can use that while you're in town. Don't go near Blake's wife. I'll look into things there, all right?'

Wilf nodded. There would no doubt be a good reason for that.

'And be ready at six tonight. I'm taking you out for a drink with one or two people you may just recognise.' He leaned back and looked at Wilf, his expression serious. 'Sure I can't persuade you to join me here in London permanently?'

'No. I've had my fill of that sort of thing. I just want a peaceful life now – once this present mess is sorted out. Besides, I've found a home in Heyshaw and good friends, almost like a family. When I find a job, I may even have a wife as well.' He didn't need to explain further. They'd chatted together on long wakeful nights and Hugh knew all about his background, had been there when he'd wept for his brother. This man was the least officer-like of anyone Wilf had served under and yet he'd got things done and everyone had respected him.

As he walked away Wilf smiled. He felt alive again, of use to his country. He had missed that sense of worth lately. And although his help was essential to Grandad Gill, it wasn't the same as having a proper job with regular wages. Should he accept Hugh's offer and come down to London to work? He shook his head. No, he'd give it a bit longer in Lancashire. He didn't want to leave Jenny, not while there was even half a chance of marrying her one day. Didn't want to leave Aaron and the lads, either, come to that.

After he'd dumped his things in the tiny flat, he spent a pleasant hour ambling along the bank of the Thames, studying the people as much as the sights. These southerners looked more prosperous and there were fewer men begging. Clearly things weren't nearly as bad down here. Once, however, he came across a group of Welshmen singing with an upturned cap set on the pavement in front of them. He stopped to listen. A sign proclaimed *OUT OF WORK EX-SERVICE-MEN* and he could see the shame in their eyes as they stood there. Their singing was beautiful. He tossed half a crown, almost all his own remaining money, into their cap and wished them luck.

The evening brought him into contact with three other old friends, and he eagerly exchanged news with them, reliving old times and repeating old stories and jokes.

'Come and see me at eleven tomorrow morning,' Hugh said as they parted.

Wilf walked slowly back to the flat, which felt very luxurious after Grandad's little cottage, with both electricity and a proper bathroom. But Wilf knew where he'd rather be – and who he'd rather be with.

The following day he was shown straight into Hugh's office and found a senior police officer sitting there as well, so stood to attention in the old way and didn't take a seat until asked.

Hugh took charge. 'We've been hunting a group of villains for a while now, Wilf, with the help of the police, because it's both Army and civilian stuff. We think Blake is part of a conspiracy that dipped its fingers into every pie it could, from stealing stores over here during the war to burgling our allies' châteaux in France and even looting our own dead. Nothing too big, nothing too small for this lot. There's a lawyer chappie in Heyshaw who has contacted the police about some concerns he has over Blake.'

'Not Eric Beaman?'

The police officer nodded.

Wilf whistled in surprise, then wondered why. Beaman was a canny sort and staunchly patriotic, noted for it in the village.

'Acting on Beaman's information, we've sent for Blake's wife. He may be the key to our breaking the network.'

'Blake? I can't see him knowing the ringleaders. He's slippery, I'll grant you that, but look how he messed up the wedding, and his wife seems to have traced him easily enough. No, I can't see Blake as a master criminal. Why, he hid valuable stuff in the garden shed of a house that didn't even belong to him, protected only by a simple padlock. Bloody stupid, that. And now he's moved it to Sid Linney's. Even stupider. Sid's known in the village for poking his nose into anything and everything, whether it concerns him or not.'

Hugh grinned at the inspector. 'When Wilf talks like that, it's worth listening. He's as shrewd as they come, for all his quiet ways and refusal to accept promotion during the war.'

The other man grunted acceptance of this and studied him with more interest.

Hugh turned back to Wilf. 'We don't think Blake is a boss. A junior officer in the gang, perhaps, or a renegade who's double-crossing them. Oh, and we've traced one of the crests already. The silver was stolen from a château in Northern France quite early in the war. It was a big haul and was never traced. A bit embarrassing, that, since it could only have been one of ours who did it. We don't even know whether they brought the loot straight back to Blighty or hid it over there and retrieved it later.' He sighed. 'You don't expect to be fighting thieves from your own side, do you? We'd be very happy to catch up with those concerned, because we think they're the same ones who got away with a big pay delivery later in the war, and that sticks in the gullet somewhat as well.'

Wilf allowed himself a low whistle of astonishment. The lads at the front would have gone mad about their pay being delayed.

'We've been piecing the picture together gradually, but this is the first time anyone's found a cache.' Hugh gave a thin smile. 'We *are* getting closer to the top men through other channels, though, and think they're starting to get worried. Pieces have been sold one by one in the region round Heyshaw, offered in pawn-shops or to dealers in stolen property by all sorts of minor scum selling things on commission for someone they met in a pub. That's made it hard to trace the organisers, but one or two have mentioned a tall fellow asking them to do it and you say this Blake is tall?'

An aide came in just then and whispered in his ear.

'Ah, good. Show Mrs Blake in, please.'

The woman Wilf had glimpsed in Heyshaw entered the room, scowling at them as she took a seat.

'We'd like you to tell us about your husband, Mrs Blake,' Hugh said once she was seated. 'What's he been up to?' He watched her carefully as she stared sullenly at them. It was a surprisingly long time before she answered, and her gaze went from one to the other as if she were having difficulty deciding what to say.

'How the hell should I know?' she replied eventually. 'I hardly saw the bugger during the war and only caught up with him because someone told me they'd seen him in Leeds. I guessed then that he might be at his auntie's. He always said she was worth a bit and he was the only male Blake left.' She began to fiddle with her gloves. 'It's just like him to sponge on an old lady. He'll do anything rather than work, that lazy sod will. Actually, I don't care if I never see him again as long as he continues to pay me my maintenance.'

There was silence and as it continued, Hugh asked, 'What else do you know about him?'

She ran a tongue over her lips, seemed about to speak, then shook her head slightly and said in a flat voice, 'Nothing. What should I know? I hadn't seen the bugger since I got the "missing presumed dead" telegram. Though I wasn't surprised to hear he was alive. It's only the good who die young.'

Hugh signalled to his companion to keep quiet and she began to shift uneasily in her seat.

'I don't want anything to do with him,' she said at last. 'I just want the money.'

'Well, I doubt he'll be able to continue paying you

for much longer, Mrs Blake. The Government has some interest in his future.'

She stared at him, mouth half-open, then shrugged and nothing they said could get any further information from her. But Hugh remained certain she knew something else.

When she'd gone, he looked at the inspector. 'A little surveillance might be in order, don't you think? Can your chaps handle that?'

'Definitely.'

Hugh turned to Wilf. 'And I'd like to send someone back with you to keep an eye on things in Heyshaw. You can pretend Mac's an old Army friend and—'

'Let me do another recce first, see if Blake's still around.'

'All right. We'll try it for a week or two. But if he doesn't make any moves, we might have to take more direct action to flush him out.'

Eva took Jenny into her sitting room. 'Would you stay on in your old job, working for me and Aaron?'

'You don't really need me, love. Oh, I'll help you get straight, but I don't want any pretend job thank you.'

'It isn't a pretend job. Aaron's going to open a garage, build it in front of the house. He'll repair cars and bikes, sell petrol and bits and pieces, perhaps even cars. There's only the South Heyshaw Motor Company round here and he says there's easily enough business for two garages. The richer members of our community still have money to spare, it's the poorer ones who're feeling the pinch, mostly. And I'm going to help him in the office.' She gave Jenny a rueful smile. 'I think I'd go mad just being a housewife. Polly loves it, but Lizzie helps in the shop and I think I'm more like her, really.'

Jenny swallowed hard. 'Then you're – not just making work for me?'

'Definitely not.'

'Oh, Eva love, I can't think of anything I'd like better than to stay on here.' Her voice quavered with emotion.

'There's one condition.'

'Oh?'

'You're not to call me Mrs Brierley. Never, ever. You're my friend, the very best friend I've ever had, and I want it to stay that way.'

Jenny flung her arms round her and the two women hugged one another, both with over-bright eyes.

'There's another thing,' Eva said as they drew apart again. 'Do you think Wilf would do the garden for us – just until he gets something else?'

'If it's a real job.'

'You know it is, though it's only a few hours a week. Aaron will be busy setting up his garage, you see, and it's a big garden. Alice would have hated it to go untended.'

The next day being a Saturday, Eva took the girls into Heyshaw and bought them some new clothes. She watched in delight as Molly kept beaming down at her new skirt and stroking the material. Eva had insisted she wear it straight away because her other one was so ragged. The little girl kept staring down at her feet as well, which were now shod in sturdy new shoes.

Even Gracie, also clad in new clothes, was marginally less grumpy today.

'When your voice comes back, Molly,' Eva said casually as they walked back up the hill to North Hey, 'I'm going to teach you to sing. I like a good sing-song, don't you?'

The child frowned at her.

'Her voice might never come back,' Gracie said promptly.

'Oh, I think it will. It's no wonder it vanished with your mother being ill for so long, but now, gradually, things will get back to normal again. And you'll be able to help her.' She knew Gracie was very jealous of her position as her little sister's protector.

'I will?'

'Yes, of course you will. That's what big sisters are for. Lizzie always helped me when she could. You'll like my sisters. We'll go over to visit Lizzie and Peter one Sunday on the train. They have a grocer's shop in Overdale. And maybe in the summer we can have a holiday in Stenton with Polly. She has a little boy called Billy and Richard is her second husband, so she has a stepdaughter from him as well. They've all settled down very happily together.' She let that sink in and added casually, 'Have you ever seen the sea?'

They both shook their head.

'Then that's something else to look forward to.'

She left it at that, hoping the seeds she had sown would bear flowers.

★　　★　　★

As the days passed without a sign of Wilf, Aaron fretted visibly, trying to settle to planning his garage and failing. He busied himself with doing small repairs around the house and could not even be persuaded to go down to the pub for a drink in the evenings.

'I'm not leaving you on your own and that's flat,' he told Eva when she suggested it. 'I don't believe we've heard the last of Blake.'

'Jenny can come across to sit with me while you're out.'

'It'd not be safe enough.'

That worried her. What was he frightened Gus might do? She was praying Alice's nephew would leave Heyshaw soon and that they'd never hear from him again. Clearly Aaron did not expect that to happen. She tried not to let him see how worried she was, because he had enough on his mind at the moment. Stan now came every evening to do a night watchman's job while Aaron slept, so she provided Stan with tea and sandwiches and took care always to lock the doors, except for the sitting room where he sat and from where he patrolled the garden at irregular intervals.

It felt like the lull before the storm. There was so much unresolved, for all the plans they were making.

And Gus Blake not only stayed on in Heyshaw, but turned up at the pub with Sid Linney most nights, as loud and confident as ever, Grandad Gill said.

Why?

Wilf kept his return so quiet that the first they knew of it was when he slipped across to the house after dark, tapping on the kitchen window and nearly making Jenny jump out of her skin. When she let him in, he pulled her towards him and gave her a kiss, saying by way of explanation, 'I missed you.'

She stared at him in mingled shock and joy. 'Does that kiss mean what I think it does?'

'It doesn't mean anything till I have a job, then I'll speak my piece.' He took a step away from her, stared at the floor and said gruffly, 'I shouldn't have kissed you, really, but you looked so fresh and bonny, I couldn't help myself.'

'I don't want you to help yourself,' she said with simple honesty.

'That's all right then.'

Hearing voices Aaron came to investigate, greeting his friend with, 'About time you got back!'

Wilf dragged his eyes away from Jenny. 'We need to talk, all of us.'

They went into the large sitting room, now smelling of polish and with a cheerful fire blazing in the grate. The girls were still up and Wilf looked from them to Aaron, who said, 'Why don't you two go and get washed ready for bed? You can come down again afterwards and have some cocoa.'

'I'll come up in a minute and check that everything's all right,' Eva told them.

'I can manage perfectly well,' Gracie said. 'I *am* ten, you know. I'm quite used to the bathroom now. And Molly *likes* me to help her.'

Eva sighed as she sat down again. Gracie was still reluctant to accept her new role in their lives.

Wilf quickly explained what had happened in London.

'So you think Mrs Blake knows something she's not telling?' Aaron asked when he'd finished.

'I'm sure of it, though I've racked my brain and can't think what it is.'

'We need to check that the boxes are still at the farm, so that you can let Major Grimmond know.'

'Yes. But what about the farm dogs?'

'Oh, they know me. I think we can get into that barn unnoticed if we go in the middle of the night.'

But before they could do anything, Sid Linney got curious about the boxes. He waited till Gus had gone off on another of his little selling trips then went out to the barn.

What he found there made him whistle in surprise. Small objects but valuable if the jewels were real, and they looked real. No wonder Gus was making no attempt to find work, the lucky devil! Sid wished *he* didn't have to work so hard. It was no sinecure being a sodding farmer and having a wife who ran off to live in luxury with her old auntie rather than do her duty by her husband. But he knew Angela would carry out her threat to reveal some of his wartime dealings in food, if he chased after her so he did nothing.

After he'd put Blake's stuff away again, he went back to sit in front of the fire, wondering if he could get a share of Gus's profits. After all, if it was stolen property, he was running a risk too by having it here.

When Gus returned the two men spent a pleasant

evening at the pub, then came home to demolish most of a bottle of whisky – or rather Sid did while Gus tipped some of his into a plant pot.

After Sid had stumbled up to bed, Gus waited for the snoring to start before going out to the barn. What he found made him angry. Someone had been tampering with his boxes, someone very careless.

It was probably Sid. After all, who else would have such easy access to the locked storeroom at the rear of the barn? He went to bed and lay there seething with anger at both himself and Sid. He should have realised what the man was like. Hail fellow well met, a drunkard and a babbler. Nosy bastard, too.

When the dogs began to bark in the small hours of the morning, he stirred in his bed and listened carefully, but it was a brief outburst, probably at some passing fox, and they settled down again almost immediately. It was good having them to keep guard.

But they couldn't guard Sid's tongue. He'd have to do that himself.

Aaron and Wilf waited with the dogs until they were certain no one was coming out of the house to investigate the barking. They were more patient about this than either Sid or Gus would have been, but then they'd learned their patience in a very hard school. Eventually Aaron laid one hand on Wilf's arm and led the way into the barn, which didn't even have a padlock on the outside door.

Inside he waited for his eyes to adjust to the darkness, then led the way across to the small storeroom.

Wilf examined the door, but found no obvious traps. However, it was locked. 'I'll have to pick the lock,' he whispered.

'Hang on a minute.' Aaron fumbled on the lintel. When he found the key he whispered, 'It's still here.' It had always been kept there in old Linney's day, though the storeroom had never been locked then. The key felt rough with rust, but turned easily in the lock, which must have been oiled recently. With a couple of flashes of the torch he guided the other man inside.

Several piles of boxes stood there, the same ones as had been in the shed at Rose Villa.

'Someone's opened them,' Wilf muttered. 'And clumsily.'

Aaron grinned in the darkness. 'I bet it's Sid. He wouldn't be able to resist having a look.'

'How do you think Blake will react to that?'

'I don't know. He's an unknown quantity, isn't he? Rotten for Eva, him being Alice's nephew. It upsets her, I know.'

'Want to check inside them? It'd be child's play to open them again.'

'Just one or two. We'll send a telegram to Grimmond tomorrow and he can send up his observers. We've played our part now.'

They went home, slipping quietly through the darkness undaunted by the light rain that was falling and greeting Stan, who reported that all had been quiet at home.

'I'll be glad to be rid of Blake,' Aaron said as they parted. 'I don't feel as though I can get started on anything else until we've cleared up this mess and I worry about Eva and the girls. If I thought they'd go away, I'd send them somewhere till it's over.'

'Your Eva wouldn't stand for that. Neither would my Jenny.'

'Is it "my Jenny" now?'

'Aye. But nothing's going to happen till I'm able to support a wife. And I'm grateful for the gardening job, but that's not a *real* job, is it?'

'Part-time garden, part-time garage later, maybe? Until things pick up, then it can be full-time at the garage. I'll need help and, no, it's not made-up work, I promise you.'

Wilf stopped, glad the darkness hid his face. 'Do you mean that?' he asked gruffly.

'Yes. But it'll be lean pickings for a while.'

'At least it'll be a start. Thank you, lad.'

The next evening Gus was all smiles until the farm workers had gone home and he was sitting down with Sid to an excellent meal prepared by the housekeeper, who always left as soon as it was served.

When they had finished eating, he said quietly, 'You shouldn't have gone poking around in my boxes, Sid. That stuff is none of your business.'

'How did you . . . ?'

'I have my ways of telling, though you were so careless about how you put them together again a child would have known they'd been tampered with.'

Sid shrugged, feeling secure and affable in his own home. 'No harm meant. I just wanted to know what I was storing for you.'

'And?'

'And I hadn't realised how valuable their contents were. There's a small fortune out there.' He leaned forward. 'If there's a chance of getting a share of whatever you're into, I'd be very interested.'

Gus stared at him. 'I'll remember that. For the moment, just make sure you don't mention those boxes to anyone – *anyone at all!*'

Sid nodded. 'I won't, I promise you.'

Stupid bugger! Gus thought as he lay in bed that night. He knew he couldn't trust Sid to keep quiet for long. When he left Heyshaw he'd have to do something to shut the farmer's big mouth. Permanently.

In London Clara Blake answered a knock on her door and was shoved backwards into her hall. Two men followed her, caps pulled down over their eyes, mufflers up round their faces.

She opened her mouth to yell for help but one of them had his hand over it before she could do more than gurgle. 'If you scream it'll be the last sound you ever make.' He slowly let her go and pushed her into the back room. 'Now, we're here to ask you some questions and if you answer them truthfully, we'll not need to trouble you again.'

He was dressed shabbily but his voice sounded educated, and that worried her for some reason. The other man hadn't spoken at all, just kept staring at her. 'What do you want to know?' she asked.

'Where's your husband?'

'I might have known it was to do with him! That sod's never given me anything but trouble!'

'Just answer the question!'

'He's in the north, in a place called Heyshaw.'

'Did he take any boxes with him?'

'I don't know.'

The man grabbed her and slammed her against the wall. 'The truth, mind!'

'It *is* the truth. I only found out where he was recently by chance and my brother and I went up to see him to get my maintenance money. As long as he pays up, I don't want to see him again.'

'I think you should get yourself a job,' the man said. 'He definitely won't be paying you for much longer. He owes us too much, you see.'

She scowled. He was the second person to say that.

'Who were the men you went off with in the car?'

She let out a long shaky breath. Caught between the devil and the deep blue sea here. 'They were from the Government,' she said cautiously. 'They wanted to know about Gus, too.'

'What did you tell them?'

'Same as I've told you. Where he is.'

'You didn't mention Ted Lowder?'

She sucked in her breath in shock, then shook her head vigorously. 'No.'

'Good.' He stepped back. 'I think you'd be wise to forget you ever saw us. And forget our friend in the north, too. If you enjoy living, that is. Is that clear?'

She nodded. What else could she do?

23

The next day Gracie looked flushed and feverish, complaining of a sore throat, so they decided to keep her home from school.

She immediately burst into tears. 'Molly can't go without me! Those girls will bash her.'

'I'll take her to school myself,' Eva said quietly. 'And fetch her back.'

'I can go if you're busy,' Aaron volunteered.

'No, you stay here and keep an eye on things. I need to do some shopping anyway. Jenny's going to clear *his* bedroom out this morning.'

When they left the house she took Molly's hand. The child did not pull away. Eva talked quietly to her as they walked into Heyshaw together.

As they got near the school, Molly dragged her feet and looked up at Eva pleadingly. 'I don't feel well,' she whispered.

Eva laid a hand on her forehead. 'You're not feverish and you can't stay off school for no reason, dear. But I won't forget to come for you this afternoon, I promise.' She gave her a little push and Molly walked slowly into the playground, shoulders hunched. Two other girls came to talk to her.

Eva moved away, but as she was turning the corner, she looked back and saw Molly's friends move away hurriedly when a bigger girl came up to them. She was one of the three Eva had once caught bullying Molly.

Miss Deevers was standing by the door watching all this, but made no attempt to intervene when the big girl started to push Molly around. Outraged, Eva ran back through the gate and across the yard, dragging the bigger girl away. 'You stay away from her, Christine Smart!'

'Wasn't doing anything wrong, just playing.'

'Play with girls your own age and leave Molly alone from now on.'

Miss Deevers came up. 'Parents are not allowed in the yard,' she said – as if Eva had not been a former colleague, as if there hadn't been a genuine need for her to intervene.

Eva turned round to look her in the eye. When they had worked together she had always been a bit nervous of the older woman, but now all she felt was anger. 'When *you* keep a better eye on things there will be no need for me to enter the yard, but I won't stand by and let Molly be bullied. That child is terrified of coming to school. What are you going to do about it?'

Red spots flew into Miss Deevers' sallow cheeks. 'Children are always bullying one another. Your step-daughter must learn to stand up for herself, as others do.'

'Against a child twice her size?'

'Against anyone.' She glanced round, clicking her tongue in annoyance at the audience standing round them, listening avidly. 'Go and line up, girls.' Turning her back on Eva she marched across to the school doors, blowing her whistle.

Now I know how mothers feel, Eva thought as she watched Molly join her classmates and shuffle unhappily towards the school door. As the bigger girls marched past her, Christine poked her in the side and said something that made Molly wince.

Why is Miss Deevers letting this happen? Eva thought angrily. When she was a teacher she would have noticed bullying of this degree, though you could never stop all the nasty little tricks children played on those weaker than themselves.

Mr Comper came out to watch the last pupils enter the school and looked at her in puzzlement, for she was still standing in the centre of the playground, arms folded.

She didn't let him nod and vanish into the school but hurried across to join him. 'Christine Smart and her friends are still bullying Molly, Mr Comper, and I'm very worried about it. They even waylay her after school if they can so that someone has to bring her here and collect her in the afternoons.'

He sighed. 'I'll keep an eye open. Perhaps when the new teacher starts after Christmas things will be better.'

'They can hardly be worse for Molly, can they? She's terrified of coming here.'

'I – um – believe we have to offer you our congratulations. Mrs Brierley now, isn't it?'

'Yes.'

'You'll have your hands full with those two. Gracie can be very difficult.' He turned away with a nod and hurried back into the school.

Silence fell on the yard, broken by the good morning choruses from inside the classrooms, then the shuffling of feet and banging of desk lids. Eva swallowed a lump in her throat. She still missed teaching, always would.

Lost in thought she walked slowly home, stopping on the way at the butcher's for some stewing steak for tea, then speeding up as she approached Rose Villa. She was hoping to discuss the garage with Aaron this morning.

She found him pacing out the front garden with Wilf, gesticulating. He looked up with a smile as she walked through the gates and she was delighted to see the glow of hope still there in his eyes. She wanted to keep it there, make him happy.

When he came to put his arm round her she felt suddenly shy. She didn't know if she was supposed to put her arm round him, but gave way to the temptation and did so, loving the feel of his warm body against hers.

'I've been telling Wilf about our plans,' he said.

Wilf beamed at her. 'It sounds smashing.'

'We have to go into Heyshaw now to make a phone call,' Aaron said. 'Make sure you keep all the doors locked while we're away.'

Somehow she found herself walking with him to the side door. Their steps matched. The fact that he wanted to put his arm round her in public made something feel soft and warm inside her. Maybe she'd been worrying about nothing.

She went into the house and started making the beds, something the girls found incomprehensible. Lil could not have been a good housewife. Well, Aaron had admitted she was untidy. But as she worked Eva couldn't get the memory of Molly out of her mind. As she tucked in corners and tidied Aaron's room, she kept seeing the child's unhappy eyes, so like her father's.

When she went to check on Gracie, she found her curled up under the covers looking flushed and heavy-eyed. 'Can I get you anything, dear? How about a nice cup of tea and a piece of toast?'

'All right.'

When she took it up, Eva sat down on the bed. 'Why do they pick on Molly?'

Gracie's face immediately took on a shuttered look.

'I can't help her if you won't talk to me. I spoke to Miss Deevers today, but I'm afraid I may have made things worse, because I told her she should do something about the bullying.'

'Did you really?'

Eva nodded. 'And then I spoke to Mr Comper about it as well. There's a new teacher coming after Christmas for Molly's class, because Miss Deevers is retiring. The headmaster hopes things will settle down then.'

Gracie unbent enough to ask, 'You won't forget to pick Molly up on time this afternoon?'

'No, I definitely won't forget.'

Eva sat on, staring out of the window while the girl sipped her tea. 'They used to hit my sister Polly at school,' she said after a while, 'and Lizzie protected her, just like you protect Molly. And they used to call me a swot. But I was big enough to stand up for myself. Molly's too little yet.'

Gracie began playing with the crumbs on her plate. 'Will she really be able to speak again one day?'

'Oh, yes. I'm quite sure of that.' Eva picked up the empty cup and plate. 'Now try to get some sleep and maybe I'll have a nice surprise waiting for you later.'

She went up to the third floor where Jenny was scrubbing out the room Gus had used. The smell made her wrinkle her nose in distaste. 'It still stinks of those dreadful cigarettes. We'll have to keep the windows open on fine days. I'm just going to find something for Gracie.' The rear part of the attic was one big open space and contained the accumulated rubbish of three generations of Blakes, plus some things of Eva's.

Jenny came out of the bedroom to survey it with her. 'It's a right old mess up here, isn't it?'

'Yes. Alice and I always meant to clear this out properly one day. I don't know why we never got round to it.'

'Because it took all the hours of the day to keep downstairs nice, she was so pernickety.'

'Was she? I suppose so. Do you think I'm pernickety?'

Jenny grinned. 'Yes, but I'm going to train you out of it. Clean is one thing, pernickety is a waste of time.'

Eva went across to her own boxes. In the one containing her few treasured childhood books she found *The Magic Unicorn*. 'It sometimes helps to be a hoarder,' she told Jenny, brandishing the book. 'I promised this to Gracie.' She hoped her stepdaughter would love it as much as she had.

There was no sound of movement from the girl's room, so Eva went to make a start on the garden room, which was in a sad state. They seemed to have been trying to catch up with the housework ever since they'd moved back to Rose Villa. Later, as she went into the kitchen, she stared out at the front garden, acknowledging to herself that she would be sorry to see the roses replaced by a garage. They were so beautiful in the summer.

But Aaron's happiness must come first.

When she next went to check on Gracie, she took the unicorn book with her. 'I found this.'

Gracie stared at the book and made no move so Eva laid it on the bed in front of her. The child traced one finger round the unicorn on the cover and stared at her hopefully.

'It's yours now. I'm too old for it and it was waiting for a girl who loves stories about unicorns.'

Gracie swallowed hard. 'Thanks, Eva. I'll look after it, I promise.'

Eva set off in plenty of time to pick Molly up from school, but an encounter with old Mrs Garston delayed her and she could not bring herself to cut the old lady short too abruptly. By the time she reached the school, most of the children had left. She scanned the playground but could see no sign of Molly. After checking everywhere she went inside and asked the caretaker if he had seen the child.

'Some of the big girls hustled your little lass off towards the fields,' he said. 'Saw them shoving her along the back lane. Getting too big for their boots, they are. We'll all be glad when they leave school next summer. They'll be in for a shock if they try to play their nasty tricks at work. Why, I remember when I was a lad and . . .'

She left him still talking and ran towards the back lane, terrified of what she would find.

Gus was so bored he went for a walk, avoiding Sid and taking a well-marked path across the fields. Time he made some plans to leave Heyshaw. He'd lingered too long, really, but it wasn't easy to find a suitable place to stay and store his things. And if truth be told he was sick of running and dodging.

He'd hoped to settle down here for a while, but bloody Clara had put paid to that. Ironic, really. He might try Tyneside next. You couldn't get much further away from London than that. There were plenty of people out of work up there in the north-east who'd be willing to risk pawning stolen property for him. Of course, prices were bound to be lower up there as well, but he had a fair amount of money saved now and after he'd got rid of the rest of the stuff, he intended to head off to the colonies, change his name and disappear once and for all.

As he was passing through a grove of trees he heard a group of children shouting. They couldn't be playing because the shouts had a nasty edge to them. Children could be little sods sometimes. When he came up to them, he saw they had the little dumb kid prisoner in their circle and were pushing her from one to the other. Tears were running down her cheeks and she looked utterly terrified, but she wasn't making any noise, apart from little mewing sounds in her throat. Well, she couldn't, could she? If he hadn't come along, no one would have known.

He should have walked on and minded his own business, because it was best not to get involved, but something about her mute misery upset him. Before he knew what he was doing he had yelled, 'Hoy!' and marched forward yelling, 'Just stop that!'

'We're only playing a game,' the biggest girl said, pushing her victim behind her.

'Then play it with people your own size,' he snapped and shoved her aside, dragging the little dumb girl into the protection of his arm, touched by the way she clung to him. He wasn't sure what to do next, so simply said, 'Bugger off home and don't let me catch you doing this again.'

They ran away, but the big one paused to shout, 'We'll wait for you tomorrow, Molly Brierley.'

Which left him with a shivering, weeping child on his hands. What the hell did you do with one in this state? He fumbled in his pocket for his handkerchief. 'Here. Wipe your eyes.'

Did she understand him? For a moment he thought not, she looked so wild-eyed, then she gave a huge shudder, wiping her eyes and blowing her nose. But he could feel her trembling still.

'Run along home now,' he said bracingly.

She looked at him in terror and then stared in the direction the girls had taken.

'Go on! They'll have gone by now.' He turned and began walking back towards the farm. But when he looked round, she was following him. She was such a thin little thing he didn't have the heart to shout at her, so stopped with a sigh. 'Want me to take you home?'

She nodded, looking up at him trustingly and slipping her hand into his. Poor little sod! Brierley should look after his children better. Gus hid a grin. Fancy him rescuing that bugger's child! Fancy him rescuing any child.

As they were approaching the rear of the school, Eva came rushing round a corner, stopping dead when she saw him. The child let go of his hand to hurl herself at Eva and cling to her.

'I found a group of kids bullying her,' he said. 'Chased them off.'

'*You did?*'

He grinned. 'Yes. Surprised me, too.' Then he shrugged and turned away.

'Thank you, Gus.'

He waved one hand and left it at that. But he chuckled several times on the way home. Knight errant was hardly his usual role! He'd bet it galled Brierley to have to be grateful to him.

Eva alternated between guilt and fury as she walked home with Molly, who had stopped weeping now but looked absolutely washed out.

Jenny exclaimed in shock at the sight of the child, muddied and rumpled. 'What's happened?'

'They've been bullying her again. We'll talk about it later. Now I want to wash Molly and see how badly they've hurt her. Where's Aaron?'

'Out scouting round, he said. Didn't say what he was scouting for, though.'

Upstairs Gracie saw them through her open bedroom door and came rushing out. 'You let them hurt her!'

'I was delayed.'

'I told you they'd hurt her. I hate you!'

Eva pushed her back into her room. 'Stay away from Molly! You don't want to give her your cold, do you?'

Gracie scowled, but trailed back to bed.

Molly's thin little body had several bad bruises on it, some yellowing. It looked as if they had been thumping and pinching her for a while. Eva washed her gently and put her into her new nightie and dressing gown for comfort. She felt racked by guilt. What sort of a mother would she make if she couldn't even protect her own child?

Her own child?

Yes, Molly and Gracie felt like hers now. It was only Aaron who didn't feel like her husband yet.

Aaron got back a short time later and came into the kitchen radiating enthusiasm. Before she could speak he said, 'They're sending two men up from London to deal with Blake. They'll be here tomorrow.'

'That's good. Aaron, I—'

'I had to go and hire a car for them, pretending it was for me. I went to the South Heyshaw Motor Company. Well, there's nowhere else round here, is there? They charge ten shillings a day, plus sixpence a mile. Can you believe that? Highway robbery, it is. While I was there I had a good look round – not that we can start a garage on that scale – but I studied the prices and how things were set up. It's so busy I reckon I'll easily attract customers from this end of the village. I heard them telling one fellow they couldn't see to his car until next week. Anyway, I've serviced cars for a few of the folk round here already and they know I do a good job. That place looks all right from the outside, but it's in a right old mess round the back. They'd have had our guts for garters in the Army if we'd been so slipshod in our ways. It's a wonder they can find their tools at all, they just set 'em down anywhere.'

She opened her mouth to mention Molly but he was off again.

'I'll consult old Beaman, I think, before we do anything. He's a wise old coot and seems to have taken a shine to you. We'll have to get the Council's permission to put a new building up and I definitely want a petrol pump out in front. We're well placed here with the main road running past the door. Folk driving through will stop for petrol because it's convenient. It's a right job with those two-gallon cans of petrol. Whoever designed them was thinking only of storage, not of use. You have to pour the petrol into the car through a funnel and it's hard to measure accurately. And at two shillings a gallon, no one wants to waste the stuff.' He laughed. 'Eh, listen to me going on? You'll be sorry you offered to set me up.'

'No, I won't. I'm going to join in your dream, if you'll let me, learn to type and do accounts so that I can be your secretary.'

'You're a grand lass, Eva. It shouldn't be long before we sort out Blake, then we can make proper plans, not just for the garage but for ourselves as well.'

His smile held a promise that made her heart give a little skip of happiness.

'And in the meantime, how are my lasses?'

Guilt flooded through Eva. 'Gracie's still in bed. She's got a dreadful cold. And there's been trouble with Molly.' She explained to him what had happened. 'I blame myself,' she finished. 'If I hadn't been late picking her up . . .'

He sighed. 'You can't be there every minute for them, however much you'd like to. All parents learn that. And the Deevers woman is right in one sense. Molly will have to learn to stick up for herself. Gracie's been too protective this past year.' He paused to shake his head. 'I can't believe Blake rescued her.'

Eva gave him a wry smile. 'I think he surprised himself, too.'

'I'll go and give Molly a cuddle and tell her to kick out at them next time. Gracie will know who's doing the bullying, so perhaps I can talk to the parents. I'm a poor sort of father, aren't I, going on about my garage when I have two girls in the wars today?'

'It's Christine Smart who's the main bully, I think.'

He paused. 'Amy Smart will be mortified. She lost

her husband at Ypres and she's had a hard time of it since. Maybe we'll give it another day or two before we do anything.'

Eva had enjoyed seeing his shining enthusiasm about the garage. For a time he had seemed almost to glow with happiness. Now the joy had faded and care lines had replaced it on his face.

She hoped the men from London would drive Gus Blake away from Heyshaw. She felt uneasy, knowing he was just across the fields from them, and kept worrying about what he and Sid might be planning and whether it would involve trying to hurt Aaron.

No one in the village trusted Sid Linney, and Gus might have rescued Molly but she still wouldn't trust him an inch. If he found out that Aaron and the lads were keeping an eye on him, he might do something desperate.

It was hard to start a marriage in such circumstances, very hard.

In London, Clara Blake began to feel uneasy, for no reason that she could fathom. As if she was being followed. She took to peering out from behind the bedroom curtains and several times caught sight of the same fellow, idling on the corner. Men did idle around if they were out of work. But he was always on his own.

She didn't like it. She didn't like it at all.

Was it the police or was it *them?*

In the end, she could bear the suspense no longer and chose what she considered to be the lesser of two evils. She sought out Hugh Grimmond, offering to tell him more in return for police protection.

The next day passed with no trouble for Molly that Eva could see, though the child seemed very quiet. The men from London turned up at dusk and found their own way to Rose Villa. The first Eva knew of it was when Aaron answered a knock on the door and brought in two strangers, the first a tough-looking man with a battered face, the other thinner, rather nondescript in appearance.

'Mac and Chas are from London,' he said. 'Do you think we could put them up?'

'Happy to sleep on the floor,' Mac, the bigger man, said. 'Better not to take rooms in the village. Like to keep our presence quiet, if we can.'

'Of course we can put you up and we have proper beds as long as you don't mind sleeping in the attic.'

'Thank you, Mrs Brierley. Now, is Wilf Horrocks around? We need to talk to him.'

'Jenny, will you fetch Wilf?' Aaron asked, then took the men into the sitting room.

Eva looked at her friend, indignation bursting out. '*Well!* It's as if we weren't involved, isn't it? We've only had our whole lives turned upside down, but I suppose that doesn't count.'

Jenny shivered. 'I don't know that I want to be involved. I won't be a minute then I'll help you make up their beds.'

While they were in the attic, Molly came and peeped round the edge of the door. 'Who are the beds for?' she whispered.

'Two visitors from London, friends of Wilf.' Eva hesitated, then said, 'Don't tell anyone at school they're here. It's a secret.'

Molly nodded solemnly and continued to watch. Eva had taken the child's mattress into her own bedroom, not wanting Molly to catch Gracie's cold, and she seemed lost without her older sister to cling to.

'Come on, let's go down and make them some food,' Eva said when they'd finished. 'They must be hungry.' When she held out her hand, Molly took it with a shy smile.

Although the men accepted the sandwiches gratefully, they didn't linger over them and soon all four were getting ready to go out for a recce, wearing dark clothes, faces smeared with dirt, expressions grimly determined.

Eva heard them come back just after midnight and waited until the noise of people settling for the night had died down. Molly was fast asleep and didn't stir as she crept out of the bedroom.

She tapped on Aaron's door and heard him get out of bed, saw the line of light under his door as he switched on the light.

'Eva! Is something wrong?'

'No. I just wanted to know how you went on tonight.'

'Better come in a minute, then. We'll disturb the others if we talk here on the landing.'

She perched on the edge of his bed as he dragged on an old Army greatcoat and realised suddenly that the girls were not the only ones in need of new clothing. 'I just – felt left out. I can't help feeling curious.'

He sat down a little distance away from her. 'I was only showing them round tonight. We went to the farm and then round the village.' He smiled. 'I'd forgotten about creeping through the darkness, shivering and wishing you were tucked up in a warm bed.'

'What's going to happen next?'

'Not sure. They're going to make proper plans in the morning. I think they'll need the lads' help to keep watch. It'd be quite easy to spot anyone coming up here. I gather the police have dropped a few hints in certain quarters in London, in the hope of flushing out those involved in this conspiracy. If that doesn't work, they want to spook Blake into packing up and leaving in a hurry, so that they can at least catch him with the boxes and get some names out of him.'

'That sounds dangerous.'

'It could be.'

'I don't want you getting hurt again.'

He smiled and clasped her hand for a moment. 'I'll do my best not to, but I can't let others take all the risks, can I? Not on my own territory.' He raised her hand to his lips. 'And afterwards, perhaps we can think about ourselves, Eva love. If you still want to make something of this marriage of ours, that is?'

She gave him a shy smile. 'I do.'

'Good. So do I.'

He drew her to her feet, but to her disappointment only planted a chaste kiss on her forehead, then put his arm round her and guided her towards the door. 'Now go and get some sleep, Mrs Brierley.'

It was the first time he had called her that. She liked it

and she definitely didn't want to leave him. But she didn't dare betray that fact, was still not sure how he'd react. The only time he'd really confided in her was about his dreams for a garage. She needed more than that before she could tell him how fond she'd grown of him. She wasn't sure if this was love, she only knew she wanted to be a proper wife, wanted to be with him, wanted to mother his children and have children of her own.

She smiled. She had once thought she was a born spinster. Well, she knew better now, didn't she?

Eva got up first the following morning, leaving Molly to finish dressing. When the child did not come downstairs, she went to look for her and couldn't find her anywhere.

Jenny hadn't seen her, either. 'Poor little mite's frightened to go to school. Why don't you keep her at home today?'

'It's not just my decision or I would.' Eva peeped into Gracie's room, then Aaron's, but found no sign of the child. Their two visitors had not yet made an appearance so she crept up to the attics. Surely Molly hadn't come up here?

Then she saw that the door of the old wardrobe in the corner was not properly closed. She knew she hadn't left it like that. When she opened it, Molly sobbed and cowered into a corner. Eva had to drag her downstairs. It felt eerie because the little girl didn't speak above a whisper, just wept and whispered pleas not to be sent to school.

'What do you think?' Eva asked Aaron quietly as Jenny tried to persuade the child to eat something. 'Should we let her stay at home for a few days? She's in a right old state.'

He shook his head. 'No. But I'll take her to school myself and give those girls a good talking-to. If that doesn't stop the bullying, I'll go and complain to the headmaster myself.'

She hated to see how the worried look had settled on his face again and threaded her arm through his for a minute. 'It's hard to know what to do for the best sometimes, isn't it?'

Molly went off to school with her father, shoulders drooping.

Eva shed a tear as she watched them go and could not get the picture of the unhappy child out of her mind all morning.

24

Gus was growing tired of Sid continually asking questions about his boxes: how he had obtained the contents, how he intended to dispose of them, what they were worth. When he came back unexpectedly and found the other man in the inner store room looking through the contents of a box of jewellery which had been at the bottom of the pile that morning, he grabbed the plump farmer by the throat and flung him away from it so violently that Sid went sprawling on the floor.

'I told you to leave them alone. If I find you *anywhere* near these boxes – *ever again* – I'll make sure you regret it.'

For a minute or two Gus thought Sid was going to attack him, so ugly did his expression become. Amazing how like a pig the man was. He'd noticed that the first time he'd seen him then forgotten it, as you do once you're used to someone's face. Now the image came back to him: an ugly old boar with bristly skin and small bloodshot eyes, a face not to be trusted even by a fellow conspirator.

After a moment during which tension throbbed between the two of them, Sid stood up and brushed himself down, saying, 'Given the risk I'm taking, I should have a share of that stuff.'

'Should you, now?'

'Yes, I bloody should.'

'And how are you going to make me give it you?'

'I could always tell the authorities about your little hoard. There'd probably be a reward.'

Gus stood very still and willed his anger down. Sid still continued to spend lavishly on booze, but complained all the time about the cost of food and housekeeping. He must be short of money. He seemed an indifferent farmer, for all his boastful talk of finding opportunities his father had missed. He wasn't liked in the village and Gus didn't blame the wife for running away from him.

In fact, he'd be no loss to anyone if the worst came to the worst, but it'd have to be planned carefully . . . Gus forced a smile. 'In that case I'll make sure you're well rewarded for your help before I leave, won't I? You won't find me ungenerous, Sid, but I don't answer well to threats and I *don't* like people messing with my things.'

Sid's face cleared. 'That's all right, then. All I ask is that you act fairly by me.'

Gus stuck his hand out and kept the smile on his face as they shook to seal the bargain.

It was definitely time to leave, so he spent the morning repacking the contents of the boxes. Four fewer than last time. He'd got rid of quite a bit of stuff while in Lancashire and Yorkshire, though for nothing like its true value. But his nest egg was mounting steadily and at a pinch he could take off any time he chose and simply abandon everything that was left – or even take the best stuff abroad with him.

He spent the afternoon in Rochdale making arrangements to move the boxes. When he'd pinched the stuff from his fellow thieves, it'd been sheer luck that he'd got away with it. Now he knew exactly how to send his stolen treasures around the country by strictly legal methods so that they'd be waiting for him later elsewhere.

He felt pleased with himself as he drove back. He'd be glad to get away from Heyshaw and from seeing Eva everywhere. The bitch was a constant reminder that he'd just missed out on an easy life that would have been totally legitimate. If only Clara hadn't turned up! She was another one he'd like to make rue the day she'd ever tangled with him.

The following morning a carrier arrived at the farm to collect the boxes Gus couldn't fit into his car, the ones with the less valuable pieces in them.

Sid came out of the barn to watch it all, his expression suspicious. 'You're leaving soon, then? Don't forget your promise.'

Gus went over to clap him on the shoulder. 'Don't worry, old chap. You'll get compensation for your trouble before I go and you won't find me ungenerous. We've had some good evenings together, haven't we? Since I'm heading out in two days, let's have a farewell booze-up tomorrow night, eh? We can start off with fish and chips, then bring back a bottle of whisky for a nightcap or two. I'll have your present ready for you – and you won't be disappointed. You can open it there and then, make sure you're satisfied before I leave.'

Sid's face brightened. 'Bloody good idea.'

When he went up to his bedroom Gus wedged the door shut and took his revolver out of its hiding place, noting that his possessions had been gone through in here as well. But Sid didn't seem to have found the revolver, and the nest egg was safely in the bank with the bankbook always on Gus's person.

After loading the revolver carefully, he hid it again, ready for later use, and walked into Heyshaw to buy some cigarettes.

As he passed the school he saw it was playtime. The boys' yard was full of shouting, wrestling little savages. Hell of a racket they made. As he passed the quieter girls' yard, with its skipping ropes and little groups, he saw the dumb kid standing on her own in a corner. The group of bullies he'd driven away once were whispering nearby, threatening her by just hovering.

When the kid noticed him, she ran across to smile at him through the railings. There was something about her trusting little face that made him stop. Well, it cost nothing to offer a kid a kind word, did it? 'How are you going? Not letting them catch you?'

She whispered, 'No.'

The bell rang and he watched the girls rush to form lines. It was as bad as the bloody Army. He'd hated the regimentation. It wasn't till he'd fallen in with a group of like-minded chaps that he'd seen how to turn the war to his advantage and had never looked back since.

He walked on whistling, amused that the kid had turned round to watch him go. He hadn't had much to do with children before and the little girl's shy smiles touched him.

You're getting soft in your old age, he told himself. Better watch it.

Gracie got better only slowly and her illness reminded Eva of the dreadful 'flu epidemic just after the war, so she kept the girl home from school and fussed over her. Not that Gracie said thank you, but her hostility was definitely lessening and the unicorn book was often in her hand. Eva would guess from the reverent way she handled it that Gracie hadn't had any books of her own before, though she'd kept some of her mother's magazines which she guarded jealously, not even letting Molly handle them.

Well, the child would have books from now on, as many of them as she wanted. Eva might not be allowed to teach any more, but she could still help develop the minds of the two stepdaughters who were now partly her responsibility. And any children of her own. She sighed at that thought. She had discovered how much she liked Aaron touching her in small ways and was beginning to wonder what it would be like to make love. Lizzie said it was wonderful with the right man. It felt to Eva as if Aaron was the right man, it really did. She only hoped she was the right woman for him.

They were all playing a waiting game. It was so frustrating. Even Aaron's plans for opening a garage had been suspended until the situation was resolved.

Jenny said Wilf was the same, with his mind on other things than her and their future.

The next morning Molly again wept and begged not to be sent to school.

'Has that Christine touched you since I spoke to her?' Aaron demanded.

She shook her head.

'Then why this fuss?'

Molly looked at Eva and whispered, 'She says things. She frightens me.'

Eva looked pleadingly at her husband, but he shook his head. 'She's got to go to school.'

'Can I speak to you in the sitting room?' she asked, not wanting to quarrel with him in front of his daughter.

He followed her out. 'If you're going to try to persuade me to change my mind, you won't.'

'You've decided that before you've even listened to me, have you?'

'Eva—'

'All those years I spent as a teacher don't count? I don't know anything about children, is that it? Well, let me tell you, I know a lot about children and I'm seriously worried about Molly. I think we should take her to see a specialist about her voice. I'd hoped that when life settled down after her mother died she might start speaking again, but she hasn't made the slightest improvement. And she won't while she's terrified of those bullies. Let me go and see Mr Comper about her, then keep her at home and teach her myself for a while.'

'What about Gracie?'

'Gracie too, if she wants, though she can look after herself, I'm sure.'

'She looks after Molly too.'

'But she isn't at school just now and Molly's absolutely terrified.'

'She's safest there. I wish Gracie were with her. I'd thought of sending all three of you away for a few days, just till we sort this out. Would you do that? Go away somewhere?'

'Certainly not.' She stared at him, amazed by his suggestion. 'You think Gus is that dangerous?'

'Could be. He's mixing with some rather dangerous folk, that's for sure.'

'Well, this is my home and you're my family now. I'm not going.'

And there they had to leave it. Stiffly polite, they returned to the kitchen.

'You ready now, love?' Aaron asked, ignoring his daughter's pleading look.

At the school gates he stopped and sent Molly into the yard with a quick kiss then, as she still didn't move away from him, a gentle push. She stumbled forward a few paces but stayed near the gate. The group of bullies were near the school entrance. He didn't like the looks on their faces, so decided to come back at playtime and watch what was happening. Maybe Eva was right and he was being too harsh with Molly.

But he was getting more concerned about his family's safety every day. Blake was not only under investigation by the police and military wallahs, but word from London was that he seemed to have offended some well-known criminals as well. Wilf said the investigations threatened to expose people in high places for what they had done in the war, so Grimmond had warned them all to be extremely careful of their own and their families' safety.

Besides, Aaron didn't trust Blake an inch, because he had seen others like him, weak men behind the bluster, men who could go off like hand grenades if panicked.

That afternoon a car drove into Heyshaw and its two occupants, a husband and wife, booked a room for the night at the Red Lion. They were smartly dressed in sombre colours, and spoke of attending a funeral in Carlisle and now being on their way back to London.

They tipped generously and dealt very genially with any staff who served them, showing an interest in the village, which they said was very picturesque.

But Mac had asked the lads to tell him of any strangers who came to the village in a motor vehicle, a rare enough occurrence to warrant checking, and when he heard about the newcomers he frowned. 'They could be just who they say they are, but I'd rather check out every stranger who comes till this is over. I'd better go and have a drink in the bar at the Red Lion, see if I can catch a glimpse of them. Wilf can come with me. It'll look better if there are two of us celebrating a win on the horses.'

In the Red Lion he and Wilf found a table in a corner, then Mac went out, ostensibly to the toilets.

Instead he found the dining room and went across to study the menu in its glass case on the wall. As he glanced through the doorway he gaped in shock, then retreated quickly and hurried back to the bar.

'It's Davies, a well-known hatchet man from the East End,' he said in a low voice. 'What the hell is he doing up here in the north? Drink up and let's get out of here before he recognises me. This can't be a coincidence. I need to phone my boss.'

Only they couldn't phone from the hotel in case Davies saw them. And although the post office sported a sign which said: 'Public Telephone – You may telephone from here' that was no use at this time of day.

Mac snarled in annoyance as they passed it. 'What the hell use is that when the place is closed in the evenings? What I wouldn't give for one of the new telephone kiosks they've got in London, with a penny in the slot mechanism on the door. Now that's real progress.' He stood frowning for a moment or two. 'This news is too important to wait. Do you know of anyone in the village who has a phone and who'd let me use it, Wilf? Preferably someone who can keep his mouth shut?'

'How about Mr Beaman? He's a lawyer and as tight-mouthed as they come.'

'Take me to him.'

They strode back to North Hey at a brisk pace and knocked on Beaman's front door.

'You can prove who you are?' he asked when they told him what they wanted.

Mac produced an identity card and waited while Mr Beaman studied it.

'I'm happy to help the authorities in any way I can.'

When he had finished making the phone call, Mac rejoined Wilf and their host, grim-faced. 'They want us to keep watch over the Red Lion tonight, in case Davies goes out wandering. If he doesn't leave tomorrow, they'll send reinforcements. Will the lads help as well, do you think, Wilf?'

Eric Beaman looked from one to the other. 'If there's anything else *I* can do . . . ?'

'Thanks. I gave my boss your phone number. If you can pass on any messages immediately, that'd be a big help.' Mac looked at them both.

'Miss Blake would be horrified at her nephew being involved in such dealings,' Beaman said sadly. 'Eva had a lucky escape there.'

Mac hesitated, wondering whether to tell them what his superiors had confided in him, then decided not to. Not yet, anyway. You didn't dish out information till you had to. Tonight they'd keep a very careful watch on both Blake and Davies. 'Do any of your lads have guns?' he asked Wilf as they walked back to Rose Villa.

'No.'

'Pity.'

That night Gus and Sid went out to get some fish and chips, eating them in the street as they walked along and then going on to the Dog and Duck for a few pints. They walked home afterwards with Gus joining Sid in a few drunken choruses as they staggered arm in arm down the lane. Gus had had more to drink than he'd planned, but not nearly as much as Sid.

Once in the house they started on the whisky, though Gus again tipped his into the plant pot when Sid went out for a pee or got up to fill his glass.

'Well, what about my reward?' he asked after a while, brandishing a newly filled glass of whisky and slopping some on the carpet.

'Ah, yes. I think you're going to be very pleased with what I've set aside for you. Of course you'll have to dispose of the items yourself. I can't do that before I go. I'd advise you to go on a trip somewhere and visit the pawn shops. Harder to trace that way.'

Whistling softly he ran up to his room, put the revolver in his jacket pocket and carried down the packet he'd prepared. 'There you are.' He laid it in the other man's lap and sat back, smiling gently as Sid tore it open.

'What the hell . . .' Sid gaped at the parcel of gravel and small stones he'd just opened, then goggled at the revolver trained on him.

'You haven't done anything to earn a share of my property,' Gus told him, smiling. 'Now, get up and start walking towards the barn. You're going to have a cold, uncomfortable night, I'm afraid, but perhaps that'll teach you not to mess with professionals.'

He didn't say that he intended to leave no one behind who could point a finger at him. No use alarming Sid and making him harder to handle.

But as they walked out of the sitting room, Sid made a sudden dash towards the rear of the house.

Furious, Gus sighted the revolver and pulled the trigger. There was a click and nothing happened. Swearing, he pulled the trigger again, with the same result.

Sid laughed and brandished a rifle at him. 'I unloaded your gun earlier. Wasn't sure whether you'd check it or not. Worth the gamble, I thought. *Stand still!*'

As he pointed the rifle, he held it steadily enough for Gus to decide to obey.

'I can hold my booze better than anyone I know,' Sid boasted. 'I've won a lot of bets about that in my time. You really should have checked the revolver, you know. That's not at all professional in my book. People think I'm stupid because of this,' he pointed to his own face, 'but I'm not. Angela knew that. Which is why she behaved herself while she was with me.'

Gus threw the revolver at him, at the same time jerking sideways. There was a loud explosion, then a burning sensation in his leg. He yelled in both pain and shock, then as Sid moved forward to hold the barrel of the rifle very close to his head, lay still. 'What do you want?'

'Everything. Why not? You're not going to need it any more.' Sid laughed. 'Get up. We'll finish this out in the barn.'

'I'm not moving. I'm injured.'

'Show me. And move slowly.'

Gus hitched up his trouser leg, grimacing at the blood but relieved to see that it was only a flesh wound in his calf and that the bullet had only grazed him.

'That's nothing,' Sid scoffed. 'And if you don't start moving, I'll shoot you in the guts. Your choice: a quick easy death or a slow, agonising one.' He waggled the rifle. 'I'm pretty good with this. If you hadn't thrown that gun at me, I'd have made sure of you first time. Have to be good at destroying vermin when you're a farmer.'

Gus, who had seen men die in lingering agony from belly wounds, shuddered. He could not believe this was happening. How had it all gone wrong? He'd planned it so carefully. Damn this sod!

Sid moved the rifle lower, aiming it at his belly, so Gus levered himself slowly to his feet. 'I need a walking stick,' he gasped. 'Can't put any weight on this leg.'

Sid laughed and tossed one at him from the umbrella stand by the door. 'Lift that above your ankle and I shoot.'

They made their way slowly out to the barn. Gus's leg was throbbing and growing more painful by the minute. He tried desperately to work out a way of getting the rifle off Sid. He had to do it before they reached the door of the inner barn or he'd be in trouble.

But as he got there and swung out desperately with the stick, the world exploded around him and the last thing he felt was fury at dying like this.

The following morning, as soon as Mr Brierley had walked away from the school, Christine and her friends pushed Molly into the toilets. While her friends kept the other children outside, Christine began punching Molly anywhere the bruises wouldn't show. 'I'll teach you to tell tales to your dad!' she said viciously, sending the smaller child back hard against the wall. 'And next week you'd better start bringing money to school again. Other kids manage to find a penny or two to give me and so can you, now that you've got a rich new mummy.'

So terrified she acted only on instinct, Molly took her tormentor by surprise, kicking out at her and diving past while the older girl was still gaping in surprise at this unexpected show of rebellion from one who had only cowered before her previously.

Blind panic sent Molly running away from the yard full of noisy children, heading towards her old home, seeing her mother's face.

She didn't stop running until she was in sight of home. But a stranger came out of the door to shake a tablecloth and Molly stopped, with a whimper of dismay. It wasn't her home any more. Her mother wasn't there any more. And her father kept sending her to school.

She couldn't think what to do, utterly terrified that Christine might come after her. But when she listened there was only the sound of the rising wind and a woman's voice in the distance calling out to someone.

It was cold and she'd lost her gloves and her dad was going to be really mad at her. She heard the sound of a car coming along the lane and nipped through a gate to hide behind a wall. It was Mr Linney in his lorry, leaving the farm.

When he'd vanished down the lane, she moved on, darting from one hiding place to another. Maybe she could hide somewhere till home time this afternoon and pretend she'd spent the day at school? One of the farm dogs came up to her, wagging its tail. When she waved it away it went back to its kennel.

She slipped through the open door of the old barn and stopped dead at the sight of the man's car, shivering with cold now. Perhaps she could sit in it till it was home time? There was a rug on the back seat. No, Mr Linney would see her through the windows, and anyway, how would she know what time it was? She had to find somewhere else to hide.

She knew from when her dad worked here that there was another room at the back of the barn, a place not much used. Maybe she could go in there? But the door was locked, and she heard Mr Linney's lorry coming, so she ran and hid behind a pile of straw. Wriggling down under it, she poked a small hole through it and watched as Mr Linney came tramping into the barn. She didn't like him. He shouted at you if he saw you near the farm yard.

When he opened the door of the back room, she saw inside the man who had once helped her, lying on the ground asleep. What was he doing there? Hadn't he got a bed? She watched in astonishment as Mr Linney said something to him and kicked him, but he still didn't wake up.

When the farmer came out, he left the door of the room open, so she waited till he had left the barn and crept into it. Perhaps the man would help her again. She went over to him, but just as she was going to waken him, she heard the sound of footsteps coming back across the barn. Panic-stricken, she looked round for somewhere to hide and saw the pile of boxes. There was a little space behind them, so she squeezed into it, pressing herself flat against the cold stone wall.

Mr Linney came and dumped a jug and cup beside the man. 'I know you're only playing dead,' he said loudly.

Molly peeped through a gap between the piles of boxes and saw that the man's hands were tied in front of him. She didn't understand what was happening, but the old fear of Mr Linney kept her silent.

'I reckon you can reach the jug,' Sid said. 'Don't want you dying on me, do I? But I'll have your revolver with me every time I come here, so don't think you can get away.'

He went out again, locking the door behind him.

The room was nearly dark because there was only a small window high up in one wall. Molly waited to be sure Mr Linney wasn't coming back then crept out from her hiding place. She crouched down next to the man. 'Wake up,' she begged him. 'Please wake up.'

When he didn't, she began to weep.

'I haven't seen Blake this morning,' Mac said as he came in for his breakfast after a night spent watching the farm. 'He's usually up by now, walking into the village for a paper and some cigarettes. His car's still there, though.'

'Have you had time to look at those boxes he left with the carrier yesterday?' Wilf asked, lounging in a chair while Jenny served some bacon and eggs.

'Chas and I went through them last night. The locks on that firm's warehouse wouldn't keep a child out. It's not the valuable stuff, but it should be enough to convict Blake of theft, because there are some marked pieces. Good thing one of your lads noticed what was happening yesterday. The boxes are destined for Newcastle, but I'll arrange for them to be intercepted en route.' He grinned and filled his fork with crispy bacon.

'The lads are quite enjoying themselves,' Aaron said.

Eva, who had been worrying about Molly, picked up her shopping basket. 'I'm just nipping down to Mrs Arden's. Won't be long.'

The two men sat and talked, then Mac looked at his watch. 'I'd better go and check whether Davies is staying on at the Red Lion. Then I'll phone the inspector and let him know what's happening.'

Aaron cleared their things away and went up to see Gracie, but she was drowsy and didn't want to talk. She had a bit better colour today, though, he was glad to see.

He went downstairs, looking forward to spending a little time with Eva when she got back. In fact, he decided to walk along the road to meet her. Jenny would keep an eye on Gracie.

Before Eva did the shopping she decided to go and check how things were at the school. It was nearly playtime and she arrived in time to see the children march out and scatter. Miss Deevers' class came out last, but Molly wasn't with them.

Eva called over a child she knew. 'Has Molly Brierley been kept in?'

'She didn't come to school today, miss.'

'Yes, she did. Her father brought her.'

The girl waved another child across. 'Molly Brierley didn't come to school today, did she?'

The second child looked so uncomfortable Eva was sure she knew something. 'Tell me!' she pressed, but the girl shook her head and ran away.

Christine drifted over. 'Is your Molly sick today?' she asked, all wide-eyed.

For some reason this made Eva feel utterly certain something was wrong. The bell rang and the children lined up quickly and marched into the school. She stared round the empty yard and after hesitating for a few moments, followed them inside. Making her way to Miss Deevers' classroom, she stood in the corridor staring in through the upper panes of glass that separated the classroom from the hall. Molly was definitely not there.

Miss Deevers looked up, saw her, scowled and muttered something.

Eva beckoned and after a few moments the older woman came to the door at the rear of the classroom.

'This really has to stop, Mrs Brierley. You're not a teacher any more and must leave us to get on with our job.'

'My husband brought Molly to school this morning, but the other children tell me she hasn't been seen.'

Miss Deevers gave a sniff of annoyance. 'Then she's run off and if you don't punish her, you're a bad mother.'

'Run off? Molly? Why should she do that?'

'Who knows with a child who refuses to talk and is pampered instead of chastised for it?'

'Look, could you ask the children if anyone saw her leave? Please!'

With an irritated sigh, Miss Deevers turned round. 'Kindly remain at the back of the classroom while I speak to my pupils.'

Her questions were so staccato and her irritation so obvious that Eva wasn't surprised when none of the children spoke up. But the same little girl looked uneasy, so Eva moved forward and said to her, 'Molly could be in danger. If you know something, *please* tell us.'

The child burst into tears.

Miss Deevers opened her mouth to speak, but Eva said quickly, 'I'll take her outside, shall I?' She raised her voice. 'Anyone else who knows anything can come out with us.'

The elderly teacher threw up her arms in a gesture of leaving her to it, so Eva put her arm round the still sobbing child, looking round and nodding encouragement to a few others who were looking at her hesitantly. She found herself outside with five children.

'Tell me,' she said simply.

So it all came out about Christine and the way she demanded money from them, how Molly hadn't given her anything since her mother died, so was being picked on. Someone had seen the older girl hit Molly in the girls' toilets that morning and another girl had seen Molly squeezing past the rubbish bins and running out of school the back way.

'She might have gone to see that man,' one of them volunteered. 'He came and spoke to her through the railings yesterday at playtime.'

'Which man is that?'

'The one who stopped them beating her up after school.'

Mr Comper came out of his office at the far end of the hall and stared at them in surprise.

'Let's go and tell the headmaster about it,' Eva whispered. She saw fear on their faces and put her arms round the two nearest to lead them across the hall. The others tagged along behind them.

After the explanations were complete, she said, 'I'll leave you to deal with Christine and her fellow thieves, Mr Comper. I have to find Molly.'

She was beginning to get really worried because she was not at all certain that Gus would do the right thing by her stepdaughter and who knew what the distraught child would do then?

25

Eva hurried down the lane towards the farm, calling first at the cottage where the Brierleys had once lived. The young woman who answered the door remembered that she had seen a child in the distance earlier that morning, but hadn't thought anything of it. Children were always playing truant.

Gathering her courage together Eva went on to the farm and rapped smartly on the door. Sid Linney answered, swaying on his feet, clearly drunk, which surprised her so much at this hour of the day that she couldn't think how to deal with him.

'What do *you* want?' he growled, clutching the door frame.

'I'm looking for Molly, Aaron's younger girl. She's run away from school and we think she might be hiding somewhere near her old home. Would you mind if I searched the barns for her?'

'Yes, I would bloody mind! This is a working farm not an asylum for dummies.'

Eva drew herself up. 'There's no need to talk about her like that.'

'I'll talk about her how I like on my own farm. And I'm not having you or anyone else messing around in my barns upsetting the animals. Clear off or I'll have you charged with trespass.'

She walked away, disgusted by his attitude. But as she was starting back down the lane, she found one of Molly's gloves. There was no mistaking it, because Molly had chewed the thumb and Eva had darned it. So the terrified child had gone towards the house where she'd lived for so long. Was she still nearby, hiding somewhere, alone and afraid?

Eva was determined to search so made her way across the fields to approach the farm buildings from the rear. Whatever Sid Linney said, she wasn't going home again till she'd checked everywhere. Molly was upset and needed help.

Gus discovered that he wasn't dead, after all. He tried to move and groaned as pain stabbed through him. His head was throbbing and he was seeing two of everything, but he was still alive. Sid must have clouted him on the head and knocked him out cold. And it must have been a hell of a blow, because it was light now and had been dark when he came in here.

Someone whispered, 'Man!'

He blinked. Was he hearing things? It sounded like that funny little kid. He tried to turn his head and moaned as pain stabbed through it, then realised that his hands were bound in front of him. None of this made any sense. Sid had said he was going to kill him, so why hadn't he done so when he had the chance?

Gus's mouth felt as if it were stuffed with cotton wool but his vision was clearing slowly and by moving very gently he managed to turn his head enough to see the whisperer. Damnation, it *was* the child! He tried to bring saliva into his mouth so that he could speak, but his throat was dry and his voice came out as a rasp. 'What are you doing here?'

Tears filled her eyes. 'I've runned away from school.'

There was the sound of someone approaching the door and since it could only be Sid, Gus said urgently, 'Hide quickly. Mr Linney's a bad man!'

As she slipped away, he closed his eyes. The door opened and Sid came in, shaking him so hard he could not help groaning.

'Ha! You're awake at last.'

Gus stayed as limp as he could. 'What – happened?'

'You tried to escape, so I crowned you one.'

'Need – water.'

'I left you some.'

Gus didn't move. 'I'm seeing double. Where is it?'

Roughly Sid lifted him up and shoved a tin cup of water to his lips, spilling some down his chest.

Gus drank thirstily then let his head fall back, pretending to be more befuddled than he was. 'Can't think,' he muttered.

With a laugh Sid stood up. 'Better sleep it off, then. You're going nowhere till I say so.'

Gus watched him leave through half-closed eyes. How the hell was he going to get out of this? Or was Sid planning to kill him? Though if so, why he had not done it already was beyond Gus's understanding. And his head was aching, dammit.

*   *   *

Eva started searching the largest of the barns, reasoning that no one would hide in the cow shippon where the animals were milked twice a day. She had seen one of Sid's labourers in the distance as she crossed the field but the farm buildings seemed deserted. Hugging the shadows she made her way across to the barn door.

Hearing voices from inside she crept to the back to see who it was. To her astonishment she saw Gus Blake lying on the floor with his hands bound and Sid bending over him. When he stood up she heard him say, 'Better sleep it off, then. You're going nowhere till I say so.'

She swung round, looking for a place to hide before Sid came out, but her arm came in contact with a rake and it fell over. It took some other tools with it and they made so much noise she stopped trying to hide and turned to run away.

But she was behind some machinery and Sid caught her just as she reached the barn door. Although she struggled desperately, kicking and scratching, she was no match for him. Laughing, he twisted one of her arms behind her back and the pain was so intense she stopped even trying to get away.

'If you don't do as I tell you,' he growled in her ear, 'I'll break this arm, snap it like a twig.' He frogmarched her towards the store room at the rear where he was holding Gus prisoner. 'If we go on at this rate, we'll have the whole bloody village in here,' he said loudly as he shoved her through the door, still keeping her arm twisted behind her.

He laughed down at Gus, who was gazing up at Eva

in open-mouthed astonishment. 'She must still have a fancy for you, Blake.'

'I told you, I came here to look for Molly!' Eva protested.

'Shut up, you stupid bitch.' Sid forced her across to the side of the room and fumbled through some bits and pieces for a rope. 'Put your other arm behind your back, you, unless you want a good clout round the ears.'

Eva did as he told her and the pain eased as he tied her arms together.

When he had finished, he shoved her to the floor and she fell awkwardly, unable to save herself. The breath was thumped out of her and the side of her head hit the wooden floorboards, making her cry out.

'Serve you right for poking your bloody nose in!' Sid taunted as he bent over her to tie her legs together then tie them to a ring set in the wall. 'This'll teach you to mind your own business in future. But while I'm deciding what to do with you, you can stay here in my little guest room. There'll be no one near enough to hear you call out, believe me, and this part of the barn was built over a hundred years ago so the walls are nice and thick.'

Laughing, he walked across to Gus and rolled him across to tie his feet to the far wall. 'Don't want you two getting together, do we? Who'd have thought these old rings for tying up stock would come in so useful?'

But as he strode back to the farm, the pleasure he'd taken in showing them who was master faded and he began to scowl. What the hell was he going to do now?

He'd tried to shoot Gus last night while he was un-
conscious, had held the rifle to his former friend's head
and willed himself to squeeze the trigger. Only he
hadn't been able to. Shooting a man wasn't like killing
a cow or sheep. Sod it, he wasn't cut out to be a
murderer. And for all his boastful words, he knew he
couldn't kill a woman.

Maybe if he had another drink he'd be able to think
of some other way out.

'You all right?' Gus called across the store room.

With some difficulty Eva rolled over to face him.
'More or less.'

'Well, I have a surprise for you. Come out again,
little girl!'

To Eva's dismay Molly slid out from behind the
boxes, her face tear-stained and her eyes wide with
terror. 'Oh, no! Darling, what on earth are *you* doing
here?'

Gus gave a snort of laughter. 'She's run away from
school.'

Molly edged past him and ran across to flop down
beside Eva. 'Why did Mr Linney tie you up?' she
whispered.

'Because he's a bad man and wants to hurt us. If you
hear him coming back, you're to hide at once,' Eva told
her. 'Promise me you will?'

Molly nodded.

'But in the meantime,' Gus said, 'maybe she can
untie us. Can you do that, little girl?' He held his bound
hands out towards her. 'Come and have a try.' He

looked across at Eva. 'Of the three of us, I'd be the best at dealing with Sid, don't you think, so she should untie me first?'

She couldn't argue with that. 'See if you can do as he asks, Molly dear.'

When Aaron didn't encounter Eva anywhere along the road, he went into the shop, but Mrs Arden hadn't seen her at all that morning.

'I passed her earlier,' one of the customers volunteered. 'She was going into the school and she didn't look best pleased.'

'Thanks.' Aaron hesitated outside, then went down the hill and stood in the school yard for a moment, listening to the various sounds from inside the building: the chanting of times-tables from one side, another class singing a song, the grunts and puffs of physical exercise from the boys' yard in time with the teacher's orders.

Surely Eva wasn't still here?

But he couldn't turn round and go home, not when he was worried about both her and his younger daughter, so he went inside and crossed the hall to the headmaster's office. What Mr Comper told him sent him hurrying along the lane behind the school, which led towards the farm.

Like his daughter and wife before him he thought it prudent not to advertise his presence to Sid, so cut across the fields.

What the hell was going on?

*　　*　　*

Eva watched as Molly tried to undo the ropes that bound Gus's hands. The child picked away at the knots, her tongue sticking out of one corner of her mouth to aid concentration, but she didn't make any progress.

After a while she began to weep. 'I can't do it! The knots are too tight.'

'Don't cry, dear,' Eva said soothingly. 'We'll have to think of another way to do it.' She looked across at Gus. 'Can you see anything she could use to cut the rope?'

He stared at her then let out a rumble of annoyance. 'I think the blow on my head must have scattered my wits. There's a small penknife in my pocket. Can you get it out, Molly? It's in the top pocket inside my jacket.'

She found it almost immediately.

'Open it up,' he said impatiently. 'We can't cut anything with it closed.'

But she couldn't. It was too stiff for her little fingers.

'Put it near my hand and hold it tight. Maybe I can pull the blade out.' He fumbled, muttering under his breath in annoyance as his fingers kept slipping. Then suddenly the blade opened. 'There you are. Can you cut the rope with it now?'

She sawed away at the rope and suddenly the strands parted.

He grabbed the knife and freed his feet, then went across to cut Eva's bonds. She immediately gathered Molly into her arms and cuddled her close.

'Very touching!' Gus scoffed as he looked round.

'But you'll be of more use to her if you help me look for a way to get out of here. That window is too small and the door's solid oak.'

'Is it worth shouting for help?'

'Only if you want to bring Sid down on us again. No, we're going to have to wait till he returns and catch him as he comes through the door. And we'll only get one chance at that, so we'll have to work together. Your job will be to distract him.'

'I'll try.' She looked down at the child, who was pressing close to her. 'Molly dear, if Mr Linney comes back, you're to hide behind those boxes again. As far behind them as you can get. You hear me?'

Molly, who had her thumb in her mouth, nodded.

They did not have to wait long before they heard Sid's heavy footsteps.

Eva pushed Molly away and lay down, pretending still to be tied up. In the dimness of the store room it would take Sid a minute or two to notice that she was not bound – or so they hoped. Gus went to stand to one side of the door with a chunk of wood in his hand.

There was a fumbling and they heard Sid cursing.

When the door banged open, Eva began shrieking, which drew Sid's attention, and Gus slammed down the wood on their captor's head. With a grunt he fell to the ground and Gus picked up the revolver that had fallen from his hand.

Sid had not moved and blood was pouring from a scalp wound.

'Is he all right?' Eva worried.

'Who the hell cares? Pass me those ropes. He's a strong bugger and I want him safely tied up before he regains consciousness.'

She did as he asked. 'What now?'

He grinned. 'Now I lock you all in here and make my getaway.'

'But you can't! I need to get that child home. She's upset and—'

'Do I look stupid?' he demanded. 'If I let you go home you'll be telling everyone what's happened. I'm not going to hurt you and they're bound to find you before nightfall. There's even a jug of water.' He nudged Sid with one foot. 'And *he* won't be able to hurt you unless you're foolish enough to untie him.'

'I still won't agree to it.' Eva tried to push past him.

He shoved her back inside the room. 'You don't have a choice.'

'She does, you know,' said a voice and Aaron stepped out from behind the door.

With a curse, Gus pushed Eva aside and grabbed Molly. He held the child in front of him, using her as a shield and keeping the revolver pointed at her. 'Don't move!'

Both Aaron and Eva froze. Their eyes met for a moment, then they stared at Gus.

'I think this young lady will have to come for a little ride with me in my motor car,' he said. 'And if we do this gently, without any shouting and fussing, she won't be afraid.' He grinned as he saw Eva and Aaron both sag in dismay. 'I think you should move two steps back, Brierley. But I'll need you to come with me, Eva, to hold the child. No tricks, though, because I'm desperate enough to shoot you both, believe me.'

She did believe him. Stomach churning with apprehension, she moved forward, taking Molly's hand and saying quietly, 'It'll be all right, dear.'

Gus slammed the door of the store room shut and locked it, laughing as he tossed the key into the untidy mass of hay. 'Right, then. Let's go for a ride.' As he urged them towards his car, Molly suddenly cried out, 'Daddy! Daddy!' and started sobbing.

Inside the store room, Aaron heard his daughter's voice for the first time in many months and thumped his fist against the door in frustration.

'You going to stand there all day weeping like a great soft babby or do you want to get out of here an' get after them?' Sid asked.

Aaron spun round. 'How do we do that?'

'Untie me and I'll show you.'

'Oh, no. I don't trust you.' Sid was definitely stronger than he was.

'Then you don't get out of here.'

Aaron folded his arms. 'And neither do you.'

After glaring at him for a moment, Sid made an angry grunting sound and said, 'There's another spare key on the window ledge. It's badly rusted, but it ought still to work. Good job my father never threw owt away, isn't it?'

Aaron clambered on a box and found the key then fitted it into the door. He heaved a sigh of relief as it turned easily enough. Flinging it open, he strode out.

'Hoy!' yelled Sid from the store room. 'Come back

and untie me, you stupid bugger. You can't leave me like this.'

Aaron didn't even bother to answer. He ran out into the yard and started up Sid's lorry. He'd see if he could find out in the village which direction Gus had taken and follow him. Maybe, if he was very lucky, he'd be in time to save his wife and daughter. They were both very precious to him and he wanted most desperately to tell Eva so and to hear his daughter's voice again.

In the car Eva sat with Molly on her knee and Gus put the revolver into his jacket pocket on the side away from her. As he drove she thought about jumping out, but the car was travelling too fast. As they turned out of the end of the lane, they passed Ben Luccan, sitting outside his door as usual in his basket chair, which he did every day as long as it wasn't raining. She cuddled Molly close and at the same time pressed her face against the car window, hoping he had seen her. Gus didn't seem to notice.

When they drove straight past Rose Villa, Molly made a soft sound of dismay and stretched out her hand, as if she had expected them to stop there.

'Where are we going?' Eva asked as they left the village behind.

'I'm going as far away from here as possible. You're not.' Gus laughed at her horrified expression. 'I'm not going to kill you, you stupid fool. I'm a thief, not a murderer – though I might have made an exception for Linney.'

'What are you going to do with us, then?'

'Probably drop you on the moors, so that by the time anyone finds you, I'll be long gone.'

She wondered if she dared trust him on that. Perhaps he was just saying it to keep her quiet. If there was any chance of getting away from him, she'd take it, she decided. If he slowed down enough, she would jump out of the car.

'Eva?'

She realised suddenly that the child was speaking. Molly's voice was quiet and hesitant, but it was a voice again. 'Yes, darling?'

'Eva, I've got my voice back. Just like you said I would.'

'Yes, dear. I'm so pleased for you.'

'You're good with children,' Gus said. 'Pity Clara turned up when she did. I'd have enjoyed giving you one or two of mine. I'm a lazy sort of chap. I'd have been quite happy to settle down here, you know, and idle away my days.'

Eva shuddered. 'I didn't really want to marry you, but both you and Alice pushed me into it.'

'You didn't know what you wanted then. Life's taught you a few things since, hasn't it?' He gave a scornful sniff. 'It always does.'

A short time later he began to whistle, but the sound cut off abruptly as he saw a large black car pull out of a gateway and start to follow them. 'Hell and damnation! How did he get up here?'

'What's wrong?'

'I know that car. And if it's who I think it is, I definitely don't want to meet the owner. Hold tight.'

He pressed down the accelerator and the car speeded up.

But the other vehicle seemed to have no difficulty in keeping up with them. Eva and Molly were thrown from side to side as Gus screeched round corners and took short cuts across the middle of the road.

'Please slow down,' she begged. 'You're going to kill us all.'

'Not bloody likely.'

As they rattled on, he patted the gun as if to reassure himself it was still there and Eva began to wonder if it was worth risking hurling herself and the child out of the car door, even at this speed. She didn't want to be caught in cross-fire.

Aaron stopped the truck at Ben Luccan's house and leaned out to yell, 'Have you seen Blake's car?'

'He went that way.' Ben pointed along the road.

'Was my wife in it, did you see?'

Ben nodded again. 'Aye. She had her face pressed against the window and was holding your Molly on her lap.'

Thank God for an intelligent woman, Aaron thought. 'Thanks. Can you get a message to Wilf as quickly as possible to tell him Blake's driven off and is holding my daughter and Eva hostage? Tell him I'm following.' Even before Ben could answer he drove off, cursing the slowness of the lorry, able to do nothing but follow at a sedate pace along the road that meandered in a north-easterly direction across the moors. At least there were no turn-offs for a while, except for farm lanes, and he didn't think Blake would be interested in those.

What did that bastard intend to do with his hostages?

Would Aaron be in time to rescue them? At the thought of anything happening to either of them, his heart contracted and a lead weight seemed to settle in his guts. He'd delayed and kept his distance from Eva, calling it 'giving her time', but now he wished he hadn't. Wished it quite desperately. She didn't even know he loved her. But he did. He was utterly certain of that now. Seeing her so helpless in Blake's power had nearly broken his heart.

'Come *on!*' he begged the old motor, but it could only wheeze and groan in protest as he tried to make it go faster.

Suddenly there was a loud crack and glass splintered in the rear window.

'Get down! They're shooting at us!' Gus yelled.

Clutching Molly to her, Eva slid down as far as she could and positioned herself so that she could open the door if they slowed down at all.

Gus was cursing steadily, throwing the car from side to side in an attempt to avoid giving their pursuers an easy target. But the next shot blew out a tyre and the car slowed down considerably of its own accord, bumping along in a way that made Eva's teeth rattle. With her hand hidden by Molly's body, she took hold of the door handle, but before she could open it, the car behind speeded up and slammed into the back of them, sending them skidding helplessly sideways into a dry stone wall. Somehow, Gus managed to get control of the car again and pull away.

'Get out, quick!' he yelled.

Eva opened the door and threw herself and the child out.

They hit the ground with a sickening thud that squeezed all the breath out of her and flung Molly out of her arms. She blinked and tried to pull herself together, but her head was spinning and her arm hurt.

She must have lost consciousness for a minute, because she suddenly became aware of Molly crouching beside her, weeping uncontrollably. 'Are you all right, Molly?' she asked.

The child wailed even more loudly. 'I thought you were dead.'

Eva raised her head and looked round. Of the two cars there was no sign. How could that be? Where had they gone? 'You're not hurt?'

'I've cut my leg.' Molly stuck it out to show her the graze.

'But you can move your arms and legs?'

'Yes.'

Eva realised suddenly that the car which had been pursuing them might come back and struggled to get up. Only then did she realise she'd broken her forearm. 'I've hurt my arm. Don't touch it, Molly.' She bit back a moan and tried to hold it steady with her other hand while she dragged herself to her feet, but it seemed to take a long time and by then she had heard the sound of a car approaching. 'Go and hide behind the wall,' she told the child. 'Climb over it quickly.'

But Molly only shivered and pressed herself closer.

So Eva turned to face the vehicle, pushing Molly behind her with her good hand. It was the black car which had been pursuing them. It slowed down and she stared into it expecting at any moment that its driver would shoot at them. He had a cloth cap pulled down low, hiding the upper part of his face, and a scarf wrapped round the lower part. And he was definitely holding a gun.

He slowed down and for a moment they stared at one another.

She thought she wasn't even going to see the face of her murderer and wondered if her body would protect Molly from the bullets, or if they would both die here on this lonely road?

He turned the car round, jerking it to and fro on the narrow road. When he was facing away from Heyshaw again, he raised the gun as if in salute and drove past them.

She could only stand there, feeling stupid, watching the car pull away into the distance, hearing the sound of its engine grow fainter and then fade into nothing.

A chill wind tugged at her skirt, clouds scudded over them, heavy with rain, and there was no sign of a farm or other habitation nearby. She knew she couldn't walk far with a broken arm.

When she heard another car, she thought for a minute it was Gus coming back for them, but realised almost immediately that the vehicle was coming from the direction of Heyshaw. A ramshackle lorry came into view, chugging slowly along the road. When the driver saw them he slowed down and she waved her good hand, stepping forward into the road so that he could not drive past.

But he didn't even try to do that. He slammed to a halt and as the driver's door opened, Aaron clambered out awkwardly.

'It's Daddy!' squealed Molly, rushing forward and banging Eva's arm as she passed.

The world vanished in a dark sea of pain.

When Eva came to she was lying on the muddy verge with her arm bound to her body by a piece of material. She was cold and it was starting to drizzle, but the sight of Aaron's face leaning over her filled her with such relief and joy she forgot the discomfort for a moment. 'You came,' she said. 'You came after us.'

'Good thing I did. How did you manage to break your arm?'

'Rolling out of a moving car.' She explained what had happened and he frowned. 'You say the man who pursued you stopped?'

She nodded. 'He slowed down. I thought – Oh, Aaron, I thought he was going to shoot us. But he didn't, he just turned the car round, waved and drove away.'

'What did he look like?'

'I don't know. He had a cap pulled down and a scarf tied round his face.'

'Good.'

'Why do you say that?'

'Because he's a known hit-man and you'll be safer if you remember nothing about him. He'll have an alibi,

anyway, and say his car was stolen. Mac was telling me
about him. They've suspected him for years, but he
can always prove he was somewhere else when a killing
occurs.'

'Why didn't he shoot me to be sure I wouldn't tell?'

'Who knows?' He shuddered at the mere thought.

'What do you think's happened to Gus?'

He shrugged. 'I'm not even going to try to find out. I
want to get you to a hospital. You need that arm
setting. It must hurt like hell.' He reached out to
smooth her tangled hair back from her forehead. 'I
thought you might be dead. I knew then how stupid I'd
been, not telling you how I felt, not making you my
wife properly.' As Molly nestled against him, he smiled
down at the child, then looked at Eva again. 'I felt
guilty, you see. It was such a short time after Lil's death
that it seemed terrible to care about you already.'

'You – care about me?'

'Love you. I'm not good with words, but I can say
that one. To you. Only to you. And I'll go on saying it
to you till you're sick of hearing it.'

She forgot the pain for a moment, feeling a glow of
joy. 'I shall never be tired of hearing it, because I love
you too, Aaron Brierley.' She glanced at the weary
child and added, 'I love your children as well. Isn't it
amazing that in all this Molly has found her voice?'

The little girl raised her head to say, 'I can speak
again, Daddy.'

He ruffled her hair. 'I suppose that means you'll be
turning into a chatterbox like you used to be.' Then he
looked back at Eva. 'We have to get you into the truck,

love, and I can't carry you with this damned leg. It's going to hurt like hell to move, I'm afraid.'

Suddenly there was the sound of a vehicle approaching.

'It's not –?' Eva began.

He listened for a moment longer, then grinned. 'No, it sounds like my old motor bike. It'll be some of the lads, I expect.'

And when the bike topped the rise, they saw Wilf driving it with Mac hanging on behind him and Chas in the sidecar.

The next few minutes passed in a blur for Eva as the men talked in low voices, then lifted her into the back of the truck where she lay with her head in Aaron's lap. Wilf got behind the wheel, with Molly beside him, and drove them slowly home. Mac and Chas went ahead on the motor bike to see what had happened to Gus.

She could almost hope he'd got away because he'd been kind to Molly once and was Alice's nephew. Her friend would have been so mortified to know that a Blake had been involved in theft, and perhaps worse.

'Maybe now we can build you that garage,' Eva said on the way back.

'More important, we can start to become a real family, Eva love.'

'Has our Eva broken her arm?' Molly asked. 'A lad at school did that.'

'Yes, she has.' He looked down at his wife. 'But you and me and Gracie will look after *our Eva* till she gets better, won't we?'

Molly nodded solemnly.

In spite of the pain, Eva smiled at him. His answering smile was young and loving and full of hope again, the same hope that filled her.

26

When the truck had driven off in the direction of Heyshaw, Mac kick-started the motor bike. 'Right, lad, let's go and see if we can find Blake. He's going to be shut away for a long time and he richly deserves it, that one does.'

But a mile further on they found a smoking wreck crumpled against a rocky outcrop, with Gus Blake's body trapped in the twisted metal, his eyes staring sightlessly up at the sky.

'Was the car nudged off the road or do you think he was simply driving too fast?' Mac asked.

The two men examined everything.

'Driving too fast from the looks of it,' Chas said glumly. 'That Davies sod might have been the cause of it, but we'll never be able to prove anything.'

Mac thumped one fist into the other. 'They're going to get away with it again, damn them.'

'For the time being. We've a better idea of who to watch now, though.'

Mac made a scornful noise in his throat. 'We've had a fair idea of who was involved all along. Fat lot of good it did us. There are some people involved with useful friends in high places.' He shrugged. 'Well, I suppose we're a little further along. One day . . . Toss you for who stays and who fetches help.'

He lost and went to perch on an outcrop of rock and wait for someone to come and take away the car and body. He'd be glad to get home to London.

After a while he got bored and went to look in the back of the car. It contained a pile of crumpled newspaper which had been used to pack things. The man pursuing Blake must have had a quick check through the boxes before taking them away. Some corners of white paper were sticking out at one side, crumpled among the others. Mac pulled them out, wondering what they were.

When Chas returned with a big lorry commandeered from the South Heyshaw Motor Company, he found his friend grinning like a fool.

'We've got 'em,' Mac said simply, flapping some pieces of paper at him. 'Blake must have been intending to blackmail the others. He was very thorough in collecting the details and writing them down. These must have been stuffed into one of the boxes.'

Chas had a quick read of the papers, then stuck his hand out.

Mac shook it solemnly, then could hold his jubilation in no longer.

The man from the South Heyshaw Motor Company watched in bafflement as they thumped each other on the back, yelled and did a wild dance, cheering and waving their hands. Bloody southerners! You never knew where you were with them. Fancy dancing about like dervishes when there was a corpse lying trapped in a car.

'You'll have to help me push that car on to my lorry,' he said sourly when they calmed down a little. '*If* you have a minute to spare. But if you want to go on cuddling one another, don't let me stop you.'

The minute Grandad Gill saw Wilf and Aaron return to Rose Villa, he slung on his overcoat and hobbled across the road, determined not to be left out. 'Did they catch yon bugger, then?' he demanded as he opened the kitchen door and walked in.

Jenny set her hands on her hips and pretended to be annoyed. 'Couldn't you even wait till someone came to tell you? And don't swear in front of the children.'

'No, I couldn't wait – and them childer have heard worse words nor that. Besides, he *is* a bugger. And where's Eva?'

Jenny's smile faded. 'She's in hospital with a broken arm.'

'Eh, how did she get that?'

'Leaping out of a moving car.'

He sank down on the chair his granddaughter was holding. '*Eva did? Eva Kershaw?* Well, I'll –' he caught sight of the two children watching him and amended it to '– I'll go to the foot of our stairs!'

Jenny's smile returned. He always said that when he was surprised but needed to stay polite. She said it herself sometimes, but it was a stupid thing to say, really.

'What's happened to that Blake fellow?' he demanded.

'We'll have to wait to find out,' she said. 'Now, who's for a cup of tea?'

A little later Aaron came back, looking somewhat the worse for wear.

'Is our Eva badly hurt?' Gracie demanded at once. She'd been fidgeting about the kitchen ever since her dad had brought Molly back, annoyed at being left out of a real adventure.

As he realised what she had just said, Aaron smiled at her. It was the first time his elder daughter had said 'our Eva' and he hoped it meant she'd now accepted his new wife. 'She's bruised, like this young lady here,' he gave Molly a hug, 'but the broken arm will heal in a few weeks. Come over here and give me a cuddle, love.'

Often Gracie would refuse this request, but today she edged across and allowed him to put his free arm round her. 'I didn't look after Molly well enough,' she muttered. 'Mum said I was always to look after her.'

'Well, you've got a new mother now so you don't have to do it all yourself, love.'

'Anyway I can talk properly again now,' Molly said suddenly, speaking aloud for the first time since their return.

The room fell silent as everyone stared at her. Grandad was the first to speak, 'Eh, flower, that's champion! I bet you'll talk our ears off now.' He looked round in disapproval. 'And it's not like you, our Jenny, to stand doing nowt when there's folk needing a cup of tea.'

Hiding a smile, she turned to set the kettle on, but swung round, mouth open in shock as she heard his next words.

'And as for you, Wilf Horrocks, I reckon it's about time you married that granddaughter of mine. I keep expecting to hear that you're engaged from the way you look at one another, but you seem frit of asking her.'

Wilf glared at him. 'I'm not frightened of anything, and I can do my own asking in my own time, thank you very much.'

'Oh, aye? I'll believe that when I see it.'

Wilf marched across the room. 'Right then. Watch this. Jenny Gill, will you do me the honour of becoming my wife?'

'Of course I will.'

'Good.' He turned to stare challengingly at the old man, who was grinning broadly at them.

'About time, too. You can come and live in the cottage. I need someone with a strong arm. It'll belong to both of you one day, anyway.'

'Both of us?' Jenny demanded.

'Aye. In case I popped off sudden-like and couldn't give you a nudge when you needed it, I made another will.' He turned to smile at Aaron 'And you owe me a quid, lad. Remember saying you'd never marry again and me betting you would?'

'You old devil!' Jenny said.

Aaron could hold his laughter back no longer. 'But he got his own way, didn't he? And here's your pound, Grandad. I'm more than happy to pay up.'

When the laughter died down again, Wilf said

quietly, 'We'll have to wait to marry till I get a proper job, though, Jenny love, and a bit of money behind me. You do realise that?'

'I told you before, you can come and work with me in the garage,' Aaron said. 'Your upholstering skills will come in useful and I can teach you the rest. If that's not a proper job, I don't know what is. What's more you can help me build the garage. We'll get some timber in and knock it up ourselves. If you and Jenny have got somewhere to live rent-free, you'll only need to buy your food – and Jenny has a job as well.'

'I allus swore I'd support my wife,' Wilf said stiffly.

'Well, I don't see why I should stop work until I need to,' Jenny said. 'Besides, no one's asked me, but I've got over two hundred pounds saved up and there'll be Miss Blake's legacy as well. There's no reason you can't become a partner in the garage. And I want to get wed as soon as we can.'

Everyone stared at her, then Grandad let out a cackle of laughter and after a moment the other men joined in.

'We're in terrible trouble, you and me,' Aaron told Wilf, 'both marrying rich women.'

Jenny was watching Wilf anxiously. She knew how proud he was.

He looked at her and they both forgot the other people in the room. 'You can do better than me, Jenny.'

'No, I can't,' she said softly, her love shining in her eyes. 'You're the one I want, the only one.'

'I swear I didn't know you had so much money saved.'

'I know. And I didn't mean to embarrass you by blurting it out like that.'

He walked across and took her in his arms. 'Eh, Jenny, I love you and I can't refuse.'

Gracie and Molly watched with great interest as he kissed her and Grandad had to wipe a tear from his eye as he saw the proof that his granddaughter would be properly cared for after he'd gone.

To Eva's intense annoyance the doctor at the hospital insisted on keeping her in overnight once they'd set the arm. By the time he did his rounds the following morning and gave permission for her to leave, she was in a fret of impatience.

When she saw Aaron walk into the ward an hour later, her heart filled with love and pride. Limp or no limp, he was a fine-looking man, *her* man.

'How are you, love?' he asked, his glowing smile saying what he could not voice in front of the interested occupants of the nearby beds.

'More than ready to go home.'

Outside was not the motor bike, as she'd expected, but the farm lorry.

She stopped in amazement. 'Did Sid lend you this?'

'Not exactly. He's been arrested and when the police contacted his wife, she asked me to run the farm for her till things are sorted out. She can't drive so she said we could use the lorry. Wilf and I will be keeping an eye on things for her and earning a bit that way. It'll help keep the wolf from the door till we get our garage up and running.'

'That's wonderful.'

When Eva was settled in the front of the lorry, she asked, 'What's happened to Gus?' As he hesitated, she said firmly, 'I have a right to know.'

Aaron hesitated, then decided she deserved the truth. He didn't intend to keep her wrapped in cotton wool as Miss Blake had, and Eva had more than proved that she was a strong woman. 'He's dead.'

'Oh. Did that man in the car shoot him?'

'He didn't need to. Blake's car careered off the road and smashed into a rocky outcrop. The impact killed him.' Aaron glanced at her. 'If you hadn't jumped out with Molly, you might both have been killed too, and I don't think I could have borne that. Not now that we've just found one another.'

She gave a shaky laugh. 'It was worth the broken arm, then. Aaron . . .'

'Yes, love?'

'Do you think you could kiss me before we set off? And say that word again?'

'I might just manage it.' He pulled her towards him, taking care not to jolt her arm. Before he kissed her he stared into her eyes. 'You're a brave lass, and a pretty one, too. I'm a lucky fellow and I love you very much.' Then he bent his head and kissed her, a long slow kiss that made her whole body sing with joy and hope.

Afterwards they sat close together, oblivious to the cold until he realised she was shivering and set her gently aside. 'I'd better get you home again, love.'

*   *   *

They arrived back at the same time as Mac and Chas came to collect their things.

Mac tipped his hat to Eva and followed them into the hall. 'Glad to see you're all right, Mrs Brierley. You had a lucky escape yesterday.'

She nodded. 'I'm just glad Alice died before it all came out. It'd break her heart to know that her nephew was a criminal.'

'He wasn't,' Mac said.

'But he stole all those things.'

'The man you knew as Gus Blake was actually the cook in Gus's regiment. After the war he pretended to be Blake, who'd been killed in one of the final skirmishes. Our fellow was hurt and when they found he had a dicky ticker he was invalided out and vanished. Nobody realised what he'd been up to until quite recently, when Mrs Blake told us.'

'But she stopped the wedding! Why did she pretend he was her husband then?'

'Because he offered to pay her to keep quiet. Ironic, isn't it? He was actually free to marry you.'

She shuddered at the thought, then asked, 'What was he really called?'

'Ted Lowder. Does it matter?'

She nodded. 'It does to me. I'd rather not go on talking about him as a Blake, for Alice's sake.'

Not long after those momentous events Christmas was celebrated in style at Rose Villa. Polly came to stay and catch up with all the exciting things that had been happening, driving over from the Fylde Coast with her husband Richard and her stepdaughter Connie, not to mention her son Billy, who was making excellent progress now, able to talk and walk again, albeit slowly.

Lizzie and Peter drove across from Overdale for the afternoon, and Billy and Percy sat in the back of the van with Lizzie's children, also agog to hear every detail of what had happened to their Eva.

'Emma says she'll come and see you when she's had the baby,' Percy said, as he took Eva in his arms and gave her a careful hug. 'She says she's too big now to go bouncing around the countryside in the back of a van, let alone it might bring on the birth.'

'I'll look forward to that.'

'My turn next for a cuddle,' Lizzie said, pushing him out of the way. She held Eva at arm's length and studied her face. 'Eh, I never thought I'd see my quiet sister getting mixed up with thieves and murderers. And you've changed,' she added in surprise. 'You don't look half as soft as you used to.'

'I don't feel it. Come and talk to Aaron and the girls.'

As Eva turned round to survey the room and smile in pleasure at having so many of her family gathered under her roof, Polly asked quietly, 'How are you feeling now, love?'

Everyone fell silent to wait for her reply, so Eva told them the simple truth. 'I've never been as happy in my whole life.'

Which meant Aaron just had to go across and give her a hug, while Gracie nudged Molly and beamed at her.

Fifteen people sat down to a meal that had taken

Jenny and Polly all the previous day and all morning as well to prepare. Since Eva's arm was still in plaster, she had supervised the girls who had been in charge of setting the table.

Richard Mercer had brought some wine and when it had been poured, they all drank the health of the newly-weds, while Aaron held Eva's hand and smiled at her besottedly.

Afterwards Lizzie banged on the table and said loudly, 'Shush, you lot. I'm going to propose another toast.' She raised her glass high. 'To the Kershaw sisters. We've none of us done it easily, but we've all found good husbands –' she looked severely at Aaron '– at least, I *think* we've all found good husbands, and you'll answer to me Aaron Brierley if you don't make my sister happy.'

'I will,' he promised softly, squeezing his wife's hand under the table.

She nodded. 'Right then, raise your glasses, everyone, and drink to us.'

'The Kershaw sisters!' they all chorused.

''Specially our Eva,' muttered Gracie rebelliously.

Anna Jacobs is always delighted to hear from readers and can be contacted:

BY MAIL:

PO Box 628
Mandurah
W. Australia 6210

If you'd like a reply, please enclose a self-addressed envelope, stamped (from inside Australia) or with an international reply coupon (from outside Australia).

VIA THE INTERNET:

Anna now has her own web domain, with details of her books and excerpts, and invites you to visit it at:

http://www.annajacobs.com

Anna can also be contacted by e-mail at:

anna@annajacobs.com

If you'd like to receive the latest news about Anna and her books by e-mail every month or two, you are cordially invited to join her announcements list. Just e-mail her to be added to it.